Claiming
THE
TEXAN'S HEART

Claiming

THE
TEXAN'S HEART

Cathy Gillen
Thacker

Tina
Leonard

Amanda
Renee

MILLS & BOON

CONTENTS

The Texas Valentine Twins

Cathy Gillen Thacker

Books by Cathy Gillen Thacker

Lockharts Lost & Found
His Plan for the Quadruplets

Texas Legends: The McCabes
The Texas Cowboy's Quadruplets
His Baby Bargain
Their Inherited Triplets

Texas Legends: The McCabes
The Texas Cowboy's Triplets
The Texas Cowboy's Baby Rescue

Visit the Author Profile page at
millsandboon.com.au for more titles.

Cathy Gillen Thacker is a married mother of three. She and her husband reside in North Carolina. Her stories have made numerous appearances on bestseller lists, but her best reward is knowing one of her books made someone's day a little brighter. A popular Harlequin author, she loves telling passionate stories with happy endings and thinks nothing beats a good romance and a hot cup of tea! Visit her at cathygillenthacker.com for information on her books, recipes and a list of her favorite things.

Chapter 1

"When were you going to tell me?" Wyatt Lockhart demanded. He was obviously furious.

Adelaide Smythe looked at the ruggedly handsome rancher standing on the front stoop of her Laramie, Texas, cottage and tried not to react. An impossible task, given the way her heart sped up and her knees went all wobbly any time he was within sight.

Purposefully ignoring the intent look in his way-too-mesmerizing smoky blue eyes, she picked up both duffel bags of baby clothes, blankets and burp cloths and carried them to her waiting SUV.

Aware he was still waiting for an answer, she stated coolly over her shoulder, "I wasn't."

Wyatt moved so she had no choice but to look up at him.

He looked good, but then he always looked good in the way of strong, tall and sexy. Radiating an impressive amount of testosterone and kick-butt attitude, he stood, brawny arms folded in front of him, legs braced apart. Back against the rear corner of her vehicle.

His gaze drifted over her, as if he were appraising one of the impeccably trained cutting horses that he bred and sold on his ranch. "You didn't think I would find out?"

Adelaide tensed. Of course she had known.

She shrugged, her carelessness in direct counterpoint to his concern, and slid the duffels into the cargo area next to the boxes of diapers and formula.

Finished, she lifted her chin defiantly and looked into the piercing gaze that always saw way more than she would have preferred. "I knew your mother might mention it, eventually." Just as she had intuited that the most cynical of the Lockhart sons would be more than just a little unhappy when he heard about the arrangements.

Wyatt stepped back as if to ward off a punch. "My mom knows?"

It was her ranch. Of course Lucille Lockhart knew Adelaide and the twins were moving temporarily into the Circle H bunkhouse the following week!

Wondering how Wyatt imagined she could manage this without the matriarch's explicit permission, Adelaide favored him with a deadpan expression. "It was Lucille's idea, obviously." As was the notion that Adelaide start bringing over the things she was going to need now, instead of waiting and trying to do it and transport her six-week-old twins all at one time.

Again, Wyatt shook his head as if that would clear it. His sensual lips compressed into a thin, hard line. "I know the two of you have always been close."

An understatement, Adelaide thought. In many ways Lucille Lockhart had been the loving maternal force her life lacked. Even before her father had betrayed everyone they knew and taken off with a gold-digging floozy. "Yes. We have."

Wyatt took off his hat and shoved his fingers through the thick, straight layers of his wheat-colored hair. Frowning, he settled his Stetson square on his head and met her gaze head-on. "I still find it hard to believe my mother talked you into this travesty."

Adelaide didn't see what was so difficult to understand. If Wyatt had a single compassionate bone in his body, he would have extended a helping hand, too. If for no other reason than their two families had once been very close. "Lucille knows how I've been struggling to manage in the six and a half weeks since my children were born. She thought some assistance..." Some help feeding and diapering and rocking...

His brow lifted. He cut in sharply, all harsh male judgment once again. "Financial, I suppose?"

A mixture of embarrassment and humiliation filled Adelaide with heat. She'd never imagined needing a helping hand. But since she suddenly did...she would accept it on behalf of her twins

Adelaide marched back to the porch, tension shimmering through her frame. Aware only a small part of any of this was her doing, she picked up the large monogrammed designer suitcase that held her own clothing. The one that, unfortunately, had been given to her as a high school graduation gift. And had accompanied her on another, fortuitously ill-begotten, trip.

The way Wyatt was eyeing it said he remembered, too.

Refusing to think about what he might be recalling about their hopelessly romantic—and ill-fated—adventure, she continued, "If you consider being guests at her ranch for a couple months so I won't have to pay rent on top of my mortgage and new construction loan..."

He definitely did.

She squared her shoulders and admitted reluctantly, "Then yes, I do need some financial help, and in many other ways, as well. Things have been hard for me, since my father left Texas..."

Seeing how she was struggling under the weight of her bag, Wyatt reached over and took it from her. In two quick strides he carried it to the cargo area and set it next to the two smaller duffels. "Don't you mean since he embezzled funds from my family's charitable foundation and then fled the country?"

Her shame over that fact only increased as time passed. Adelaide tossed in a mesh bag of soft infant toys. Figuring she had done enough packing for now, she slammed the lid on the cargo hold. "I've apologized every way I know how for that." A fact that Wyatt very well knew, gosh darn it.

She stomped closer, determined to have this out once and for all, so they'd never have to discuss it again. "Everyone else in your family has forgiven me," she reminded him.

He remained where he was. Which was…too close. Far too close. He leaned down, inundating her with the scent of sun-warmed leather and soap. "So they're more foolhardy than I am," he said.

Adelaide glared at him. She knew Wyatt was still angry with her. And that his anger was based on a lot more than the sins of her father. The thing was, she was grief stricken over their failed romance, too. The knowledge that their dreams were never going to come true.

Ignoring the heat and strength radiating from his tall body, Adelaide stepped around him and headed wearily for the porch. Unable to help the defeated slump of her slender shoulders, she asked, "When are you going to let our last mistake go?"

He caught up with her and joined her on the small porch. Hooking his thumbs through the loops on either side of his belt, he murmured silkily, "I never said making love with you bothered me."

It had sure as heck bothered her! To the point she barely slept a night without reliving that reckless misstep in her dreams. Refusing to admit how many mornings she had awakened hugging her pillow as if it were the answer to her every wish and desire, Adelaide challenged him with a smile.

"Then that makes two of us," she drawled, refusing to admit how small his six-foot-three frame made the four-by-four-foot square beneath the portico feel.

Wyatt paused. His gaze roamed her postpregnancy frame, dwelling on the voluptuousness of her curves. "Enough to go again?" he taunted softly.

So that was it, she realized with a mixture of excitement and resentment. He still desired her every bit as much as she yearned for him. Fortunately for both of them, she was sensible enough not to repeat their error. Even if her obstetrician had given her the go ahead at her last checkup.

Adelaide stiffened. "Not if we were the last two people on earth," she vowed.

The look in Adelaide's eyes had Wyatt believing her.

The knowledge of what she had done—or more precisely *hadn't* done—convinced him otherwise.

Wishing he no longer found her thick mane of chocolate-brown hair and wide-set sable eyes so alluring, he stepped closer still. Deliberately invading her personal space, he let his gaze drift over the elegant features of her face, lingering on her slightly upturned nose, the prominent cheekbones and lushness of her lips.

Body hardening, he demanded, "Then why did you concoct such a harebrained plan with my mother?" If that was indeed the case. He still found it hard to believe that his mother had played matchmaker.

Adelaide blinked at him and furrowed her brow. "Why do you care where the twins and I live while the addition is being built on my home?"

Her innocence was real enough to be believed...had he not been the recipient of her heart-rending, soul-crushing antics. He knew, better than anyone, what she was like deep down. Reeling him in, and promising one thing, then actually delivering on another...

Luckily, his broken heart had mended.

"Even if it is technically on your mother's property," Adelaide continued irritably.

It was his turn to do a double take. He studied the riotous blush of pink on her pretty face. "You think I'm ticked off about you and your kids moving into the bunkhouse on the Circle H?"

Adelaide lounged against the opposite post. She folded her arms in front of her, the action plumping her newly voluptuous breasts even more. She regarded him with contempt. "Aren't you?"

He wouldn't lie. "I think it's a bad idea." One of the worst, actually.

Her lower lip thrust out in the way that always made him want to haul her into his arms and kiss her. "Why?"

He remained on his side of the small covered porch with effort. Getting emotionally entangled with this woman again would not serve either of them. "I don't want to see my mother taken advantage of by your family again." The first time had been bad enough.

Adelaide sent him a withering glare. "I'm not my father."

She was right about that. In some respects, she was worse. Paul Smythe's actions had been aimed at the bank account. Adelaide's targeted...the heart.

He pulled a folded envelope from a back pocket of his jeans. Still holding her turbulent gaze, he handed it over. "I would have believed that if I hadn't seen this," he told her gruffly.

Adelaide stared at the logo on the outside of the folded business letter, announcing the information was from the Texas Metro Detective Agency. Farther down, it was addressed to Wyatt Lockhart, regarding background information on Adelaide Smythe.

The color drained from her face. He watched her shiver, although the temperature was mild for the last day of January. She stared up at him in disbelief. "You actually had me investigated?"

She'd given him no choice. "The minute I heard my mother had invited you-all to stay at her place indefinitely. And you made her Jenny and Jake's godmother and 'honorary grand-mother.'"

Adelaide looked like she wanted to kick him in the shin. "You really are unbelievable," she sputtered.

Refusing to allow her indignation to sway him from the facts, he countered harshly, "Don't you want to know what I found out?"

Recovering, she handed him the report, said with cool disdain, "Well, obviously you're dying to tell me, so far be it from me to stop you."

If she wanted to play dumb, he could draw it out mercilessly, too. "Remember Vegas?" The most wildly romantic and absolutely soul-crushing time of their teenage courtship?

Her spine turned as stiff and unyielding as her mood. "I'd rather not."

He agreed with her there. Their hasty elopement hadn't turned out the way he'd envisioned. Her, either, judging from the blotchy red and white hue of her skin.

"It wasn't just the wedding night you had trouble following through on," he told her sarcastically, still not sure this wasn't some kind of ruse cooked up by her, long ago, left to wreak havoc on him now. Seeing he had her complete attention, he continued, "You had a little difficulty with the paperwork, too."

For a moment, she seemed not to even breathe. She regarded him warily. "What are you talking about?" she bit out finally.

His worst nightmare come true, obviously. "We're still married."

Chapter 2

A whisper of fear threaded through Adelaide. What Wyatt was suggesting was even worse than the thought that he might have somehow discovered the disturbing messages she'd been getting through her social media accounts. Messages that were also tied to her past, although in a different venue.

This was dangerous territory. "Stop clowning around."

Scowling, he stood with his hands on his hips. "Do I look like I'm joking?"

No, he most certainly did not. A fact that unsettled her even more than the person *pretending* to be her MIA father. "Look, I don't know who you talked to, Wyatt, but I signed everything and paid the lawyer the wedding chapel recommended before I left Nevada."

His jaw took on a don't-mess-with-me tilt. He stepped close enough she could almost touch the rough stubble lining his impossibly masculine jaw. "Then why isn't there any record of the dissolution of our marriage?" he demanded gruffly.

Deciding being close enough to kiss was a terrible idea, Adelaide backed up. "I don't know. Maybe you hired an incompetent private investigator."

"And maybe the annulment was never filed," Wyatt bit out. "Which is why I've asked Gannon Montgomery to meet us here in five minutes."

The former Fort Worth attorney, now married and living in Laramie, had handled lots of clients with family money, fame and fortune, including a case involving the former Dallas quarterback's son.

Adelaide should have known that her ex would revert to a legal solution to a very personal problem that, had they both been reasonable, would not have required any outside intervention.

"Fine," she huffed, ready to call in her own ace attorney. She whipped out her cell phone. "You want lawyers involved? I'm calling mine, too."

Luckily, it was the very end of the work day, and Claire Mc-Cabe was still in her office. She agreed to come right over. So by the time Adelaide had brewed a pot of coffee, Claire Mc-Cabe and Gannon Montgomery had both arrived.

Big and handsome, Gannon was a few years older than she and Wyatt. Claire was in her midfifties. She had two adopted children, and was the go-to attorney in the area for families who had children in extraordinary ways. Adelaide had always found Claire sympathetic and kind, and today, to her relief, she seemed to have extra helpings of both ready to dish out.

"So where are the twins?" Claire asked warmly.

"Upstairs, sleeping." Adelaide glanced at her watch. "Hopefully for at least another half an hour."

"Then let's get to it, shall we?" Claire suggested.

Gannon sat at the dining table next to Wyatt. Claire sat next to Adelaide. While she poured coffee, Gannon and Claire perused the documents, then did quick searches on their laptops for any verification of an annulment. "I'm not finding any," Claire said. "Under either of their names."

"Nor am I," Gannon added. "Although their marriage comes up right away, on Valentine's Day, almost ten years ago."

"So that means the detective agency is right," Wyatt presumed, big hands gripping the mug in front of him. "Adelaide and I are still legally married?"

He looked about as happy as Adelaide felt.

Claire and Gannon nodded.

Adelaide did her best to quell her racing pulse. Even bad situations had solutions. "What will it take to get an annulment?" she asked casually.

More typing on the computers followed as both attorneys researched Nevada law.

"Were you underage?" Gannon asked.

Adelaide admitted reluctantly, "We were both eighteen. No parental permission was required."

"Incapacitated in some way?" Claire queried. "Mentally, emotionally? Either of you intoxicated or high?"

Wyatt and Adelaide shook their heads. "We knew what we were doing," he said.

In that sense, maybe, Adelaide thought, recalling how immature they had been. They hadn't had any idea what it really meant to be *married*. Since both of them had remained single, they probably still didn't know.

Gannon exhaled roughly. "Then you're going to have to claim fraud."

"I'm not doing that," Adelaide cut in. Not with her family's reputation.

"Well, don't look at *me*. I'm not the one who changed my mind and backed out," Wyatt said.

Claire lifted a hand and intervened gently. "Why don't you tell us what happened?"

Adelaide flushed. Reluctant to discuss how foolishly romantic she had been, when they had set out for Vegas, after both had fought with their parents about the too-serious nature of their relationship. How determined they were to do something to show everyone, only to find out how scary it was to truly be in over their heads.

Adelaide drew a deep breath. "We eloped without thinking everything through."

Wyatt sat back in his chair, the implacable look she hated in his smoky blue eyes. "What she's trying to say is that she got cold feet."

"Came to my senses," Adelaide corrected him archly, irritated to find he still hadn't a compassionate bone in him. When he merely lifted a brow, she continued emotionally, "You did wild and reckless things all the time, growing up, Wyatt. I didn't."

He scoffed, hurt flashing across his handsome face. "Well, we sure found that out the hard way, didn't we?"

She knew she had disappointed him. She had disappointed herself. Though for entirely different reasons. Adelaide turned to their attorneys, explaining, "I was fine all through dinner, but when it came time to check into the hotel and consummate our union, I…" Choking up, Adelaide found herself unable to go on.

All eyes turned to Wyatt, who recounted dryly, "She panicked. Said she loved me, she just didn't want to be married to me, not yet." Accusation—and resentment—rang in his low tone.

Adelaide forced herself to ignore it, lest she too become caught up in an out-of-control emotional maelstrom. "I wanted to go home to Texas, finish our senior year of high school. And I wanted everything we had done, undone, without our families or anyone else finding out."

Wyatt, bless his heart, had agreed to let her have her way. Unlike now.

Exhaling, he continued, "We went back to the wedding chapel and asked the justice of the peace who married us if he could pretend we had never been there. He refused. But he gave us the name of someone who could help us."

Adelaide remembered the relief she had felt. "So we went

to the attorney's office the next day and asked him to file an annulment."

"I had a rodeo to compete in that evening, in Tahoe, so I signed what the attorney told me to sign and took off, leaving Adelaide behind to wrap things up."

"Which I did," Adelaide said hotly.

Wyatt lifted a brow. "You have a canceled check to prove it?"

His attitude was as contentious as his low, clipped tone, but she refused to take the bait. "No. I paid his fee in cash."

Wyatt rocked back in his chair, ran the flat of his palm beneath his jaw. Finally, he shook his head and said, "Brilliant move."

Resisting the urge to leap across the table and take him by the collar, Adelaide folded her arms in front of her. "I was trying not to leave more of a paper trail than we already had."

Wyatt narrowed his gaze at her in mute superiority. "Learned from the best, there, didn't you?" he mocked.

Adelaide sucked in a startled breath. "*Do not* compare me with my father!" she snapped, her temper getting the better of her, despite her desire to appear cool, calm and collected. "If not for me, and all the forensic accounting work I did, people still might not know where all the money from the Lockhart Foundation went!"

An angry silence ticked out between them. Broken only by his taut reminder, "If not for *your father*, the foundation money might still all be there. My mother would not have been put through hell the last year."

Their gazes locked in an emotional battle of wills that had been years in the making. Refusing to give him a pass, even if he had been hurt and humiliated, too, she sent him a mildly rebuking look, even as the temperature between them rose to an unbearable degree. "Your mother knows I had nothing to do with any of that. So does the rest of your family." Ignoring the perspiration gathering between her breasts, she paused to let her words sink in. Dropped her voice another compelling notch. "Why can't you accept that, too?"

The hell of it was, Wyatt secretly wished he could believe Adelaide Smythe was as innocent as everyone else did. He'd started to come close. And then *this* had happened.

He had seen Adelaide taking advantage of his mother's kindness and generosity, decided to investigate, just to reassure himself, and found even more corruption.

Claire and Gannon exchanged lawyerly looks. "Let's all calm down, shall we?" Gannon said.

Claire nodded. "Nothing will be gained from fighting."

Adelaide pushed her fingers through the dark strands of her hair. It spilled over her shoulders in sexy disarray. "You're right. Let's just focus on getting the annulment, which should be easy—" she paused to glare at Wyatt "—since we never consummated the marriage."

Once again, she was a little shady on the details. "Not then," Wyatt pointed out.

Adelaide paled, as if suddenly realizing what he already had.

Claire's brow furrowed. "You've been together intimately in the ten years since?"

Wyatt nodded, as another memory that had been hopelessly sexy and romantic took on a nefarious quality. "Last spring. After a destination wedding we both attended in Aspen."

A flush started in her chest and moved up her neck into her face. In a low, quavering voice, Adelaide admitted, "We have a penchant for making terrible mistakes whenever we're alone together. But since we didn't know we were married at the time, that can't count as consummating the marriage." She gulped. "Can it?"

Stepping in, Gannon stated, "Actually, whether or not you slept together really doesn't affect the marriage's legality in the state of Texas. Hasn't for some time."

Wyatt and Adelaide both blinked in surprise.

"Emotionally, it might have ramifications," Claire interjected.

No kidding, Wyatt thought. Their one and only night together had sure left him feeling as if he had been rocketed to the moon, his every wish come true, and then...as soon as Adelaide had come to her senses...sucker punched in the gut by her. Again.

"Unless, of course, one of you is impotent and concealed it, which is clearly not the case," Gannon continued.

No kidding, Wyatt thought, remembering the sparks that had been generated during his and Adelaide's one and only night together.

"You're saying we can't get an annulment?" Adelaide asked.

"Too much time has elapsed—nearly ten years—for you to request one from the court," Gannon said.

Claire soothed, "You can, however, get a divorce."

Wyatt knew what Adelaide was thinking. An annulment was a mistake, quickly remedied. A divorce meant being part of a marriage that had failed. That didn't sit well with her. He hated failing at anything, too.

"But we went to a lawyer at the time!" Adelaide protested.

Claire looked up from her computer. "Who, according to public record, has apparently not been a practicing member of the Nevada bar for nearly a decade."

Wyatt nodded. "The private detective agency said Mr. Randowsky had quit his practice and left the state shortly after we saw him. His practice dissolved accordingly."

Adelaide looked both shocked and crestfallen. "So there's no record of us ever being in his office? No real proof we ever tried to get an annulment?"

"None," Wyatt confirmed irritably. He had already been down that avenue with the private investigators. "I couldn't even locate anyone who worked in his office at the time."

Adelaide buried her head in her hands. "Which means that getting Mr. Randowsky or his former staff to testify on our behalf is a lost cause."

"Plus, there are children involved now," Claire pointed out.

Adelaide sat up abruptly, her pretty face a mask of maternal ferocity. *"My children,"* she stated tightly. "I went to a fertility clinic and was artificially inseminated two weeks before I saw Wyatt in Aspen."

Gannon looked at Wyatt. "You knew about this when you were together?"

Even as Wyatt shook his head, he knew it wouldn't have made any difference if he had. When he had seen her again that night, so happy and glowing and carefree, he had wanted her. She had wanted him, too. Recklessly. Wantonly.

And the rest was history.

"Adelaide didn't tell me she was starting a family until after I slept with her in Aspen." *"Nice as this was, and it was nice, nothing else can happen, Wyatt. I've got other plans…"*

She tossed her mane of glossy dark hair and gave him a defensive look. "It was a one-night stand, Wyatt. A kind of whimsical 'what if' for both of us ten years too late. I didn't think my pregnancy was relevant."

He hated her habit of downplaying what they had once meant to each other. Even if she hadn't had the guts to follow through. He looked her up and down, refusing to let her pretend any longer. "Oh, it was as relevant as the protection I wore."

Adelaide's mouth opened in a round O of surprise. "Wyatt!"

"Don't mind us," Gannon said dryly. "We're lawyers."

Claire added, "We've heard it all."

"Anyway," Wyatt stated, "I know what you're thinking." What he'd thought before reality and statistical probability crept in, given the fact that she'd already been inseminated and he'd worn a condom *every* time. "But the twins are not mine."

And he was glad of that. Wasn't he? Given the fact he still felt he couldn't quite trust her?

Adelaide's slender shoulders slumped slightly. "Thank heavens for small miracles!" she muttered with a beleaguered sigh.

She turned her glance away, but not before he saw the look of defeat in her eyes.

Wyatt felt a pang of remorse. So, the situation had ended up hurting her, too—despite her initial declarations to the contrary. Maybe he should try to go a little easier on her.

Certainly, they had enough strife ahead of them...

Oblivious to the ambivalence within him, Claire went back to taking notes. "So this... Adelaide's decision to have children via artificial insemination and sperm bank...is why you parted acrimoniously. Again."

Wyatt only wished it had been that simple. "I wouldn't have cared about that," he said honestly, ignoring Adelaide's embarrassment and looking her square in the eye.

Adelaide returned his level look. "Over time, you might have." She glanced at the baby monitor, as if hoping it would radiate young voices. It was silent. She cleared her throat, turned to regard their lawyers. "In any case, the insemination at the clinic took place before Wyatt and I ever saw each other again and were...reckless."

Reckless was one way to describe it, Wyatt mused. There was also passionate. Tender. Mind-blowing...

"And I was already sure I was pregnant...from the way I was feeling..."

Which was why, Wyatt thought, she'd been so happy. In retrospect, he could see that it'd had little to do with seeing him again.

And for reasons he couldn't explain, and didn't want to examine, that stung, too.

More lawyerly looks were exchanged between the two attorneys.

Clearly, Wyatt noted, there was another problem.

Claire's brow furrowed. "Is the donor's name on the birth certificate?"

Adelaide shook her head. "No. Just mine. But I know exactly who the biological father is. Donor #19867 from the Metroplex Fertility Clinic's sperm bank, where I was inseminated."

More glances between attorneys.

"This is a problem," Claire said.

Gannon agreed. "Under Texas law, any children born during a marriage are *legally* the offspring of the husband, unless and until proved otherwise. Meaning court-ordered DNA tests are going to be necessary."

"Why court-ordered?" Wyatt asked, his impatience matching Adelaide's. "Can't we just have them done on our own?"

"Not if you want them to be part of any legal record," Gannon said. "When DNA tests are court-ordered, a strict chain-of-custody procedure is followed, ensuring the integrity of the samples. Everyone who has contact with them has to sign. This protects against tampering, or ill-use."

Made sense.

"Then court-ordered it is," Adelaide said grimly, as Wyatt nodded.

"Luckily, we can formally request this online." Gannon was already typing. "I'll follow it up with a call to the judge to make sure it goes through immediately."

"While you do that, I'll call my cousin Jackson McCabe, who is chief of staff at Laramie Community Hospital, and ask him to write the medical orders for the blood tests." Claire rose, cell phone to her ear. "And arrange to have them done as soon as possible."

Not that it would matter, Wyatt thought, as Claire stepped into the next room and Gannon, when finished, walked out onto the front porch. They all knew what the tests were going to reveal. Once that happened, he and Adelaide would go their separate ways.

Forever.

Unable to sit still a moment longer, Adelaide rose, gathered the mugs and took them to the kitchen sink. "I wasn't finished with that," Wyatt called after her.

No one had been, Adelaide knew. But she needed something

to do before she exploded with tension. "Hold your horses," she said over her shoulder. "You'll get a fresh mug in a minute, and more hot coffee to go with it. Unless you'd prefer something more dainty." She turned his way to give him a too-sweet look. "Like tea?"

He shot her a deadpan look.

They both knew he hated tea. All kinds.

He didn't like iced coffee, either.

Or at least he hadn't.

What if he had changed?

Then again… Doubtful.

Gannon walked back in, just as she sat four fresh mugs and a platter of cookies on the table. "We've got the court order."

Claire returned, too. "Jackson expedited everything on the hospital's end. The hospital lab will be open until eight this evening, so you can both go over now if you like." She paused. "If you want to write this down…?"

Adelaide plucked a notepad and pen from the charging station, then returned to the table, carafe in hand. She slid the former across the table to Wyatt.

He ignored her helpful gesture. "I'll just type it in." He pulled out his smartphone, gaze trained on the oversize screen, paused again, then brought up the appropriate menu.

Just scribbling the info on paper would have been faster. Then again… "It's probably best," Adelaide quipped, in an effort to lighten the mounting exasperation. "No one can read his chicken scratches anyway."

Wyatt squinted at her, his expression partly annoyed and the rest inscrutable.

"Unless something's changed?" she continued, determined to be just as provoking and ornery as he was being.

It hadn't just been the love notes he'd passed to her in class she hadn't been able to decipher. It had been anything and everything he wrote. Worse, he had seemed to take perverse delight in everyone else's frustration. Just as he was enjoying her impatience now. She didn't know why he had to be such a pain sometimes.

"You've taken a class in penmanship…?" she taunted lightly, aware they had temporarily reverted to their worst selves from their teenage years.

"You wish." Smugly, Wyatt looked at Claire, his fingers poised over the keyboard on his man-size smartphone. "Ready when you are."

Barely suppressing her own exasperation, Claire returned to her own handwritten notes. "The tech who's going to be doing the test is Martie Bowman. The outpatient lab is on the first floor of the main building of the hospital, in the east wing. Suite 111."

Wyatt quickly typed in the information. "Do you want to email that to me, too?" Adelaide asked.

"Not necessary," Wyatt said. "I've got it."

He was also as impossibly chauvinistic as ever. Adelaide sighed. "How long until we have the results?"

"They're going to put a rush on it. So three or four days at most."

"What about the rest of it?" Adelaide asked.

"It would be advisable to proceed with the divorce only when the DNA results are back," Gannon said.

Adelaide decided to give it one last try. "Are you sure it has to be divorce? Can't we remedy this mistake—" and it had been a big one, the biggest of her life "—some other way? Maybe just invalidate the marriage on some technicality, or… I don't know…" She was grasping at straws, and she knew it.

Wyatt grimaced. "I agree. I'd prefer to find another way to end this, too."

"There isn't one," Gannon decreed.

"You've not only consummated the marriage, but had children during the term of the union, which has lasted nearly ten years," Claire reminded sagely.

Gannon agreed. "Like it or not, divorce is the only way to dissolve your marriage."

No sooner had Claire and Gannon left them to discuss their pending trip to the hospital lab than a wail sounded on the baby monitor. A second swiftly followed.

Adelaide looked at the alarmed expression on Wyatt's face. Suddenly, she was in no hurry to have cheeks swabbed or blood drawn. At least with him standing right next to her. "I've got to feed the twins, so…" She waved him off. "If you want, you can go ahead to the hospital without us."

He stood firm. "I prefer we all go together. Just get it done."

It wasn't as if they didn't already know the results.

Irritated, she took the stairs quickly, as the cries quickly escalated to a fever pitch. "Well, some things won't wait."

He lagged behind at the foot of the stairs. "How long…?"

Adelaide threw the words over her shoulder. "If you want to make it fast, then give me a hand, cowboy."

Never in a million years did she think he would take her up on the suggestion. By the time she bypassed the tiny master and reached the even tinier room with the twin cribs, the volume had been turned up nearly as loud as their little lungs could go.

Unable to bear to hear her children sobbing, Adelaide quickly picked up little Jake and snuggled him in one arm. His sobs subsiding, she walked over to Jenny's crib and scooped her up, too. Hence, it was suddenly blissfully quiet, as she carried both to the changing stations set up side by side.

"You're going to change both their diapers simultaneously?" Wyatt lingered in the doorway, the same cautious, awestruck expression he had on his face whenever he saw a new foal.

Except this wasn't one of the cutting horses he bred on his ranch.

Adelaide shrugged. "Neither one of them is all that keen on going second."

"Then how do you…?"

"When I was nursing, I put one on each breast."

She knew it was too much information. She also figured too much information might incent him to leave.

He seemed to know that was what she wanted, so, as ornery as ever, he strolled languidly into the room.

Jenny and Jake lay on their backs while she worked at unsnapping their onesies, letting their legs go free. Fortunately, both diapers were just wet.

"They look like you," Wyatt said softly.

No surprise there. She had picked a donor with the same shaped facial features, dark wavy hair and bittersweet chocolate eyes as her own.

The tender regard in his expression made him all the more handsome. "Their eyes are blue, though."

Pure blue.

His were blue-gray.

The wistfulness he was suddenly evidencing forced her to recall he had always wanted kids, too. "Most fair-skinned babies are born with dark blue or dark gray eyes that can change color several times before their first birthday."

He stuck his hands in his pockets. "Did not know that."

Did not know a lot of things. Finding it a relief to be able to distract themselves with information, she explained, "An infant's eye color changes as he or she gets older and melanin levels increase."

He watched as Adelaide eased away the wet diapers, quickly wiped down their diaper area and slid on the new.

Wyatt turned to her, his broad shoulder nudging hers in the process. "When will you find out?"

Ignoring the electricity of the brief contact, she fastened one, then the other. "By their first birthday, I'll know if their eyes are going to be blue or brown or green or gray."

Not that it mattered.

They would be adorable regardless.

She turned back to the man she had once loved. Suddenly, he wasn't the only one feeling wistful. Had their elopement worked out, the way they both had hoped, these children could have been theirs. But they weren't. So...

She sighed, aware Wyatt had gone back to observing her children. He leaned closer, regarding them contentedly. For a person who'd had zero interest in ever laying eyes on the two babies she'd had on her own, he was certainly fascinated.

"I think they have your nose, too. See the way it turns up slightly at the end?"

She certainly recalled Wyatt kissing her nose. And her cheek, and her temple, and...

Best she not go there.

She really should not go there.

"Your eyelashes, too," he mused.

Aware this situation was getting far too intimate too fast, she challenged him with a droll look. "Is that a good thing or bad?"

He straightened. As their gazes collided, it was hard to tell what he was feeling.

"Fact."

"Whew!" She pretended to wipe perspiration from her forehead. "For a moment, I thought you were paying me compliments."

His low laugh filled the room, bringing back a slew of unwanted memories.

Simmering with emotion, Adelaide scooped up Jenny in one arm, Jake in her other. She headed down the hall. He followed, close enough she could feel his steady male presence. "You're really going to go down the stairs like that?"

He was a man. Of course he wanted to take charge. "Very carefully. And yes, I am."

He still looked skeptical.

With good reason, had she not already done this dozens of times.

Figuring as long as she had a pair of helping hands nearby she might as well use them, Adelaide turned and handed off little Jake. For a moment, Jake gazed up at Wyatt mutely, studying the handsome rancher's unfamiliar face.

Blinking in confusion, Jake let out a howl loud enough to wake the entire neighborhood.

"Now what?" Wyatt mouthed, looking every bit as panicked as Adelaide had felt the first moment she was confronted with two in the hospital. When all she had ever signed up for was one baby. Until Mother Nature had intervened. Adelaide held out her free arm.

Wyatt slid Jake back into her hold.

To everyone's relief, the crying ceased.

Adelaide continued on downstairs, as originally planned. Once in the kitchen, she had no choice but to put both babies down in their infant seats, as she prepared their bottles. Luckily, they were so focused on watching her, each other and their visitor, both forgot to voice their immense impatience, as per usual.

Wyatt stood next to her, his arms braced on the counter on either side of him. Was it her imagination, or did he look completely besotted by her precious offspring?

"When did you stop nursing?"

"Our doctors made me stop when they reached four and a half weeks. I wasn't able to provide enough milk for both and trying to do so was having an adverse effect on my health." She sighed her regret. "Since I'm all they've got, I had to do what was best for all of us. Even if that meant making concessions I would really have rather not." She paused to give her babies adoring looks. "I thought it might be hard for them, moving from breast to bottle, but they adjusted really easily. Maybe because they were already getting supplemental formula feedings."

He nodded. Understanding in a way she didn't expect.

Telling herself this was no time to start feeling kindly toward him, Adelaide put one bottle in the warmer, waited for it to ding, then added the other. Finished, she tested the liquid of both on the inside of her wrists. Scooping up both babies, she inclined her head at the bottles. "Mind bringing those in for me? You'll save me a trip."

"Sure."

Adelaide walked over to the sofa and settled both infants into the supportive indentions on the extra-large twin nursing pillow already there, then she sat and carefully moved it onto her lap. Wyatt handed over the bottles one at a time, and she tipped the nipples into Jake and Jenny's mouths. Then all was silent as they drank. For the first time in a while, Adelaide felt herself begin to relax and really breathe. Until she looked up again and saw Wyatt watching her with the kind of respect she had always yearned to see.

Telling herself that his newfound admiration didn't matter, that this situation would be over as quickly as their one-night stand had been, Adelaide bent her head and did not look up at him again.

An hour later, they were on their way. Thankfully in separate vehicles. Four cheek-swab DNA tests later, they again split up. Wyatt returned to his horses and his ranch. Adelaide took the twins home and thus began the wait for results.

They came in late on the third day.

On the morning of the fourth, she found herself back at the hospital. This time in Dr. Jackson McCabe's office. To her surprise, Wyatt was there, too.

Jackson indicated they should sit, even as Adelaide's palms began to sweat. "I understand you requested this test to disprove Wyatt's paternity of the twins."

Wyatt and Adelaide nodded.

"It proved the opposite. Adelaide Smythe is their biological mother, Wyatt Lockhart their biological father."

"But that's…" Adelaide sputtered. She thought this was just

a formality! "I was artificially inseminated before Wyatt and I ever hooked up. So it can't be! He can't be!"

She slanted a look at Wyatt, who was not moving or reacting in any way.

"Apparently the AI did not take," Jackson explained.

That was impossible. "We used protection when we were together!"

Not because she had felt she needed it, since she had been convinced she was already pregnant by then, but because she hadn't wanted to stop and explain her circumstances, a move that surely would have spoiled the romantic aura of the evening, as surely as it had the morning after. And she had wanted that one night with Wyatt so very badly. To make up for everything heartbreaking and awful that had come before.

"No birth control method is one hundred percent effective." Jackson handed over two sets of lab results. "The tests were conclusive. Both children are Wyatt's. So—" he rose, reaching across the desk and shaking their hands "—congratulations to both of you."

Chapter 3

Wyatt was still reeling from the news that he was a dad, when his younger sister met them at the door of Adelaide's home, where she had been babysitting the twins. Sage caught the equally shell-shocked look on Adelaide's face. "What happened to you?" Immediately incensed, his sister swung back to him and demanded, "Are you responsible?"

If Sage only knew, Wyatt thought ironically. Feeling joy—that he finally had the kids he had secretly wanted for a long time. And shock—that the woman he'd once thought—erroneously—was the love of his life, was the mother who had provided them.

He had no idea why fate kept propelling them together this way. When it was abundantly clear he and Adelaide could not be more wrong for each other.

Yet there was nothing of the cruel joke of nature when it came to the sweetly slumbering children, he thought, gazing down at Jenny and Jake in reverence and awe.

They were perfect.

And they were his.

As well as Adelaide's...

Oblivious to the ambivalent nature of his thoughts, Adelaide turned back to Sage and made a shushing motion with her hand. "It's complicated," she told his sister.

Sage looked them both up and down. Sighed, as a twinkle came into her eyes. "Isn't it always with the two of you?"

Reluctantly, Wyatt turned away from the twins, who were still sleeping angelically in their Pack 'N Plays. Eager for some time alone with them, he grabbed his sister's coat and bag and ushered her toward the door. "Thanks for babysitting."

Sage dug in her heels. "I can stay awhile longer if you need me."

Adelaide's expression broadcast the need for privacy. "Wyatt and I have some things we need to discuss."

Which probably, Wyatt admitted grudgingly, should be done before the twins woke up.

"Uh-huh." Sage shrugged on her coat and patted Wyatt's arm. "Be good to Adelaide, big brother."

As if he had ever wanted to be anything but, Wyatt thought grumpily. Even if things hadn't worked out.

Sage shut the door behind her.

Adelaide's small house felt even tinier.

Looking as tense and upset as he felt, she went to the kitchen, stood on tiptoe and pulled out a bottle of Kahlua. Wyatt knew how she felt. He could use a good stiff drink himself. Even if it was barely ten in the morning.

Hands trembling, she made two drinks. Wordlessly, they each took a stool at her kitchen island. "What are we going to do?" she asked in a low, jittery voice, lifting the glass to her lips.

He sipped the concoction of milk, ice and coffee-flavored rum. "The only thing we can. Raise them together."

She looked down her nose at him. "I'm not staying married for all the wrong reasons."

He grimaced as the too-sweet mixed drink stayed on his

tongue. "I'm not asking you to stay married," he retorted in exasperation. "I still think we should get a divorce."

"Good." Relief softened her slender frame. "I'm glad we agree on that, because the last thing I want Jenny and Jake to suffer through is a marriage like my parents had," she vowed, her cheeks turning an enticing pink. "With both of them fighting all the time."

He gazed into her eyes. "I promise you. For the sake of the kids, we won't fight." And especially not the way Paul and Penny Smythe had, before Penny had died in that Jet Ski accident when Adelaide was fourteen. He could still remember how unmaternal Adelaide's mother had been, her dad only a little more interested in their only child. Had it not been for the teachers, camp counselors and horse-riding instructors who had taken an interest in the shy but eager to please little girl, he wasn't sure what would have happened to Adelaide.

Her face grew pinched. "I promise you, too. We'll keep things civil in the way we haven't managed to in the past."

Regret tightened his gut. It wasn't the first time he had felt remorse over having given her such a hard time. "Then, we had no reason to buck up," he admitted shamefully.

She nodded, accepting her own culpability in the ongoing tension between them. "Now, we certainly do."

The unmistakable ache in her tone caught him unawares. He studied her, realizing for the first time she might wish that things had turned out different for them, too, despite her avowals to the contrary.

Silence. She lifted her eyes to his, then looked at him long and hard. "The question is, how are we going to arrange it?"

He drained his glass. "I don't want a judge to tell us how the twins are going to divide their time."

She pushed her unfinished drink away. "I don't want them to divide their time at all," she said firmly, sending him a probing look that sent heat spiraling through him. "Not when they are this young."

It took everything he had not to touch her again. Haul her into his arms. And… "What are you suggesting?" he bit out.

She angled her chin. "That we work together to get you up to speed on all the daddy stuff and make you and the twins comfortable with each other."

That sounded good in terms of the kids, but there were still wrinkles to work out. "I'm not moving into my mother's bunkhouse, Adelaide." He anticipated enough family interference as it was. From his mother, who never seemed to trust him to be able to succeed without her help. And his way too idealistic younger sister, Sage, whose own unsatisfying love life prodded her to look outward for her fix of romance.

"Well, we can't stay here. The work on the addition to my home is due to start in two days, and the movers are coming to take the bigger items, like the twins' cribs and changing tables and so on, tomorrow." She rose and carried her glass to the sink.

Wyatt took his over, too. "I don't understand why you just didn't buy a bigger place to begin with when you moved here from Dallas last fall." Their shoulders touched as they leaned over to put the dirty dishes into the dishwasher.

Adelaide shut the lid and straightened. "I thought about waiting until spring, when more properties were likely to be on the market, and renting something else in the meantime, but I also knew that the modest price and the location of the cottage—just blocks from downtown where I work—couldn't be beat. So I put an offer on it that was immediately accepted."

Okay, that made sense, even if his urge to kiss her again did not. "Why didn't you do the addition before the twins were born?"

She raked her teeth across her lower lip. "Because Molly and Chance were both busy with other jobs, and I wanted one or both of them to handle it for me."

That he could also understand. His contractor brother and his fiancée had the best building teams around.

Adelaide moved away, giving him a brief, enticing view of her curvy backside in the process.

She swung back to face him, picking a piece of lint from the knee of her trim black wool skirt. "I also didn't think the twins would need separate bedrooms for a couple of years. But, given the way they keep waking each other up, I figured it would be better if they each had their own space now. A dedicated space for me to work in, when I do work at home, would be nice, too. And since I was able to get a low-interest construction loan from the bank and Molly and Chance were able to fit my project into their schedule... I went for it."

"Makes sense." Even if it would cause a lot of temporary upheaval.

Adelaide removed the coated elastic band from her wrist, gathered her wavy dark hair into a knot on the back of her head and secured it there. "Unfortunately, the babies can't be around construction dust and fumes. It's not safe."

The good thing about Adelaide was that she could be easily persuaded to do what made sense logically. The bad thing was that she often came to regret her ready acquiescence if the situation did not continue to align with her wants and needs. Still, she was also known for making the best of whatever situation she found herself in. A propensity he knew would be helpful to both of them in the coming months. Briefly he covered her hand with his own. "You and the babies can stay at Wind River with me. I've got plenty of room at the ranch."

She pinched the bridge of her nose and looked even more stressed than she had in Jackson McCabe's office. "That will cause a lot of talk."

Why did people always think gossip was the worst thing in the world? When what really sucked was hiding the truth out of *fear* of scandal. He shrugged. "There's going to be a lot of talk anyway."

Adelaide looked like she wanted to thrust herself against him and hold on to him for comfort. But of course she didn't.

She ran her finger along the edge of the granite countertop. "How are we going to handle that?" she asked anxiously.

Wyatt worked on keeping his emotions in check, too. This situation was hard enough without adding messy feelings to the mix. He looked Adelaide in the eye. "For starters? By getting my family together."

Adelaide couldn't recall ever being this nervous. "Are you sure you want to do this right now?" she asked, as she bundled up the twins and strapped them into their car seats.

Wyatt grinned, as confident as she was on edge. "Sage already knows something's up. Garrett works at the hospital, so he may have heard we were there with the twins earlier in the week. Then there's the court-ordered bloodwork, the fact that both our attorneys were at your house with us. Singularly, none of those details may have caused much gossip, but all together..."

Trying not to notice how he towered over her when they stood side by side, she shut the rear passenger door.

"Besides—" he rested his big hands on her shoulders "—the fact I have two children, that the twins have a daddy to love and watch over them, is fantastic news."

"You're right." She stepped back, aware having his kids was, in many ways, her deepest held romantic fantasy come true.

She'd never imagined it would actually be possible, though. Or dreamed he would ever be able to forgive her for changing her mind about marrying him. Because it had been more than his pride that had been destroyed that day. Her actions had eradicated his trust in her. And in them. She still wasn't sure his faith in her would ever be resurrected, at least not entirely.

And without that, even becoming friends again would be a challenge.

But, given the situation, there was nothing to do but try to forge some peace.

Go on from there.

* * *

They took both vehicles out to his mother's ranch, the Circle H. By the time they arrived, the Lockhart family was already there, save Wyatt's brother Zane, who was on assignment with Special Forces.

The rest were gathered in the main room of the bunkhouse. Garrett and Hope, and her eleven-month-old son, Max. The newly engaged Molly and Chance, and her three-year-old son, Braden. Wyatt's sister, Sage, and his mother, Lucille.

Adelaide settled the twins, who were still fast asleep in their carriers, at one end of the long plank table, while Wyatt asked them all to have a seat toward the other end.

"So what's up?" Sage asked.

Adelaide's pulse raced as Wyatt moved to stand beside her. She hadn't expected to ever want to rely on him again, but right now, she did.

Especially with his family looking at them so curiously.

"Adelaide and I eloped in Vegas on Valentine's Day, when we were eighteen," Wyatt announced, as if it were no big deal.

Brows rose all around.

"We thought we annulled it before we left the state, but apparently we were mistaken."

Garrett cocked his head, clearly as shocked and disbelieving as everyone else. "So you're still married," he concluded.

Adelaide lifted her hand. "Yes, but we're getting a divorce," she clarified quickly.

Wyatt frowned. "Eventually," he said.

Lucille pressed a hand to her heart, her joy surfacing as the reality sunk in. "You're going to give the marriage a try?" The matriarch of the Lockhart clan looked delighted. There was nothing she wanted more, Adelaide knew, than to have all five of her children married and living happily-ever-after.

"No," Adelaide corrected hastily, glad to see that at least Lucille did not look disappointed in them. At least not yet. "But we have to learn how to live together because..." She cleared her throat. Oh heck, she really did not know how to put this.

The man of the hour did.

Casually, Wyatt related, "We hooked up a while ago, at a wedding, when Adelaide thought she was already pregnant via artificial insemination, and long story short—" he couldn't quite suppress a triumphant grin "—we just found out the twins are mine. Ours."

A second really shocked silence reverberated around the table.

Glad to see this, too, was happy news, Adelaide added, with an outer confidence she couldn't begin to feel, "Naturally, we want to do what is best for everyone. So Wyatt and I have decided to join forces and move in together at his ranch, until such a time as we can figure out a way to be a family without being married or living under one roof."

Chance and Garrett exchanged looks. "How long do you expect this to take?" Chance asked.

Adelaide had no clue. The only thing she knew for sure was that she was in no rush to let the twins out of her sight for more than a few hours every day. Given how quickly he was stepping up to the plate, she assumed Wyatt would soon feel the same.

"A year. Maybe more," Wyatt said.

"However long it takes us to consciously uncouple," Adelaide agreed.

Sage tilted her head, looking every bit as happy as her mother, Molly and Hope. "Well, if it works for the Hollywood stars, why shouldn't it work for the two of you?"

Chance and Garrett both guffawed.

"This is serious." Lucille frowned. "Under the circumstances, I think you should both forget about ever getting divorced. And have a proper wedding, here on the ranch, as soon as possible, with all your friends and family present."

The pressure of that kind of public hoopla made Adelaide

reel. "Not going to happen, Mom," Wyatt said. A little too quickly for Adelaide's taste.

Was the thought of doing what was best for the twins in the conventional sense really so distasteful to him? Did he hate her that much?

On the other hand, she knew he was certainly being practical in wanting to go into the arrangement with their eyes wide open.

"We should at least have a party to officially welcome Adelaide and the twins into the family," Lucille insisted.

"Once the dust settles on the news, that is probably a good idea," Hope concurred, her considerable expertise as a crisis manager and public relations expert coming into play.

"How do we get the word out?" Sage asked.

Hope smiled. "The usual way—via announcement."

The women promptly went to work. Fifteen minutes later, they had a rough draft of the whimsical announcement. There was a border of hearts, with a stork across the top, carrying two babies, one in pink, one in blue. Followed by the words:

And just when you think you've heard it all...

Nearly ten years ago, on Valentine's Day, at the tender age of eighteen, Adelaide Smythe and Wyatt Lockhart eloped.

They soon got cold feet. And had it annulled. Until fate intervened, and they met up again on another starry romantic night.

Twin babies and a surprisingly still legal marriage were the result!

Please join us on the Circle H Ranch, on Saturday March 1, at 4:00 p.m., to welcome Adelaide and the twins, Jake and Jenny, into the Lockhart family, and celebrate the unconventional events that brought them all together. And brought all of us such happiness and love.

"It can be a combination belated wedding reception slash baby shower," Lucille decreed.

Wyatt and Adelaide exchanged worried looks. Adelaide was willing to go along to get along, to a point. Not add more deception to the mix. "I think we might want to add something about our plans to eventually amicably divorce," she said. "Otherwise, we will just face even more scandal down the road."

"Nonsense," Lucille huffed. "If you two want to consciously uncouple, that is your business and can be done privately until such time as you are actually ready to divorce. Right now, the emphasis has to be on the twins. They deserve the kind of fairy-tale entry all children merit as they enter this world. When they look back on these events, as they certainly will someday, I want them to see an unconventional beginning brimming with love and joy."

As much as Adelaide wanted to, she could not argue that.

Chapter 4

"Why are they crying?" Wyatt asked in alarm several hours later. He and Adelaide carried both twins in the front door and set the carriers on the sofa.

Adelaide eased Jake out of the straps and hooded jacket and blanket confining him, and handed him to Wyatt to hold. "A lot of reasons." Tossing her own coat aside, she bent to retrieve Jenny from her carrier, too. "They saw a lot of new faces tonight."

No kidding, Wyatt thought. After the news had set in, everyone in the family had wanted to congratulate them and cuddle the twins. His mom had persuaded them to stay for an impromptu family dinner. He'd agreed as readily as Adelaide. Mostly because he hadn't figured out how to be alone with her yet, under the startling new circumstances.

He wished he had one-thousandth of Adelaide's ease as a parent.

Horses, he knew. Kids, not so much. He'd never had the golden touch with them. Well, except for his nephews Max and Braden. Those little tykes had taken right to him. Maybe because he bore a resemblance to their own daddies…

"Do you think they're still hungry?" He and Jake edged closer to Adelaide and Jenny. His daughter hadn't lessened her wailing, either. "Because they were fed and burped right before we left the ranch." Less than thirty minutes ago. "Their diapers changed, too."

Adelaide inclined her head, indicating he should follow suit. She carried Jenny up the stairs. "I think they're just wound up and overtired." They moved into the nursery. "Nothing a little walking the floor with them won't cure. Unless…" Adelaide squinted at him thoughtfully. The crying was so loud now she had to practically shout to be heard. "You'd like to go on home now?"

Wyatt shook his head. He had responsibilities now. "I'll stay until they are asleep," he vowed firmly.

She pressed a kiss onto the top of Jenny's head. He did the same with Jake.

"Your horses…?" she asked.

"Troy and Flint, my hired hands, have already taken care of them."

Briefly, Adelaide looked disappointed. As if she'd been counting on his work to take him away from them. Heaven knew it wasn't the first time she'd used an excuse to put distance between them. It stung, just the same.

He told himself her reaction was understandable. Had it not been for the babies they now shared, he would have been out the door hours ago, new dissolution papers filed.

Instead, he was here with the three of them, trying to make sense of what had happened. Figure out how the heck they were going to proceed on a practical level.

It was one thing to promise to care for the kids together.

Another to actually make the situation work.

Luckily, right now, all they had to concentrate on was easing the persistent crying of their children.

He watched as Adelaide shifted Jenny's head onto her shoulder and tried somewhat awkwardly to do the same. While Jenny cuddled sweetly against Adelaide's soft breast, her head resting against the slender slope of her mommy's neck, Jake resisted doing the same. Recalcitrant, he arched his little spine, tilting the back of his neck against Wyatt's gently supporting palm.

Wyatt was tempted to give up, hand his son over. But given the fact that Adelaide had her own hands full, and Jenny was finally starting to settle down, just a little...

Adelaide mouthed the words, "Move him up a little higher. So his head is..."

Wyatt tried. Little Jake arched again. Opened his mouth wider and the largest belch Wyatt had ever heard came out. Followed swiftly by a flood of curdled, really foul smelling sour milk. Like an erupting volcano, the messy goo went all over Wyatt's shoulder, the front of his shirt, inside the collar, onto his neck. Trying not to get it on Jake, too—who was remarkably unscathed by the flood—Wyatt lifted his son slightly away from him, still holding him gently with both hands, and that's when two things happened. Jenny finally fell sound asleep. And Jake spit up again, this time all over the rest of Jake's shirt and pants.

Gently, Adelaide eased Jenny into her crib. The little darling slumbered on.

Wyatt expected Adelaide to reach for Jake, who, now that he'd emptied the contents of his tummy, was looking incredibly sleepy, too. Instead, she disappeared into the hall bath and came back, a damp washcloth in hand.

By then, Jake had put his head on the only other spit-up free zone of his daddy, Wyatt's other shoulder. His eyes were drifting closed.

Adelaide wiped the curdled milk from her son's face. "Want me to take him?" Adelaide murmured softly.

Wyatt shook his head, feeling incredibly proud and relieved he had done what just a few minutes ago had seemed impossible—nearly put his wildly upset son to sleep. "I've got this," he said.

And to his surprise, he did.

* * *

Adelaide had seen new dads cuddling babies. But nothing had ever affected her the way the sight of Wyatt, so tenderly cradling their son, did.

Aware she was near tears that if started would not stop, she turned away. She went into the bathroom, grabbed the lone towel off the rack and returned just as Wyatt was easing Jake into his crib. Her son slept on, looking incredibly peaceful and unscathed.

Wyatt, on the other hand, was a mess.

He looked like he'd been hit by a massive eruption of spoiled milk. He had a little bit in the edges of his hair, along his nape. He smelled even worse. She handed over the towel and another damp washcloth. He dabbed ineffectually, smearing spit-up into the terry cloth rather than removing it from his shirt.

She knew exactly how he felt. "I don't suppose you have any clean clothes in your pickup truck."

He shook his head regretfully.

Adelaide winced. She had nothing that would fit, and even worse, the smell of the sour milk was clearly making them both feel ill. "Experience has taught me the best way to clean up is just get in the shower. If you want to do that and toss the clothes out to me, I'll put them in the wash. An hour and fifteen minutes—you'll be good as new."

For a second, she thought he would argue.

A deep breath had him wincing in disgust and simply saying a gruff, "Thanks." He disappeared into the hall bath.

Twenty seconds later, the door eased open. The clothes, soiled towel and washcloth were handed out. Adelaide took them and disappeared down the stairs.

Luckily, the denim shirt, jeans, black boxer briefs and heavy wool socks could all go in one load. The snowy-white T-shirt and towel would have to go in another. Trying hard not to breathe in the stench, she pretreated the stains, added a detergent that was formulated for baby laundry and switched on the machine. Then she went to thoroughly wash her hands.

Wondering what she was going to give Wyatt to wear, which was maybe something she should have figured out before she had him strip down to nothing, Adelaide started back up the stairs.

Then went back down to get a fleece-lined navy lap blanket from the back of her sofa.

Halfway to the second floor of her cottage she realized two things. First, the shower had stopped. And second, in her urgency to get the river of baby vomit off him, she had neglected to give Wyatt something even more important.

A towel.

She hurried all the faster, reaching the upstairs hall and rounding the corner. Wyatt, never one to stand around waiting to be rescued, had quietly begun his own search for the linen closet. Never mind he was dripping wet and smelling of her lavender shampoo, from head to toe, his only clothing a pale pink washcloth that had already been in the shower, held like a fig leaf over his privates.

The ridiculousness of the scene, the sheer unpredictability of their situation, coupled with the sight of all those sleek, satiny muscles beneath the whorls of hair covering his tall body, had her catching her breath.

Memories flashed.

Laughter bubbled up in her chest.

He grinned, too—sheepishly now. But blissfully, kept his hand, and the washcloth, modestly in place.

That, too, hit her, hard.

The laughter came out.

Wilder now.

Uncontrollable.

Then, just as swiftly, turned into loud, wrenching sobs.

The kind that could wake her babies.

Tears streaming down her face, hand pressed against her mouth, smothering the increasingly hysterical sounds, Adelaide stumbled into the master bedroom.

The next thing she knew Wyatt's hands were on her shoulders. Warm. Soothing. He was spinning her around, pulling her close, wrapping his arms around her, holding her tight. And still she cried, and laughed, and cried some more. Her emotions spinning as out of control as her life.

She lifted her head, opened her mouth to jerk in a breath. And then his lips were on hers, drawing her in, and she was as lost in him as she had ever been.

His emotions just as out of control as Adelaide's, Wyatt folded the woman who had once been so much a part of his life, even closer. She was soft and vulnerable, feisty and sweet, and when it came to any sort of reconstituted relationship between them, stubbornly resistant as all get out. Yet when he held her in his arms, kissed her with such fierce abandon, she was all yearning, malleable woman. And right now he wanted her that way.

Not laughing and crying as if her world were splintering apart. Not angry and confused at the unexpected twist their lives had taken. And definitely not as furious as he had been since the last time they'd spent a night together, just under a year ago. When she had finally gotten the courage to make love with him. And then left him again anyway.

He didn't ever want her to feel as gut-punched as he had, when he had discovered she had chosen to have a baby with an anonymous donor rather than risk having a family with him.

Only to find out what he had wanted all along had come true anyway.

The undeniable fact was that after all this time he still wanted her, wanted this. Wanted the chances they'd never had. Most of all, he wanted to take advantage of the gifts they had been given. The kids. And through them, another chance, this time to get it right…

He'd half expected her to offer some resistance, even if it was only token. He ran a hand down her spine, pressing his hardness into the softness of her body.

She moaned at the onslaught of pleasure engulfing them both. Lifting his mouth from hers, he strung kisses along her jaw, her nape, the open vee of her blouse.

Lifting her arms to wreathe his shoulders, she pressed against him and kissed him back with a wildness beyond his most erotic dreams. Went up on tiptoe, her hands sliding down his spine, lower, lower still.

His body throbbing, he felt her end the kiss and then watched her step back. Damn if she wasn't the most beautiful woman he had ever seen.

Pink cheeks still wet with tears, dark eyes glowing, she sucked in an impatient breath and shimmied her skirt down her thighs. Toed off her suede flats and stripped off her tights.

He caught her hand before she could remove her blouse, undo the clasp of her bra. "Let me."

Her breath stalled. Holding her arms akimbo, she said softly, her eyes still holding his. "If you insist…"

Oh, he insisted all right.

Her blouse went the way of her skirt, and her skin felt soft and silky beneath his fingers.

Whole body thrumming with need, he undid the clasp and eased her ivory bra down her arms. Her breasts were fuller than he remembered, taut and round, the nipples rosy and erect. She wore matching panties that were slung low across her hips.

He hooked his thumbs into either side of them and tugged them down. Past the damp curls, her sleek thighs, past her knees. She gasped as he lowered her to the edge of the bed, parted her knees with his hands and buried his face in her sweet warm softness.

"Wyatt…" She caught his head in her hands, quivering now.

"Shhh." He found his way to the feminine heart of her. "Busy here."

She laughed softly. Shakily, as if on the verge of a new flood of tears.

Determined to help her find the release she sought, he dropped butterfly kisses, slow and deliberate.

She shuddered again but did not resist as he ran his thumb along the feminine seam, coaxing her to let all her worries, all her inhibitions float away, to open for him even more. She whimpered low in her throat and gave him full rein. He suckled the silky nub and stroked inside her, fluttering his tongue, until she caught his head in her hands and let her thighs fall even farther apart.

She quivered as he cupped her bottom with both hands, lifted her farther back on the mussed sheets of her bed. Pausing only long enough to grab the condom he carried in his wallet, he covered her and penetrated her slowly. She closed around him like a wet, hot sheath, her entire body shivering with need.

Feeling a little like the conqueror who had just captured the fair maiden of his dreams, he kissed her again, slowly tenderly, even as she draped her arms and legs around him and arched up to meet him. Her response, as true and unashamed as he always hoped it would be, he plunged and withdrew, aware of every soft whimper of desire, every wish, every need.

Until there was no more holding back for either of them.

She came apart in his hands. He free-fell right after her. Together they spiraled into ecstasy, and then slowly, breathlessly returned to the most magnificent peace Wyatt had ever known.

For long moments they held each other tightly, still shuddering, breathing hard. Loving the warmth and softness of her, he rolled so he was on his back. Stroking one hand through her hair, he held her nearer still.

Finally she lifted her head, and her hand came to rest in the region of his heart, even as a wry smile curved her kiss-swollen lips.

"So," she whispered with unexpected playfulness. Ready to do what she always did, which was downplay the import and strength of their connection. "Is this part of our conscious uncoupling, too?"

Chapter 5

"We're really going to throw that term around, as pertaining to us?" Wyatt asked lazily, doing his best to ignore the disappointment churning in his gut.

He knew Adelaide wasn't the least bit romantic. She had made that clear to him numerous times. Part of it was the way she had grown up, with a family that didn't seem to know the first thing about love.

Another was the linear nature of her chosen profession—as an accountant, numbers either added up or they didn't, and if they didn't, there had to be a concrete reason.

The rest was her unwillingness to forgive him for pushing her into an elopement she clearly wasn't ready for when they were kids, and letting her talk him into a reckless consummation years later, when he had known, deep in his gut, she hadn't been ready for that, either.

And tonight they'd done it again.

Made love on a reckless whim. For a whole host of reasons, all of them, obviously, in her retrospective view, wrong. Which likely meant, deep down, she was mad at him. Again. Even if she wouldn't let herself admit that, either.

Adelaide extricated herself from his arms, and grabbing a velvety pink blanket, wrapped it around her as she rose from the bed. "Conscious uncoupling is what we're doing."

He thought about how she looked and felt when she was on the brink, and, despite his effort to be the gentleman he'd been raised to be, got hard all over again.

He waggled his brows. "Funny, that felt more like coupling to me."

"Ha, ha." Adelaide grinned and tossed her head. "And you know what I mean. We have to figure out a way to get along with each other and peacefully co-parent. This—" she waved a hand down the length of her body, then his, before pulling on her bra and panties once again "—can only get in the way of that."

Aware he had nothing to put on save the washcloth he'd utilized earlier, he lounged in the mussed sheets of her bed. "Or make things more pleasant for both of us. After all, we're both healthy human beings in our prime. We have needs."

Bypassing her skirt, she walked to the closet and plucked out a pair of jeans.

He got even more aroused as he watched her draw them seductively up her long, sleek legs.

She wrinkled her nose and met his eyes with her own. A flicker of vulnerability shone in the dark chocolate depths. "Are you seriously using that line on me?"

Wyatt lay back on the pillows and folded his arms behind his head. His pulse amped up as she drew another quick breath. "I admit this isn't an itch that needs to be scratched on a regular basis unless I'm with you. Then…" He watched her draw a sweater over her head, only to get it briefly twisted up over the soft luscious curves of her breasts. "I'll be honest. I do want to forget being celibate." He paused, thinking about how passionately she had responded to him. How sweet and seductive she still looked now. "Can you honestly tell me you don't feel the same?"

Adelaide looked at the expression on his handsome face, the rock-hard muscles on his tall, broad-shouldered frame. A whisper of need swept through her, followed swiftly by a yearning that went soul deep.

"You're right. Normally I'm so busy I don't even have time to think about sex. Not the way I do when I'm with you," she admitted with a reluctant shake of her head, "and then…"

All common sense was gone.

His eyes drifted possessively over her. "It's chemistry. Right?"

She ran a brush through her hair, restoring order to the silky waves, but could do nothing about the just loved glow of her skin. Flushing, she snatched up the thick shearling-and-velour lap blanket she'd brought up for him and tossed it to him. "Unfortunately, given the fact we're all wrong for each other and you're probably never going to forgive me, yes." She turned her back as he took the hint and rose reluctantly.

"Forgive you for what?" His wheat-blond brow furrowed.

Adelaide led the way to the decidedly less intimate first floor. "Not figuring out what my father was doing before he stole millions from the Lockhart Foundation."

Wyatt followed, blanket wrapped around his waist. "None of us had a clue about that, Addie, until it was too late," he said softly.

There he went with his nickname for her again. There he went, looking at her like he loved her again.

Ignoring the quivering sensation low in her belly, Adelaide pushed on to the laundry room.

"Or getting cold feet the time we eloped." She plucked his clothes out of the washer and tossed them into the dryer. She caught a drift of his scent, as she leaned past him to punch the speed dry button. He smelled like soap and sex and lavender-scented bed sheets.

He shrugged, as if he'd suddenly found a way to let all that go. His gaze tracked hers, serious now. "We were way too young to even be considering marriage."

True, but...

She recited another reason he would never completely forgive her. "Botching up the annulment."

An affable grin deepened the crinkles around his eyes. "We hired the wrong lawyer. That was all."

He hadn't been this understanding four days ago.

She recited her most unforgivable sin of all. "Sleeping with you in Aspen without first telling you I already had plans to have a family alone?"

With a satisfied grin, he pulled her into his arms and held her close. "If you hadn't done that, I wouldn't be the father to twins," he said, his smoky blue gaze skimming her intently. "Jake and Jenny would be yours, not ours." He sifted a hand through her hair, tenderly cupped the side of her face. "And neither of us would have any clue just how good we are together, in bed—and possibly out."

Resisting the crazy urge to make love with him all over again, right here in the laundry room, she splayed her hands across the hard musculature of his bare chest. "It sounds suspiciously like you're about to let bygones be bygones."

"On two conditions," he declared.

Struggling to regain her equilibrium, she took a step backward and inhaled a shaky breath. "I'm listening."

He moved closer once again, dimples appearing on either side of his wide smile. "You forgive me for being a jackass where you're concerned, for most of the last ten years."

Her heartbeat quickened at the unexpected culpability in his low tone. She thought about the kisses they had shared and how quickly he had rocked her world. Again. She drew a bolstering breath. Swallowed to ease her parched throat. "I think I can do that."

He lightly caressed the back of her hand. "And we agree not

to lie to each other or keep things from each other from now on." He paused to let his words sink in. His expression turned calm, inscrutable. "I'm serious, Addie. Because I can't do this on-off again thing or have you run away and put a stop sign in front of your heart again. Like you did in Vegas. And Aspen," he told her quietly, gaze narrowing. "I don't want to feel like I'm not good enough for you to hitch your future to."

Not good enough! Was he kidding her?

"Where did you get that idea?" Adelaide retorted, unsure whether it was emotion or nerves causing her to respond so emotionally.

Looking impossibly manly with only a blanket knotted around his waist, he shrugged. "You were obviously holding out for something back then." Folding his arms in front of him, he braced his legs a little farther apart. "I kind of didn't think it was something *worse* than what I had to offer."

"Don't joke around," Adelaide said harshly.

Their eyes met and held for a breath-stealing moment. An expression she couldn't read passed across his face.

"Look, I'm okay if you don't love me. I'm not sure I love you anymore, either, or even if I ever did, but I have never stopped wanting you, or wanting to be with you. And if we are going to be together like this, then we have to be all in or all out," he warned, with a tone edged in steel. "Otherwise, I'm going to feel played again and resent you. And the tension between us will be unbearable—and that would be bad for the twins."

He was right about that.

They did need to be honest about what they each desired. Mindful of not just the twins' welfare, but their own feelings, as well.

"All right. I'm all for a physical relationship with you while we are living together. As long," Adelaide said, lifting a cautioning hand, "as it is a bed buddies, no-strings type of thing."

He studied her. "That's what you want?"

No, but it was realistic.

So she would settle for that. Because she had no other choice. Not trusting her voice, Adelaide nodded.

The reserve was back in his stormy eyes, along with lingering desire. "And one other thing," he said gruffly.

Her heart skittered in her chest.

She braced herself. "Yes?"

"If you have reservations about anything, I want you to tell me, and I promise I will do the same."

"Okay."

As for the rest...

The fact someone had been posting crazy messages on her social media pages, pretending to be her father, and then deleting them as soon as she'd read them...well, she didn't want to go into all that. There were some things that did not bear discussing. Not anymore. Not if they were going to have the peace they all desired.

"What all is going on the truck?" the two local movers asked Adelaide late the following morning, as she cradled Jenny in her arms.

"Everything from the nursery, including the two cribs, changing tables slash dressers, and rocker glider. And...?" Adelaide turned to Wyatt, who was holding Jake. "Do you have a guest bed at Wind River?"

"No."

The thought of them sharing sheets every night was definitely too much, too soon. She wanted them to be co-parents—not feel married. Even though, of course, technically they still were.

"Room for one?"

He tracked the pulse throbbing in her throat. Grinned. "Yes."

A self-conscious flush flooding her face, she swung back to the movers. "You'll also need to bring my bed. And all the assorted baby gear I've stacked in the living room."

Wyatt squinted, as the movers stripped her linens and dissembled her bed. "Sure you want to do that?"

They had made love again and slept together the night before, but that didn't mean they would want to do so every night hereafter. Since he didn't have a guest bed, she would bring her own.

"They aren't going to open up the walls on both floors until the addition is actually framed out. When they do, though, I was advised to cover everything in the vicinity with protective cloths, even though heavy plastic sheeting will be hung in the entryways to keep out the construction dust. Not having my bed there will mean one less thing to cover."

Wyatt wasn't fooled.

He knew she was still keeping one foot out the door and clearly wasn't happy about the idea. However, he might feel differently the first time sharing space got on their nerves. As she was sure it would eventually.

Luckily, they had no more time to discuss it.

The truck was loaded. "We're going to Wind River Ranch, not the Circle H," Adelaide told the crew.

Wyatt gave the address and directions.

And off they went. Adelaide could only hope they were doing the right thing.

Half an hour later, they reached Wind River, the horse ranch Wyatt ran. She'd heard it had been pretty run-down when he inherited it, but it looked to be in good shape now. With a long inviting drive, plentiful tree-lined pastures, outdoor and covered training arenas, and well-maintained outbuildings.

Wondering why Wyatt had parked beside them and directed her and the moving truck to do the same, Adelaide got out of her SUV. "Where's the ranch house?"

Wyatt blinked as if she had asked him the obvious. He pointed to the freshly painted slate-gray barn in front of them.

"You're kidding."

He wasn't kidding.

Upon closer inspection, she saw there were windows on both

floors, and the double doors in the center had dark black pulls on them, and a doorbell to one side. "You live here?"

Wyatt rubbed the flat of his hand beneath his jaw. "Surprised you hadn't heard."

Actually, she had heard some jokes from his brothers about him acting like he lived in a barn sometimes, but she thought they had just been razzing him.

Wyatt opened the rear passenger door of her SUV, while she opened the other. "Let's get the twins inside."

She plucked one infant carrier from its base, he undid the other. Together, with the sleeping twins still cozily ensconced in their travel seats, they headed up the walk.

Wyatt opened the door, using the numbered security pad, and held the door for her.

The interior was large and sweeping, sporting a beautiful wide-planked oak floor, creamy white walls, heavy masculine furniture, and dark beams overhead. A living area stood at one end, a kitchen, dining and laundry took up the other. A center staircase—also made of gleaming oak—led to the second floor.

As below, there were abundant windows along the sides and back. At one end of the mostly open space was a king-size bed; the other end held what appeared to be a sparsely appointed home office. A peek into the only walled-off area showed a large steam shower with glass walls, a private commode and a single vanity-sink.

"There's a half bath downstairs, tucked beneath the stairs," he said.

"Very nice," Adelaide murmured, panic beginning to sink in. She looked around. "But where are the twins and I going to be?" Where was her privacy? Her own space? Apart from him, and the desire he aroused in her?

Wyatt shrugged. "Anywhere you want. We can put you where my office is, if you like. Or in the center of the upstairs loft, close to the stairs, if that would be easier. There's plenty of open floor space."

But no walls.

And sometimes, good walls—with doors that shut firmly—made good housemates. No wonder his mother had such reservations about Adelaide and the twins moving in here!

Wyatt stared at her. "You seriously had no idea I lived in a converted barn?"

Adelaide shook her head.

She had tried to learn as little as possible about Wyatt and his life to avoid dwelling on mistakes made and lost opportunities. "Everyone in your family knew better than to try to discuss you with me, or vice versa. It was too upsetting to both of us."

"True."

Adelaide bit her lip. Too late, she realized she should have asked pertinent questions about his home before agreeing to move out here. Since they hadn't begun unloading the truck yet...

She swung back to him, her heart racing. "Sure you don't want to take advantage of your mother's offer and just move into the Circle H bunkhouse, with its six bedrooms and six en suite baths, in the interim?" Her bed could go into storage. Or better yet, back to her home. The twins could each have their own bedroom. Ditto her and Wyatt.

He scoffed, a mutinous look crossing his handsome face. "And have my mother pressuring us daily to make this a real marriage?"

His grim prediction brought her up short. "You're right. It's not what we want," she retorted, just as firmly.

She would go along to get along, just the way she always had.

However, she would *not* make the same mistake she had ten years ago and allow herself to get pressured into a lifelong romantic commitment that she was not ready to make.

Especially when they both knew that a real marriage was the only thing that would satisfy the very traditional-minded Lucille Lockhart.

She and Wyatt could craft a businesslike temporary schedule

that included lovemaking—when they both were in the mood—and plenty of time apart, in their own beds, when they weren't so inclined. They could split up care of the kids. That alone would keep them plenty busy.

"We're just doing this for the babies," she said out loud.

His expression unreadable, he nodded. "Because it's the right thing to do for everyone." Wyatt glanced out the windows. "The movers are getting restless. What do you want me to tell them?"

Adelaide carried the still sleeping Jenny to the master bed and set the carrier in the center of it. She motioned for Wyatt to do the same with Jake. "Have them bring everything that was on my second floor up here. We'll just have them set it up in the center for now. My bed on the office side, and the twins' nursery on yours."

Then they would go from there.

"You're sure you need the bottle warmers?" Wyatt asked later that afternoon, aware how cozy and domestic this all was. And even more surprising how much he already liked it. He paced back and forth, a sleeping Jenny in his arms, watching while Adelaide laid a sound asleep Jake in the Pack 'N Play they had set up.

"If it were just that…" Adelaide reached for Jenny and placed her in the identical bed next to her brother's. Keeping her voice low, she walked back to Wyatt, continuing, "I would wait until tomorrow. But I also forgot the baby first-aid kit and my laptop and work files for my clients, which really shouldn't be left in an unattended home. Plus half a dozen other things we might need, so it's best I go now."

She picked up on his unease. "The twins were awake most of the afternoon, watching the movers and getting acquainted with their new surroundings, so they should sleep most of the next two hours. I can probably be back in a little over an hour. But if you would be more comfortable, I could call your mom.

She's just down the road… If Lucille's home, she could be here to help out in five minutes."

The thought of another lecture on why he and Adelaide should just bite the bullet and stay married—for real—instead of trying to figure out how to untangle their lives and success-fully co-parent, brought a frown to Wyatt's face. "I've got it," he told her firmly. After all, what could happen in an hour that hadn't already?

Plenty, as it turned out. Jenny woke practically the moment Adelaide's SUV disappeared from view.

No worries.

Adelaide had showed him how to offer a pacifier.

Only problem? Jenny wouldn't take it.

His precious little girl didn't like the fact he was offering it to her, either. She looked around, tears glistening on her lashes, appearing to search for her mommy. And found only him. A poor substitute, in her view. She screwed up her little mouth into a deep frown, glared at him, then let out a howl of outrage.

Ignoring Adelaide's instructions, which had been to offer a pacifier and see if she went back to sleep first, he hastily picked Jenny up.

Too late.

Jake was already awake, as well.

And when he looked around and did not see his mommy, either, he became just as furious as his twin sister. Then pro-ceeded to open his mouth and squall until tears ran down his cheeks.

Meanwhile, Jenny was ignoring all attempts to soothe her and kept on crying as if her little heart would break.

Wyatt had options.

The question was, which should he take?

Her cottage was oddly quiet when Adelaide let herself in. Starting the following day, as the foundation for the addition was dug out, framed and poured, it would be pure chaos. But for now with the late-afternoon shadows slanting through the windows and a chill filling the interior, it was almost eerie.

Adelaide shook off her unease and went straight to her laptop. Gloomy atmosphere or not, she needed to check her work email before any more time elapsed. See if there were any crises with clients that would need handling right away.

She booted it up. Waited for her usual screensaver—a photo of the twins in the hospital nursery, taken just hours after they were born—to come up.

Instead, to her amazement, another photo of a child appeared. Adelaide blinked at the image of herself, at age six, with both her parents, and then another, when she graduated from SMU, in cap and gown, standing with her very proud dad.

"What in the world...?" Adelaide gasped, as the pictures she was looking at disappeared right before her eyes, and the picture of the twins that should have been there all along popped up behind the usual icons.

Adelaide continued staring at the screen.

Had she really seen what she thought she had? she wondered in alarm. If so, how was that possible? Or was whoever had been messing around on her social media pages, posting then removing messages as soon as she'd read them, playing even more tricks on her?

There was only one way to find out. With shaking hands, she reached into her purse and pulled out a card that a local law-enforcement officer had given her when she'd moved to the area. Dialed.

Short minutes later, Kyle McCabe, deputy detective in the Laramie County Sheriff Department, arrived at the house. He'd been off duty when she called but had headed right over.

While the head of their cyber crimes unit set down his messenger bag and shrugged out of his jacket, Adelaide briefly explained what had happened. "It was just there for a second. I almost think I imagined it." But she knew she hadn't.

Kyle examined the programs running on her laptop. "Did you put a remote log-on on your computer?"

"No!"

"Well, someone has. And it looks like the IP address is from Venezuela."

Her pulse began to pound. "How long has it been on there?"

He pointed to the installation date on the screen.

"That was when I was in the hospital, giving birth to the twins."

He studied her. "You're not surprised."

Adelaide told him about the messages she'd received on her social media pages that had also disappeared as soon as she had read them.

"When did they start?"

"Shortly after I got home from the hospital. I had posted Jake and Jenny's photo on my Facebook page and Instagram accounts, and I got a reply that said, 'Twins! I am so proud!'"

"And the post simply disappeared?"

"As soon as I read it. Then I got another a few weeks later that said, 'It was never my intention to leave you behind.' That one just came out of thin air one night when I was getting ready to upload some new pictures on my Instagram page, and again disappeared as soon as I read it. I was so sleep deprived at the time, so torn up over my lack of any real extended family I thought maybe I had dreamed it."

Kyle attached a device to her computer and began making a high-speed copy of all the data. "Why didn't you call me?"

Adelaide shivered and began to pace. "I was hoping that if it really had happened, and again, I wasn't entirely sure it had, that it was just one of the crackpots that harassed me after the scandal with the Lockhart Foundation first broke."

She paused, regretfully reflecting on the many hateful comments that had initially caused her to shut down all her social media until after the birth of the twins. When she had hoped enough time would have elapsed for it to be safe from harassment again.

"Were there any others?"

Reluctantly, Adelaide stopped and turned. "I received the last one two weeks ago." *Well before her life had imploded with the news she and Wyatt were not only still married but shared twins.* "It said, 'We can be part of each other's futures.'"

"You think it was him?"

Adelaide shrugged. "It certainly wasn't Wyatt." She massaged her forehead. "Sorry." She didn't know why she had just blurted that out.

Kyle smiled sympathetically. "Congratulations, by the way."

Adelaide flushed. She still found it embarrassing to have everyone know that she and Wyatt had slept together. "Thanks."

"Does Wyatt know about any of this?"

Her personal misery increasing tenfold, Adelaide shook her head. "He was so angry before. I didn't want to mention it."

"And you shouldn't," Kyle said firmly. "If these messages are from your father, we don't want anyone outside the cyber crimes unit here having a clue."

The low warning in his voice got to her. "You don't think my dad would mean me and the twins any harm?"

"Not from the sound of it, but he could still inadvertently put you in legal jeopardy for aiding and abetting."

"I've already told you," Adelaide choked on another wave of bitterness. "If I ever see him again, I'm turning him in."

Kyle nodded appreciatively. "In the meantime, the sheriff's department needs to keep the GPS tracker on your phone and SUV, and I'd like to put a keystroke recording device on your laptop, too. That way, if there are any other remote log-in attempts on it, we'll get an immediate alert down at the station, and we'll be able to record and track the activity on our surveillance system in real time."

Adelaide swallowed, as her next thought hit. "You don't think my father...he wouldn't be back in the country, would he? Not without being detected?"

"The Texas-Mexico border is porous. With fake ID, a change in his looks, yeah, he could do it."

"But why?"

"Maybe he just wants to see you and meet his grandkids. You are all the family he has, you know."

"He has Mirabelle Fanning," Adelaide reminded him bitterly.

"If they're still together. Once a crime is committed, the co-conspirators often split up."

Adelaide thought about that, and knew it wouldn't make any difference to her if they had. She was never going to be able to forgive her father for what he had done. "Or maybe he wants me to steal for him. Or he wants to steal *from me*." Angry tears blurred her eyes.

"Check your bank accounts and credit cards."

Adelaide sat and quickly pulled everything up. She breathed a sigh of relief. "My accounts are all fine."

"Clients?"

She relaxed even more as she realized none of those files, which had elaborate security protecting each and every one, had been breached. "Also fine."

He opened his leather messenger bag. "I'd like to sweep the house and then put some listening and recording devices in."

Adelaide envisioned a team of law-enforcement personnel storming her house, much as they had in Dallas after the initial scandal broke. The fact she had requested their presence to see if they could find anything there had not made it any easier to bear. "Won't that cause a lot of talk?" Talk that would be sure to get back to Wyatt and the rest of the Lockharts?

"If I do it while you're still here, no one will be any wiser."

Adelaide watched as Kyle put tiny devices behind pictures, under lamps. Another minuscule camera was trained at the front door. "People could wonder why you're staying so long."

Early evening, Kyle had already been there an hour. While

Wyatt was back at the ranch with the twins. Who, most likely, were still sleeping.

Casually, Kyle provided their cover story. "If anyone asks, you're doing my taxes for me."

Made sense. She was a CPA who often met with clients at her home.

Kyle cast her a brotherly look. "It'll be okay, Adelaide."

"Good, because I really can't afford to be at the epicenter of another scandal right now. Nor can the Lockharts. And if this turns into a mess..."

Kyle guessed where she was going with this. "You could easily find yourself in the middle of a custody battle."

Adelaide nodded miserably.

Kyle walked into the attached garage and put a device just above the back door. "Wyatt's a good guy."

Adelaide knew that.

But like her, he wasn't without his faults. "Just not the most forgiving type. Which is," she said, squaring her shoulders and drawing a deep breath, "another reason why I don't want Wyatt to know. We're trying to become a family right now..."

"Nothing will be leaked from the department," Kyle promised.

"That's good," she said in relief. Because she was pretty sure if her dad was back, Wyatt would not understand. Or forgive.

Chapter 6

Adelaide hoped to find peace upon her return to the ranch. And, thankfully, the converted barn was quiet, except for the whisper of the double-stroller wheels gliding across the wide plank floor.

It was Wyatt who looked on the verge of parental exhaustion, a feeling she knew all too well.

Guilt mingled with regret. Wondering just how long he had been pushing the stroller around, she set down her belongings and quickly shrugged out of her coat. "Sorry that took so long," she said, moving toward him.

He stayed where he was, gently moving the stroller back and forth. Nodded, as if to say, "I'll bet."

She hated withholding stuff from him, had sworn she wouldn't do so again, and yet here she was, forced, for all their sakes, to hide what was really going on with her.

Aware Wyatt always noticed much more than she wished, she closed the distance between them. "I got caught up. I had a problem with my laptop, which—" she sighed in real frustration "—I was eventually able to resolve. And then Kyle Mc-

Cabe dropped by." She choked out the fib, knowing that if her "husband" heard about it, it should be from her. "He wants me to do his tax return."

"You couldn't have called?" Wyatt asked brusquely.

Of course she could have, but she had needed the time to gear up for the half-truths she was going to have to tell if she were to keep him—and the twins—out of the mess her life was quickly becoming. "You're right. I should have."

He gave her a telling look but made no reply.

She knelt to look at her little darlings. "What's been going on?"

Seeing her, both babies spit out their pacifiers and burst into tears. With a *shhh* sound, Adelaide steered the stroller to the rocker-glider. She put on the brake, sat, then gathered first Jenny, then Jake into her arms, cuddling them against her breasts.

"They've been awake the entire time," he reported grimly, his emotional exhaustion mirroring hers in similar situations. "The only thing that soothed them was that." Looking tough and sexy in his usual indomitable way, he pointed to the stroller.

As Adelaide rocked the twins, slowly, but surely, their cries subsided. "So you've been wheeling them around the entire time?" *For three hours?*

"When I wasn't changing them and feeding them another bottle, which by the way, neither seemed to really want."

She hated that he'd had such a hard time. She allowed herself to admire the width of his shoulders and the flex of his muscles beneath his shirt. "Why didn't you call me? Or your mother?"

Wyatt's brow furrowed. "I didn't call my mother because she already lacks faith in my ability to do this on the fly."

Adelaide knew Lucille could hover. Particularly where her Wyatt was concerned, but she had never realized it bothered him. "Did Lucille do or say something…?"

He was silent a long moment, his expression inscrutable. "She emailed me a slew of articles on being a good dad and husband."

Adelaide swallowed around the sudden ache in her throat. "Husband?"

"Yep."

The tension within her intensified. Only it was a different kind of heat and tension. The kind that usually preceded their lovemaking. "Lucille knows we're not planning to stay married."

His gaze caressed her face. "Yeah, well, she says the key to being a good father is being a good husband. So, according to her, if I really want to do it right, I've got to figure out a way to make us work, too."

"I'm sure she means well," Adelaide soothed.

He cocked his head. "I take it this means you didn't get any articles?"

"Ah. Not yet." *Hopefully never.* "But," Adelaide said, trying to stay positive, "even if she did send them, I would not take offense because your mom has become a second mother to me."

In fact, Adelaide wasn't sure what she would have done the last year without Lucille. "I'm sure it's just her way of helping," she continued.

He rested his hands on his waist and gave her a dubious glance. "Well, here's hoping Mom offers a lot less assistance in the future."

Adelaide watched him walk into the kitchen and pour himself a glass of chilled water from the outside spigot on the fridge. Big body tense with frustration, he drained two-thirds of it in one gulp.

"Okay, I get why you didn't call Lucille when you could have used some help with the twins," Adelaide persisted, curious, "but why didn't you call me?"

He drained the rest, then looked at her over the rim of his glass. "Because I thought you'd be home any moment."

Home. Adelaide liked the sound of that, despite her inner caution not to let herself get as wound up in her relationship with Wyatt as the Lockhart matriarch wanted.

He let out a rough exhalation of breath, oblivious to her simmering guilt and tension. "And I didn't want to worry you if
you were driving." He edged closer, peering at the snoozing
babes. "Especially since things were sort of under control," he
admitted softly.

Adelaide stopped rocking long enough to meet his smoky
blue gaze. "You did a good job with them."

He sent her a skeptical glance.

"Seriously. With anyone else they didn't really know, if they'd
been awake that long, they would have been howling at the
tops of their lungs when I walked in. The fact they stayed calm
must mean—" she drew a deep breath, determined to get this
out whether he wanted her to or not "—they realize on some
instinctive level that you're their daddy."

He paused. "I doubt—"

"Can't you feel the connection? With me...in the hospital...
it was innate."

He hunkered down beside her, his expression one of almost
unbearable tenderness. Reaching out, he gently stroked the side
of each baby's cheek. "Yeah." He surprised her by admitting
softly, reverently, "I felt it the first time I saw them at your
home, even before we had any idea they were ours. That's why
I couldn't stop looking at them. And noticing everything about
them. I feel it even more now. I just didn't know *they* did."

"Well, they do," Adelaide said fiercely. Powerful emotion
welled within her for this man, the children they shared.

"And if you'll help me now, I think we can put them down
in their cribs. At least for a little while."

"How do you feel about brisket tacos?" Wyatt asked, when
they came back downstairs.

Glad the tension had eased between them once again, Adelaide smiled. She took a seat at the island while he moved
around the counter. "Love 'em."

He pulled an armload of items out of the fridge. "Good, because I'm starving, and that's all we've got for dinner that can be ready in about ten minutes. What's that look for?"

Adelaide shook her head in a mixture of apology and regret. "I'm usually so linear about planning, but all I thought about this morning was making sure I had enough supplies to feed and diaper the twins."

"That's why you have me," he joked.

She wished it were true. That he was there to see to her needs and wants, as well as just the twins. But that wasn't the deal they had made.

"I guess you have to be prepared out here in the country." She rested her chin on her upraised fist, and watched him chop up a pound of smoked brisket, then slide it into a skillet. A smattering of southwestern spices and splash of beef broth followed.

Apparently Sage wasn't the only chef in the family, she thought as the tantalizing aroma of Tex-Mex soon filled the air. "You can't exactly call for takeout."

He flashed her an impish grin. "Not unless you want to drive an hour round-trip to pick it up."

As the mood began to lighten, she found herself relaxing, too. Maybe this arrangement of theirs would work out after all. "Next time I'm in town, I'll check with you before I leave."

He set another skillet on the stove and began warming flour tortillas. While he worked, he poured grated Monterey Jack cheese and slaw into serving bowls. Then got out some chips and tomatillo salsa. "When do you need to go back in to Laramie?"

She dipped a crispy corn chip into the fragrant salsa. "The twins have their two-month checkup next week."

"Can I go?" He helped himself, too.

Adelaide savored the spice on her tongue. "You are their dad."

He grinned, obviously liking the sound of that.

"But yes, to answer your question more directly, I really would like your help," she admitted, the heat in her mouth nothing compared to the heat rippling through her, whenever he neared.

He looked at her, listening intently.

"They're going to have immunizations," Adelaide continued. "And I'm a little nervous about it. The Hep B injections they had at one month didn't go so well."

Wyatt put the softened tortillas in the warmer, turned off the heat under both skillets and covered the meat mixture with a lid. Then came around to sit beside her. "What do you mean?"

Their blue-jeans-clad legs nudged as they faced each other. "Well," Adelaide confessed, a little embarrassed, as he took her hand in his, "they'd never had a shot before. And they cried. And then I cried." Adelaide welled up just thinking about it. "I was supposed to be calm and reassuring, and instead I was almost as much as a mess as they were. At least for a couple of moments. Luckily, your mom had offered to go with me to help out, and she was much more composed."

Wyatt tightened his hand on hers. Stood, and guided her off the stool and into his arms. "That was nice of her," he murmured, stroking a hand through her hair.

Adelaide rested her head against his shoulder. "That's when I got the idea to ask her to be their godmother. Even though what I really wished—" Wyatt's understanding glance helped her admit "—was that Lucille was their grandmother."

He pressed a kiss onto the top of her head. "Looks like you got your wish," he commented in a low gravelly tone. He pulled her tighter against him, his gaze warm, possessive. Sliding his hands down her hips, he planted his hands on either side of her, trapping her between the counter and his tall hard frame. "And for the record, I'm glad we gifted my mother with two more grandchildren, too."

His head slanted downward, and he gazed deep into her eyes. Then his lips shifted over hers, as he delivered the kiss they'd been avoiding all day. Adelaide knew they should slow things down. Get to know each other again first before attempting intimacy. But she couldn't do that this time any more than she had been able to the last time he took her in his arms.

She'd been frightened today.

And she still felt unnerved.

Holding and kissing him felt safe.

Wreathing her arms about his shoulders, she opened her mouth to his and kissed him back with all the pent-up emotion of the day.

Not just once. But again and again.

Sensation swept through her. And suddenly everything she had held back, everything she wanted and needed, came pouring out of her. And what she wanted most was a do-over with Wyatt.

Maybe they couldn't go back to the innocent place where they had left off. But they *could* replace the heartbreak they'd felt when they split with happier memories. They could use the erotic connection they had to deepen the bond between them.

So she kissed him feverishly, until their hearts pounded in unison. Until her mind was rife with all the possibilities she had been forcing herself not to consider. The God's honest truth was, she wanted to be more than just co-parents with him. Or casual partners. How crazy was that?

As if sensing the direction her thoughts were going, he unbuttoned her blouse, undid the clasp on her bra. Then stepped closer again and kissed her until her breasts pearled and her knees weakened.

His eyes dark with desire, he cupped her breasts and ran his thumbs across the jutting crests. She caught her breath as he ran his hands over her ribs, unzipped her jeans, eased them—and her panties—off, too. The next thing she knew, he had shifted a knee between her thighs. Still kissing her, he showed her a new way of giving and receiving pleasure.

That quickly, she trembled on the precipice. All because of his lips and hands and rock-hard thigh. She moaned again. Pushed him away. "I want us to come together."

He grinned. Grasping both her wrists, he pinned them on either side of her, kissed his way down to her breasts, languidly exploring her nipples. "We can do that, too…"

Impatient to feel him all the way against her, she wrested free, undid his jeans, stroked him silkily. He extracted a condom from his wallet, then tensed as she helped him roll it on. The next thing she knew, he'd lifted her onto the counter. Hands circling her hips, he tugged her toward the edge.

Their eyes locked. Desire and something else…something a lot more powerful…reigned. Her muscles tautened, trembling as he found his way home in one slow, purposeful slide.

Allowing her the time to adjust to the weight and size of him, he went deeper still. Kissing her, rocking into her, slowly, patiently, until she writhed in ecstasy with each stroke. Surrendering to him completely, until there was nothing but the intense driving need, the giving and the taking. Nothing but pleasure and a sweet, swirling oblivion that led to the most magnificent peace Adelaide had ever known.

Gradually, their breathing eased.

Their bodies stopped shuddering.

Adelaide had never felt more like a woman—*his woman*. Shaken by how emotional she felt, she knew she had to change the mood to a much more practical level before she ended up doing something really reckless, like fall in love with him all over again. She opened her eyes and lifted her head.

He looked just as besotted as she felt. "Wyatt?"

"Hmm?" His gruff, sexy voice made her quiver all over again.

She took a deep breath and squared her shoulders resolutely. "That food smells really good. And I'm starving."

Wyatt wasn't surprised Adelaide wanted to put their lovemaking into the Just Sex category. The part of him that had crashed and burned in his prior relationship with her wanted that, too. It would be so much easier. Especially now that they had kids to consider. So, with an easy smile, he conceded to her wishes. Concentrated simply on enjoying their dinner.

By the time they finished, the twins were awake again. Two sets of hands for the diaper changes, and the bottle warmers she'd brought back with her, made quick work of heating up the formula and settling down to feed the babies.

The only problem was, Wyatt noted in disappointment, that neither Jenny nor Jake really wanted him to be the parent caring for them. Both much preferred to be in Adelaide's arms, in their sole rocker-glider. He couldn't really say he blamed them. She was a far sight more adept at all of this than he was. Hopefully, though, with her help, that would soon change.

In the meantime, they had important matters to discuss. "I forgot to tell you earlier. Gannon Montgomery called while you were gone."

Adelaide gestured for him to head up the stairs, toward the "nursery" now set up in the center of the open loft. "And...?"

Aware Jenny was increasingly drowsy, she put their daughter on the changing table and swaddled her.

Watching, learning, Wyatt paced back and forth, Jake curled up against his chest, peering over his shoulder.

Not sure if it was too soon to discuss this or not, Wyatt told her, "Gannon wanted to know if we are considering any kind of name change for the twins."

Adelaide took Jake and put him on his changing pad, then handed off Jenny to Wyatt to cuddle. Her brow pleated in wary confusion. "You mean call the twins something other than Jake and Jenny?"

"No." Wyatt breathed in the baby-fresh scent of the infant in his arms, not sure when he had ever felt as happy as he did in this instant, with a family of his very own. No wonder all the women he knew, his age, were so baby crazy. He looked Adelaide in the eye, glad she had given him this gift, even if she hadn't actually meant to do so. "Their first names suit them perfectly," he said sincerely.

"Good. For a moment, I thought…" Adelaide broke off with a shake of her head, then slid a folded blanket beneath their son and swaddled him, too.

Wyatt knew Adelaide feared he would barge into their lives, like a bull in a china shop, and try to control everything. Which was why he was trying so hard to give her as much space as she needed, so she wouldn't instinctively withdraw and put up a wall around her heart again.

A move that would make things difficult for them on every level.

"But I would like them to carry the surname of Lockhart," he continued, forthright.

Adelaide picked up the yawning Jake and walked over to gaze out the windows overlooking the south end of the ranch. "How would you feel about a hyphenated last name?"

Wyatt joined her and turned the not quite as drowsy Jenny, so she too could enjoy the sweeping views of the training rings and moonlit pastures that held his cutting horses during the day.

"Smythe-Lockhart?" He tried it on for size.

Adelaide paced toward the area where his office had been set up, and now contained her queen-size bed. It had been placed beneath the arched windows that overlooked the drive leading up to the ranch.

Noting she looked as weary as he felt, he admitted, "I'd prefer Smythe as a middle name, for both, and Lockhart for the last. It's more traditional, especially in rural areas like this. But if you object…"

"I don't." Adelaide carried the now snoozing Jake to the crib. She laid him gently on his back and turned on the musical mobile. The upstairs was suddenly filled with the soothing Brahms lullaby. She took Jenny from Wyatt's arms, settling her in her crib, on the other side of the twin changing tables, beneath her mobile, too.

Straightening, she continued, "The name Smythe still carries negative connotations. Whereas 'Lockhart' will open a lot of doors for them."

They moved slightly back, away from the well-separated cribs. Watched as the children's lashes slowly closed. "So we're agreed?" he asked softly.

Adelaide nodded, looking as relieved as he felt that the twins were finally asleep. "We are."

Unfortunately, the quiet didn't last. Jenny woke at 9:00 p.m. and roused her brother. They got back to sleep by ten, only to have the reverse happen at eleven. Again, she and Wyatt were able to get both twins asleep by midnight.

The moment they tried to set them in their cribs, however, Jenny and Jake kicked up a fuss that continued for the next two hours.

Both were given bottles, burped, changed and held.

And absolutely nothing worked. The twins were determined not to fall back asleep. Finally, at two in the morning, Wyatt declared, "We tried it your way all evening. Now let's try mine."

He wasn't exactly the expert here. She was. "They are not going to fall asleep."

He oozed testosterone. "We'll see."

Her heart skittered in her chest. "Where are you going?"

"To set things up."

Leaving her in the rocking chair, with both babies in her arms, he bolted up the stairs. She heard him moving around, back and forth, from one end of the loft to the other. From the sound of it, moving the cribs, too. Finally, he came back down. Clad—like her—in pajamas this time. The flannel pants fit loosely. The long sleeved dark T-shirt hugged every masculine muscle. The sight of him, ready for bed, made her mouth go dry.

Luckily, there would be no more lovemaking tonight. Not, given what they were dealing with. And that was a good thing. Wasn't it?

Oblivious to her unexpectedly amorous thoughts, he eased Jake from her arms. Helped her to her feet. "Follow us, ladies."

With Wyatt in the lead, they mounted the stairs.

Every pillow—and there'd been half a dozen of them—had been removed from her bed and piled against the headboard of his. The cribs had been repositioned, one on either side of his king, at the head of the bed.

Once again, he saw much more than she would have liked. He gazed indulgently down at her. "What's wrong?"

"I was trying to approximate their nursery at home. The problem is, without walls separating the rooms, the acoustics are so different. They may not be able to see things are so different here, but they can hear it and feel it."

And then, there was the lack of privacy she had, too. The feeling she was oh so vulnerable.

He sauntered closer. Leaned down to kiss her temple.

"Maybe what they need to see is Mommy and Daddy. Sleeping peacefully—or at least pretending to sleep—nearby."

Aware he was going to be very hard to resist, if he kept up the charm offensive, she drew a breath. "So what's the plan, Daddy?"

He grinned at the endearment. "We stop rocking and singing and walking the floor with them. Get into bed, relax and let them snuggle against our chests."

She refused to get sucked in by the blatant sexiness of his gaze. "And then they will magically go to sleep," she countered dryly.

He grinned, optimistic, his wishful thinking stronger than ever. "Probably not right away, but eventually."

At this point, they had absolutely nothing to lose. Except maybe the last of the emotional distance between them.

Tossing a sassy look his way, Adelaide sat on the side of the bed. She swung her legs around and eased back onto the pillows, a swaddled Jenny still in her arms. Wyatt did the same with Jake. They lounged side by side, their legs stretched lazily out in front of them, shoulders, necks and heads nestled comfortably against the heap of pillows.

Unable to help herself, Adelaide let out a long, easy breath.

He nudged her arm playfully. "Feels good, hmm?"

You feel good, pushed up against me like that.

Plus, his sheets smelled like the masculine soap and shampoo he used. Well, that and him. And her pillows smelled like her perfume. The comingling of the scent brought even more sensual memories to mind.

It was a good thing they both held a baby in their arms.

Because otherwise…given the fact this was her very first time to ever climb onto his bed with him…

"Wyatt?" Adelaide lazily tracked the moonlight sifting through the loft.

"Hmm?"

She yawned, suddenly worrying. With sex out of the equation and her baby snuggled in her arms… "This is suddenly making me very, very sleepy."

Wyatt nodded. "Jenny and Jake, too."

Surprised, Adelaide looked down. Sure enough, the twins were nestled against Adelaide's and Wyatt's chests, their faces turned into their necks. Eyes closed, rosebud lips pursed, they were the picture of sweetness and innocence.

Adelaide yawned again, really struggling now. "It won't last," she predicted in a weary whisper, "once we put them down."

He elbowed her lightly again. "'O ye of little faith.'"

Rising ever so carefully, he eased off the bed and placed Jake ever so tenderly in his crib. Then watched as Adelaide reluctantly did the same.

Jenny barely stirred.

Jake slept on.

Adelaide stood there, looking down.

Wyatt took her hand. Drawing her back down, this time between the sheets. "They need to see us if they do wake up, remember?" he whispered in her ear.

84   *The Texas Valentine Twins*

Nodding, Adelaide relented. She turned toward Jenny's crib. Wyatt climbed in and turned toward Jake. Spines touching from shoulder to hip, they watched and waited for the next interruption of restful peace.

Chapter 7

"I don't understand why it's not working," Wyatt said five hours later, when they again tried and failed to put the fed, changed and lightly sleeping twins down in their respective cribs, which had been moved to the right and left sides of his king-size bed.

Seven in the morning, he should be out working with his horses. Instead, he and Adelaide were still trying—fruitlessly— to resituate Jake and Jenny. So Adelaide, at least, could get a few more hours of much-needed sleep.

She sighed and ran her hand through the tousled strands of her dark hair. "I think it's because it's daylight and they can see they're in a strange place."

"You think they'll go back to sleep if we put their cribs elsewhere?"

She drew a breath that lifted the soft curves of her breasts. "I think it's a worth a try."

He tried not to think how intimate it felt, to be standing there with both of them in their pajamas. Or how much he loathed moving furniture on a whim. "Where do you want them?"

Adelaide pointed. "Next to your office area."

"Both cribs?"

"Separated by the changing tables, yes."

Hadn't they already tried that? In the middle of the open second floor, the previous night? Only to have Jake and Jenny continuously wake each other up?

Adelaide set Jenny in her crib. "Putting their beds next to the light-colored walls might make it seem cozier and more familiar."

Wyatt put Jake in the same bed, next to his twin.

The two babies now sobbed in unison.

Together, she and Wyatt carried the other crib to the far end of the loft. "Here?" Wyatt asked, as the sound of the babies crying lessened the farther they got away.

Adelaide raked her lip with her teeth, surveying the space. "I think we should move both cribs in that corner, where it's not so bright. But it means we're going to have to move your desk a little bit."

Wyatt moved one end of the heavy desk.

"It's crooked."

But there was now room. He waved off her objection. "Doesn't matter."

"But…"

"I don't want to have to unplug everything," he said tersely.

She stepped back. "Oh."

Aware they were on the brink of having their first "marital tiff," he softened his tone and suggested gently, "Let's just move the cribs where you want them now. If it works, we'll worry about finalizing the details later."

Together, they moved one crib, and two changing tables to the corner. "Better?" he asked.

She nodded. Listening. Her brow furrowed as they locked gazes. "Did they stop crying?"

Not sure whether that was a good or bad sign, they both turned and moved to the side of the remaining crib.

"Well, what do you know," Wyatt murmured, as they stared in disbelief.

Jake and Jenny had both wiggled themselves out of the top of their swaddling. Their little hands were outstretched to each other, fingers touching. Heads turned, they were cooing drowsily.

"Amazing," Adelaide whispered proudly.

Wyatt wrapped his arm around her shoulders and tucked her against his side. He wanted to memorize this moment forever. "They really are."

And it wasn't just the twins.

This whole arrangement. Adelaide. It was all remarkable, too.

Jake and Jenny fell asleep shortly thereafter. Adelaide and Wyatt decided to take advantage of the quiet to shower and dress for the day. Adelaide showered first, then went down to the first floor, while Wyatt had his turn.

She had just finished drying her hair when she heard a car in the drive. A look out the windows had her opening the door to Lucille, Sage and Hope.

All three were carrying gifts. Lucille and Sage both had wind-up infant swings. Hope had a large basket of baby toiletries and toys.

"We figured it wasn't too early," Lucille said.

Glad to be welcomed so warmly into the Lockhart family, Adelaide ushered them in. "Not at all."

Wyatt walked down the stairs to join them. His hair was damp, his shirt buttoned but untucked over his jeans. He looked sexy and approachable. Tired, but happy, too. "What's up?"

"We brought you something to make your life a little easier," Lucille said, as she and her only daughter set the swings down, side by side.

"All my friends with babies love them," Sage added. "They tell me it's a surefire way to ease crankiness and put a fussy infant to sleep."

"I just wish I'd had one when Max was small," Hope said.

"Of course, sometimes only rocking will do," Lucille continued. She eyed the rocker-glider Adelaide had positioned on the first floor, then looked at her son.

"Don't worry, Mom," Wyatt said dryly. "I'm spending time there, too."

Lucille paused, clearly worried. "If you need advice..."

Briefly, her son looked irritated. "We've got it covered, Mom." He gestured amiably. "So if that's all..."

"Actually," Hope put in, suddenly looking very much like the crisis manager she was, "we need to talk to you."

Adelaide recognized trouble when she saw it. Had another computer been surreptitiously hacked with remote log-in software? "Did something happen at the Lockhart Foundation?" she asked nervously.

Wyatt sent her a look.

"This time," Hope said gently, "the scandal revolves around the four of you." She handed over a multipage printout containing the recent headlines from Texas gossip and parenting blogs and websites.

Scandal Rocks One of Texas's Famous Families Again! stated *Texas Weekly* magazine.

Surprise—It's Not Just a Decade-Old Elopement, but Twins! blasted the *Dallas Morning Sun* society page.

The popular Lone Star Mommies blog ran with, Parenthood with Both Feet Out the Door?

"And last but not least from the salacious but widely read *Texas Grapevine Online*," Hope said, while Wyatt and Adelaide read with increasing dismay: *Lucille Lockhart, disgraced former CEO of the Lockhart Foundation, had what she terms a happy surprise. Adelaide Smythe, the daughter of longtime family friend and embezzler Paul Smythe, former CFO of the Lockhart Foundation, secretly eloped with her son, Wyatt, nearly a decade ago. Flash-forward to a romantic—or was it preplanned?—rendezvous in Aspen last spring, and suddenly due to a snafu with the paperwork (where have we heard that before?) not only are Wyatt Lockhart and Adelaide Smythe still married, but thanks to the sparks that still exist between them, have given birth to twins.*

Now, trying to figure a way out of this mess, the lucky—or prodigiously unlucky!—couple has decided to move in together.

Once the legal issues are worked out, an amicable divorce is predicted to occur. That is, if a property settlement can be reached. Our legal experts tell us that ten years together makes nearly everything fair game financially for the ambitious new Lockhart Foundation CFO, and only daughter of criminal-at-large, Paul Smythe. A fact that should encourage rancher Wyatt Lockhart to firmly stake his claim on his kids and bide his time, exiting the precarious relationship...

"Lovely," Adelaide deadpanned, before she could stop herself. Even though neither she nor Wyatt had made a secret of their plans to become a family first, then consciously uncouple over the next year or so, it still stung to see it in print.

Hope frowned. "There are half a dozen more articles like this, and the news just got out a few days ago, when people started receiving their invitations to the party Lucille is giving on your behalf."

Wyatt narrowed his gaze. "I thought you said embracing the situation would lessen the scandal."

Hope smiled. "That's the good news. It probably has."

Adelaide sniffed miserably. "It doesn't feel that way."

"From a public-relations perspective, the real problem is Adelaide's father," Hope told them gently. "If Paul had been arrested and tried..."

"And were sitting in jail somewhere," Wyatt theorized, his need for justice as strong as ever.

"...the case closed," Hope continued, "then it would be old news. The fact he remains on the FBI's Most Wanted list keeps the story alive."

It was a good thing Wyatt didn't know someone was either

contacting her on her dad's behalf, Adelaide thought with dread, or pretending to be Paul...

She swallowed. All the facts weren't in yet. There was no point in borrowing trouble. They had enough already. "So what should we do?" she asked, wondering if this were going to impact her small salary as Lockhart Foundation CFO and the small accounting practice that kept her financially afloat.

"Well, you all know what I think," Lucille said.

"We're not staying married indefinitely, Mom," Wyatt warned.

Lucille wrung her hands. "But as long as you are, even for a little while, couldn't you just bow to public opinion, give this relationship your all and renew your vows to in some way lessen the talk?"

"No!" Wyatt and Adelaide said in unison. Thankfully, of one mind about that.

"We're not going to let our emotions—or anyone's else's—regarding our situation overrule common sense!" he insisted.

Adelaide agreed. "I've let myself be pushed into saying yes too many times in my life, when I really should have said no." She straightened to her full five feet seven inches. "This is one of those times."

"I agree." Wyatt wrapped his arm about her shoulders.

"It was just a suggestion," Lucille huffed, "but I still think you should keep in mind giving this marriage a real try."

"As much as I hate to differ with you, Lucille," Hope said, tactfully taking on her mother-in-law, "I would advise the opposite to curtail this kind of loose talk and speculation, if Wyatt and Adelaide are indeed still planning to divorce."

"We are," Wyatt and Adelaide said again in perfect unison.

Wyatt dropped his arm.

Hope accepted their decision in a way Wyatt's mom apparently could not. "The fact that the two of you have announced you intend to co-parent the children amicably and become a family is admirable. I haven't seen a single negative remark in print about that. But, the fact you've moved in together and everyone knows your marriage is still legal muddies the waters considerably. It's inviting speculation. Such as, how long will they actually all be under one roof? Will they or won't they stay married? Is it going to work out? If not, why not? In situations like this, rumors can go wild."

And with rumors came more embarrassment for Lucille and the rest of the Lockhart clan. "We really don't want that," Adelaide said quietly.

Hope understood. "Then, the sooner you wrap up all the legal details, as to the future plans of the two of you, and get those out there as a matter of public record, the better."

Wyatt and Adelaide called their respective attorneys and set up an appointment for the following afternoon, while Molly and Sage babysat the twins.

"We think it might be better if we go ahead and set our divorce in motion," Adelaide said, as she and Wyatt met with their lawyers in the conference room at Gannon's office.

Wyatt didn't know if it was the fact that the two of them hadn't made love again since learning of the new scandal, or just the fact they'd been really busy with the twins, but there was definitely renewed tension between him and Adelaide. He didn't like it. He also suspected it might disappear when they had the legalities wrapped up. At least for now. "So how long will it take?" he asked impatiently.

Claire McCabe explained, "Texas has a mandatory sixty-day waiting period. Which means the earliest the divorce can be granted is on the sixty-first day after the petition is filed."

Adelaide looked anything but relieved about that. "Does it ever take longer?" she asked.

"The average time is three to six months in an uncontested divorce," Gannon said.

Wyatt resisted the urge to reach over and take Adelaide's hand only because he sensed comfort was not what she wanted from him. "Is there anything prohibiting us from living together once the papers are filed? Like there was if we had wanted to go for an annulment?" he asked.

Gannon shook his head. "Not if it's an uncontested divorce."

Adelaide paled. "Can we pursue the dissolution in a way that doesn't assign fault to either of us?"

"Yes," Claire replied, "as long as you both swear under oath that the marriage can no longer continue because of differences that can't be resolved."

Gannon warned, "You will also have to agree on child support, visitation schedule and parenting times. Who gets the children on which holidays. And the division of any property."

Wyatt looked at Adelaide who seemed as overwhelmed as he was. She blew out a breath. "The property is easy enough."

Wyatt read her mind. "We'll both keep what's ours."

"As for the rest..." Adelaide relaxed slightly. "Can't we just tell the court we'll decide on a day-to-day basis?"

Both lawyers shook their heads firmly. Claire said, "The court wants it all agreed upon—*in writing*—at the time the divorce petition is filed."

"And that's good for you all, too," Gannon chimed in, "since you will have a set of rules to follow if and when any disagreements do come up."

Which meant they couldn't go forward with anything until decisions were made. Wyatt swore silently.

Claire soothed, "We'll give you each work sheets to fill out. Take the time to think about what you each want. Then call us, and we'll all sit down together and hash out a final version that works for everyone."

"What are you thinking?" Wyatt asked when he and Adelaide left and headed toward the parking lot.

Her lips twisted ruefully. "That I don't think I'll ever be able to split up our time with the kids the way it sounds like we're going to be required to do...at least on paper."

He followed her to his pickup truck. "Me, either."

Adelaide leaned against the side of the vehicle while he unlocked it and opened the door for her. "But, I see the point. It's not as if we intend to stay married."

He caught her hand before she could slip inside. "Do you want to date anyone?"

She gave him a shocked look. "What?"

"Do you want to date anyone else?"

"No." She sounded affronted. "Do you?"

"No." He flashed her a reckless grin, continued wryly, "So, that being the case, why do we have to divorce at all? Why not just stay legally married indefinitely, the way we first thought we would? Until we both feel the time is right for us to split up. Taking care of infants is a lot of work. Even with both of us, we're exhausted."

She clamped her arms in front of her, as if warding off a sudden chill. "That's true." Worry clouded her eyes. "But there's still all the gossip to be quieted. Much as I'd like to just ignore it, we can't. We need to protect your mom and our families' reputations."

Wyatt studied her closely. "And that means no more scandal." He exhaled roughly. "The question is how? We can't do what my mother would prefer and recite vows we don't mean."

"I totally agree. We already did that once."

You *did that once*, Wyatt thought bitterly. *I meant mine then with all my heart and soul.* The question was, would he ever be able to mean them again if they did ever find themselves contemplating entering into a real marriage? Not just one that was continuing out of expedience.

"And we can't divorce." Oblivious to his thoughts, Adelaide rushed to add, "At least any time soon. So what do we do?"

Wyatt gave her a hand up as she climbed inside the cab. He watched her tug the hem of her skirt down to her knees. The glimpse of silky thigh filled his body with need. Deliberately, he pushed the desire away. "Let's talk to Hope. See if she has any more ideas."

Luckily, the crisis manager was available when they stopped by her office. "There must be another way that doesn't involve renewing our vows or getting a divorce," Adelaide said.

"Some middle ground," Wyatt persisted with a terse nod.

"Well, actually, there is one thing you can do." Hope rocked back in her desk chair. "You can always fight fire with fire."

Chapter 8

"I can't believe we're doing this," Adelaide said the following morning.

Wyatt emerged from his pickup truck and walked around to open her door. He gave her a gentlemanly hand down, much as if they had been on a date. Leaning over, he brushed his lips across her temple. For show? Or for real? It was impossible to tell.

Straightening, he smiled down at her. Then promised, "It's just a few hours."

Adelaide shivered, whether from the wintry February air or nerves, she did not know. "And a lot of scrutiny."

Wyatt wrapped a protective arm about her waist as he led her down Main Street toward his sister's coffee shop and bakery, The Cowgirl Chef.

"From afar." He leaned down to whisper in her ear, "Hope promised the paparazzo she hired to follow us around on our errands wouldn't get closer than a thousand feet."

Adelaide leaned into the curve of her husband's body, appreciating the warmth and strength. Her pulse pounding, she stopped to turn and look up at him. "Problem is, we don't know in which direction Marco Maletti will be shooting us from," she whispered.

Wyatt tucked a strand of hair behind her ear. "Like Hope said, it's best we don't know. Otherwise, it wouldn't look as if we were getting surreptitiously photographed. It's got to seem like these are unguarded moments."

When something was happening between them.

Something romantic, Hope had stressed.

Adelaide felt the heat pour into her face. "I don't know if I'm cut out for this," she confided in a trembling tone. She already felt ridiculously self-conscious.

He leaned down, and his lips brushed hers. "Then just don't think about it," he murmured huskily.

The next thing she knew, his arms were wrapped all the way around her, and his mouth was on hers. Hot and insistent. Patient and sweet. Caressing. Tempting. Her body responded with a tidal wave of lust.

Telling herself this was all for show and not what she really wanted deep down in her heart, Adelaide wrapped her arms about his neck and rose on tiptoe, pressing her body fully against the hardness of his. Avidly, she met his kiss.

And that was when they heard it.

Guffaws. Followed by a loud cough.

They broke apart and turned in time to see two of Wyatt's brothers, Chance and Garrett, grinning from ear to ear.

Both were in on Hope's plan to battle the rumors with an emerging "story" of their own. "Too bad Mom's not here to see this," Chance ribbed.

Garrett ran a hand along his jaw, teasing, "She'd think her fondest wish was coming true."

Lockhart family unity was also on Hope's agenda of things to be publicly demonstrated. Although in this case the action synched with Adelaide's instinct, too.

The members of the Lockhart clan were famously strong individually. United, they were invincible. It made her feel a lot safer, knowing that she and the twins were now part of the famous Texas family.

"Nice to see you." Adelaide went to give both big men a warm and welcoming hug. Like Wyatt, his brothers were tall and fit, with rangy muscular frames.

Chance winked. "Mom'd probably also tell you to get a room." Adelaide blushed, and they all laughed.

Garrett flashed a devilish smile. "Where are the little ones?"

Glad to have something else to focus on besides her PDA with their brother, Adelaide answered, "At the Circle H. Lucille and Hope are going to bring them into town in a little while."

Arm locked around her waist, Wyatt wheeled Adelaide in the direction of his sister's bistro. "Meantime, we've got a breakfast to get."

"Lots of luck." The brothers inclined their handsome heads down the street, where a line was coming out the door. "Sage has her usual crowd."

All of whom, as it turned out, wanted to congratulate Adelaide and Wyatt on their "news."

"Looks like love is in the air," the mayor said with a wink. "And it's not even Valentine's Day yet."

"Didn't the two of you elope on Valentine's Day?" his wife asked.

Wyatt grinned proudly. "Ten years ago."

"So you've got an anniversary coming up," Nurse Bess Monroe observed.

Her twin, Bridgett, winked. "The traditional gift is tin."

Family law attorney Liz Anderson said, "That's changed with the times. These days, the gift is supposed to be diamonds."

"I can't see Wyatt wearing diamonds," Rebecca Carrigan-McCabe said teasingly.

Octogenarian Tillie Cartwright squinted. "He'd look good in tin, though."

Chuckles abounded.

"Speaking of Valentine's Day, are the two of you volunteering for the Laramie Chili Festival?" the mayor asked.

It was a major fund-raiser for the community. As well as a good time.

"I'm manning the cutting-horse training demonstration at the fairgrounds," Wyatt said.

"Adelaide?"

"I'm on the planning committee for the Lockhart Foundation, and I also signed up for shifts in the LF Information booth as well as the WTWA Go Fishing game for children."

"She's also going to be assisting me," Wyatt added.

Adelaide whirled, a question in her eyes.

"Looks like it's news to your wife," Travis Anderson observed.

Adelaide batted her lashes comically. "I guess that must mean we are married."

Everyone laughed.

"Well, we're happy to have you both," the mayor said.

They chatted a little more, enjoying the warm congratulations from the community, then Wyatt and Adelaide walked out and headed across the street to the local park.

They sat side by side on a bench, munching on iced Danish pastry, stuffed with almonds, and made in the shape of bear claws. "You have to work today?" Wyatt asked.

"For about four hours this afternoon," Adelaide said, aware how cozy this all was.

"Can it be done at the ranch?"

"It's work for the foundation, so I need to do it at their office, on their computer system."

Which had state-of-the-art cybersecurity protection and more firewalls than anyone thought was necessary. But after the embezzlement scandal the previous summer, Adelaide wasn't about to take any chances. Or make it possible for her father, the foundation's previous CFO, to strike again.

Intuiting her need for comforting, Wyatt draped his arm along the back of the bench. "What about the twins?"

She snuggled against him, loving his warmth and his strength. "I've been taking them with me when I have to go in. There's usually no shortage of people willing to pitch in and hold Jake and Jenny if need be. Although most of the time they usually sleep. Probably because there actually *are* an abundant number of people willing and ready to hold them," she quipped. Unable to help herself, she scanned the surrounding landscaped areas. Saw nothing. No one. Which meant what? The paparazzo wasn't here yet, or he was? In any case, they wouldn't be able to spot him at that distance.

She turned back to Wyatt. Unlike her, he was totally relaxed and oblivious. "You?" she asked.

Playfully, he nudged his thigh against hers. "Troy and Flint can handle things at Wind River today."

"Do you have anything else you need to do today?"

He grinned sexily. "Just be with you."

That should have been comforting. Having him shadowing her. There to help with their twins while she recorded the latest donations, did the foundation payroll and updated the LF books. But right now all she could think about was her unoccupied home. Feeling more jittery than ever, Adelaide took another hasty sip of coffee, started to rise. "Listen, as long as we're in town, why don't we...?"

Firm hand on her shoulder, Wyatt tugged her back down and delivered another long, toe-curling kiss.

Finding she was just as susceptible to his brazen seduction as ever, Adelaide drew back breathlessly. "What was that for?"

He waggled his brows. "In case Marco Maletti didn't get the last one."

"Is he here?"

Wyatt's eyes twinkled. "I assume so."

She let her gaze rove over his handsome face and powerfully built frame. "Meaning you haven't seen him?"

He looked at her, as if completely besotted. "Haven't really tried." He traced her lips with the pad of his thumb. Bent down to kiss her again. "I've been too busy looking at you."

"I really don't think..."

He captured her lips with his. When she could finally breathe again, Adelaide said, "You're enjoying this."

He caught her hand and held it over his heart. "Aren't you?"

"Heck, yes. But I'm not in the habit of making out in the middle of Laramie."

He tunneled his hands through the windswept strands of her hair, bent his head. And kissed her...cheek. "Maybe you should be." His lips ventured to the sensitive area just beneath her ear. As he worked his magic, it was all she could do not to moan out loud. There was absolutely nothing she could do about the dampness between her thighs.

Adelaide shut her eyes as another wave of desire sifted through her. Heaven help her. The reckless, wild boy—the one who had caused her so much trouble in her youth—was back.

"Your mother wouldn't approve," she argued weakly, sensing he was about to try to kiss her—really kiss her—again.

"Actually," Wyatt said with a grin, "I think she does."

Adelaide bolted upright. "What?"

He nodded. "She's over there, parked in front of the coffee shop. Waving. Looks like she was about to send Hope over to get us. To let us know the twins are here."

Was this Step 3 or 4 or 5 of their fight-fire-with-fire plan? Adelaide couldn't remember. She was so dazed from their smoldering hot make-out session.

She rose on wobbly legs. "Time to take them on a stroll?"

"Apparently so."

They walked across the street. A delighted Lucille approached them, just as the sun peeked through the clouds. "Everything's going well, I take it?"

"Oh, yes," Adelaide said. If you could discount how real it all felt, that was.

As Wyatt got the convertible double stroller out of the rear seat of his pickup truck, her phone went off.

She stepped back to answer it. Saw a Snapchat had come in from someone she'd gone to college with.

Curious, she tapped on the icon and instantly her screen was filled with a photo. Not of any of her pals, but of a deeply tanned fiftysomething man, with spiky peroxide bleached-yellow hair, a salt-and-pepper goatee, tropical shirt and cargo pants. He had a camera slung around his neck, earrings glinting from both ears. Sunglasses covered his eyes. She couldn't say how tall, but five feet ten inches seemed about right. He was a little chunky around the middle and had a gorgeous beach behind him. The message *Can't Wait To See You and the Kids!* flashed across the screen.

Causing Adelaide to take another, harder look.

Could that be…

My God.

Was that *her father*?

His nose was all wrong.

And he'd gained weight. Changed his hair.

But the rest of him…

The image disappeared. Meaning ten seconds had passed.

Wyatt and Lucille were both looking at her. "Is everything okay?" Lucille asked.

Adelaide thought about everything the matriarch and her entire family had already been through. Thanks to her criminal dad.

A chill went down her spine.

Ignoring the curiosity and concern in Wyatt's eyes, she forced a smile. "Yes. I just remembered something. Is it okay if I meet the two of you over at my house? I really need to check out the framing for the foundation of the new addition. See how that's going."

Without waiting for permission, tacit or otherwise, she rushed off.

* * *

"This wasn't the plan," Lucille said worriedly as Adelaide drove off in Wyatt's pickup truck, while he and his mom pushed the double stroller down Main Street. Wyatt knew that, and even worse, he sensed his wife was keeping something from him. *Again.* He hoped it was just about her house. Some unexpected—and probably costly—problem there she did not want to discuss.

He soothed his mother with a reassuring smile. "Adelaide and I can walk Jake and Jenny in her neighborhood, instead of the park, Mom. It will be fine." Which, as it happened, was only three blocks from historic downtown Laramie anyway.

Lucille fretted. "She looked white as a ghost to me."

To me, too, Wyatt thought. But there was no need to worry his mom. He pointed out casually, "Renovating can be nerve-racking, even when you have a normal amount of sleep."

His attempt to change the subject worked. "How are things going with the twins?" Lucille asked.

They make great chaperones. "We're still trying to get them on a schedule," he admitted.

"It'll happen. Although, in addition to the wind-up infant swings we brought you, you might try…" His mom proceeded to give him a dozen tips. Most of which went right in one ear and out the other because he was so focused on wondering what was going on with Adelaide.

Lucille squinted at him as they reached the front of Adelaide's home. Construction trucks were parked all around. "You think I'm interfering, don't you?"

I think you don't trust me to be as capable as my siblings would be in this situation. And we both know why.

But figuring it was best to let the ghosts of old problems recede into the past where they belonged, he said instead, "I think we're all doing our best, Mom, which is all we can do. Right?"

Lucille offered a smile so dubious it hurt. "Right."

Wyatt pushed aside his resentment. "Do you want to come inside?" he asked politely.

At the rear of the cottage, there was a lot of sawing and hammering going on. Lucille wheeled the stroller in the opposite direction. "I think I'll walk a little more. I don't want the construction noise to wake up our little darlings."

"Okay. I'll get Adelaide and be right out."

Familiar voices floated toward him as Wyatt walked in. Although the rear walls of her home were still intact, big drapes of heavy duty plastic had already been hung from ceiling to floor. Through the windows, Wyatt could see half a dozen workers putting together the frame for the addition to the cement foundation.

In the kitchen, his brother Chance and his wife, Molly, stood with Adelaide, who looked increasingly uneasy.

"So everything looked good to you, when you got here this morning?" Adelaide was asking.

The couple nodded. "Yeah. It was fine," Chance said.

Molly put her hand on Adelaide's shoulder. "Are you worried about your house being unoccupied?"

Adelaide hesitated as Wyatt closed the distance between them. "A little," she admitted as he took his place next to her.

"In a city as big as Dallas, that might be warranted," Molly soothed. "But here? No one is going to bother your stuff, Adelaide. Even if you left your door unlocked, it would still be fine."

Wyatt had the feeling that wasn't it. "Okay," Adelaide said.

"You ready to walk the twins?" he asked.

Behind him, more footsteps sounded. After a short rap at the door, Deputy Detective Kyle McCabe walked in.

Adelaide had only to look at Wyatt's face to know he had completely misunderstood why the uniformed lawman was there. Figuring she'd know how to deal with that later, she smiled and said hello to their visitor, who also happened to be one of the first people she'd met in the community she now called home.

"Hey, Adelaide." Kyle gave her an affable hug, then turned to Wyatt. After the two men shook hands, Kyle continued, "I didn't know if you'd be by to check on the renovations today..."

He did however know about the creepy message she had just received, Adelaide thought. And—thanks to the surveillance software the department had installed on her phone—exactly where to find her. Not just now, but at all times.

"...but I'm glad I saw your vehicle because my parents tasked me with giving you a baby gift."

"That's sweet of them."

"They know how it is to deal with multiples..."

Adelaide chuckled. "I guess so, since they had five boys—triplets and twins!"

"Anyway, they thought whatever the gift is might help. So—" Kyle gave her a look that signaled he needed to speak with her privately "—it's out in the squad car."

"I can get it," Wyatt offered.

Guilt and anxiety flooded Adelaide. She had promised not to keep things from Wyatt but she had also privately vowed not to ever hurt him—or his family—unnecessarily again.

She would tell him everything—as soon as she could. Meantime, she would do what had to be done.

So, tensing with the duplicity required, Adelaide turned back to her husband. Aware it was all she could do not to wring her hands, said, "Actually, would you mind going up the block and seeing if your mom needs some help? That double stroller can feel like a lot to push after a while."

Wyatt paused. Then met her gaze with a completely inscrutable one of his own. "Sure." He shook hands with Kyle again. "Nice to see you."

"Likewise."

While Wyatt headed off to catch up with his mom, who was almost to the next cross street, Adelaide walked out to the squad car with Kyle. The beautifully wrapped present was sitting on the front seat. "Is that a real gift or just a ploy to see me?"

"Both."

"You saw the photo-message on Snapchat?"

Kyle nodded imperceptibly. "Was it your dad?"

"I think so," Adelaide said nervously. "I mean his nose and his entire look were different, but yeah, I think so." It was an effort to stay casual. "Were you able to record the photo?"

"Yep." Kyle reached into the front seat and got the package. "Have you told your husband what's been going on?"

Guilt flooded her anew. She and Wyatt had promised to be direct with each other...and here she was, already lying and hiding. "No."

"Good." Kyle handed the box to Adelaide. "Don't."

"He's going to get suspicious," Adelaide warned.

"The last thing we need is him interfering with our investigation by trying to protect you. You can tell him everything when it's all over." Kyle paused meaningfully. "But nothing, not a word, Adelaide, before then. I mean it."

Adelaide gulped nervously and nodded her head. She prayed this didn't backfire.

Chapter 9

Hours later, Wyatt and Adelaide were back at the Wind River Ranch. Evening chores completed, Jenny and Jake asleep—at least for the time being—they finally had a chance to sit together on the sofa and open the gift from Annie and Travis McCabe.

Wyatt stared at the padded black cotton canvas garment with the thick straps and two open envelope-style pouches with holes along the bottom. "What is it?"

Adelaide's dark eyes dazzled with excitement. "A kangaroo-style carrier for twins."

"For one person?"

"And two babies. One in front, one in back."

He turned to face her, his knee nudging her thigh. "I didn't know they made those."

"I did." Adelaide's smile widened. "But it seemed impractical because I couldn't figure out how I was going to get both babies strapped in their compartments and then put it on by myself." She studied the accompanying literature, then leaped to her feet. "Mind if we try it on you?"

All for whatever made her happy, he said, "Sure."

She had to reach up to slip the contraption over his head. Her hair brushed against his chest and shoulder as she adjusted the length of the harness and fastened the clasps on either side of his waist.

It took a while.

He didn't mind.

She was gorgeous, with her delicate brow furrowed and her soft lips pursed in concentration.

Inhaling the sweet womanly scent of her, he stood, legs braced slightly apart, his arms akimbo as she walked around him, her hands sliding between the carrier and his body as she checked to make sure it was on securely.

"Now let's see if we can put something akin to two babies in it." She moved to the box of baby toys and returned with two stuffed teddy bears, one pink and one blue. "These are about the size of Jake and Jenny." She fit one in, facing his chest. Safety-strapped it in.

Then walked around behind him and did the same with the other.

Plucking the phone from her pocket, she opened it and stepped back. "Say cheese!"

He mugged at her comically. His pulse revved up even more as she sashayed back to him.

It had been several days since they'd had the opportunity and energy to make love, and he wanted her more than he had imagined possible.

Oblivious to the lusty direction of his thoughts, she beamed and held the photo out for him to see. "See how cool this is? We'll be able to carry both Jake and Jenny at one time, at least until their combined weight is thirty-five pounds."

Wyatt knew he would. He doubted Adelaide would be able to comfortably carry both for too much longer, given the way they were growing.

It was a good thing he was going to be around.

Adelaide picked up the note that had come with the present.

She read it, then handed it over for him to peruse. "Annie and Travis McCabe said they used a similar one when Kyle and Kurt were infants, and they were still corralling their six-year-old triplets, Teddy, Tyler and Trevor. I'll have to call them in the morning and thank them."

Here was his chance to ask some of the questions that had been nagging at him all day. He wasn't normally a jealous guy. Maybe because he'd never had to compete for the attention of any woman he was interested in. But something about Kyle Mc-Cabe's visits, the past couple of days, didn't feel right to him.

It was almost as if he and Adelaide were hiding something.

What, he couldn't imagine.

"Why do you think Annie or Travis didn't stop by in person to deliver this to us? Their ranch is just five miles from here."

For a moment, she went very still.

"Do you think it's because you and Kyle are no longer dating? And Annie McCabe thought it might be awkward?"

Still wary, Adelaide lifted her chin. "I didn't know you were aware I dated Kyle when I first moved to Laramie."

For a moment, Wyatt let himself drown in the depths of her dark brown eyes. "Kyle McCabe is the only one of his brothers not married with kids."

She shrugged. "So?"

He inhaled the sweet smell of baby lotion clinging to her skin. "You were pregnant at the time, with no daddy in sight. Of course people took notice."

Just as he was now noticing Kyle's dual appearances.

She unhooked the belt buckles at his waist. Stepped back. He eased the carrier over his head and handed it to her. She turned and walked away, still not saying anything. He could practically see her emotional armor sliding back into place.

"Don't you have anything to add?" he asked quietly. The last thing he wanted was for them to go back to the anger and mistrust they'd experienced before they learned about the twins' parentage.

Whirling, a distant look came into her eyes. "I'm not sure what you want me to impart," she returned with unusual stoicism.

He couldn't shake the feeling she was protecting someone. "Was there a reason he stopped by in person a couple of days ago to ask you to do his tax return, and delivered the gift from his parents to you personally today?"

She stalked into the kitchen and stood on the other side of the island, where they'd made love a few days before. "First of all, a lot of people have asked me to do their federal taxes for them. And I expect even more will before the April filing deadline. Second of all, he delivered the present to *us*."

Thanks to the tumultuous events in their past, Wyatt had a sixth sense when she was holding back from him. She was definitely doing so now. The force field around her heart had never been more fortified.

He had to find out why.

"So the fact the two of you stopped dating was mutual. Kyle's not interested in you romantically any longer?" he prodded.

To his frustration, her emotions became even more obscure. "We're...friends."

Who had spent at least ten minutes talking, their heads bent together, before Kyle left. Even half a block away, pushing a stroller, he had been able to see the subject matter had been both serious and intimate. "What's going on, Adelaide?" he persisted. He knew there was something she was withholding.

Worse, she knew that he realized it.

And that knowledge broke the dam.

She threw up her hands. "Look, I know the whole hiring Marco Maletti plan was supposed to stay just within the Lockhart family, but I'm not so sure it's a good idea not to clue in at least someone in the sheriff's department."

Suddenly, her fierce defense and the defeated slump of her slender shoulders made sense. "So you went rogue on us and contacted Kyle?"

"No!" She circled around to stand in front of him again. "I had no idea Kyle was going to stop in when he did this morning. But then he was there, and he already knew stuff was going on...about us..."

"You mean he read the tabloid stories."

"He heard about them. Everyone in town has. They're just too polite to say anything to us about it directly."

"But Kyle did."

"No. But he—he wanted to know how I was, and so I just... I blurted it out. I told him in confidence that for the next few days or weeks we are going to be intermittently trailed and photographed by paparazzo Marco Maletti. And that it was with our permission, as part of a fight-fire-with-fire strategy. So that if someone saw something and reported it to the sheriff's department, Marco would not be arrested."

That certainly explained the ten-minute conversation with their heads bent together, Wyatt thought in relief.

Adelaide sighed. "And then I felt like maybe I shouldn't have told Kyle without first discussing the option with you-all. Which is what I should have done in the first place anyway."

He wrapped his arms around her waist. "Then why didn't you?"

She splayed her hands across his chest. "Because clearly I was the only one who thought keeping anything from local law enforcement was not a good idea."

He stroked his hand through her hair, pushing it away from her face. "So you went along to get along, the way you always do."

"Yes." Her chin trembled. "And then, because I didn't speak my mind," she admitted hoarsely, "I ended up getting myself in more trouble with you."

She bit her lip as her eyes searched his. "I know no one is supposed to know about our scandal-rebuttal plan but the Lockhart family. But, given how protective of their fellow citizens the residents of Laramie can be, I thought it was the right thing to do. For everyone."

Silence fell between them, followed by a wave of guilt.

Wyatt had to admit he hadn't given any thought to the jeopardy the freelance photographer Hope had hired could possibly be in.

He praised her foresight. "Sweetheart, I think it was a smart move. I'll let everyone else in the family know what you did, and why."

"And for the record? You have no reason to be jealous of Kyle McCabe."

The intensity in her low tone made him smile. "Is that so?"

"There was never any chemistry between us." She threw her arms about his neck and went up on tiptoe. Looking deep into his eyes, she whispered, "Not like what you and I have."

She pressed her lips to his, kissing him sweetly and evocatively. Each brush of her lips deeper and more intimate and searing than the last.

Though she had always been quick to respond, he had always been the one making the first move. It was a thrill to feel her melting against him helplessly, wanting him as much as he wanted her.

Resolved to cherish and care for her the way she deserved, he continued making out with her, slow dancing their way up the stairs to his king-size bed. In the glow of the moonlight pouring in through the windows, they faced each other once again.

He let her strip her sweater over her head and shimmy out of her jeans, just because it was so exciting to see her begin a striptease. But when it came to her bra and panties, it was all him.

When they were both naked once again, he kissed her long and hard and deep, until she made that low sound of acquiescence in the back of her throat.

Determined to make her his, he positioned himself between her legs, making lazy circles, moving up, in, until the moisture flowed. Eager to please her even more, he drew her onto the bed.

"My turn," she whispered.

The silk of her hair sliding over him, she kissed and caressed her way down his large, muscular body, molding and exploring, erotically laying claim. Supplying him with everything that had been missing from his life.

Tenderness. Desire. The feeling of being not just wanted but needed.

Sensations ran riot through him. Taking him to the brink.

He found a condom.

She rolled it on.

Stretching over her, he slid his palms beneath her and lifted her in his arms. She arched against him, open and ready, and he slid into her, slowly pressing into her as deeply as he could go.

She was everything he had ever wanted.

Everything he needed. And more. And then there was no more thinking, only feeling, no more holding back, only hot, wet kisses and hotter pleasure.

She shuddered and cried out.

He caught the sound with his mouth, and then he too was catapulting into oblivion.

They held each other tight. Surrendering to whatever this was. Always had been. And always would be.

Wyatt eased away from her, moving onto his side, drawing her into the warm inviting curve of his body. As she shifted to face him, pillowing her head on his broad shoulder, Adelaide buried her face in his chest. The comfort she should have felt after making love with Wyatt was only partially present. Undercut by the deep sense of guilt she felt.

They had promised they would be completely candid with each other this time. Stop holding back whatever was going on with each of them. So they could forge a better foundation for their family, whether they eventually divorced or not.

But she couldn't do that.

Not when it came to the situation with her dad. He was a

criminal, and he was still at large. And apparently trying to contact her with an intent to see her and his grandchildren.

Which meant if her father wasn't back in Texas, he would be soon. A fact that could put them all in danger. Especially Wyatt, if he knew, because her husband would want to protect her and their babies, and personally bring her father to justice.

It wasn't necessary, given her ongoing, secret cooperation with authorities. She just wasn't sure Wyatt would accept that.

Or forgive her for holding back the truth now.

"What are you thinking about?" Wyatt rasped, pressing a kiss into her hair.

Adelaide sighed and cuddled closer. He felt so good. So big and strong and solid. Reassuring herself that the secrecy certainly would not be required for much longer—one way or another law enforcement would be able to solve the case—she snuggled even closer. "I was wondering if we had time to make love before the twins wake up again."

As if on cue, the baby monitor crackled. An indignant cry filtered through the air.

"Guess not." Wyatt chuckled ruefully.

Adelaide bussed his nose, teasing, "It's nothing that can't be picked up later." She grabbed her robe. "I better get there before Jenny wakes up Jake."

Wyatt tugged on his jeans. "You know it's her?"

Adelaide headed for the cribs. "Can't you tell their cries apart?"

"Not yet."

"You will." She scooped up Jenny. Miraculously, little Jake slept on.

"Maybe we should wake them both up," Wyatt suggested.

Adelaide shushed him with a finger pressed against his lips. "This way I only have to feed and change one at a time."

He caught her hand and kissed the back of it. "We," he corrected her, the light evocative caress reminding her of just what a tender and compelling lover he was. He followed her to the changing table. "And since I'm here, I think we should care for both now so we can all get the maximum amount of uninterrupted sleep later."

Adelaide studied him. Wyatt was right—she was no longer a single parent. And although the day or night would come when he wasn't with her at times like these, right now, in this instance, he *was* here.

So she handed him Jenny to hold while she woke up their sleeping son. "You're right. Let's do this together."

Chapter 10

The following morning, Wyatt again let his hired hands handle the horses and elected to instead help Adelaide with the twins. Who were both pretty darn fussy, Adelaide noted, after another only slightly less restless night.

A softly whimpering Jenny ensconced in his arms, Wyatt attempted to settle his big frame into the rocker-glider. Not an easy task. The chair that fit Adelaide's five-seven frame perfectly was at least 30 percent too small for him. Frowning, he shifted Jenny a little higher on his shoulder. "What we need is a man-size rocking chair."

No kidding. He looked like Papa Bear sitting in Mama Bear's chair.

Adelaide knelt and put Jake in the seat of the indoor baby swing. "Way ahead of you, cowboy," she said over her shoulder as she strapped the audibly complaining Jake into the seat, then cushioned him at the waist with rolled-up receiving blankets. Rising to her knees, she pushed the button on the top that would provide thirty minutes of gentle uninterrupted swinging back and forth.

Jake's expression turned from grouchy complaint to one of surprise as he began to move.

Back and forth. Back and forth.

Adelaide sat in front of her son, where he could see her. She smiled encouragingly.

He smiled back.

To Wyatt, she said, "I called the online baby superstore and express ordered their largest rocker-glider. It's supposed to be delivered here today. Once it arrives we'll be able to rock the kids at the same time."

Wyatt looked her over. "Will we have to stay in rhythm? Or be woefully out of synch, like old folks on the porch of the nursing home?"

Her heart pounding at the memories of when they'd last made love and the urgent need to do so again, Adelaide snickered. "Funny."

He waggled his brows in a way that let her know his thoughts were going in exactly the same direction. "Thanks."

Noting Jake had stopped fussing entirely, she said, "Want to try this with Jenny?"

"Sure." He rose and walked toward her.

Still on her knees, Adelaide moved the other baby swing right next to Jake's. With Wyatt's help, she situated Jenny, too.

Jenny's eyes widened in pleasant surprise as she began to swing.

A peaceful silence reigned. Wyatt extended a hand. "We're going to have to thank my mom for these."

Slanting him a curious glance, Adelaide rose. "So you admit Lucille really does know a thing or two about caring for children?"

He let go of her palm reluctantly. "Almost anyone would know more than me, but yeah, she was right about this."

And maybe other stuff, as well, Adelaide thought.

Like giving their marriage more of a chance than they had.

Pushing the unwanted notion away, she accompanied him

to the kitchen. Adelaide brought the wheat flakes out of the pantry. Wyatt retrieved the milk and a pint of fresh blueberries. They fixed their bowls. "So how much do I owe you for the rocking chair?"

Surprised he would turn what had been a thoughtful gesture into a transaction, Adelaide hid her hurt with a smile. "Nothing." She took her breakfast and slid onto a stool at the counter. "It's a gift."

He lounged against the counter beside her, bowl held against his chest. "A tenth-anniversary gift?"

"No," she said dryly, watching him eat with the same appetite he did everything else. "An 'I expect you to use it frequently to help us all out' kind of gift."

He poured more cereal into his bowl. "I think I can manage that."

"So what's your schedule like for the rest of the day?" Adelaide asked.

"Troy and Flint are taking care of the horses this morning, but I really want to work Durango myself once my mom and Sage get here."

Adelaide batted her lashes. "You don't want to spend two hours working on the menu for the Welcome to the Family party for the twins?"

He fed her the last blueberry from his bowl. "I think you know I might have five minutes of patience for that."

She fed him her last wheat flake. "I think you know that's about my limit, too."

He set their dishes aside, then pulled her into his arms. "So why not let Sage and Mom babysit the twins and come with me?" He wrapped his arms about her waist. "You probably should ride the horse you're going to be using during the Chili Festival."

"I thought I was just going to be assisting you during the cutting-horse training demonstration at the fairgrounds."

"Like Vanna White?" He mimed the graceful movements of the TV game-show hostess.

Adelaide rolled her eyes. "I don't think an evening gown will work in the arena."

He rubbed his jaw. "You look mighty fetching in a pair of jeans and boots, though."

She blushed at his sexy once-over. "Seriously..."

"Seriously." Catching her hands once again, he reeled her in. "I'd really like you to join me out on the ranch this morning. It'll be good for both of us. Getting some fresh air." He pointed to the now happily snoozing twins in their matching baby swings. "And you know the Lockhart women can handle it."

Was this a date?

It felt like a date.

"Consider it our date morning," he drawled, reading her mind.

She hesitated.

"PG rated."

The twinkle in his eyes was irresistible. When was the last time she had played at anything? "All right," she agreed recklessly. "I confess... I'm dying to get back in the saddle again."

"Go get ready. I'll handle things down here."

By the time they had both dressed for the excursion, Sage, who had the morning off from her bistro, arrived. Once again, looking a little wan and definitely tired.

"Before you two head out to work with the horses, I have a favor to ask," Sage said. "You two really should have anything you want for the party."

"But?" Adelaide prodded.

Sage inhaled. "I'd really like it if you vetoed everything involving shrimp."

Adelaide was as shocked as Wyatt looked. It wasn't like his little sister to shy away from any ingredient. In fact, the cowgirl-chef liked to joke she could put a southwestern spin on any dish.

Sage held up a palm. "I got sick on it in early January, when

I had that really awful stomach flu…and just the thought, the smell, anything to do with it. I can't…"

"Fine with me," Adelaide said cheerfully.

"Me, too," Wyatt agreed.

Sage sent them looks of gratitude and relief, just as a car engine sounded outside. Adelaide glanced out the window. "There's your mother now."

"So what do you know about Sage that I don't?" Wyatt asked after the preliminary menu had been approved—sans shrimp— and the two of them went out to the stables.

Oh, dear. She had been hoping he wouldn't ask. "Nothing," Adelaide fibbed.

Wyatt blocked her way to the tack room. "What do you intuit, then? 'Cause something is sure as hell going on."

Adelaide bit her lip. Reluctant to betray.

"Fine." He brushed by her, blanket and saddle in hand, and entered Buttercup's stall. "I'll ask Sage directly when we get back to the ranch house."

Adelaide watched him put on the halter, secure the reins. "No. Don't do that. I have a feeling your mom already suspects anyway."

Wyatt brushed past her and went back to the tack room. "Suspects what?"

Adelaide followed. "That Sage's life, like ours, is about to become a lot more complicated."

"How?" Wyatt carried the gear to Durango's stall. "She's not dating anyone." He sent Adelaide a sharp look over his shoulder. "She hasn't since she finally called it quits with TW and left Seattle for good."

"I know." Adelaide lingered in the aisle. "But she's become really good friends with Nick Monroe since she moved to Laramie."

Wyatt adeptly saddled the big black gelding. Taking the reins, he led him out. "Isn't Nick intent on getting out of here?"

"Taking his family's Western-wear business public via venture-capital expansion? Yes."

Wyatt motioned for Adelaide to go into the courtyard, then paused at the next stall to get Buttercup, too. "So why would Sage get involved with him if he's leaving Laramie? Maybe even Texas altogether?"

Adelaide put her left foot in the stirrup, her hands on the horn, and swung herself up into the saddle. "I didn't say that she had."

Wyatt watched as she got settled, then handed her the reins. "But...?"

"Every time I go in The Cowgirl Chef, Nick's either just coming in for a quick cup of coffee or just leaving."

Wyatt moved lithely into the saddle. "So? Their businesses are both on Main Street." Bypassing the arena next to the barns and heading toward a pasture the size of a football field, he swung down to open a gate, then proceeded to hop back on his horse.

"It's more than that," Adelaide insisted. "She's close to him."

Wyatt frowned. "Hooking up close?"

Aware how good it felt to be out in the cold, crisp winter air, Adelaide shrugged. "I don't know exactly what's going on between them, Wyatt. Maybe Nick and Sage are just good friends, the way they keep telling everyone."

"And yet...?" he prodded.

"She seems different somehow and she's gained weight, despite having the stomach flu several times over the last few months. Then there's her new aversion to shrimp. When I was pregnant, I couldn't handle the smell of Swiss cheese for some reason. It just made me want to barf every single time. In fact, I still can't handle it."

Amusement flickered in his eyes. "I'll make an effort to keep it out of our fridge."

She returned his droll look. "Much appreciated."

Now if she could just keep him from breaking her heart again...

Where had that thought come from?

Misinterpreting her frown, Wyatt continued, "Back to Sage. If she is pregnant and is finally getting the baby she always wanted, why haven't she and Nick told anyone? I mean, he seems like the kind of guy who would step up whether it was planned or not."

Adelaide shrugged and adjusted her flat-brimmed hat against the late-morning sun. "Who knows? Maybe it isn't his. Maybe Nick doesn't know. Maybe it is their baby, and they just don't want to get married or do anything that would in any way complicate or interfere with his business plans right now." She sighed. "Or maybe she decided to have a family the way I thought I had, via artificial insemination, and then got involved with Nick...and now it's all too complicated to figure out."

Wyatt paused. "You really think Sage got inseminated, too?"

"All I can tell you is that last summer, when she and your mom and I were investigating the foundation scandal, and driving back and forth from Dallas to the ranch, we had a lot of time to talk about other stuff, too. I had just started my second trimester, and I was over the moon about finally becoming pregnant. Sage asked me a ton of questions about where I went and how it all worked, and confessed she had been thinking about going that route, too. Your mom blew up at her because she wanted Sage to find her own knight in shining armor and fall in love first, and then have kids."

Wyatt's gaze narrowed. "How did Sage react to that?"

"She just stopped talking about it. And your mother never mentioned it again, either. But if this is what Sage has done, then my sense is your mom is not going to take the news well. Especially if Sage is also falling for Nick. Because that would go back to your mother being right, that your sister should have waited."

Wyatt scowled, as fiercely protective of his family as ever. "Should I talk to Sage? Or Nick?"

"No! To both! And don't you dare tell Sage I suspect anything, either. This is her news to tell, in her own time. Assuming it's true. It might not be."

Wyatt directed his horse to do a right turn and motioned for Adelaide to do the same. "On the other hand, if Sage is pregnant, she can't hide it for long. So why doesn't she just tell Mom?"

"Probably because she's feeling hormonal and vulnerable and doesn't want this to become yet another family crisis." Adelaide brought her horse to a halt next to Wyatt's. "And she's probably right to protect Lucille, since we aren't out of the woods yet with our own Texas-size scandal. Speaking of which…" Adelaide scanned the countryside. "Do you think Marco Maletti is out there somewhere right now, taking photographs of us?"

"I can't spot him, but he's sure supposed to be."

Adelaide studied the vast acres of yellow winter grass, the strands of cedar and live oak. "I can't see anyone, either," she murmured, but she still couldn't shake the feeling that she was being constantly observed.

For reasons she didn't dare reveal.

Wyatt mistook the reason behind her unease. "Relax, sweetheart. This is going to be easy. Buttercup—the mare you're on—is fully trained as a cutting horse. Durango," he said, petting the two-year-old gelding's neck, "is still a work in progress, but he's coming along."

Happy to have something else to concentrate on, Adelaide held the reins and smiled. "What exactly are we going to do today?"

"First order of business is to take them straight and forward. Get them comfortable."

He waited until she drew up beside him, then moved Durango, taking care to keep them at the same steady easy pace. "We're going to speed up just a bit," Wyatt explained. "And then slow down… A little more…"

Back and forth, they moved across the pasture. Their horses alert and eager to please.

Eventually, Wyatt led them to a small wooden bridge, where

they worked on stepping up and down, and backing. Buttercup responded to the lightest touch of reins and leg. Durango was a little less sure of himself, but Wyatt was swift to offer gentle pats to the neck and murmurs of encouragement.

By the time their work session at the bridge was over, Durango was stopping and starting and moving over and around it with the same ease as Buttercup. Better yet, it was clear the horse not only trusted Wyatt to keep him out of trouble, he adored him.

"You're really good at this," Adelaide said, admiration in her tone.

Wyatt tipped his hat. "Why, thank you, Addie." His eyes twinkled as they rode toward a stand of trees. "You're not so bad yourself."

"A little rusty." Especially at love. Not that her husband seemed to notice...

They stopped next to the pond, then dismounted to let their horses get a drink.

"How long since you've been on a horse?" Wyatt asked curiously.

Adelaide's inner thigh muscles were humming with the tension a long neglected workout brought. "A decade."

"You used to love to ride when we were kids," he recalled. It was how they had gotten close. Taking riding lessons every weekend. Later, when they'd both become old enough, they'd assisted with classes of younger kids. She'd focused on Western pleasure riding; Wyatt had taught cutting, reining and barrel racing. And competed in rodeo events, too.

Adelaide glanced at the wintry clouds, looming on the horizon. "After we broke up, I didn't want to go to the riding academy anymore."

He caught her gloved hand in his. "I figured you just changed your teaching times to avoid me."

Shrugging, she turned back to face him. Even through the leather, she could feel the warmth and strength of his fingers.

A shiver of awareness swept through her. "No chance at all of us crossing paths if I didn't go there." She sighed and leaned back against the trunk of a live-oak tree. "It was bad enough seeing you at school." Every time she had seen him, it had felt as if her heart would shatter.

He lifted her hand and kissed the inside of her wrist. "Yeah, the end of our senior year pretty much sucked."

Adelaide let him put both arms around her. "Big time." They'd both skipped their prom and barely made appearances at post-graduation parties.

He smoothed the hair from her face. "I was surprised when you went into accounting. You'd always said you wanted to teach riding."

Adelaide rested both her hands on his chest. "I did."

"Then...?"

She breathed in the masculine fragrance unique to him. "There was a lot of pressure on me to follow in my dad's footsteps." She pushed back the ache of disappointment her father's crime had brought, and moved to get back on her horse. "It seemed like a way to get close to him, which was something I had always wanted."

Wyatt got back in the saddle, too. Reins in hand, he guided his horse through the beginning of another set of training exercises. "And did you?"

Adelaide followed his lead, taking Buttercup in a straight leisurely line, moving her mare's front end, then her rear. "Yes and no. I'm not sure anyone ever really knew my dad."

Wyatt worked Durango in a circle. "What do you mean?"

"He always resented the success of people like your parents. The hedge fund they built gave them wealth beyond their wildest dreams. My father felt he worked just as hard, managing the money, and doing the books for people like your folks. Yet, his net worth was so much less."

Wyatt pointed toward the windmill at the far end of the pasture. They rode off, side by side, adapting another easy, well-controlled pace. "Paul's resentment never showed."

"He had excellent social skills."

Wyatt slowed even more. When Durango showed fear and uncertainty as they neared the windmill, he guided his horse away in a smooth easy motion.

They rode a distance away, then turned and started back, this time from a wider, even easier vantage point. "Did you see what happened at the foundation coming?" Wyatt asked.

The unexpected question brought the heat of shame to her face. "No." With effort, she met Wyatt's searching gaze. "I was as shocked by the disappearance of the funds as everyone else. In fact, that's the real reason I headed up the initial forensic investigation for your mom. I was sure I'd exonerate my father."

His expression reflected his sympathy. "Only, you proved the opposite."

"And cleared everyone else at the foundation in the process." Adelaide paused. "It was important to me that no one but my dad and his mistress, Mirabelle Fanning, the bank VP who helped engineer the fraud on her end, were blamed."

Wyatt approached the windmill again. Durango got significantly closer, but when he tensed, he moved him away again. "Paul never explained anything to you?"

She sighed. Maybe it was good they were finally discussing this.

"No." Although Buttercup was showing no fear, Adelaide turned the mare away, too. Keeping pace, she continued, "It's probably good that my dad never hinted what he was up to, because if he had, I would have had to turn him in." Her heart clenched in her chest. "And what happened was hard enough as it was."

For once, Wyatt seemed to understand the depth of her loss. "I'm sorry your dad put you through that."

Adelaide's lower lip trembled. Without warning, her throat was clogged with tears. "I'm sorry he put us all through it."

Wyatt caught her reins and brought her and the mare in close. "It's all going to be okay, sweetheart," he reassured her.

And in that moment, Adelaide could *almost* believe it.

"How did the riding go?" Lucille asked when they walked back in several hours later.

Wyatt looked around, surprised at the difference a family could make. His ranch house had always been comfortable, but it had never been what anyone would call warm and cozy. Now, with Adelaide at his side, blushing prettily from the exertion of their afternoon, Jake and Jenny napping angelically in their travel cribs, his sister Sage in the kitchen, whipping up something that smelled delicious, and his mom in front of her laptop computer, still working on the details for the Welcome to the Family party for Adelaide and the twins, it was downright homey.

Who would have thought?

"Our session with the horses was great!" Adelaide went to the kitchen sink to wash up, her dark wavy hair tumbling about her face. "Wyatt got Durango to go all the way up to the windmill and stop. No problem."

Sage made a comical face. "And that's a plus because…?"

Wyatt had to admit, at the moment, Adelaide did sound like she had it bad. For him. A notion that made him grin.

Oblivious to the brother-sister teasing, Adelaide enthused, "A good cutting horse has to trust his rider, so he can go where he needs to go and do what he needs to do without even thinking about it. He's also really got to trust and like his trainer. And even though it's clear that unlike Buttercup—who's a cowgirl's dream—Durango is still a newbie at all this. I swear he would follow Wyatt anywhere."

Sage burst out laughing. "Maybe she should do your advertising."

Before he could stop himself, Wyatt said, "Or join me in the business."

At that, all three women blinked.

"Adelaide *has* a profession," Lucille said.

"But she's always wanted a career teaching riding," Wyatt informed her.

More stunned looks. "Is this true?" Sage asked.

"I thought you liked working at the Lockhart Foundation!" Lucille said, hurt.

In salvage mode, Adelaide swiftly lifted both hands, palms out. "I do."

"Then?" Lucille pressed, looking even more distressed.

"She would like working with me more," Wyatt insisted, matter-of-fact. Having just had a taste of how great life could be, if they just went back to a simpler time when they'd both been happy, before all the heartache and divisiveness of the last ten years, he turned to Adelaide. Who, to his surprise, was suddenly heading for her phone. Head down, gaze averted. He paused, wondering if he had gotten this all wrong. "Wouldn't you?"

"Doesn't matter," he thought he heard her mutter. She whirled back to face him and his family, the closeness they'd shared during their ride suddenly gone. Gaze serious, she said, "I think we've had enough changes."

An awkward silence fell.

Sage perked up. "Speaking of changes, have you seen the latest from the online gossip sites? The stuff that was posted late last night?"

Adelaide and Wyatt shook their heads.

Beaming, Lucille tapped on her keyboard. "I've got them bookmarked," she said, then proceeded to pull them up, one after the other.

The *Daily Texas Dish* featured a photo of Adelaide and Wyatt kissing outside Sage's bakery, his two older brothers looking on. It was next to another photo of Adelaide and Wyatt cooing over the twins in the stroller, on the sidewalk outside her home. The headline proclaimed: Infant Twins Have Made the Wyatt Lockhart–Adelaide Smythe Love Match a Family Affair!

Another from the *Dallas Morning Sun* gossip page showed Wyatt and Adelaide strolling hand in hand through the Laramie town park, sharing a sidelong glance. The caption proclaimed: As Valentine's Day Approaches, Is Love in the Air?

The third was on the website for *Personalities!* magazine. It showed Adelaide and Wyatt emerging from the bakery, under the banner: Secret Marriage Brings Peace to Texas Family Feud!

Appearing shaken, Adelaide moved uneasily onto a stool. "I can't believe we made a national magazine with this."

Deciding they both could use a drink after their rigorous outdoor activity, Wyatt went to fix two tall glasses of electrolyte-infused ice water.

"We made the national news with the embezzlement scandal at the foundation last summer," he reminded her.

"I much prefer these headlines," Lucille retorted happily, getting up to give Adelaide, then Wyatt, then Sage, all reassuring hugs. "And peace between our two families."

"It sure beats the stories that were out there a few days ago." Sage sighed.

Wyatt nodded. "We all owe Hope a debt of gratitude."

"And there were will be a fresh batch of photos posted tomorrow," Lucille added. "From the activities on the ranch today."

"Speaking of which," Adelaide cut in, "now that we've replaced the negative with the positive, do you think we can finally call off Marco Maletti and end the clandestine paparazzo-stalking?"

Chapter 11

"I'm all for ending the tabloid stuff, too," Wyatt admitted after his mother and sister had left.

With the twins still sleeping, he and Adelaide went up to change out of their horse-riding clothing and shower.

Not sure how much time they actually had, Adelaide stripped down to her skivvies. "Then why didn't you back me?"

Wyatt followed her into the master bathroom. "Because if Hope—a renowned crisis manager—says it's too soon to stop feeding positive stories and accompanying photos to the press, then it is." He pulled off his own shirt and jeans. Picking up his electric razor, he ran it over the stubble on his jaw. "Why does it bother you so much?" he asked.

Adelaide turned on the water in the shower, peeled off her undies and stepped into the masculine-tiled stall. She tipped her hair back, beneath the warm invigorating spray. "I don't like the idea of someone surreptitiously following us. Photographing…everything. It makes me feel vulnerable and exposed."

He opened the glass door and walked in, his gaze roving appreciatively over her naked body. Taking her into his arms, he dropped hot, openmouthed kisses along her jaw. "Like this…?"

A delicious shiver went through her. "Wyatt..."

He gripped her tighter, his mouth capturing hers. Lower still, she felt the force of his arousal, hot and demanding. A river of need swept through her. Hands sliding down her back to her hips, he urged her back against the wall and nudged her legs apart with his knee.

He kissed her again, one hand skimming a nipple, the other moving between her thighs. Drawing her into a sweet and pleasing current of desire, making her as wild for him as he was for her. Helplessly, she lifted herself against him. Wanting, needing. Trying to...then unable to...wait.

He held her until the aftershocks passed, then left her just long enough to roll on a condom. Stepping back into the shower, he lifted her so her legs were wrapped around his waist. Thrilled by the raw, primal need she saw on his face, she sank onto him, cresting together through wave after wave of seductive pleasure.

Wyatt knew Adelaide was wary of the future, as well as the here and now. He also knew this was the one thing—the only thing—that would make her feel better. And if it helped him, too, he thought as a sigh rippled through her, and then a moan, if it helped them get even closer, then so much the better.

He kissed her softly and tenderly, sliding into and out of her, possessing her rough and hard. Until she peaked again, exquisitely and erotically, and this time he came with her.

Afterward, with the babies still quiet, Adelaide wrapped herself in her cozy white terry-cloth robe. Emotions awhirl, she went to the suitcase containing her clothes.

He stopped drying his hair with a towel and ambled closer. "I can make room in my closet for you, you know."

His scent—all warm, sexy man—sent another thrill thrumming through her. "That's okay."

His smoky blue eyes leveled her. "Don't want to get too comfortable here?"

She rose, undergarments in hand, determined to be practical, even if he wouldn't be. "More like I don't want to overstep my bounds. Become even more intrusive to your living space than the twins and I already are."

"Hey." He caught her arm and reeled her back to his side. "Why so formal, sweetheart? I thought we had a good time this afternoon."

She smiled. "We did." Heaven help them, they did. In fact, if nothing stood in their way, they'd be making love again right now.

He let her go and rocked back on his heels, still searching her face. "Then...?" he prodded relentlessly.

"What? Are you sorry we made love again? Regretting we moved in together...?" His frown deepened in consternation.

Now he was definitely unhappy.

Adelaide swallowed. "No. Of course not. It's just..." Ignoring the way his gaze scanned the vee of her robe, she pulled the bodice modestly closer, angled her chin and tried again. "You and I have made a lot of changes really quickly."

In under two weeks, they had gone from finding out they were not actually divorced, to discovering *they* had twins, to moving in together, albeit temporarily.

"Because we had to," he countered, all implacable male. "What I want to know is why you're suddenly running so hot and cold again. Having fun with me, wanting to make love with me one minute, putting up all the barriers the next."

Exasperated, Adelaide ran her hands through her hair. "I'm unnerved because we're doing what we always do. Getting way, way ahead of ourselves!"

Wyatt gathered her in his arms. "No," he countered gruffly, "we're catching up."

Head lowering, he delivered another smoldering kiss.

"You see," she said breathlessly, throwing up her arms and pulling away. "There you go. Seducing me into being reckless again." *Making me feel really, truly married to you. Instead of in the process of consciously uncoupling.*

He shrugged affably. "What's wrong with that?"

Not about to reveal how vulnerable she felt, or how tempted she was to do as he had suggested earlier, and at least go back to teaching riding lessons part-time, while still continuing her work as CFO for the Lockhart Foundation, she folded her arms in front of her. "I like to think things through first." Not just react emotionally.

He dropped his towel and tugged on a pair of snug black boxer briefs. "Mulling over anything is overrated."

She tore her eyes from his lower half. "Says you."

He pulled a T-shirt over his head. "I like to go with my gut."

She turned away to slip on panties under her robe. "Well, when I go with my first instinct, and let myself be impulsive, I usually make the wrong decision." She slipped into the bathroom to put on her bra and camisole.

"Like...?"

Walking back out into the room, she looked him in the eye. "Agreeing to elope with you."

He sat on the edge of the bed. "Why did you do that, anyway? And then run away?"

Wyatt had never asked anything about that, never wanted to understand. From his vantage point, things were just the way they were. So Adelaide knew even wanting to talk about it was a big step for him. Just as her making love with him, after he had said they were either all in or all out of a physical relationship for the duration, was a big step for her.

So she took a leap of faith, too. She sat next to him on the edge of the bed, and told him what was in her heart, too. "I wanted to be with you, Wyatt. Really, really bad. I just wasn't ready for marriage when we set off for Vegas, and—" she was ashamed to say "—I knew it."

He craned his neck and asked softly, "Then why didn't you tell me that?"

"Because it was still what you wanted. And what the reckless part of me wanted. But the more logical part knew it was a mistake."

"So you bolted."

They sat in tense silence.

Finally she looked into his eyes and asked the question that had haunted her. "Why were you so insistent we get married as soon as we both turned eighteen? Why were you in such a hurry for us both to grow up?"

"Because I didn't want the future my parents were trying to push on me. And the only time I felt good about myself, or really happy, was when I was with you."

Same here.

He grimaced, recalling that tumultuous time. "I was afraid if you went off to college, and I didn't, you would leave me behind."

"But you did go to A&M."

"Only for two years. And I pretty much flunked everything but the ranching and equestrian courses."

She waved off the defeat. "Only because you weren't interested in the other stuff. You were bright enough to ace any course."

Falling silent, he pulled on the rest of his clothes.

"Is that why you spent your summers working rodeos as a pick-up rider?" she persisted, pulling on a pair of black yoga pants and a long-sleeved red T-shirt.

He gathered up their soiled riding clothes and tossed them into the hamper. "How do you know about that?"

"You and I might not have had a word to say to each other, and been very good at managing not to run into each other, but I knew what was going on with you. Through Sage and your mom."

His lips curved wryly. "They made sure I knew what was happening with you, too."

But had he been interested to hear? His expression gave no clue. Telling herself she had no reason to be disappointed if he hadn't been, Adelaide grabbed the hamper of baby laundry. They headed downstairs.

While she added clothes to the washer, he lounged nearby. "Is my lack of college degree why you wouldn't want to go into business with me, teaching riding and training horses?" he asked as they entered the laundry area off the kitchen. "'Cause I thought we had a good time out there today. I thought you were finally having a taste of your dream career."

"Well, it's either that or your atrocious handwriting," she joked.

Not funny. Okay. Adelaide sobered. "You're right. I loved training the horses. But I can't make a life-altering decision like that on a whim. Because whenever I impulsively do something like deciding to buy the cottage in town..."

He picked up a stray bootie, their fingers brushing as he handed it to her. "Hey, that's a nice cozy house. Conveniently close to work, like you said."

Adelaide added soap and turned on the machine. "Yes, and I knew in the logical part of my brain that it was never going to be big enough for me and the twins unless I renovated it."

He shrugged. "You thought you could wait on that."

"And now that the twins are starting to sleep better because we figured out they need to be able to see each other to feel secure, I realize I could have waited a couple years to do the renovation, like I originally planned. But instead I was so anxious to get everything settled and comfy and right..."

Clearly intrigued, he met her gaze. "Just the way you are here?"

Back to that. "Keeping my clothes in a suitcase reminds me that this agreement we have to live together, for the sake of our kids, is only temporary."

And she needed to be reminded, lest she do something really foolish, like fall head over heels in love with him, all over again.

"What if it isn't?" Wyatt asked quietly, coming closer yet. He cupped her face in his big hand. "What if you and I like being together, taking care of the kids together, making love together?" His voice dropped a husky notch. "What then?"

It would have been easy to say they should forget the divorce and stay together if it had been months, rather than mere days, that they had been bunking together.

But that simply wasn't the case.

Determined not to hurt him, Adelaide chose her words carefully. "It is great things are working out better than we could have envisioned at the outset."

He lifted a speculative brow. "But…?"

Trying not to think what his low, gruff voice did to rev up her insides, she said, "We're still in the honeymoon period. Immersed in the wonder of being together again in a way we never thought was going to be possible, and of having kids."

He slanted her an annoyed look. "You say that like it's a bad thing."

She lifted her palm. "I'm saying it's why we have to continue to be *cautious*. Whether we stay together as lovers for the long run is not as important as the fact that we're going to be the twins' parents for life." She paused to let her words sink in. "We have to make sure we can make that part of our relationship work ad infinitum before we even consider changing anything else."

"Don't you look like you just lost your best friend," Chance teased the following morning, when he and Molly dropped by Wind River with a basket of traditional German breakfast breads and cookies, three-year-old Braden in tow.

Braden frowned, looking around. "Where's the babies?" he asked, tipping his little cowboy hat back. "There's supposed to be babies! Two of 'em! A girl. And a boy!"

Molly elbowed Chance. "Told you we should have called first."

Chance elbowed the love of his life right back. "Told you Wyatt might have said no to just dropping by."

"So where are they?" the little boy persisted.

"Adelaide had to go in to town to do some work at the foundation, so she took little Jake and Jenny with her."

Braden walked over to the baby swings. He pushed the buttons on top before anyone could stop him. The swings began moving back and forth. "Can I try?" He lifted a leg as if to climb in.

Chance hit the off buttons and quickly stopped the motion. "No, buddy, you're too big for these, but we can take you to ride the horses like we promised." He turned to Wyatt. "If that's still okay?"

Wyatt had given his bucking-bull-rancher brother and loved ones permission to ride on his property at any time.

"No problem."

Molly assessed Wyatt quietly. "Why don't you two fellas head on out to the barn? I'll catch up with you in a minute."

"Sure thing." Chance shepherded the little boy out the back door.

Molly set her gift on the kitchen counter.

Wyatt tensed. "Something you want to talk to me about?"

"Yes, actually, there is."

Adelaide had just about wrapped up the accounting for both the Lockhart Foundation and the West Texas Warriors Assistance nonprofit, when Wyatt's sister-in-law, Hope, stuck her head in her office doorway.

Her hands hovering over the computer keyboard, she tensed. It wasn't unusual to see Hope there—not only was she married to the physician who ran both organizations, but she also handled the public relations for both organizations.

Still, Adelaide had to ask, "Everything okay with the twins?"

Hope waved off Adelaide's new mom tremors with a big grin. "Oh, yes. Currently, Lucille and Garrett are holding court with the rehabbing soldiers. My Max, no slouch, is doing the play by play. Which, due to the fact he's not quite one year old, amounts to a lot of clapping and laughing, and pointing and smiling. And the occasional 'dada,' 'nana,' and 'baby' thrown in for emphasis."

Adelaide rocked back in her chair. "I never have to worry about Jake and Jenny getting enough attention here."

"An understatement. Listen, Tank Dunlop's wife, Darcy, is here, and so are Sage and Molly—"

"I thought Lucille said that Molly, Chance and Braden went out to Wind River to ride today." Apparently Adelaide had just missed them.

"She did, but we had something come up this morning regarding the foundation's Chili Festival fund-raiser, so she left the guys there and came back into town to meet with us. Since you're on the steering committee, too, I was hoping you had time to join us in the conference room."

"Sure. Just let me shut everything down here and I'll be right in."

"So what's up?" Adelaide asked when she joined the group.

"The mayor called," Hope said. "Advance ticket sales have been through the roof. Nearly double what they were last year. So he's asking all the participants to make sure that they have enough to accommodate the extra crowds."

"So we want to know if we should either expand our Kids Go Fishing Family Fun booth to double the capacity," Molly said, "or add an additional activity geared for the four-to-ten-year-old set."

"We're going to need to order extra prizes, too," Sage said. "Although some of those could come from my bakery in the form of cookies or cake pops."

The group talked some more.

Adelaide ran the figures on cost. They looked at their budget, the potential profits each idea could potentially make, and then decided to just have two go-fishing games, set up side by side.

Darcy agreed to line up additional ex-military and/or their spouses to supervise the activities. "So what are you getting each other for Valentine's Day?" Darcy asked as the meeting wound down.

Adelaide tensed at the thought of the traditionally romantic holiday.

"What my man always desires." Molly laughed. "More home-baked German pastries and cookies! In the shape of hearts, of course. Braden will help me make them."

Darcy turned to Hope. "Garrett and I arranged an overnight at a luxe hotel in Dallas—the weekend after. Max is going to stay with Lucille while we have our adults-only ooh-la-la!" Everyone laughed.

"Adelaide?" Darcy asked.

Oh, dear. Adelaide flushed. "Um… I don't know. Haven't even thought about it yet."

"Well, you should get him something," Sage, who was practically glowing with good health, said. "After all, it is your tenth wedding anniversary."

So everyone kept reminding them. Adelaide lobbed the ball right back into Sage's court. "Are you getting Nick Monroe something?"

"Actually, yeah." Squaring her shoulders, Sage beamed. "Since we're otherwise unattached, we agreed to give each other something jokey." She turned to Darcy, the only one of them who had been married to active duty military, and had to help her husband battle back from life-changing injuries. "What about you?"

Darcy radiated hard-won serenity. "Well, maybe it's because I nearly lost Tank when he was injured overseas. But I always make sure I give him something that lets him know I will always love him with all my heart. Because I never ever want him to feel taken for granted."

A collective "ahhh" filled the room.

A few tears were shed.

The women had just finished exchanging hugs all around, when a volunteer loomed in the doorway. "Adelaide? Kyle McCabe is here to see you."

* * *

"Sorry to interrupt," Kyle said when Adelaide met him in the hall. "But my twin brother, Kurt, has this baby buggy they used when his triplets were infants. It's been gathering dust. And he and Paige thought you might want to have it."

Adelaide smiled, hoping this was just a casual visit. And not anything related to her dad. "That sounds wonderful."

"It's in the back of my pickup truck now," Kyle continued, "if you want me to transfer it to your SUV."

Amused by how oblivious the single lawman seemed to the admiring female glances turned his way—what was it about a man in uniform?—Adelaide said, "Great. I'll walk out with you." She and Kyle took the elevator to the first floor, then walked through the lobby, past the glass-walled PT unit where rehabbing ex-military worked with physical therapists to regain their strength.

Kyle held the door for her and they strode side by side through the parking lot. As soon as they were out of earshot, Adelaide asked, under her breath, "Is this the only reason?" *Please say yes.*

He sobered. "No. Mirabelle Fanning was picked up yesterday with Interpol's help."

The hair on the back of Adelaide's neck stood up. "My dad?"

The deputy detective lowered the tailgate of his personal vehicle. "Still at large. Allegedly with most of the money they stole."

With effort, Adelaide kept her expression casual. "He left her?"

Kyle lifted out the collapsed buggy and set it on the ground. "Mirabelle Fanning says he was headed back to the States to see you and the twins."

The knowledge her dad might be coming to Texas hit her like a sucker punch to the gut. Not because she feared him harming them in any way; she knew he wouldn't. It was the thought of how Wyatt would take the news, and what that might do to their newly healing relationship, that scared her.

Kyle carried the collapsed buggy to the other end of the lot, where Adelaide's SUV was parked. "Has there been any other contact?"

"Aside from my phone and computer?"

He nodded. "Anything out of the ordinary?"

She pushed the button and watched the cargo door lift. "No."

Kyle moved a few things in order to set the collapsed buggy inside. He looked down at her genially. "You'll let me know if that changes."

Telling herself everything was going to be okay, Adelaide promised, just as cheerfully, "First thing."

In the meantime, they had another more immediate problem to solve.

Wyatt parked at the far end of the lot. Chance got out and removed Braden and his car seat. They all watched Kyle try to put a huge collapsed pram into the back of Adelaide's SUV.

"Doesn't look like that's going to fit," Chance observed.

Especially with the twins' safety seats in the second row.

"Too big," three-year-old Braden pronounced solemnly.

Wyatt tried not to react to the sight of Adelaide with Kyle once again. To his knowledge, the two of them hadn't seen each other this much when they were dating. And why was the set of Adelaide's shoulders so tense while she was gazing up at the uniformed lawman?

Fighting back a worried frown, Wyatt said, "I'll see if they want to put in my truck."

"Hey, thanks for the horseback adventures and ride into town," Chance said.

"Yeah! Thanks, Uncle Wyatt!" Braden yelled.

"Anytime." Eager to see what was going on, Wyatt strode off.

Nearing the deputy detective's vehicle, he noticed Adelaide was as white as a ghost. The usually affable Kyle was sober, too. The innate male need to stake a claim on one's territory surfacing quickly, Wyatt flashed a lazy grin. "Problem?"

Adelaide turned with a guilty start. "Yes," she said, frustration and something else he couldn't quite identify flashing in her dark eyes. Closing the distance between them quickly, he wrapped his arm around her shoulders for a hug hello. "Kyle's brother and his wife, Paige, are lending us a pram to use for the twins, but it won't fit in my cargo area."

Noting Adelaide had not relaxed into his embrace the way she usually did, Wyatt let her go. "No worries, sweetheart. It'll fit in my pickup."

"Problem solved." Abruptly, Kyle looked as anxious to get out of there as Wyatt was to see him go. Still, manners required a little more conversation. Wyatt extended his hand to the lawman. "That's really nice of your brother and his wife."

"Yes." Adelaide reacted in kind. "Thank you all so much!" She stepped forward to give Kyle the kind of casual southern hug that served as both goodbye and an expression of gratitude.

Wyatt had seen her make the gesture hundreds of times over the years, but this time, despite her aura of distraction, it seemed to carry the kind of emotional weight that made Wyatt feel he was still missing something.

Not love.

Not attraction.

But *something*...

Kyle tipped his hat. "You-all have a nice day." He ambled off.

Adelaide turned to Wyatt. "Do you want me to take this back inside the building and deal with it later, or put it in your truck now?"

"Let's do it now." He wanted a chance to talk to her and get a better handle on what was going on. "I think it will fit in the rear passenger compartment if I fold the seats."

Adelaide touched his arm as he picked up the pram. "I'll walk with you," she said quietly He nodded as they headed toward his truck. Maybe he was reading too much into the situation between Adelaide and Kyle. It was possible that because the two had briefly dated and then transitioned to friends, the situation between them was still awkward at times.

"Where are the twins?" he asked, folding the rear seats and setting the pram in his pickup.

"Inside with your mother and Garrett." She looked up at him and paused, her teeth raking across her lower lip. "Would you mind if we collected them and went back to the ranch now?"

Ignoring his instinct, which was to pull her all the way into his arms and hold her until her distress faded, he studied her instead. "And skip the grocery shopping and early dinner in town?"

She held his gaze, her expression pleading. "We can do both tomorrow. Can't we?"

He stroked a hand through her hair, then tucked a strand behind her ear. "Are you okay, Adelaide? You'd tell me if there was anything wrong, right?"

"Yes...of course." She drew a breath that lifted the swell of her breasts. "I'm just really ready to go home."

"Sure," he said, wrapping an arm around her. Maybe a night at Wind River was just what the four of them needed.

Chapter 12

"So this is 'tummy time,'" Wyatt observed later that same evening. They had spread blue and pink blankets in the middle of his king-size bed, and put the freshly bathed and pj'd twins on the center of each. Both were cooing as they waved their arms and kicked their feet. He and Adelaide stretched out beside the kids and kept them entertained, waving rattles and soft small stuffed toys in front of their faces.

Adelaide smiled with maternal tenderness as their babies played. "Well, it will be, as soon as we flip them over onto their tummies. First, I want them to get acclimated and know we are here to support them in their ongoing quest to be able to lift their little bodies up on their arms and look around."

"They certainly seem up for it tonight." Cheerful, not a fuss or complaint in sight.

The easy tenderness she bestowed on the twins was suddenly directed at him. "That's what an exhausting visit to town and a good nap will do."

He thought about the way she'd looked when she'd curled up on his sofa after they got home. Her dark hair spread out on the pillow, a soft knit blanket covering her abundant curves. Hours later, her cheeks still glowed a contented pink.

"For all of you?" he teased, watching her smile spread to her pretty dark brown eyes.

"Yes, well, sometimes new mommies need naps, too."

Noting Jake looked ready for a little more action, he asked, "Ready to do this?"

Nodding, she gently turned Jenny onto her tummy.

Wyatt followed suit with Jake.

Initially the twins seemed more befuddled than happy. Which was understandable, Wyatt thought. Babies weren't supposed to be put facedown unless they were supervised. "I think it might go better if they can see each other."

They positioned the twins so they were facing each other. For a moment, both babies lay with their heads to the sides, taking in their new position. Then Jake pushed himself up on his arms. Lifted his head. Saw his twin do the same. He grinned widely, gurgled. And fell back down, only to push up again.

Jenny mimicked her brother's actions, gurgling all the while.

Contentment drifted over them. "I can see why this would build strength," Wyatt said softly.

A connection, too.

Adelaide rested her head on her upraised hand and met his eyes. "This is how infants eventually learn to roll over. Get up off their tummies, onto all four limbs, then rock back and forth and crawl."

Wyatt tried to imagine that. Found he preferred just staying in the here and now. Things were so damn good. Surprisingly good...

Adelaide seemed to want to savor the moment, too. She watched the twins a few more minutes, her face suffused with pride. Then noted with amazement, "They're just *perfect*, aren't they?"

So far as we know. Wyatt tensed. Unable to help himself, he asked the question that had been nagging at him from the beginning. "But what if they're not?"

Adelaide blinked, not sure she followed. "What?"

"Perfect," Wyatt repeated soberly.

Adelaide rose to a sitting position. "But they are." How could he look at their children, with their gorgeous expressive faces and sturdy, healthy little bodies, their intent interest in the world around them, and think otherwise?

"They might not be." He gave her a hard look. "What if Jake turns out to have a learning disability? What if they both do?"

Okay, she could handle this. "Where is this coming from?" Adelaide asked calmly.

"I have the three Ds—dyslexia, dyscalculia and dysgraphia."

She shook her head. "That's not possible."

He just looked at her.

Adelaide's heart began to pound. "Wyatt, I went to school with you at Worthington Academy from second grade on. I think I would know if you'd had learning disabilities."

He exhaled roughly. "You would have if my parents hadn't employed expensive private tutors to teach me to read and if my parents hadn't convinced everyone that there was no need to put it on my records because it could be held against me in future endeavors. My grades were bad enough."

Adelaide defended him hotly, much as she had back then. "You were a C student because you didn't care, Wyatt. You didn't even finish the tests we took at school."

"Not because I didn't want to, but because I ran out of time. After a while," he said, puting his hand in front of little Jenny, and watching her latch on to his pinkie, "I adapted a who-gives-a-flying-squirrel attitude because it was easier. It made my lousy academic standing a badge of honor instead of a mark of shame."

Adelaide stretched out again and imitated Wyatt's move. "Did your siblings know?"

Little Jake latched on to her pinkie.

"Nope." Wyatt replaced his hand with a soft cloth rattle. "My parents knew my self-esteem was bad enough without adding fuel to the fire."

"Your sibs would have teased you?"

"We were *kids*. And growing up, as you probably recall, the four of us boys were rowdy as hell." His lips quirked. "Of course they would have teased me! And then suffered the consequences. But by then it wouldn't have mattered because the damage would have been done. So my parents never said anything to them, and I was grateful for it. 'Cause—" he jerked in a ragged breath and sat up "—I didn't want anyone to know, either."

Adelaide studied his stricken expression. Seeing the babies were beginning to tire, she turned them onto their backs and got the swaddling cloths. "You should have told me."

Wyatt scoffed. "Miss A-Plus Student? If you recall, you were always telling me to hit the books a little harder."

Her turn to feel stinging shame, Adelaide swallowed. "I'm sorry. I—"

"Don't be." He swaddled Jenny as well as she swaddled Jake. "As you can see, I succeeded despite everything." He leveled her with a glance. "I just want to know that if it does turn out that our kids have any similar deficit…" he said huskily.

"I—we—will find a way to help them overcome it, just as your parents did for you," Adelaide promised vehemently. She reached across the bed to clasp his hand. "But we won't keep it a secret. We'll make it a badge of honor, a symbol of raw courage and grace, from the get-go."

He squeezed her hand back, hard. Briefly they stood and embraced. Yet it still felt like so much was left unsaid, so Adelaide came back to him after they had put the sleepy twins to bed. His look said he knew she wanted to ask him something. Just wasn't sure how to do so.

"Yes…?" he prodded gently.

Adelaide got two beers out of the fridge. "Were the 'three Ds' the reason your mom has sort of always hovered over you a little more than your sibs?"

He added a hunk of sharp cheddar and a package of crackers. They carried their treat to the living room and settled on the sofa. With a fire burning cozily in the grate, the house quiet, it was the perfect time to talk. "In retrospect, I can see they were trying to protect me. To keep me from making the wrong decision and/or failing and being hurt, but it was their lack of faith in me that really stung."

Adelaide tipped her bottle to his. "Is this why you rely so heavily on your gut?"

"Yep." He savored the first taste of the golden brew. "I can't allow myself to overthink anything. Otherwise, I become paralyzed with the fear I'll let everyone close to me down."

She wished she could make every past hurt fade away. "I believe in you."

He returned her quiet glance with a wry smile. "One of the things I've always loved best about you."

Loved, Adelaide mused, as another silence fell. How she wished that were true, more desperately than she had realized. But she knew better than anyone that loving something about someone or even loving the way they could make you feel was not the same as being *in* love with him or her.

Yes, they got on well. Shared twins now. Made spectacular love. But would that be enough? she worried. It was for now. But always...?

He misunderstood her silence. "It's okay, Adelaide," he said gruffly, setting aside their beverages and taking both her hands in his. "I never meant for this to be that big a deal with us. I just wanted you to know because of the pediatrician appointment coming up... I plan to ask the doctor about it. See at what point testing can be done."

"Except it's not okay, Wyatt." She leaned toward him. "It's still going on, isn't it? With your mom? It's the reason she sent you all those articles on being a good parent and husband straight off the bat."

"That—and she was matchmaking."

Adelaide shook her head. Wondering if Lucille knew how much her continued lack of faith was quietly devastating her son. "Because she didn't want you to blow it."

His brow lifted. An inscrutable expression crossed his face. "Am I?"

"No." She shifted over onto his lap, so she could wrap her arms around his shoulders. She buried her face in the comforting crook of his neck and hugged him tightly. "Not at all," she whispered in his ear.

"Good." He grinned. "Because that's the last thing I want."

His mouth came down on hers. Powerful. Evocative. She knew he needed to make love as much as she did. Needed the intense intimate connection that only the physical could bring.

Had they been in love again…

But they weren't.

Might never be.

She wasn't sure it was necessary, though, not when they had so much else going for them. The least of which was the children they adored.

Needing him naked, she unsnapped his shirt, tugged it off, then the T-shirt beneath. He paused to grin indulgently at her. "Taking the lead tonight, darlin'?"

"Appears so." She went to work on his jeans. Tugged those off, too. Found a condom, rolled it on. "I need you inside me."

His eyes heated. "Inside you is good. Very good. And to that end…"

He drew her to her feet, stripped her bare, then sank on the sofa, pulling her back onto his lap. The insides of her thighs rubbed against the outside of his. The hardness of his erection teased the feminine heart of her. As he moved to push all the way inside, the burden she'd been carrying for what seemed forever began to fade. Guilt and regret replaced by raw, aching need. Something that went deeper than lust and was far more satisfying than simply sex.

Making love with him pulled at her heart and stirred all her senses. The clean musky scent of him, the smooth warm satin of his skin. The hardness of his muscles. The pulsing heat and force of his erection.

All combined with the tempting quest of his lips, the erotic sweep of his tongue, the all-encompassing way he could kiss her, until she was awash in pleasure.

Wyatt knew she'd reached out to him out of empathy and a need to comfort him. A better man would have rejected that. Not him. Not when he wanted her the way he did. In his house, with his kids, and with him. In bed and out, she was the best thing that had ever happened to him. And he wanted her to know it as he ran his hands over her supple curves and kissed her with an intensity that took their breath away. Whether or not she realized it, Adelaide had been his destiny, and she his, the first moment they'd met. He saw it in the way she'd always looked at him, like the sun rose and set in his eyes. He'd enjoyed it every time he made her laugh or smile. And felt it in every touch, every lingering caress.

Satisfaction unfurled within him as he turned her so they were stretched out, facing each other, her leg thrown across his hip. His own body quaking with the effort it took to suppress his own needs, he slid home once again. Gliding a hand between them, he caressed her gently, kissing her all the while, dragging his chest across her creamy breasts and rosy nipples, until her skin was so hot it burned and her hips rose instinctively to meet his, her open thighs rubbing with delicious friction against his. With a soft moan of delight, she kissed him with deep, urgent kisses that washed away all the heartache of the past and rocked his soul.

His own need spiraling, he shifted positions so she was beneath him. As he entered her again, she shuddered with pleasure and whimpered low in her throat, surrendering to him, to the two of them, as never before. He pinned her arms above her head, going slow and deep, until her body took up the same timeless rhythm as his, trembling and clenching around him. And then all was lost in the heat and tenderness that surrounded them.

The next day, while getting ready for the pediatrician appointment, Adelaide brought the conversation back to a topic he had hoped was closed. At least for now.

Adelaide packed the diaper bag. "I think you should tell your siblings. Not just because LDs can run in families..."

As he looked at his wife, Wyatt was almost sorry he let the information out. The empathy and compassion of the night before felt like pity this morning. Which was the hell of learning disabilities. He never knew if he was being oversensitive, or suddenly just aware of how others saw him. Somehow deficient. Less than... In need of...

He forced himself to sound casual. "Been reading up on it?"

They eased the twins into their matching white fleece outerwear.

Adelaide's cheeks turned pink. "A little." She handed him the diaper bag, looped her shoulder bag over her arm. They scooped up the twins and carried them out to her SUV. The day was crisp and cold, but sunny. "I plan to do a lot more."

He liked the way she protected him. It felt right somehow. Always had. "You're a great wi—" He stopped at the frozen expression on her face. "Ah, friend," he corrected. "Anyone ever told you that?" He bent to make sure Jake was securely strapped in.

She did the same on the other side of the vehicle, for Jenny.

"Not the 'wife' part. But friend, yeah."

They straightened and climbed in. He returned her wry grin. "Sorry. I didn't want to offend you."

She watched him fit the key into the ignition. "You won't."

He liked the fact she let him drive. "I don't know." He gave her the slow, sexy once-over. "Some of those articles my mom sent me said some new moms can be pretty sensitive."

She snorted at his teasing. "I wouldn't worry about riling me up. But we do need to be concerned about being late to our appointment if we don't get a move on…"

Wyatt had planned to ask Adelaide what to expect as they drove into town. Unfortunately, she had a call from Molly and Chance regarding her renovation. There were several issues that needed discussion and resolution, and Adelaide spent the entire time working those out.

They arrived at the medical arts building and because they were the first appointment after lunch, were immediately ushered into an exam room by the nurse.

"So who have we here?" the nurse asked, looking at Wyatt.

"This is Jenny and Jake's daddy, Wyatt Lockhart."

"Right. I think I heard something about the two of you being married." Her glance went to their bare left hands. "Or, ah," she stammered, embarrassed to have possibly spoken out of turn.

"No. We are, actually," Adelaide said.

"And have been for the last ten years," Wyatt added.

The nurse shot him a look. "It's a long story," he said.

She looked torn between bemusement and concern. "I imagine so. Well, get the babies undressed down to their diapers. I'll be back in to weigh and measure them and then Dr. McCabe will be in."

"You said they have to get shots today?" Wyatt took his last chance to ask the questions he hadn't been able to voice earlier.

"Yes," Adelaide whispered back. "And let's not talk about it. I get nervous just thinking about it. And I don't want Jake and Jenny to feel my anxiety."

The odd thing was, Wyatt was beginning to feel a little worried about it, too. Which was weird, since he'd given plenty of shots to his horses. And never had a problem watching anyone else get an immunization, either.

Lacey McCabe breezed in. The mother of six grown daughters, the veteran pediatrician was known for her warmth and understanding. Which was why, Adelaide had explained to Wyatt the previous day, she had chosen Lacey as their babies' primary physician.

"So how is it going?" Lacey asked, checking the soft spots on Jake's head. She looked into his ears and eyes. "Get them on a schedule yet?"

"Sort of," Adelaide said.

Lacey examined the inside of Jake's mouth, then his skin. She paused to put a stethoscope in her ears, then bent to listen to Jake's heart and lungs. The little guy was so patient and cooperative, Wyatt couldn't help but be proud of him.

Lacey palpitated Jake's's abdomen, gently tested the movement of his hips and legs. Then undid the diaper and checked out that area, too. Finished, she handed Jake back to Wyatt and motioned for Adelaide to step forward and lay Jenny on the examining table, which she did. While the nurse took notes, Lacey began the same exam, all over again. "How long are they sleeping at night?" Lacey asked over her shoulder.

Adelaide smiled as Jenny cooed happily up at Lacey. "Four and a half hours straight if we're lucky. After that, they could wake up again anywhere from two to three hours."

Lacey grinned back at her small patient as she checked out her navel. "And how long are they awake then?"

Adelaide looked at Wyatt for confirmation. "Usually at least an hour. Sometimes two," he said. Liking the fact that Adelaide was giving him a chance to participate, too.

Lacey lifted Jenny off the table and gave her back to Adelaide. "Congratulations, Mom, Dad. Everything looks great on both of them. Now, what questions can I answer for you?"

While the nurse prepared the immunizations, Wyatt explained about his learning disabilities. Lacey listened intently. "LDs do run in families, but that doesn't mean your children will have them. We'll put notes in their charts, though, to be on the lookout. And if we find any deficiencies we'll get them the help they need immediately."

"Thanks," Wyatt said, feeling immensely relieved to have this out there.

"We appreciate that," Adelaide said.

"Anything else?" Lacey asked.

Adelaide and Wyatt exchanged glances and shook their heads.

Lacey went into efficiency mode. "Okay, we're going to get this next part over with as quickly as possible."

Thank heaven for that, Wyatt thought. He wasn't looking forward to the shots any more than Adelaide was.

"So what I'm going to do is have Daddy step outside with little Jake while we do Jenny's immunizations. And then we'll switch places, and have Mommy step outside with Jenny while Daddy comes back in with Jake."

The nurse opened the door. Just that quickly, Wyatt found himself out in the hall facing a collage of patient photos, all pinned to the middle of sunflowers. On the other side of the exam room door, he heard Lacey talking and Adelaide murmuring soothingly, followed by an indignant scream and hysterical crying.

Wyatt bit down on an oath. He couldn't even see anything and already empathetic tears were welling in his eyes. He was supposed to be the man here. His little guy was depending on him; they all were. Working to get it together, Wyatt blinked furiously as little Jake—who had no idea what was coming next—snuggled happily against his chest.

On the other side of the door, another indignant scream pierced the air, followed by more heartrending sobbing. Wyatt paced. Finally, for what seemed an eternity but in reality took only twenty seconds, the crying lessened and stopped.

The exam room door opened. Her eyes swimming with tears, Adelaide stepped out, comforting their little girl. Happy the traumatic episode was over, for Jenny anyway, Wyatt flashed Adelaide a reassuring look, then followed Lacey into the exam room.

"Let's put Jake here." She pointed to one end of the cushioned table. "We don't want Jake to be able to push the syringe away, so you're going to have to gently hold his hands above his head. Yes, that's it. The first vaccination is oral, so we're going to slip it in and let Jake swallow it."

That was easy enough, Wyatt noted nervously, although his son didn't particularly seem to like the taste.

"Next we're going to have two injections. One on each thigh. We'll do them as quickly as we can." Lacey swabbed the area on Jake's upper left thigh, rubbing the area gently in preparation. "While you talk to him to distract him."

How had Adelaide managed this? His throat wouldn't even work! Lacey gave him a look, as if wondering if he was going to be able to man up. Wyatt found a surge of testosterone and smiled down at his son. "It's okay, buddy. It's all going to be over in a minute…" he soothed.

Lacey skillfully delivered the first injection.

Jake started in shock as the needle pierced his skin, grimaced, then drew in a breath and let out a cry even louder than his sister's. He was still sobbing like his little heart would break as the nurse moved in to put pressure on the wound and bandage the left thigh, while Lacey prepared, and administered, another shot into Jake's upper right leg. Jake—who had never stopped sobbing—wailed even more.

Lacey picked him up and handed him to Wyatt, tenderly giving little Jake's shoulder a final pat. "It's all over, little one," she promised. "Your daddy will make you feel all better."

And indeed, cuddled against Wyatt's chest, Jake had already stopped his sobbing. The nurse and doctor slipped out while Jake leaned back, staring up at Wyatt with wounded, tear-filled eyes. Seeming to say, *How could you have let that happen to me, Daddy? I thought you cared about me!*

And at that, Wyatt just lost it.

Adelaide came back in the room, her face damp. "Dr. Mc-Cabe said we can get them dressed now." She caught his gaze, and seeing his overflowing emotion, began to cry again.

So Wyatt did the only thing he could. He gathered her and Jenny into an embrace with him and little Jake. Together, the four of them took the time to pull themselves together.

"Well, that went well, don't you think?" Adelaide quipped as the four of them finally made their way to her SUV, post-immunization instructions in hand.

Wyatt shook his head, knowing there was only one person in the world he could have let see him that vulnerable. Fortunately, she did not seem to think any less of him for his inability to man up there at the end. "I really did not think I was going to cry."

She poked fun at herself. "That's the difference between us. I *knew* I was going to lose it."

Aware he'd never felt more bonded to her and the kids than he did at that moment, he fell into step beside her. Soberly, he reflected, "We're going to have to toughen up before the next round of immunizations, though. Because even if the twins don't recognize a syringe in two months, they certainly will after that." They didn't want their anxiety transferring to their kids, the way his parents' fear over his LDs had transferred to him.

"You're right." Adelaide's desire to be the best mom possible came into play. "They're going to rely on us to be strong and steady and calm. Not just for shots. But throat swabs. And procedures..."

Wyatt frowned, thinking about needles. "Stitches..."

She winced. "Don't even say that."

He shrugged, already trying to brace himself for the inevitable. "They're kids. Some stuff is bound to happen. Someone is going to fall off a bike, or out of a tree..."

"Oh my God. I remember when you broke your arm in third grade, playing Tarzan!"

"Tumble off a diving board at the pool…"

"That was Zane," Adelaide commiserated fondly. "Showing off."

"Or cut her hand in the kitchen," Wyatt recollected.

"Sage."

Wyatt paused next to the car and waited for the door to read the keypad signal and automatically unlock. "Even Garrett—" the oldest son who in many ways could do no wrong "—conked the back of his head when he was inner-tubing down the Guadalupe."

"And let's not forget Chance," Adelaide murmured as they both secured the kids into their safety seats. "Who actually did wreck his dirt bike and split open a knee." Straightening, she climbed into the front.

He leaned forward and briefly let his forehead rest against hers. "It's kind of a Lockhart family tradition."

"Not for me." Looking as if she were thinking about kissing him, Adelaide moved back and fit the end of her safety restraint into the clasp.

Aware this was not the time to start making out, he slanted her a glance. There was still a lot he didn't know about her childhood. Particularly, the years before they'd met. "You never got hurt?"

She shook her head. "I was far too cautious."

And in certain ways, Wyatt thought, she still was. Whether that worked to their advantage or disadvantage remained to be seen.

"I'm glad you were there with me today," Adelaide told Wyatt hours later, when the full effects of the twins' immunizations began to surface. "And I'm really glad you're here now." She would have hated to have to handle this alone, with both of the twins so fussy.

Looking more like a family man than ever, with little Jake clasped gently in his arms, Wyatt got out of his man-size rocking chair and walked over to hers. He leaned down so she could put a hand to Jake's too-rosy cheek. "What do you think? He feels really warm to me."

"To me, too." Adelaide shifted the child in her arms. "What do you think about Jenny?"

Wyatt touched her cheek with the back of his hand. He grimaced with worry. "She's warm, too."

Adelaide went in search of the infant first-aid kit. "Do you know how to take their temperatures?"

"Do I know!" Wyatt scoffed. At her skeptical look, he amended, "At least in theory."

She chuckled. What was it about men that made them reluctant to admit to any deficiencies? "Those articles your mother sent are coming in handy." At least the ones about being a daddy. She hadn't seen him reading up on being a husband. But then, she hadn't read anything about being a wife.

He watched her remove Jenny's diaper and put her across her lap. "We really have to do it rectally?" He watched her coat the thermometer with petroleum jelly.

"To get the best accuracy when they are this young. Which is yet another reason I'm glad you're here with me."

He mugged at her joke.

"It's 99.9," she read.

"One hundred," he declared.

Adelaide consulted the printout they'd gotten from the pediatrician. "We don't have to call the service if it's under 100.4."

"Good."

"It also says we can give them baths to bring their temps down and make them more comfortable."

Wyatt sat again, Jake and Jenny snuggled against his chest. He hummed as he rocked, and the twins quieted almost immediately.

Trying not to be distracted by the tender sight, Adelaide worked quickly to set up a bathing station on the kitchen island.

"Good thing we have two baby bathtubs," Adelaide said, returning, and then reaching out to lift Jake out of Wyatt's arms.

He stood with Jenny. "Good thing we have a man-size rocking chair. I kept getting stuck in yours."

Adelaide laughed, aware that what could have turned into an extended time of misery and tears had instead turned into a sweet, joyous time she would always remember. Wishing Lucille could see Wyatt the way she did, and know just how wonderfully adept he was at nearly everything he'd tried, Adelaide kissed his jaw. "Have I told you yet what a great daddy you are?"

Grinning proudly, he leaned over to kiss her back. "In all the ways that count. Have I told you what a spectacular mommy you are?"

She nodded.

Now all they had to do was find a way to transfer the boundless love they felt for the kids to each other. And their family would be all set.

Chapter 13

"You look amazingly cheerful for someone who's just spent the last forty-eight hours caring for babies with post-immunization fever and fussiness," Lucille remarked when she came by Friday morning to help Wyatt out with the twins while Adelaide ran errands in town.

"It's probably because I had such superior help from their daddy," Adelaide teased.

Well, that and the number of times she and Wyatt had also managed to make love, she added silently. Sweet and tender, hot and passionate, slow and sensual. Their sessions had run the gamut. Leaving them both relaxed and happy and feeling surprisingly closer. Almost as if they were in love.

Wyatt winked. "What can I tell you, Mom? All those how-to articles you sent me really did the trick."

"Something did." Lucille grinned approvingly at both of them. "How long do you think your errands will take, Adelaide?"

"Not sure. I'm going to—" *pick up the special-order Valentine's Day gift I got for Wyatt and* "—um, hit the grocery. The bank and the pharmacy. And I also want to check on the progress at my house."

"I told her to take her time. She deserves a morning to herself."

"I agree," Lucille said.

Adelaide went over to the wind-up swings, knelt and kissed each drowsy infant in turn. Wyatt was there to give her a gallant hand up, so she did what she never did, went with her gut and kissed him, too.

Maybe things would work out, she thought, better than they had ever dreamed.

"Steak, potatoes, spinach and cream. That looks like the makings of a man-pleasing meal if I ever saw one," Sage teased when she ran into Adelaide in the supermarket.

With the same needling affection, Adelaide checked out her sister-in-law's shopping basket. "Roast chicken and all the fixings." *Plus saltines, ginger ale.* "What might you be planning?"

Sage grinned. "Nick Monroe is coming over for a little early Valentine's Day dinner."

Adelaide hoped Sage didn't get her heart broken again. She deserved someone who would put her first, above all else. "Where's he going to be after that?"

"Sante Fe. Houston. Phoenix. Oklahoma City."

"So he really is trying to take Monroe's Western Wear national?"

"At least completely thoughout the southwestern United States."

Adelaide thought about how happy her friend appeared whenever Nick was around. "I'm sorry."

"It's good for him."

Adelaide said gently, "I meant for you."

Sage waved off her concern. "We talk all the time. That's not going to change. So. How are things with you and my big brother?"

"Good."

"I'm glad. I've never seen him this happy."

I've never been this happy. "Being blessed with twins—" and a daddy who doted on them as much as Wyatt did "—will do that for you."

"Mmm-hmm." Sage winked mischievously. "Plus a lot of other things."

"Speaking of which," Adelaide said, flashing a smile, "I've got to get back to the ranch."

"Okay. Give everyone my love. I'll see you at the Chili Festival."

Adelaide checked out, then wheeled her basket out to the lot. She had just finished putting her groceries inside, and shut the cargo door, when she caught sight of the bumper sticker on her SUV: Grandpa Can Fix Anything.

Grandpa? Her children had no grandfather. Wyatt's dad had passed, and hers was out of the country for good.

Wasn't he?

Hands shaking, she got in her car and immediately called Kyle McCabe. "I have no idea how it got there," she told the deputy detective.

"Did you have a bumper sticker prior to this?" he asked.

Adelaide's nerves jangled. "No."

"Is the bumper sticker magnetic?"

"Let me check." Adelaide got back out of her SUV. Phone to her ear, she touched the colorful slogan on the bumper. "Yes. It is. You can peel it on and off."

"Then it's probably the sticker that was stolen off a car parked at the community center a few days ago. We've had a rash of sticker thefts the last week or so. All are ending up on other cars. Who gets what seems to be pretty random. So you're probably the victim of a teenage prank, just meant to be a silly joke."

Relief flowed through her. "Oh, thank heaven. I thought…"

"Have you had any more contact from your father?"

"No. Nothing." Adelaide drew a deep breath. "Have you heard anything more?"

"Nope. The customs and immigration service and TSA have all been notified, but as I told you earlier, it's not likely he'd try to come into the country legally."

Adelaide tried to imagine her father catching a ride with a coyote who drove people across the border in the dead of night, swam the river or climbed a fence. All options seemed impossible. Which likely meant she was overreacting. "What should I do with the bumper sticker?"

"If you have time, it'd be great if you could drop it off at the station. You can just leave it at the front desk. They'll see it's returned to the original owner."

Glad nothing was happening to disrupt her life after all, Adelaide climbed back behind the wheel. "Thanks, Kyle."

"And Adelaide? If anything else seems out of the ordinary, don't hesitate to notify me."

"Thanks for coming over to help out today," Wyatt told his mom while they sat down to give the twins their midday feedings.

Lucille settled Jenny in her arms and offered her the bottle. "You know, you still have time to go out and get Adelaide something nice for Valentine's Day."

The assumption he was still a screwup stung. Wyatt threw a burp cloth over his shoulder. "You really think you have to micromanage me in the husband department?" He'd blown off the articles Lucille had sent on how to be a good spouse, but somehow, this was different. It harkened back to his childhood, when Lucille had felt the need to shadow only one of her children.

"You don't exactly have a normal marriage." She paused meaningfully. "A really nice gift might help."

So would a lack of maternal interference in his love life. "I've got it covered, Mom," he said gruffly. He had not only figured out what he was going to give Adelaide, he knew where he was going to get it and when he was going to gift it to her, too.

"That's good to hear."

Wyatt moved his son to his shoulder for a burp. "But there is something I'd like to discuss with you. Adelaide and I talked to the pediatrician about the possibility of the twins developing learning disabilities."

Lucille did the same with Jenny. "I know you told your brothers and sister about your dyslexia, dysgraphia and dyscalculia."

He studied the stiff set of his mother's lips. "You don't approve?"

Lucille sniffed. "I don't see it as necessary, especially now, with you doing so well. Your father and I went to a great deal of trouble to keep you from being adversely labeled."

When Jake burped, Wyatt offered him his bottle again. He slanted his mother a glance. Although she'd come over to care for the babies, she still wore a silk-wool sheath, cashmere cardigan and heels. "Why did you do that?"

"Having come from modest rural backgrounds, we knew what it was like to be discounted unfairly. We worried the same would happen to you, and we didn't want you to be denied any opportunities because of your learning disabilities. Especially when we had the means to see you overcame them, privately."

Wyatt sensed there was more. "And you and Dad didn't want it known, either."

Lucille cuddled Jenny lovingly. "The rich get extra scrutiny, Wyatt. If it had been publicly known, people would have said you didn't belong at Worthington Academy."

The premiere Dallas school for the elite. "Maybe because I didn't."

"You had so many accommodations there."

Silence fell.

"Do you know how many children with reading and writing and math challenges never graduate from high school, never mind go on to college?"

Wyatt tipped the bottle so Jake could get the last of the formula. "Too many. And the term is *learning disabled*, Mom. LDs are nothing to be embarrassed about. Nothing to hide."

"Your father and I worked very hard to protect you."

And she still was, even though he no longer needed it.

"I'm not going to apologize for that," Lucille continued stiffly.

Wyatt turned to see Adelaide standing in the doorway, groceries in her arms. His sister-in law, Hope, was right beside her. Clearly, they had both overheard. And wished they hadn't.

Adelaide walked in. "Sorry to interrupt, but Hope needs to talk to us."

The other woman shrugged out of her coat and plucked a computer tablet out of her bag. "Another story has surfaced in the tabloid press. We didn't plant it."

She brought it over for everyone to see.

The screen was filled with a series of grainy photographs of Adelaide and Kyle McCabe in his sheriff's department uniform. The two were standing outside the WTWA/Lockhart Foundation building in Laramie, talking intently. Another showed Kyle lifting the McCabe's baby pram out of his truck and showing Adelaide how it went from the collapsed state to a fully extended buggy, big enough for multiple infants. Another of Kyle and Adelaide smiling, hugging. Wyatt had been standing off to the side when that happened, but he'd been cut out of the picture. And later was shown standing alone.

The story beneath was both damning and salacious: *Smythe-Lockhart marriage already in trouble as Adelaide resumes love affair with legendary Texas lawman Kyle McCabe, leaving husband Wyatt Lockhart out in the cold.*

Reading it, Wyatt snorted.

Adelaide blushed in distress. "Obviously, this was taken the other day."

"But not by Marco Maletti," Hope said. "He wasn't even in Laramie. He was off in Houston, chasing another story."

Wyatt walked back and forth with Jake in his arms. He patted his son's back gently. "Then who...?"

"An amateur who asked to be paid via an online money service with a shady reputation. At least that's what my contact at the tabloid claims. It's why the photos are so bad. But you can see they are authentic because this actually happened. Kyle did stop by to see Adelaide when she was in town the other day."

"So we're being followed by another paparazzo?" Wyatt theorized grimly.

"Or a wannabe," Hope concluded. "All we know for certain is that this person wants the story to take a salacious turn."

Adelaide looked like she was going to cry. "Oh no."

"So now what?" Wyatt asked the highly efficient scandal manager.

Hope shut her tablet. "We stick to our plan. And keep feeding interesting, touchy-feely photos and positive stories to the tabloid press until interest fades."

"Has anyone told Kyle McCabe?" Adelaide asked grimly.

Hope shook her head. "Not that I know of. I was alerted because I follow these things as part of my job."

"I'll do it," Adelaide said. Before anyone else could offer, she grabbed her phone and stepped outside.

Adelaide came back in, just as Hope and Lucille were leaving Wind River. "Talk to Kyle?" Wyatt asked.

She nodded tersely and walked over to the dual Pack 'N Plays. The twins were sound asleep. She stared down at their angelic faces, a faint smile on her face, admitting quietly, "He agreed with Hope, that it was likely the work of someone hoping to cash in or become part of the story, even vicariously."

He followed her into the kitchen. "Was that all he said?"

"Aside from the usual, if anyone bothers us, notify law enforcement? Yes." She took two thick hand-trimmed porterhouse steaks out of the package and put them into a glass baking dish.

Then, turned to look at him, the walls going up around her heart as quickly and sturdily as ever. "Why?" she bit out.

Working to corral his disappointment, Wyatt came close enough to inhale her familiar womanly scent. "I'm just wondering why you stepped outside to make the call."

Her head bent over the task, Adelaide seasoned the steaks with a spicy dry rub. "Because I feel like this is my problem to solve," she retorted stubbornly.

Once again, she was pushing him away. "I disagree," he countered quietly.

Her slender form stiff with tension, Adelaide swung back to face him. "If it weren't for what my dad did, no one would give two spurs whether our two families get along or not. Yes, people who know us would be interested to find out we are married and have twins, but the news wouldn't be written up in the press. We wouldn't be forced to fight fire with fire and or have unknown paparazzo stalking us and anyone else who came into our path."

"Like Kyle McCabe."

Turbulent emotion filled her eyes. Her lower lip trembling, she admitted even more miserably, "Not to mention the fact that your entire family is now stuck doing damage control, right along with us!"

"They don't mind. I don't mind."

"Well, I do!" She threw up her hands in frustration. "I hate the fact that my family has caused your family so much pain!"

"What happened last summer at the foundation is over, Adelaide."

She sighed, closed her eyes, and shook her head. "Don't you see?" she whispered, rubbing her temples. "It'll never be over. Never!"

"Yes," he said firmly, "it will."

Unfortunately, she didn't seem to believe him.

Luckily, her guilt and remorse about the past were things he could ease. Closing the distance between them, he wrapped his arms around her waist.

"First of all, you're part of the Lockhart clan, too, now. And thanks to our marriage, have been for years. Even if we didn't know it." He buried his face in the fragrant softness of her hair, kissed her temple.

He paused to give her a long reassuring look. "Second, you don't need to handle any of this alone. Not anymore. Not even the apologies."

Adelaide gulped. Her eyes glistened moistly. "I was trying to protect you."

Her vulnerability broke his heart. Wanting to do everything and anything he could to ease her hurt, Wyatt brought her closer still. "I don't need your protection," he told her gruffly.

He was strong enough to shield all of them from whatever came their way. He threaded one hand through her hair, looked down at the fiercely loving expression on her face. "What I need...what I have always needed...and wanted, Addie...is just you."

Relief softened her slender frame. "Oh, Wyatt," she admitted softly, "I need and want you, too." She stroked her hands through his hair. "So much..."

He lowered his head, and kissed her passionately. To his delight, she kissed him right back, clinging to him with all she had, until all the walls she'd just erected came down, and the last of her inaccessibility faded.

Figuring it was time they took advantage of the peaceful interlude, Wyatt caught her beneath her knees. "And now, as long as the twins are still sleeping," he teased, sweeping her gallantly up into his arms. He waggled his brows. "I have in mind something equally 'relaxing' we adults can do..."

She laughed shakily as he carried her up the stairs and dropped her down on the center of her queen-size bed.

"Mine?" she teased, knowing he liked space when he made love to her.

"This was closer," he told her gruffly. When she looked at him like that, all soft and sexy and needy, he couldn't wait any longer.

He stripped off her boots, jeans. Knelt on the bed to help her out of her pants, sweater and bra. She gasped as he kissed her again, ravenously, his hands discovering the deliciousness of her curves. Her nipples beading against the center of his palms, he moved lower. Past her navel. Lower still.

She arched as he caught the elastic edge of her panties in his teeth and brought it down. In a shockingly short time he had her naked and crying out.

His own body thrumming with need, he stripped down, found a condom and joined her on the bed.

"Let me." Trembling, she rolled it on, then pushed him onto his back and swung her body lithely over his. Joyously, she moved to take him all the way inside. As their bodies merged, her eyes filled with an emotion that was as elusive as it was deep. The nameless ache within him spread, infiltrating his heart. Turning her, he moved over top of her, their mouths connecting as intimately as their bodies. Tongues twining, they kissed and kissed. His hands slid beneath her hips and he lifted her, going deeper, slower, then deeper again. With a soft, low groan, she rocked against him erotically, breathlessly. She shuddered in his arms. He plummeted right after her. They clung together, sharing the ecstasy, the peace.

Worried his weight might be too much for her, he rolled onto his back, taking her with him. Cuddling her close, he kissed her temple, ear, cheek. "For the record," he whispered, savoring the increasing intimacy between them, "I adore you, too."

Adelaide would have liked nothing more than to stay wrapped in his arms, their naked bodies entwined. But she had promised herself she was going to make him dinner. And with the twins newly asleep—five o'clock fast approaching—she needed to get started.

"Where are you going?" he asked huskily as she eased out of his arms.

Damned if the sight of him, sprawled naked in her bed, wasn't the most beautiful sight she had ever seen. She pulled on her panties and secured her bra. with him watching lustily all the while.

"I got steaks. Remember?"

When she bent to pick up her pants, a small velvet jeweler's box tumbled out onto the floor.

He lifted a brow. "What have we here?"

Maybe there would be less pressure if she gave it to him now.

"Your Valentine's Day gift." She sat on the edge of the bed, pretending a casual ease she couldn't begin to feel. She searched his eyes. "Want to open it now?"

"It's February 12. I haven't had time to pick up your gift yet."

"So we'll draw out the pleasure."

His big body relaxed. "Well, now I'm curious."

"It's also sort of a fun anniversary gift," she added nervously as he took the gift box. She hoped she hadn't overstepped. "Practical, too. In the sense that maybe if we use them, we'll get less questions at places like the pediatrician's office. At least for the time being."

His brow lifted.

Adelaide drew a breath. "I'll be quiet now."

Grinning sexily, he opened the lid. Looked inside at the two identical twisted tin-and-sterling-silver tenth anniversary rings that could easily double as wedding bands.

One for her.

One for him.

There was a moment when he didn't move. At all. A moment where she wished they had never made a promise to consciously uncouple and then split up when the twins were older and the time was right.

But they had.

And with the secret she was still keeping from him, her father still on the loose, maybe even edging closer right this very second, she couldn't ask him to put a halt on any divorce plans and really try to make their marriage work.

Then he looked up at her, his eyes dark with desire, and something else she couldn't identify.

Something he, too, seemed reluctant to suggest, for fear it would somehow jinx the closeness they were already feeling, with every moment that passed.

"It's just for now," she said hastily.

"For appearances," he confirmed, his expression even more tender, yet inscrutable.

"And fun." And love... Because she was falling in love with him, all over again. And unless she was mistaken, he was beginning to want much more from her than they'd already agreed upon, too...

"This," he said gruffly, as he slipped the larger band on his left hand, then put hers on her ring finger, "is a gift as perfect as you."

There was only one problem with that, she thought, as Wyatt laid her down and made sweet and tender love to her all over again.

They had a lot going for them. *A lot.* But she wasn't perfect. Not even close. Or she wouldn't still be forced to keep so much from him.

Chapter 14

"We may have a lead on the photo of you and Kyle McCabe," Hope told Adelaide early Saturday morning as they worked to set up the go-fishing games at the Chili Festival.

Darcy lined up the troughs. "Tank told me that the guys at the WTWA have seen a guy who could be military veteran who might need help but is not yet ready to ask."

Sage followed behind, filling the receptacles with water and plastic sea life. "I saw him, too."

Adelaide tensed. "What did he look like?"

Sage grimaced as a cook-off participant went by with a great big bowl of freshly sliced onions. "I couldn't see much of his face. He had on dark glasses and a hat pulled low over his eyes. But he had a kind of mangy-looking beard. Long salt-and-pepper hair in a braid that just reached his shoulders. I hate to say it, but he sort of looked—and smelled—homeless."

That didn't seem like her dad. He had always been meticulously dressed and groomed. Then again, the last photo she had seen of Paul had been as a beach bum. Could this be another disguise? Or someone else? "Was he dressed in camouflage?"

"No." Sage unrolled the banner for the front of their fund-raising booth. "He wore faded jeans, a flannel shirt, an olive-green sweater and a really filthy shearling coat. Military-issue boots, bedroll and backpack, though."

Sage straightened and massaged her lower back. "Nick said he went into Monroe's and paid cash for some new wool hiking socks, and a couple of boxes of trail mix and protein bars."

Molly turned to Darcy. "So why would anyone think he was the person who sent the photo to the tabloid?"

"'Cause he was carrying a cell phone," she replied. "Tank said he always seems to have it out."

"And while he was in the store with Nick, some of the customers were talking about all the paparazzo photos that had just appeared online, and they were speculating how much you could get paid for something like that," Sage added.

Hope, who had been busy unpacking boxes, began setting up a second row of troughs. "It could have been one of the locals, then."

"Except for one thing," Darcy stated, adding more fish toys to the water. "The people of Laramie County take care of their own. I mean, they'll all *talk* about what's going on until the cows come home, but selling you out would go against the grain."

Adelaide tried not to be paranoid. It wasn't easy given the messages, the apprehension of her father's accomplice, Mirabelle Fanning, and the bumper sticker that had appeared on her car while she was grocery shopping.

Plus, she couldn't shake the feeling she was being followed. Although that was probably Marco Maletti, who was supposed to be surreptitiously taking more photos of them to generate positive press.

Adelaide paused to appreciate the smell of spicy chili, funnel cakes and corn dogs scenting the air. "When's the last time anyone saw this guy?"

"A couple days ago," Darcy said. She waved over a vendor and purchased a hot cup of coffee for everyone but Sage, who

declined the offer. "When you were at the Lockhart Foundation, getting caught up on the books. And speaking of catching up on things," Darcy said, pausing as she was in the act of
handing over a disposable cup, "what do we have here on your
left hand?"

Sage gasped. "Is that a wedding ring?"

Hope squinted. "Looks more like a roll of barbed wire
molded into a band to me. What kind of metal is that?"

Adelaide fought back a self-conscious blush. "It's a mixture
of twisted tin and sterling silver. I got them for us for a combination ten-year anniversary and Valentine's Day gift."

Smiles all around. "What did he give you?" Molly teased.

Adelaide released a dreamy sigh. "Don't know. He's making
me wait until this evening."

"Ahhh," everyone said in unison.

Wyatt walked along the midway. Catching them looking his
way, he waved. "He looks so cute with Jenny and Jake in that
kangaroo-pouch twin carrier."

He sure did. Wyatt had foregone his usual Stetson, and his
wheat-colored hair shone gold in the morning sunshine. To better accommodate the twins, he'd swapped out his usual denim
jacket for a black fleece. The soft warm fabric molded his broad
chest and provided a cozy resting place for the faces of their
two twins, who were both busy snuggling against their daddy
and looking around.

As their eyes caught, Adelaide and Wyatt exchanged smiles
before he got waylaid again by another couple wanting to gush
over the twins. "He's on daddy detail this morning. Lucille is
going to have them this afternoon while Wyatt and I do the cutting-horse training demonstration. And we'll both have them
this evening."

"Sounds like things are looking up," Hope said encouragingly.

They were. Adelaide just hoped nothing happened to mess
it up.

"Oh, no." Darcy looked around, then, through the empty boxes. "The gates are supposed to open any minute now, and I forgot to bring the boxes of prizes!"

"Where are they?" Adelaide asked.

"They're in the white West Texas Warrior Assistance van. I parked it in the lot about ten rows back from the gate. They're in the cargo area. They have WTWA written in red on them. And there's a dolly there, too."

"I'll run and get them. You keep working on this."

Darcy handed over the key. "You sure you don't mind?"

Adelaide winked and shook her head. "The exercise will do me good." She also needed to clear her head. All morning long she kept having this foreboding that all her worlds were about to collide, and it was ridiculous. Nothing bad was going to happen today.

Still, halfway there, she had the unsettling sensation she was being followed. She turned, saw nothing out of the ordinary, just festival-goers and volunteers moving through the parking lot to the gates of the fairgrounds.

With a deep breath, she shook it off and kept going.

She had just located the WTWA van when a man fitting the description of the homeless veteran stepped out in front of her, the intent expression on his weather-beaten face telling her their meeting was no accident. Her stomach roiled with nerves. "Can I help you?"

"Actually, Adelaide," he returned with surprising confidence, "it's more what I can do for you."

The person in front of her was a stranger. Unrecognizable. But she would know that voice anywhere. This was her secret wish and worst nightmare all rolled into one.

"Dad?" she asked hoarsely. He'd been a touristy beach bum in the last photo she'd seen. Now he was a down-on-his-luck ex-soldier, allegedly returning to his cowboy roots.

The man the world had once known as successful CFO Paul

Smythe tipped his hat but kept a casual distance. His weathered lips formed an affectionate smile. "You look good, Adelaide."

Still reeling from the shock, her knees began to wobble. Her dad looked so much older beneath the beard and long scraggly salt-and-pepper hair. As if whatever high he'd experienced after getting away with a fortune had faded fast.

"What are you doing here?" Adelaide demanded, still not quite believing her eyes. What was he thinking, returning to Laramie? Near the family he'd stolen from, of all places…!

Was he *trying* to get caught?

"I want to make amends." Paul shook his head, his lips pursing in regret. "I should never have left you, honey."

He was right; he shouldn't have. Adelaide swallowed around the increasing tightness of her throat. The tears she had long refused to let fall flooded her eyes, blurring her vision. "But you did run away with Mirabelle Fanning, Dad," she reminded him bitterly, unable to contain her hurt a second longer. "Without so much as a note, or a goodbye."

Paul set down his backpack and bedroll, leaning it on the car parked next to the WTWA van. "That was a mistake," he admitted as festival-goers several rows over headed excitedly for the fairgrounds entrance. "*She* was a mistake. And it's over."

Joy mingled with distrust. "You broke up?" She noted her father did not seem to know his former paramour had been arrested.

Her dad's jaw set. "I found out Mirabelle was going to leave me for a much younger man last November, so I bolted first, with all the remaining cash."

"And it was after that you put the remote log-in on my computer and started contacting me through social media."

He pushed the sunglasses higher on the bridge of his newly reconstructed nose. "I couldn't say much. But I wanted you to know I still cared about you. I love you, Adelaide. I know I wasn't very good about showing it in the past, but that's going to change. We have a chance to be the family we always should have been. You, me, the twins."

Finally her dad was saying the words she had always wanted to hear. And yet, they rang hollow. Her palms dampening, she said, "I can't leave Wyatt, Dad. I can't take his kids from him." *And I can't run off with an embezzler.*

Paul picked up his backpack and bedroll, and stomped closer, "Listen to me, honey. I know what it's like to be won over by a pretty face, but the *only* reason that reckless cowboy is back with you is because of the twins. And that's only temporary. The first time you disappoint him or he gets a little jealous—"

Everything clicked into place. "*You* sent the photo of me and Kyle McCabe to the tabloids!"

Her father acknowledged it with a lift of his brow. "I wanted you to see Wyatt's true colors. Put the real side of him, the ugly side, out there."

The only person who was being ugly here, Adelaide couldn't help but think, was her father. "Your ploy didn't work, Dad. Wyatt didn't jump to conclusions and think I was unfaithful with Kyle, or blame me for the additional bad publicity."

Paul scoffed and shook his head in mute remonstration. "Then it will be something else he won't be able to forgive. In the end, the result will be the same. You'll disappoint Wyatt— just the way you always have."

Adelaide really wished that weren't true. Deep down, she worried it might be. Because she always had eventually let down Wyatt in the past. To the point that if, it weren't for the twins, they wouldn't be together now.

"And when that happens, honey, he'll walk away. But this time he won't just break your heart, he and his family will take your kids, Adelaide. Just the way they took the money I should have had all along from me!"

Adelaide had always known her father could hold a grudge. She had just never imagined he would take one this far. "So the embezzlement was some sort of payback," she theorized quietly.

Just as she'd feared.

"Frank Lockhart and I built that hedge fund together. I was on board from the very first, but he's the one who walked away with five hundred million dollars in the end, while I cashed out with less than twenty-five million."

Adelaide was familiar enough with the company's books to understand why that had been the case. "Frank and Lucille took really big risks with their money. They gambled big and won big. You were a lot more fiscally conservative. And I get that. In your place, with a wife and child to be responsible for, no other land or money to fall back on, I would have been really cautious, too."

Her dad scowled. "Not in the end, I wasn't. I bet it all and walked away with half their remaining assets."

It hadn't been just the late Frank Lockhart and his wife, Lucille, who Paul had stolen from. "You bankrupted their charitable foundation."

Paul's jaw set. "I took what was mine. Now you need to do the same, Adelaide."

"I can't."

Paul hardened his stance. "You'll regret it if you don't."

What she was regretting was this conversation.

"Because sooner or later—probably sooner—you and Wyatt are going to have problems," her dad said knowingly. "And when that happens, you'll find yourself on the losing end of one heck of a custody fight."

"Wyatt would never try to take the kids from me."

Paul snorted. "If you think he'll let you have the kids, even half-time, you're fooling yourself. Wyatt is an all-or-nothing kind of guy who, like the rest of the Lockharts, will stop at nothing to get what he wants."

He paused to let his words sink in. "They're used to having it all. They won't rest until they have your kids, too."

Much as Adelaide wanted to discount everything her father said, the insecure part of her could not do that. Because he was right. Garrett had wanted Hope—against all odds, he'd made her his wife and adopted her son. Chance had enjoyed similar success with Molly and her son, Braden. Lucille wanted she and Wyatt to make theirs a real marriage, instead of a pathway to an amicable divorce, and was pulling out all the stops to facilitate that, too. And though the Wyatt she loved now would never try to deprive her of their twins, even if the two of them couldn't get along long-term, the Wyatt who had refused to forgive her before might...

"This is our second chance, Adelaide," her dad cajoled softly. "The only chance I'll have to get to know my grandkids."

She knew that, too. And as much as she wanted to reconcile with her father, to be able to forgive him so she wouldn't have to spend the rest of her life hurt and angry, it wasn't that simple. "I can't go on the run, Dad. I can't have the twins constantly needing to change their identity, the way you have, just to avoid detection."

"You won't have to. I've got it all worked out. New identities for all of you, with accompanying ID and fake passports. Transportation into Canada, and from there to a beautiful chalet in Switzerland. All you have to do," he coaxed, "is meet me at four o'clock tomorrow morning, and you and the twins will spend the rest of your lives in unbelievable luxury, same as me."

"That was some festival," Wyatt said hours later as he and Adelaide carried the sleeping twins into Wind River and up the stairs to the nursery. They'd stayed at the festival long enough to enjoy some of the prize-winning chili, and enjoy a little dancing, before heading back to the ranch.

She met his gaze, overwhelming emotion and something akin to gratitude glittering in her dark brown eyes. "Really wonderful," she whispered back.

Carefully, they placed Jake and Jenny into their cribs and eased off their winter caps and fleece outerwear.

Wyatt paused to admire their beautiful children, then took

Adelaide's hand and led her back down the stairs. She seemed curiously overwrought and on edge. "Want a glass of wine?"

She shook her head. "It would make me too sleepy. The twins will be awake again for feeding at 2:00 a.m."

Aware it was a little chilly in the house, he cranked up the heat. "Are you okay, sweetheart?"

She stared at him with an expression of calm indifference. "What do you mean?"

He watched her narrow her eyes. "You've been in a weird mood all day."

She paused, as if searching for a way to explain. "It was just a really long day."

Wyatt knew that.

"With a lot of confusion."

He knelt to light a fire, then stood and faced her. "You're kind of used to both, now that we have twins," he teased gently, sauntering closer. "Aren't you?"

She ran her hands through her hair, lifting the wavy mass away from her scalp. "Today was a whole other kind of stress."

"Is that why you slipped away a couple of times?"

Her hands stilled. "What are you talking about?"

"Sage said it took you forever to come back with the prizes for the go-fishing games. They were about to send out a search party for you."

She dropped her arms to her sides. "I got waylaid in the parking lot. Talking."

"And then this afternoon." Taking her by the hand, he reeled her into his side. "You were almost late for the cutting-horse demonstration. And no one could find you."

She turned bright pink and pulled away. Walking into the kitchen, she got herself a glass of water. "The lines were so long for the ladies' rooms, I thought it would be faster to use the gas station half a mile down the road from the fairgrounds."

He watched her make up a few more bottles of formula for the twins. "You drove there?"

She flushed all the more, shrugged. "Sometimes you just got to do what you have to do." She gave him a terse look that warned him not to pursue it.

He got the hint. Moved on, waiting until she had finished, then gently gathered her in his arms. "We still have time for my Valentine's Day anniversary gift to you."

She stiffened and pulled away. Switching off the lights in the kitchen, she returned to the hearth. "I'd rather not do that tonight."

She had to be kidding, right? He drew her into his arms once again. This time she did not pull away. "How come?"

Sighing, she said, "I think we'll both enjoy it more tomorrow evening. When we're not so tired."

She had a point. Now that he looked closely, he could see she seemed completely exhausted, emotionally and otherwise. Yet curiously wired, too. "You want to go to bed now?"

Maybe a little lovemaking and a night of snuggling was just what they needed. He kissed her neck, the sensitive spot just behind her ear. "I think I could handle that."

She splayed her hands across his chest. Clearly as averse to the idea as he was for it. "I meant separately." The walls were right back up again. "You in your bed, me in mine."

He narrowed his eyes at her. Now she was really freaking him out. "You haven't done that since you got here."

She nodded, determination radiated in her gaze. "I feel like I'm going to be restless, and I'd rather not have to worry about keeping you awake." Her voice dropped an urgent notch. "Please tell me you're okay with that."

Was this some sort of test? he wondered, bewildered. It seemed to be. If she wanted proof of the depth of his feelings, he would give it to her. "Okay," he conceded softly. "But first I want a good-night kiss." His lips claimed hers, drinking in the sweet essence of her mouth. He expected her to melt against him, really get into it, the way she always did. Instead, she kissed him back with uncommon reserve, her body drawn as tight as a guitar string.

Surprised, he ran a hand down her spine. "You really are tense, Adelaide."

"I know." She dropped her head and let it rest against his chest. "I'm sorry." She released a shaky breath, even as her fingers gripped the fabric of his shirt before flattening and smoothing outward across his pecs. Sorrow and regret were reflected in her eyes. "Forgive me?"

What could he say? She had asked for so little. Given so much. "Of course."

Her slender body relaxing with relief, she headed up the stairs.

Twenty minutes later, they were both in their beds, on opposite sides of the loft-like second floor of the converted barn, the twins sleeping soundly in their cribs.

As Adelaide had predicted, she was restless. Tossing and turning every few minutes in the moonlit darkness.

Frustration roiled through him. He wanted to go to her, convince her to come to bed with him, work his magic on her to alleviate her stress. However, she had asked for her space, and he was honor-bound to give it to her.

But still it took everything he had not to demand answers. Mostly because he knew something was bothering her, and had been for days now. What exactly, he didn't know.

In the past he would have immediately assumed it was because he was failing to meet her expectations on some level and let her withdraw without ever telling him why.

Now he wanted to know so he could fix it.

Because only then would he be able to make his move and suggest they reevaluate their initial plan to consciously uncouple.

Meantime, he needed to get some sleep, too. So that tomorrow, when Adelaide wasn't exhausted from the long day at the

Chili Festival and caring for the twins, they'd be able to enjoy the romantic late evening he had planned. And celebrate a belated Valentine's Day and tenth anniversary.

At 2:00 a.m. the twins woke. Wyatt got up to help Adelaide change and feed them before putting their exhausted little ones back to bed.

This time she did climb into bed and wrap her arms around him. He fell asleep, with her snuggled up against his chest. Only to wake two hours later to an empty bed beside him and the sound of a door downstairs softly closing.

He sat bolt upright. "Adelaide?" he called out softly.

No response.

Wary of waking the twins, he threw back the covers and padded barefoot across the top floor. His wife was nowhere in sight.

He went downstairs.

It was dark there, too.

Adelaide's coat, bag and keys were gone.

He moved to the front window. Saw her moving stealthily in the moonlight, the kangaroo-style twin baby carrier looped over her shoulders.

Swearing, he dashed back up the stairs to the cribs.

The twins were there, still sleeping soundly, their little chests rising and falling with every gentle breath they took.

So what was in the twin baby carrier?

Why was Adelaide wearing it?

And why, he wondered, as he moved to the window and saw her walking deliberately down the lane that led to the highway, a flashlight shining the way in front of her, was she going off in the middle of the night alone? Could she be sleepwalking? Attempting to meet someone? Maybe someone who was blackmailing her with other photos that could further embarrass his family?

All Wyatt knew for certain was that every instinct he had told him Adelaide was in danger.

Much as he wanted to run off after her, he couldn't leave their children behind unattended. Nor could he take them with him, without possibly putting them in jeopardy. So he did the only thing he knew to do. Called for reinforcements.

The Laramie County Sheriff's Department emergency operator patched him right through.

To Kyle McCabe.

"Stay where you are." The deputy detective ordered gruffly. "Don't turn on any lights. Inside or out. And don't call anyone else."

Wyatt was transferred back to the emergency operator. "What the hell's going on?"

No sooner were the words out of his mouth than a car drove along the highway to the entrance of the ranch. Stopped. The door opened, the interior lights of the car illuminating a figure getting out. And then all hell broke loose.

Half a dozen patrol cars and what looked like an arrest later, Adelaide was escorted safely back to the house by another officer. Rio Vasquez walked a pale, shaken Adelaide inside. "She's going to need to come down to the station later to make a statement, but right now, she should just stay put. Get some rest."

Rio thanked her again for all her help, then exited.

Trembling, Adelaide slipped off the baby carrier and sat on the sofa. Her coat still on, she removed the stuffed animals from the twin pouches, set them aside with a sigh.

He waited.

She said nothing.

Now that the danger was over, his temper rose. "I'm pretty sure I'm due some sort of explanation."

Her shoulders slumped in defeat. "My father just got arrested." The rest of the story came tumbling out.

He listened in disbelief. "So all this time, since the twins were born, you knew this could happen. Paul could show up!"

She looked at him, her gaze wary. "I knew it was possible, but I didn't think my dad would be that foolish. He's never been imprudent. Well, until he stole the money from the foundation. That was pretty crazy."

"Not to mention criminal."

A tense silence fell.

Once again, she appeared to bear the weight of what her father had done.

Guilt and compassion tempered his mood. Working to control his anger, he sat down beside her and took her hands in his. "Okay. I get why you helped law enforcement. I'm glad you did." He paused to control his mounting emotions. "I just don't understand why you didn't tell me! Let me know that you and our kids could be in danger! Especially after our agreement not to lie to each other or keep things from each other from here on out. So we wouldn't end up in situations like this!"

Adelaide pulled free, stood and walked away. She glared at him with weary resentment. "I was instructed not to inform you." Belatedly, she shrugged out of her coat.

So what? "I'm your husband," he reminded her angrily. "Or doesn't that count for anything?"

"Of course it counts, Wyatt!" Her motions stiff and mechanical, she walked over to hang it up. "But law enforcement didn't want you involved."

She, either, apparently.

He strode closer. "Why in blazes not, since this is my family we're talking about!"

He met her gaze, surprised to find her eyes shiny with tears and regret.

"Because they know how reckless you can be. They didn't want you going off half-cocked, looking for my dad and trying to bring him in by yourself! Or doing anything else that would screw up their investigation and arrest."

He forced himself to calm down. "Okay. That explains them. It doesn't explain you." He corralled his hurt. "Why you didn't tell me in confidence?"

"I already told you!" She threw up her hands in exaspera-tion. "I was following the orders I was given."

Grimly, he shook his head. "It's more than that and we both know it."

She clamped her arms beneath her breasts. "Like what?"

Disappointment churned in his gut. "You haven't trusted me in the past. You clearly don't trust me now," he accused bitterly.

She took a step back. Her eyes glittered moistly. "You're wrong, Wyatt," she said in a low, choked voice. "I do trust you."

"So why didn't you think I had a right to know?" he de-manded furiously, refusing to let her run away. "Why didn't you insist the sheriff's department fill me in, too?"

She threw up her hands in frustration. "Because I didn't want to argue with them about the proper way to proceed."

That he could buy. Jaw set, he looked her in the eye, and demanded, "Then why didn't you tell me privately? We're not just legally married, Addie, we're in a committed relationship." Or at least he'd thought they were! "You could have claimed spousal privilege. Trusted me to keep quiet and cooperate be-hind the scenes."

For a second, he didn't think she was going to answer him. Then she squared her shoulders, and locked gazes with him. Suddenly frustrated and angry now, too. "You really want to know?" she bit out eventually.

He slammed his hands on his waist. "Hell, yes, I want to know!"

"I didn't tell you because I wasn't sure you would believe me when I said I had nothing to do with my dad coming here, or contacting me."

He slowly looked her up and down. "So you lied to me, and kept things from me that I needed to know, again!"

She sent him a withering glare. "Can you blame me?"

Yes, as a matter of fact, he could.

She lifted her chin indignantly. Moved close enough to go toe to toe with hin. "You still haven't forgiven me for changing my mind about eloping. Or not telling you of my plans to have a baby on my own before we made love." Her voice took on a low, accusing timbre. "So of course I didn't *want* to tell you any of this! I worried that the mere possibility of my dad reappearing in my life would just be one more thing you'd never be able to forgive me for."

So she hadn't even given him a chance?

She'd just assumed the worst about him and left it that?

"Yet you had no problem confiding in Kyle McCabe," he retorted, incensed.

Adelaide threw up her hands and spun away. "He's a cop. He's able to keep his emotions out of it."

Great. Another low blow. "Unlike me."

Adelaide harrumphed, and pivoted back. "Where I'm concerned, yes!"

Suddenly so much made sense. "That was why McCabe kept stopping by to see you. Why you two chatted so intimately whenever you were together."

Reluctant, she nodded.

Her betrayal stung. Unexpected jealousy roiled in his gut. "Is that where you disappeared yesterday during the festival? To see him?"

Adelaide shoved both hands wearily through her hair. "My father intercepted me when I went out to the parking lot to get the boxes of prizes. So yes, I had to talk to Kyle, let him know that I had 'agreed' to take the babies and run away with my dad. I thought my dad believed me. But I wasn't one hundred percent sure. So I texted Kyle and asked him to meet me at the gas station."

Kyle. Not me. "You could have been followed."

She waved off his concern. "I had an excuse ready, if my dad had turned up there—that we needed to have my SUV ready as backup. And I did need to put gasoline in my vehicle." She released a long, shuddering breath. "But as it turned out, it wasn't necessary because my dad was already off changing his looks again, to a bespectacled, clean-cut, suit-and-tie executive."

Her courage wowed him even as her recklessness made him furious. "You put yourself in danger!"

She disagreed. "My father never would have hurt me."

"He already did."

Adelaide scoffed. "I meant physically."

The thought of something happening to her was enough to make him wild with grief. "You don't know that."

"Yes," she countered just as stubbornly, marching forward, her fists balled at her sides, "I do." Twin spots of color bloomed in her cheeks. "Dad had the chance just now to at least try something, but he didn't. In fact, he wasn't armed at all."

Wyatt blinked. Who *was* she? "You're defending him?"

"I'm saying my part in this is over and hopefully justice will finally be served and I don't want to fight about it." With an exhausted sigh, she sank in a chair.

Wyatt knelt in front of her, so she had no choice but to look at him. He took her cold, trembling hands in his.

She'd made a mistake. But he would forgive her. On one very important condition. "Promise me this will never happen again," he pressed in a voice as low and urgent as his mood. "You'll never cut me out of the loop." He squeezed her hands. "Tell me that if you had to do it all over again, you would give me a heads-up."

A myriad of emotions came and went in her eyes. Finally she sighed. "I can't do that, because I wouldn't, Wyatt. This was my family's mess to clean up. Not yours. Your family was hurt enough already. No way was I going to let anything else happen. Not to any of you!"

"So you put yourself in harm's way."

"I did what I had to do. I protected your good name. I kept you and the twins and everyone else well away from whatever illegal shenanigans my father was embroiled in. So no one else would have to suffer at his hands. Not ever again."

She was serious, even as she was courageous. Not sure whether he wanted to shake some sense into her or congrau-late her, he blurted out, "Damn it, Adelaide...!"

"Damn it, Adelaide, what?" she retorted wearily.

Her stubborn insistence on handling everything by herself was unacceptable. "I can't have you putting yourself and the twins in danger. For any reason!" he warned her quietly.

To his frustration, she stared at him for a long moment, then dug in all the harder. "I can't have you doing that, either, but sometimes life requires us to do the things we do not want to do."

Like stay married to him? he wondered. Even long enough to learn how to co-parent and consciously uncouple?

All he knew for certain was that the woman who had made love with him so tenderly, the wife who had finally started to open up her heart and soul to him, was nowhere to be found.

"You really will not admit you're in the wrong here?" he said slowly. "For lying to me, and keeping me in the dark? For not giving me the chance to be the husband I should be, the hus-band that you have every right to want and need?"

Still holding his gaze, she disengaged their hands and shook her head. Letting him know in that one instant that she was always going to shut him out. And never more routinely than when it really counted.

He stood, aware he'd never felt more betrayed and more bit-terly disillusioned in his life.

He couldn't live like that.

Neither could she.

Their kids really couldn't.

"Then the two of us having nothing else to say."

Chapter 15

"Wyatt *left* you?" Chance asked later the same day, shooting her an incredulous look.

Adelaide nodded miserably. The news of her father's arrest and the drama that had ensued preceding it had spread through the town like wildfire. By noon, it was on the news reports all over the state. Knowing it would be even more of a story if the press learned she and Wyatt had also split up over it, Adelaide was doing her best to keep the dissolution of their relationship within the Lockhart family.

Hence, she had asked Sage and Lucille to come out to Wind River to babysit the twins while she worked on finding them a place other than the ranch to live. Starting immediately.

"He got dressed and walked out midargument. I thought—hoped—he might simmer down and come back," she admitted with a weary shake of her head. *Say he was sorry. That he still wanted to be with me.* "But instead, he texted me that I could stay at the ranch as long I wanted." She drew in an unsteady breath, achingly aware just what an unacceptable idea that was, with her feeling the way she did about him.

She turned away from their sympathetic looks, swallowing hard. "Or until my place is finished. That we could alternate care of the twins with your family's help." Hot angry tears pricked her eyes. "I assume to prevent us from running into each other."

Molly moved closer, aghast. "Was all this before or after he gave you your Valentine's Day gift?"

"We never got around to that. I mean, he tried last night, when we got home from the festival, but I couldn't let him do something sweet for me when I was about to betray him."

Molly and Chance exchanged troubled looks.

"So you knew how he would likely take your secrecy?" Chance asked.

"I didn't have a choice."

Chance gave her a look that said of course she had. She could have trusted his brother to keep quiet and cooperate with law enforcement, too.

Except Wyatt would have wanted to defend her. Or go in her stead. And if her father had seen Wyatt, he would have been tipped off and bolted.

The situation would have been more complicated and precarious than ever.

Wearily, Adelaide turned her attention back to the partially framed construction of the addition to her house. "Anyway, the reason I called you both over here was to ask you if it would be possible to put an immediate hold on construction, so I could move back in with the twins."

"Sure, we can put a halt to the project," Chance said. "Happens all the time. But with the foundation poured, and some of the framing started, you may want to go a little while longer...at least get the shell up, roof on. Doors and windows on."

It would certainly look a lot better. "How long will that take?" Adelaide asked.

Molly and Chance considered. "A few weeks, if we rush," Molly said.

Only one problem. "The twins and I don't have any place to stay."

"There's always the bunkhouse," Chance pointed out kindly. "You were going to stay there before…"

…everything blew up, Adelaide finished silently. *Before Wyatt and I discovered we had twins, and I fell for him all over again.*

"Lucille's offered." To Adelaide's relief, her mother-in-law had been very kind about everything, in fact, when they'd spoken.

"But?" Chance prompted.

Guilt and misery roiled inside her. "I don't want Wyatt not to be able to see his mom whenever he wants. If I'm at the Circle H, I would interfere with their ability to see each other unencumbered. Which would in turn interfere with their making up over the whole keeping his learning disabilities a secret from everyone quarrel."

Molly squinted. "I have a feeling there's something more…"

Adelaide sighed. "She also told me I'm making a huge mistake, allowing her son to walk out on me. And that I should use every tool at my disposal—including bunking with her—to bring him back home." Especially since that proposed "arrangement" was what had brought them all together in the first place.

"Maybe Lucille is right," Molly said gently. "It is a little early to be giving up on everything you and Wyatt shared the past few weeks."

If only it were that easy, she thought in frustration. "He gave up on us first. Besides, what am I supposed to do? Beg him to stay? He's clearly never forgiven me for changing my mind about eloping, or not telling him of my plans to have a family alone before we finally made love. In his mind, this is just one more thing he'll never be able to forget."

And she couldn't bear failing. Not again. Not when there was even more at stake.

A commiserating silence fell.

Eventually, Chance asked, "Does this mean you're going to consciously uncouple after all and go ahead with the divorce?"

Adelaide released a weary breath, aware she was just going

to have to find a way to overcome a broken heart. Again. "It's not as if we were ever really together." They'd been playing house while they embarked on a wildly passionate and reckless love affair. "We were just doing what we thought needed to be done for the kids at the time." The honeymoon atmosphere they had enjoyed had been because of their babies, their growing love for them.

Brows rose.

Adelaide went to her fridge and looked inside to see what was there.

Not much, unless one counted condiments.

Making a mental note that she was going to have to go grocery shopping before she picked up the twins, she swung back around. "The good news is Jenny and Jake are too young to realize what their dad and I could have had, if only we were compatible. Which we are definitely not."

"Right now you're not," Chance agreed flatly.

As if it were all her fault!

Ignoring her mounting pain and indignation, Adelaide shrugged and looked her soon to be ex-in-laws in the eye. "Look, I wish Wyatt and I could have the kind of forever and ever relationship that the two of you have, but we don't. The bottom line is my dad was right. Wyatt is always going to be ready to walk out the door at the first disappointment, and I can't live with someone who is never going to be able to find it in his heart to forgive me for my past, present or future transgressions. So, it's better for everyone we cut our losses and part now."

Molly reached out and took Chance's hand. The couple was the picture of loving solidarity.

"We would agree if we thought it was my brother's forgiveness that you really wanted, Molly," Chance said quietly.

Eyes solemn, Molly added, "But we don't."

Wyatt returned to his ranch house as soon as he got the text from his mother. "Adelaide left?"

Lucille pulled a small load of baby clothes out of the dryer and carried the basket to the sofa. "She had to go into town to give the sheriff's department her statement. And she wanted to check on the possibility of halting construction and moving back into her home."

Wyatt looked at the twins, who were sleeping in their Pack 'N Plays, and Sage, who was in his kitchen doing what she always did when under stress—baking.

He returned to his mother's side.

He didn't want to talk about any of this, but he knew his mother wasn't going to let it go until they did. "So she told you?"

Lucille folded a blue onesie. "And of course I think it's my fault."

"What? Why?" Wyatt went to the fridge to get a bottle of water.

"The mistakes I made when you were growing up."

Not the three Ds again. He uncapped the bottle. "Mom. It's over."

"I don't think so." Lucille watched him take a long thirsty drink. "Otherwise, you wouldn't still be reliving it. Or worried Adelaide isn't strong enough to stick with you through thick and thin."

The knowledge that his wife had betrayed him—again—had filled him with a numbness that refused to go away. "Believe me, she's plenty strong enough," he groused. "Otherwise…"

His mother put a folded pink onesie next to the blue. "Not compassionate enough to help you deal with whatever lingering feelings you have about your learning disabilities?"

Wondering how long it was going to take him to recover this time, Wyatt paced. "I put those behind me years ago."

"You can't forgive her for what her dad did, then?"

Oh, for…! Wyatt swung back around. "I can't forgive her for what *she* did. Not telling me that Paul was back in her life, trying to drag her into his mess. Or, swearing afterward, that if the same thing happened all over again, she wouldn't change a thing."

Lucille put little white undershirts in a separate stack. "She's not allowed to have a different opinion than you?"

Wyatt scowled. "She's not allowed to *not trust me*, Mom."

"Did she say that?"

Of course she hadn't! Wyatt tossed his empty bottle into the recycling bin. "Adelaide's actions demonstrate it time and again! We elope. She leaves. We take a leap of faith ten years later and finally hook up. She changes her mind about turning that into something more, too. Then we find out her kids are mine, too, and decide to make the best of a difficult situation and raise our babies together. And what does she do? The one thing that will drive me around the bend! She puts herself and our kids in danger!"

"First of all, Wyatt, your children were safe in the ranch house with you. Only she went out to meet Paul. Second of all, I think she viewed it as putting herself on the line in order to keep not just you but the entire Lockhart clan out of jeopardy." She slanted him a pointed look. "And it's my understanding that the sheriff's department had been surveilling her with her complete cooperation since last summer. They knew where Adelaide was, and who she was with, at all times. And she did that *not only for our family*, but because she saw it as the best way to protect you and your kids."

"Sounds to me like a woman in love!" Sage said from the kitchen. "And if you don't want to believe that, you should see some of the photos that just hit the internet news sites on this breaking story."

She strode over with her tablet, x-ing out the screen that held the recipe she had been following. "Marco Maletti hit the jackpot with these."

Too late, Wyatt recalled that the photographer had been hired by Hope to keep taking photos during the Laramie Chili Festival to feed to the press. There were pictures of him and Adelaide together, early in the morning, before she'd seen her dad, looking happy and completely wrapped up with each other. More with them both working the festival, in the go-fishing-game booth and the cutting-horse demonstration. Photos of him, with the twins in the kangaroo carrier, taking in the sights. And shots of Adelaide being unexpectedly waylaid in the parking lot of the fairgrounds. Her expression stricken, then happy. Heartbroken. Tense. Worried. Sober. And, as she finally walked away from Paul Smythe, completely devastated.

Clearly she'd been through hell yesterday.

And what had he done?

Added to her misery.

He swore quietly.

"I can see you think you failed Adelaide," Lucille said gently.

Why sugarcoat the situation? Aware this was just another "test" he had bombed, Wyatt shook his head. "I did." And his screwup had nothing to do with his learning disabilities. It had to do with his heart.

No wonder Adelaide had run from him.

What was amazing was that she had ever stayed.

"You can still fix this," his mother said quietly.

Could he?

The larger question—was it fair of him to even try?

All this time he had thought it was Adelaide's issues keeping them apart. Now he saw it was his.

His cynicism.

His refusal to trust.

Never mind his unwillingness to understand, empathize... and forgive.

Shoulders slumping, he sat on the sofa and buried his head in his hands.

His mother put a comforting hand on his shoulder. "The point is we all make mistakes, son. You bungled it with Adelaide. Your father and I messed up with you. At the time, of course, your father and I both thought we were doing what was right for you, covering up the dyslexia, dysgraphia and dyscalculia. Shadowing you to make sure you didn't make any public mistakes that would have caused you further embarrassment. But now I wonder if maybe he and I were covering up our own inadequacies, rather than what we perceived as your deficiencies."

Aware he wasn't the only one recently who had been driven to do some soul-searching, Wyatt listened.

"You see, your dad and I had to really struggle to leave our meager beginnings behind and achieve social and financial success. We didn't want any of you children to have to fight that hard," Lucille continued pensively.

"You wanted to protect us, and do everything you could for us because we were your kids. I get that, Mom. Now more than ever because of the twins."

She nodded, accepting the partial reprieve. "But back then, I worried too much about what other people thought about us," she admitted, voice quavering. "And not enough about what I felt and knew to be true deep in my heart, which is that academic success is only a small part of a person's worth." She paused to look into his eyes. "Courage and grit and determination and kindness and compassion are worth a whole hell of a lot more."

A surge of emotion rose within him. "I'm glad you feel that way," Wyatt said gruffly.

Tears blurred his mother's eyes.

The affection she felt for him deepened her voice. "I loved you all equally. And I still do." She hugged him fiercely, then drew back to look into his face. Even more sober now. "And if I failed to communicate that, if you feel I somehow loved you less or was any less proud of you—" her voice broke and tears flowed freely down her cheeks "—then I apologize to you with every fiber of my being." She grasped his shoulders, making sure she had his full attention.

With an unsteady breath, she said, "Don't make my mistake, Wyatt. Don't let fear of being hurt drive your actions." She paused to look into his eyes. "And most important of all, don't fail to communicate what you really feel, deep in your heart."

Thanks to the offer from Lucille and Sage to babysit the twins while he cleared his head and figured out the best way to remedy the mess he and Adelaide were in, Wyatt spent the next several hours working with his horses. Decision made, he returned to the Wind River ranch house. And discovered the first glitch in his plan.

He stared at his mom. "Adelaide wants me to meet her in town?" He'd thought she was coming back to the ranch after her errands.

Lucille looked at his disheveled state. "At her home."

Aware he hadn't had time to shave and shower yet—and he needed to do both before seeing his wife—he shrugged out of his jacket. Okay, this wasn't necessarily a bad sign, he told himself. "Am I supposed to bring the twins?"

"No. But don't worry. Sage and I can continue to babysit this evening."

"Anything to help you set things right," Sage said, starry-eyed as ever, looking as emotional as he felt.

Wyatt felt a catch in his throat. What did his suddenly deeply concerned mother and sister know that he didn't? "Did she say why she wants me there?"

Reluctantly, Lucille admitted, "She wants to talk about how things are going to work with you-all going forward. She thought it would be better to get that ironed out sooner rather than later."

Damn.

He'd thought—hoped—he would have a little more time before Adelaide went into full dissolution mode and made their relationship officially a thing of the past.

Apparently not.

Which meant he was going to have to do what he loathed most. Admit he was in over his head and ask for help.

He looked at his mother and sister. Aware they had always stood nearby, ready to assist.

Resolved to prove his learning deficiencies didn't make him any less capable than the rest of his sibs, he'd rarely let them.

It looked like that, too, was about to change.

Adelaide walked back and forth, a bundle of nerves.

Where was he?

Had Wyatt changed his mind about meeting with her tonight? What could be keeping him?

A peek outside showed a cold rain beginning to fall.

It wasn't supposed to last long.

But it added an aura of gloom to the already risky evening.

What if she'd made a mistake? Like Wyatt, assumed too much? What if he didn't want what she wanted after all?

Headlights swept the front of her house. An engine cut. A door opened, then finally slammed. Footsteps moved across her porch and moments later the doorbell rang.

Heart in her throat, tears pricking behind her eyes, Adelaide smoothed her skirt and headed for the door. Jerking in a breath, she swung it open.

Wyatt stood on her porch. In tweed sport coat, pale blue shirt, pressed jeans, and boots, a black Resistol slanted low across his brow, he looked both solemn and hopeful. And ruggedly handsome as all get-out.

His gaze took in her upswept hair, figure-hugging red knit dress, and heels. She'd worried the care she had taken getting ready might be too much. Apparently it wasn't.

"You look…amazing…" he said huskily, gazing at her in a way no one ever had before, with breath-stealing tenderness.

A surge of warmth went through her as her eyes tracked his. "So do you."

He handed her a bouquet of red roses and a heart-shaped satin box of chocolate candy. "These are for you." His rough-hewn voice was tinged with apology and another more sober emotion she couldn't identify. "A belated Valentine's Day."

Regret poured through her as she thought about how she had pushed him away the evening before, when he'd been trying to celebrate their anniversary. "Thank you." Adelaide swallowed around the sudden dryness of her throat. "I have something for you, too." Opening the door wider, she ushered him inside. She'd lit a fire in the hearth and set the table for two. A big envelope sat on the entry table. She handed it to him, her heart thudding uncertainly in her chest. "This came for us this afternoon."

It had seemed like a sign. She hoped he would consider it one, too. She set the flowers and candy on the entry table while he removed the papers inside. His eyes filled just the way hers had when she laid eyes on the document. "The twins' official birth certificates."

"You're now legally their dad."

A flicker of happiness crossed his face before his expression grew solemn once again. "Thank you for showing this to me."

Deliberately, she kept her eyes locked with his. "Thank you for impregnating me."

He chuckled. "Adelaide…"

She lifted a palm. Now that the mood had lightened slightly, she was determined to get this out before either of them screwed up any more. Taking a deep breath, she began, "We've never really talked about what went wrong after our night in Aspen. And we need to, Wyatt."

He looked wary again. "I'm listening."

She moved closer. "I always regretted not giving us a chance to see if things could have worked when we eloped. So when we met up again in Aspen that night and the sparks lit, I decided to just go with it. And make love. I knew I should have told you that I already had plans to have a baby, and indeed was convinced I was already pregnant. But I didn't think you'd understand, and I didn't want to miss the chance to be with you."

Adelaide watched the regret come into his eyes and rushed on, "I just figured it was a one-night stand. A kind of 'what if' for us. But when you seemed to want more than that, I got even more scared. It hurt so much when we split up the first time, I didn't think I could bear to go through that again, so..." Pain lancing her heart, she continued, "I left you first."

"And I let you."

"That was the right thing to do then." She sucked in a breath, determined to own up to every one of the many mistakes she had made, then suffer the fallout. "I was still in victim mode, still blaming you for everything that had gone wrong between us. Still telling myself that you and I would never have anything long-term because *you* were never going to be able to forgive *me* for my past, present and future mistakes. But I've realized something, Wyatt." Her lower lip trembled as she revealed her biggest vulnerability of all. "It's never been you I needed forgiveness from," she whispered. "It's myself. I'm the one who wouldn't let the past go. Even when I saw you were willing to. I'm the one who couldn't trust.

"But I can't do that anymore, Wyatt. I can't punish myself with fear, or keep the barriers up around my heart. I'm going to accept the mistakes I've made, and there have been a lot, and forgive myself, because only then will I be able to go on and make things right."

Leaning toward her, Wyatt gathered her in his arms and held her close. As she gazed up at him, she saw something she hadn't expected—understanding.

"You're not the only one who's done some soul-searching." He stroked his thumb across her cheek. Eyes darkening, he confessed, "I was angry when I found out your father had been back in touch and you hadn't told me. But it wasn't really your participation in the law-enforcement sting that upset me. Or what your father had done."

She gripped the solid warmth of his biceps, listening intently.

"I've been ticked off because you turned away from me twice when I thought we had it all. In Vegas, and then again in Aspen. This whole time, I've been afraid to let us get too close because I was scared if I did that you'd leave me again."

How well she understood that.

"So this time," his said, lips thinning ruefully, "I took a page from your playbook, and when I found out you'd been shutting me out, I turned away first. Not because I couldn't forgive you for everything that had happened in the past, because in truth I had done that long ago. I just wouldn't admit it. Not to you, not to anyone."

Adelaide understood that, too.

They'd both feared being vulnerable.

It had been easier to simply stay at war with each other.

He searched her face. "And it wasn't because I didn't understand the situation you were in. Or accept that you were doing what you should have done—cooperate with law enforcement and follow their directions to the max. It was because I was scared, now that things had gotten complicated again, that you were going to walk out on me. Again."

"I'm not going to do that, Wyatt. *Ever.* I'm going to do what all those long-married couples do, and trust that I love you now as much as I always have, and always will, and show up every day with the kind of love and trust and commitment you and I should have had all along."

"Darlin'." His tone left no doubt about what he wanted. He lifted her face to his. Slanting his lips over hers, he kissed her tenderly until she kissed him back just as sweetly. "I love you, too. And I'm as all in now as you are," he promised gruffly.

He grinned at the tears of happiness slipping down her face, then gently brushed them away. "I want us to have that forever and ever we—and our kids—deserve. Which is why I'm going to do what I was planning to do last night. And—" he got down on one knee, removed a box from his pocket "—propose." His voice caught, moisture suddenly glittering in his eyes, matching hers.

"Marry me, Adelaide," he urged huskily. "This time, for all the right reasons."

A sob catching in her throat, Adelaide pulled him to his feet and took him joyfully into her arms. "Yes, Wyatt. I will!"

Epilogue

Two weeks later

"**Y**our mother wasn't kidding when she said she was going to spare no expense with her Welcome to the Family party for us," Adelaide said as Wyatt turned their pickup truck into the lane that led to the Circle H Ranch.

Several hundred vehicles lined both sides of the long tree-lined drive. Cowboys were doubling as valets. On the grounds between the newly renovated ranch house and bunkhouse, a dance floor and bandstand had been put up. Tables and chairs were quickly filling with the denim-clad guests.

Wyatt parked in the spot close to the house that had been reserved for them.

"How do you think Lucille's going to take our news?" Adelaide asked as they removed the twins from their safety seats.

"What news?" Lucille asked, hurrying to join them. "And what are you two doing in evening wear? I told you this party was Western casual!"

Wyatt and Adelaide exchanged cheeky grins, aware they

would both be changing later. "Do you want to tell her or shall I?" she asked.

He figured, given the hell he had put his mother through over the years, this news was his to deliver. "We're getting married, Mom."

"You *are* married!" Lucille huffed. "For ten years now!"

"Yes, but you didn't get to see it, and back then, we didn't really mean it. Not the way we do now. So…"

For the first time he could recall, his mother was completely speechless.

Tears glittered in her eyes.

She opened her mouth, tried to speak but no sound came out.

Pressing her hand to her suddenly quivering lips, Lucille hugged them both.

Recovering, she whacked Wyatt lightly on the shoulder. "You should have told me. And you're ruining my makeup."

He was beginning to get a little choked up himself. "Isn't that what weddings are for? Happy tears?" he joked.

Lucille cried all the harder.

Waving off the emotion, she stepped back to admire them both. Adelaide wore a knee-length ivory sheath with a high collared beaded jacket that made the most of her feminine curves. Wyatt was in a dark gray suit and tie.

"You look gorgeous," Lucille said, gathering her wits about her. "But we have to get everything organized."

"Relax, Mom." Wyatt nodded behind him.

His siblings were all doing their part. Directing everyone to pitch in and move the white folding chairs to the grassy expanse on the other side of the bandstand. A rose-covered arbor, originally meant as a party-picture-taking backdrop, was serving as their altar. Reverend Bleeker, from the community chapel in town, was speaking to Molly and Chance who'd been tapped to serve as their maid of honor and best man.

"So everyone knows?" Lucille asked.

"Just the sibs. The guests are as surprised as you. Speaking of which…" Wyatt nodded at the familiar man in uniform walking toward them.

"Zane!" Lucille cried all the harder at the sight of her youngest, rarely home son. "He's here, too?"

Zane reached them. He had recovered from the relatively minor mission-related injuries that had plagued him at Christmas, and had gone out on another assignment with his unit. But he was now Stateside again, at least briefly, to his entire family's delight.

"My most hardheaded, hard-hearted brother finally getting hitched to the woman of his dreams? I couldn't miss that!" He hugged them all as the band began to play.

"That's our cue."

Lucille took Jenny; Zane carried little Jake.

Sage appeared with a bouquet of flowers, and a lapel pin for Wyatt, Nick Monroe by her side, looking surprisingly protective and possessive.

Wyatt took Adelaide's hand. His family took their seats. Together, they made their way to the satin runner that had been laid out. Paused.

So much had happened over the past month he could hardly believe it, but looking down into his bride's radiant face, he knew it was true. He and Adelaide had put all the heartache of the past to rest and formed the family they had always wanted.

He had promised to become more active in the family charitable foundation. She would assist him in the training of cutting horses. In both activities, as well as with their parenting, they intended to further the bonds between them and work side by side.

Paul Smythe had been apprehended. The former CFO had pleaded guilty to all charges, and received a reduced sentence to a white-collar prison for returning all remaining cash to the Lockhart Foundation. Adelaide was still pretty hurt, but Wyatt was encouraging her to forgive her father and find a way to forge some sort of relationship. After all, Paul was the twins' grandfather, and the only dad she had. Yes, mistakes had been made. But a new path could always be forged.

Best of all, he and the love of his life were finally together and would be from this day forward. As friends and lovers, co-parents and soul mates, husband and wife, and all-around damn good time.

He took her other hand and turned her to face him. Gazing deep into her eyes, he said softly, "I love you with all my heart, Addie. You know that."

She shimmered with joy. "I do. And I love you, too, Wyatt. So very much."

Happiness floated between them, as endless as the deep blue Texas sky above.

The final strains of Rascal Flatts' "Bless the Broken Road" ended. Wyatt looked at the woman who had always meant so much to him. The life partner who had lovingly showed him just how meaningful and satisfying their life could be. He squeezed her hand. "Ready?"

The love she felt for him in her eyes, Adelaide rose on tiptoe and kissed him tenderly. "You better believe I'm ready, cowboy," she told him joyously.

He grinned and offered her his arm. The strains of the deeply sentimental "Valentine" filled the sweet, flower-scented Texas air. And the wedding they had waited their whole life for began.

* * * * *

The Triplets' Rodeo Man

Tina Leonard

Books by Tina Leonard

Bridesmaids Creek

The Rebel Cowboy's Quadruplets
The SEAL's Holiday Babies
The Twins' Rodeo Rider

Callahan Cowboys

A Callahan Wedding
The Renegade Cowboy Returns
The Cowboy Soldier's Sons
Christmas in Texas
A Callahan Outlaw's Twins
His Callahan Bride's Baby
Branded by a Callahan
Callahan Cowboy Triplets
A Callahan Christmas Miracle

Visit the Author Profile page at
millsandboon.com.au for more titles.

Tina Leonard is a *New York Times* bestselling and award-winning author of more than fifty projects, including several popular miniseries for Harlequin. Known for bad-boy heroes and smart, adventurous heroines, her books have made the *USA TODAY*, Waldenbooks, Ingram and Nielsen BookScan bestseller lists. Born on a military base, Tina lived in many states before eventually marrying the boy who did her crayon printing for her in the first grade. You can visit her at tinaleonard.com and follow her on Facebook and Twitter.

Many thanks to my editor, Kathleen Scheibling,
for believing in this series, and to Lisa, Dean and
Tim, who understand that time with family is my
personal dream. A word of gratitude to Pat Wood
for assisting me with this book during a time of her
own difficulty—Pat, you are a true friend.
Any factual errors are mine.

Chapter 1

"You reap what you sow."

—Josiah Morgan to his four sons,
a general reminder.

Late March, Union Junction, Texas

Jack Morgan stood at his father's bedside in the Union Junction hospital, staring down at the large sleeping man. Josiah Morgan had the power to impress even in his peaceful state. Jack couldn't believe the old lion was ill. He didn't think Pop had ever had so much as a cold in his life.

But if his brother Pete said Pop was weak and in need of a kidney transplant, then those were the facts. Jack took no joy in his father's situation, even though the two of them had never been close. He hadn't seen Pop in more than ten years, not since the night of his rodeo accident, his brothers' car accident and the all-out battle he and Pop had waged against each other.

It had been a terrible night, and the details of it were still etched in his mind. And then there was the letter he'd received through Pete from his father just last month.

Jack, I tried to be a good father. I tried to save you from
yourself. In the end, I realized you are too different from
me. But I've always been proud of my firstborn son.
Pop

As patriarchal letters went, it stank. Jack figured Pop
wouldn't have sent a letter at all if he wasn't sick, so he'd decided to come see for himself. He hadn't expected to care what
happened to the miserly old man; Josiah was miserly with his
affection, miserly with his money, time, everything. At least
that was the father Jack remembered. Still, Jack preferred his
father fighting.

"All right, Pop, you old jackass," Jack said, "you can lie in
that bed or you can fight."

One eye in the craggy, lined face opened to stare at him
as he spoke, then the other opened in disbelief. "Jack," Josiah
murmured.

A thousand emotions tore through Jack. "Get up out of that
bed, old man."

"I can't. Not today. Maybe tomorrow," Josiah said gamely.

"Damn right," Jack said. "Because if I'm giving you one of
my kidneys, I expect you to be jumping around like a lively
young pup."

Josiah squinted at him. "Kidney?"

"Hell, yeah," Jack said. "You and I might as well be tied
together for a few more years of agony—don't you think? It
could be the one thing we have in common. We're apparently
the perfect match for a kidney swap, which I find amusing in
a strange sort of way. Not any of my brothers—me, the perfect
donor match for you. It's almost Shakespearean."

His father shook his head and closed his eyes. "I don't want
any favors, thanks."

Jack pulled a chair close to the bed and sat. "No one's trying
to do you a favor, you old jackass, least of all me. Quit feeling
sorry for yourself, because I sure as hell don't."

Josiah's eyes snapped open, sparks of fire shooting at his son. "No one has ever felt sorry for Josiah Morgan."

Jack nodded. "Glad we got that settled. You'll need to be in the right frame of mind to get healthy for all those brats you thought you needed."

"Brats?"

"You've been bringing children into the family faster than popcorn popping. Pretty selfish of you to drag all those kids in here and then send up the white flag of surrender, don't you think, Pop?"

"I didn't ask to have rank kidneys!" Josiah barked.

Jack stretched his legs out in front of him, legs that had seen a few sprains and breaks from bulls that had taken their own rage out on him. "We all make our choices."

"I did not choose this."

"You've been 'self-medicating' for years. It's one of the reasons I don't touch a drop of liquor. I decided long ago not to live by your example."

"Alcohol didn't give me kidney disease." Josiah pulled a whiskey bottle from under the sheet and took a swallow he would have deemed "just a drop."

"Sure didn't help it, either." Jack stared at his father. "Pitiful, if you ask me."

"Well, I didn't ask," Josiah snapped, secreting the bottle again.

"It's nice to be able to tell you exactly what I think while you lie there captive. I've waited years for this moment."

Josiah looked at his son. "I guess you think paybacks are hell."

"I guess so, Pop." Jack wasn't about to give his father an inch of sympathy. The old man was mean as a snake. All the charity and benevolence he'd been throwing around in the past few years didn't fool Jack. Josiah Morgan didn't do anything without a motive.

Josiah shook his head. "So many years passed, and you didn't even let me know you were all right. You chased the one thing you cared about all your life—rodeo—and at thirty-two, you decide you're going to give up the one thing that matters to you? You can't ride with one kidney. It'd be foolish."

"I'll take the risks I want, Pop." Jack stood, staring down at his father. He didn't like the old man, would never forgive him for the harsh words over the years. Wouldn't forgive him for never being proud of him. Wouldn't forgive him for blaming him for the car accident his brothers had been in the night Jack had been carted off to the hospital. "It's just a kidney, Pop, and I'm not doing it for you. I'm doing it for my brothers, who are bringing up the families you've saddled them with. You ought to live to reap what you've sown."

"I'm proud of what I've sown!" Josiah shouted after him as he departed. Jack kept walking. It was a kidney he was giving up, not rodeo. Pop had that all wrong.

Cricket Jasper spotted the lean cowboy loping through the hospital exit and knew immediately who it was. There was no one like Jack Morgan, not in looks nor in sheer magnetism as far as Cricket was concerned. Why he was at the Union Junction Hospital she couldn't guess—he'd had very little contact with his family for years. She'd only met him a time or two in the past couple of months, and that had been purely by chance.

The brief meetings were enough to make her pray to see him again. Oh, yes, as a deacon, Cricket was fond of prayer, and she also knew that the Lord didn't always grant a person what they wanted, particularly if it wasn't in the mortal's best interests. However, she was drawn to Jack from some deep, emotional part of her soul, and she knew this could be her only opportunity for months—if ever again—to catch him. "Jack!" she called, waving.

He hesitated, glanced her way, considered, she knew, retreating in a different direction. She didn't take this personally— Cricket knew retreat was the cowboy's standard reaction when confronted with anyone connected to his family. She caught up to him. "Jack Morgan, it's good to see you."

He looked at her, his gaze skimming over her white dress. "You, too."

She smiled. "You weren't visiting Josiah, were you?" She wanted so badly to allow her eyes to do their own one-stop shopping up and down Jack's loose-hipped body, but she resisted the urge, telling herself to be patient. The hunted never wanted to feel caught, after all, and she was determined to catch Jack Morgan, even if all she got from him was a kiss.

Jack shrugged. "I wouldn't call it a visit."

"Oh, I'm sure that meant the world to him." Cricket gave him her most friendly, innocent smile. "Now all you need to truly make his day is to find a wife and kids."

He shook his head, not appreciating the joke. Josiah had managed to wrangle three of his four sons to the altar with the promise of a million dollars each, delivering Josiah the grandchildren he wanted in his golden years.

"It won't happen to me," Jack stated. "I'm giving him a kidney, not another branch for the family tree."

Cricket gasped. "A kidney!"

He shrugged. "I keep thinking I'll come to my senses and talk myself out of it, but it hasn't happened yet."

She couldn't catch her breath. It was a stunning revelation for the man who'd vowed to never even visit his father or speak to him again. "Jack, that's...wonderful."

His face was impassive. "Glad you think so."

It was clear he wanted to move on, but Cricket wanted to keep him right where he was. "When's the surgery?"

"Don't know. I need to talk to the doctor about the details. Pop says he doesn't want my kidney, but Pop doesn't always get what he wants. I can wait him out on this one."

Her eyes went wide. "No one told me."

"Maybe we don't need prayer, Deacon," Jack said.

"I'll be praying anyway, cowboy," she shot back.

They stared at one another silently, each making their own private assessment. A hundred thoughts ran through Cricket's mind. Why was he doing this? *Forgiveness. Redemption.* What Jack would never admit about himself—he loved his father, and his family mattered to him.

"You're a good man, Jack," she murmured.

"Don't kid yourself, Deacon." And with that, he walked away.

She watched him go. If he was aware that she had a crush on him, he ignored it steadfastly. She doubted he thought much about her at all. What did he know about her, other than that she was friends with Suzy, Priscilla and Laura, women who had married his brothers. There would never be anything between them. Like roping wind, she didn't have a chance of capturing Jack Morgan.

But she still felt an undeniable pull toward him, feelings that defied her normally practical heart.

This would take some thought. Josiah hadn't bothered to match make for this son because he was unmatchable. Gabe had been fixed up with Laura Adams, who had a young son and daughter. Gabe had fallen like a tree. Dane had been determined not to repeat Gabe's surrender to his father's wishes, but Suzy Winterstone had been moved into the Morgan ranch as a housekeeper, bringing with her little twin girls. Spellbound, Dane had followed his brother to the altar. Pete had wanted to give up the military for a life closer to home but never planned to marry, and certainly not the woman he called Miss Manners, Priscilla Perkins. His father had found quadruplet orphans who needed parents and persuaded Priscilla and Pete to marry. Josiah had nearly completed his family tree, and now Jack was willing to extend the old man's life, giving him the time he needed.

Jack had better watch out. Josiah lived to build his family, and while Jack might give up a kidney, he also might find himself giving up his freedom. Cricket frowned. She knew Josiah too well. As soon as he could draw a healthy breath—and maybe even before—the man would start hunting a bride for Jack. Oh,

Josiah would be very sneaky, very underhanded, but before he knew it, Jack would be roped and tied to the Morgan ranch, no matter how much he thought it couldn't happen to him.

The problem as Cricket saw it was that Josiah had always chosen women with children for his sons, and Cricket had none. Nor could she simply seduce Jack into her bed and catch him that way. Not that she would, though the seduction part was worth investigating because she had a feeling it would be a heavenly experience. As a deacon, she'd look mighty fallen to her congregation if she came up pregnant and unmarried.

Cricket mulled over her other options. There were none, as far as she could see. Walking into Josiah's hospital room, she found him surrounded by cute, young nurses. Josiah appeared pleased to have this beautiful companionship. It was public knowledge that the wealthy man had one son who was still single, and there were certainly plenty of willing bridal candidates making themselves known to Josiah. She had to make certain he didn't get that baby-making glow in his eyes for Jack. "Hello, Josiah," she said, bending down to give him a kiss on the forehead.

The nurses left the room one by one. Josiah grinned at Cricket. "What did you bring me?" he demanded.

"Cookies," she said.

"Good girl."

"I saw Jack as I was coming in."

Josiah nodded, pleased. "I always knew he'd come around."

The fact was, no one had ever thought Jack would come around—there wasn't a gambler in the county who would have taken a wager on it. Cricket smiled. "Did you?"

"No." Josiah smiled. "Just felt like bragging for a minute."

"You're entitled," Cricket said. "So I hear you might get a new kidney."

"That's what he says," Josiah said. "But I have no intention of taking his kidney."

"Why not?"

"Because he'll still ride rodeo." Josiah eased himself up on his pillow. "He just wants to make me crazy. It's his favorite thing to do, payback for the years he thinks I was a bad parent."

She looked at the elderly gentleman. "The story I heard was that rodeo was in Jack's blood. Nothing anyone can do about that."

"True," Josiah said. "but he can't ride with one kidney."

"But you know he would and that would make you crazy."

"Right." Josiah nodded. "I don't mind heading off into the wild blue yonder, but I do mind sitting around worrying like a durn fool about my durn stubborn son."

"You have a lot to live for."

"Oh, hell. You're a religious person, Cricket. You're supposed to spout that kind of nonsense. A man lives to *do*."

"So?" Cricket demanded. "What's your point?"

"My point is that I'm not taking Jack's kidney just so I can spend a few more years on this earth!" Josiah bellowed. "What good would it do me if he got bucked off and stomped? Do you know how often cowboys get stomped?"

"Perhaps some protective gear—"

"Bah!" Josiah tossed off his covers impatiently. "Have them turn down the heat in here, Cricket. It's nearly April. Why do they have the heat so high? I'm not some sissy old man who can't make my own body heat! By heaven, I'm not a corpse yet."

She smiled. "It is a bit warm in here."

"Hey, Deacon," Josiah said. "Sneak me out of this joint."

Her eyes went wide. "I can't do that. Why didn't you ask Jack to? He's the rebel, isn't he?"

"Oh, he wouldn't do it. He's Mr. Giving-My-Kidney-to-Make-Pop-Feel-Guilty." Josiah sniffed, obviously upset.

"Josiah," Cricket said, "we'd all like to see you gracing the earth awhile longer."

"Oh?" His brows beetled, white and thick on his strong fore-head. "Who are *we*?"

"Me, for one."

"Well, that's one."

"Okay," Cricket said. "What would make you feel like you have a reason to live? An important enough mission to keep your boots planted firmly on the earth, so that you can be a gracious recipient of the gift your son is trying to give you?"

He glowered at her. "I'll tell you, Deacon," Josiah said. "Find a good woman with children who needs a husband and somehow convince her and Jack to get hitched. That would be worth hanging around to see."

Cricket swallowed. "A woman with children?"

He nodded. "There's no reason to leave young children without a father when we have plenty of resources in the Morgan family. If you have a magic wand, wave it and make it snappy, say, in the next twenty-four hours, before they bring in that infernal kidney I'm getting. Grandchildren are what old horses like me live to see."

"Josiah," Cricket said faintly, "you're asking for a miracle, not a magic wand."

"Don't you do miracles? Isn't that your thing?"

She paused. "Certainly I believe in them, but Jack hasn't been... I mean, I know nothing of his personal life. He could already have a girlfriend."

"That would make your job easy."

"If she had children already," Cricket reminded him. "Just getting him to the altar would be incredibly difficult, but fixing him up with a single mother who would suit him is likely beyond impossible." Cricket tried to ignore her own racing heartbeat. There was no way she could honestly match make for Jack Morgan—not with the way her heart jumped every time she saw him. Ever since January, when she'd seen him in the bull-riding ring at the rodeo, she'd known she had the man in her sights who could undo everything rational she thought about men and marriage. A rodeo cowboy could never be the perfect man for her, and yet, her heart was drawn to the devil-may-care in him. "I can't do it, Josiah. It's not my place to do so."

"Hell's bells," Josiah complained. "A family would settle my son down, and that would be best for everyone."

"What if he met a woman he fell in love with and then made a family? Wouldn't that be better?"

"No," Josiah said stubbornly. "Because Jack will never marry unless he has to. It's kind of like visiting his old man—it's costing him a kidney. Whatever woman catches him is going to have to rope, drag and throw my son to the altar, and he'll yowl like he's trussed on a Fourth of July grill."

That was probably prescient. And she didn't want Jack "yowling" if she was the one tying him down—what woman wanted to catch her man that way? "I'll just finish the drapes for your house that you've been wanting, which Suzy and Priscilla and I promised you months ago. How about that? Wouldn't new drapes give you a reason to come home healthy?"

He shook his head. "That's the dumbest thing I've ever heard. You are no good at negotiating, Cricket Jasper, particularly as I know you have a thing for my son. However, you'll never catch him if you're planning on wrapping yourself in drapes like Scarlett O'Hara, my girl. No, to catch Jack, you'll have to be willing to lay body and soul on the line. He's not exactly the curtains type, more like cots and coyotes, if you get my drift."

Cricket did, indeed, get Josiah's drift, and considered herself well warned.

Chapter 2

Jack hesitated outside his father's door, realizing he was the topic of conversation between the pretty deacon and his father. He heard his father sneakily trying to get Cricket to romance him; he heard Cricket backing away from the idea and offering up her services as Martha Stewart instead. Part of Jack wanted to snicker at his father's failed attempt at matchmaking, the other part of him was seriously annoyed Pop couldn't just give the whole family-expansion thing a rest. But that was typical of the old man. He couldn't be happy knowing he had a chance to get well. It had to be the family and kids and happily-ever-after for Pop—as if Jack and his brother's had ever had that for one single day in their lives.

Thankfully, the good deacon was too angelic for Jack—and too crafty for Pop. Still, it shocked him that Pop thought the deacon had the hots for him. Then again, Pop was entitled to a delusion or two.

"Josiah, I'll play cards with you, but only if you quit sipping out of that bottle," Jack heard Cricket say. "Because if you don't quit, you'll be too relaxed to tell Jack that you don't want his silly old kidney."

Jack leaned close to the door, amused by Cricket's coddling.

"I hadn't thought of that," Josiah said.

"And the liquor will skew the blood tests," Cricket said practically. "It will mess up your medication, and the next thing you know, you'll be at Jack's mercy."

"You have a point." There was silence for a long while. "I do not want to be at anyone's mercy."

"Of course you don't. Who does?"

"Not me, durn it. Toss this bottle into your purse and take it home to the ranch for me, would you? Store it in my liquor cabinet."

"I will. It'll be waiting safe and sound for your return."

"And when will that be? C'mon, Deacon, I want you to spring me from this place."

"Aren't you happy here? You seem to be getting plenty of attention from the ladies," Cricket said, her tone soothing.

"My heart is already taken," Josiah said. "Anyway, I was hunting for a girl for Jack."

"When I saw him ride in January, there was a rumor going around that your son has all the female attention he wants," Cricket said. "Let's just focus on you."

"Was he any good at rodeo?" Josiah asked. "I've never seen him ride."

"He was average," Cricket said.

Jack straightened. Average! That day he'd placed first with his highest score, the best ride he'd ever had.

"Oh," Josiah said. "I was kind of hoping he was good at the one thing he's chased all his life."

"Well," Cricket said, "some men are late bloomers."

Jack blinked. The woman was crazy! She didn't know what she was talking about. He hadn't been a late bloomer at anything.

"Later on, Jack mentioned he was considering giving up

rodeo," Cricket said, her tone serene. "Let me see…what did he say he was going to do?" Jack strained, listening to the deacon spin her incredible yarn.

"Oh," Cricket said, "I remember. He said he'd decided to go into ranching. And do a little math tutoring at the high school. Did you know he got a college degree by correspondence course?"

"He did?" Josiah demanded.

I did? Jack mouthed.

"Yes," Cricket said. "From what I could tell, he's very smart and a huge believer in education."

"That makes me very happy," Josiah said. "I wish I'd known all this so that I could have told him how proud I am when he was visiting me. I didn't have a chance," he said sadly. "We always seem to get into a fight right off the bat."

"Oh," Cricket said, "Fathers and eldest sons do that."

"They do?" Josiah said.

"Sure. And eldest daughters sometimes scrabble with their mothers. I argued a time or two with mine. And my brother." Jack heard cards being shuffled. "Anyway, you can tell him how proud you are tomorrow."

"Yes," Josiah said, sounding happy. "I can. And you know, if he really wants to go into ranching, his brothers have started a new breeding business between them. They'd probably really appreciate the help. Heavens knows I've got the land. In fact," he said, lowering his voice so that Jack had to really bend an ear to hear, "it's time for me to rewrite my will."

"Oh, dear," Cricket said, "let's play Twenty-one and not think about wills, Josiah."

"Are preachers supposed to know how to play cards?" Josiah demanded.

"It's either this or dice. Pick your poison, sir." Jack heard the sound of cards being slapped down on a table.

"I'm going to have to divide up the ranch, you know," Josiah said. "Last month I realized I was going to have to leave Jack out. But maybe I've just misunderstood him."

"Most likely," Cricket said.

Jack frowned. Why was the deacon cozying up to his father on his behalf? She wasn't very honest for a cleric—she was a pretty face who told outrageous fibs. Too bad she was such a storytelling wench; she'd almost had him believing all that sweetness she was peddling. Almost. But now he knew Cricket was a woman who would say anything to get what she wanted.

He wasn't sure what Cricket wanted, but he'd know soon enough. Everybody had a price. Except him, of course.

She came out the door suddenly and squashed his toe on purpose. "That's what you get for eavesdropping," she whispered. "You're going to have to think fast to keep up with your old man, cowboy. Let's see if you can do that, okay?"

Then she popped him on the arm like he was no more than a baseball-playing buddy, tossed her enormous handbag over her shoulder—Pop could have fit a case of whiskey in that thing—and headed off, looking remarkably like a tall, but still cute Audrey Hepburn.

Jack stared after her. That was one pain-in-the-well-worn-butt woman. And unfortunately, she had the asset Jack most appreciated on a female—a very sassy derriere.

Somehow that was even more annoying.

Josiah left the hospital that night. Jack wasn't really surprised when he got the call. He would have done the same. Jack figured if anybody was like him, it was the old man. Pop wasn't going to be a burden, and like his sons, he knew how to hit the escape hatch.

It was up to him to fetch his father. This wouldn't be the easiest thing in the world because Pop didn't want his life extended by taking something from Jack. Pop would consider this gesture sacrilegious, wasteful and downright wrong.

He couldn't blame his father. Since they hadn't spoken in

over ten years, Josiah had every right to his feelings. It was bad luck that only Jack was the perfect donor match, which he'd found out after being tested—something he did only after Laura, Gabe's nurse wife, left a message for him at a local rodeo that they were running out of options with Pop. It had been a warning, not a solicitation for help. Still, Jack had felt a curiosity and an obligation to find out if he was an eligible donor. Quietly, he'd had the testing done—and bad luck as always, the prodigal son was the "perfect" match. It was the only time in his life he could remember someone using the word *perfect* to describe something about him.

He was going to have to go find Pop, somehow reel him in to the hospital. Cricket had been right—he was going to have to think hard to keep up with the old man. Pop was sharp from years of business dealings—he was focused, determined and ornery. Fortunately, Jack knew something about determination.

He'd find him. Somehow, he'd drag him back.

Cricket went to the Morgan ranch, pulling into the driveway in her old Volkswagen that had served her well for many years. The sight of the ranch and the large house that graced the property, out in the middle of nowhere, never failed to take her breath away. She parked, shut off her car, grabbed her tape measure and notepad. A promise was a promise. If Josiah Morgan was going to be on a first-name basis with the angels—unless he accepted his son's kidney, and if the operation and match was a success—she was determined he would come home to a pleasant-looking house.

No one answered her knock at the front door. Cricket decided she could call either Laura, Suzy or Priscilla and ask them to come let her in…or perhaps she could find an open door. If one of the Morgan men were here today working somewhere on the ranch, it was possible they'd left a door unlocked. They wouldn't mind her slipping in to measure, particularly as she'd mentioned her plans to Josiah.

She turned the knob.

Sure enough, it was unlocked. That meant one of the Morgans was nearby, so she carefully slid the door open and called, "Hello! It's Cricket Jasper!"

She waited for a "Hello, Deacon!" or something to that effect, but no one answered. Closing the door behind her, she walked into the hallway. "Hello! Gabe? Dane? Pete?"

All the brothers had moved into houses with their brides, leaving the ranch house to Josiah. Pete was the most recent to move, needing private space for his four new babies and wife. He and Priscilla had bought a house only a few miles down the road once the adoption was final, and Cricket was pretty certain Josiah had been crushed by the departure of the babies. "Anybody home?" she called.

Jack appeared in the hall like a ghost. "Hey, Cricket."

He startled her into the fastest heartbeat she'd ever experienced. "You scared me, Jack!"

He grinned at her. "I can't exactly claim that I'm home, to answer your question. But I'm here." He looked around, his gaze returning to the flat stare he almost always wore.

"So what are you doing here?" Cricket demanded, her heartbeat still jumping around.

"What are *you* doing here?"

"Measuring for drapes." Cricket slid past Jack, keeping an eye on him. After Josiah's warning about his son, Cricket had decided her unhealthy crush was something she needed to put away. The man was sexy, but as a deacon she had no business mooning after a hunk who had not one good side but two bad. "If you'll excuse me, I'll just measure, draw some sketches and go."

He caught her arm as she went by. Cricket jumped, snatched her arm back.

"Hey," he said, "I think you and I got off on the wrong foot."

"No," Cricket said. "We're fine. Let's not trouble ourselves about anything except getting your father well."

Jack looked at her, his gaze direct, sending a shiver over her. "I heard you telling a bunch of fibs to my father last night."

She shrugged, clearly not remorseful. "So? Is it wrong to want him to be happy? Is it sinful to put him in a happy frame of mind before he has major surgery?"

He eyed her. "A fibbing deacon."

She raised her chin. "Never you mind what's between me and the Lord, cowboy."

He grinned. "Your conscience is your own, my lady."

"Good." She started to turn away, but there was that hand again, holding her too close to him. She wished she didn't feel an unsettling sizzle everywhere he touched her. This time, she stood firm, refusing to allow him to unsettle her.

"And while we're examining your unusual conscience," Jack said. "You wouldn't help my father escape, would you, Deacon?"

Chapter 3

"What are you talking about?" Cricket demanded. "Escape what?"

"Pop left the hospital in the night. Checked himself out."

Cricket seemed to consider his words, doubting him. She finally said, "He was fine when I was visiting."

Jack shrugged. "Guess he changed his mind. Now I need to find him."

"Is he here?" Cricket's voice contained a dose of worry.

"No. Too obvious, though I was hoping he'd make it easy on me to take him back to the hospital."

Cricket held her notepad close to her chest. Perhaps she was afraid he might take a bite out of her, a very tempting thought—but he was no Big Bad Wolf, contrary to his father's opinion.

"If he doesn't want to go back, you can't make him."

Jack smiled. "Maybe you could give me your best thoughts on where he might be. My brothers haven't seen him, their wives haven't seen him. The logical conclusion was that he'd had a yen to see the grandchildren. Then we figured he might be here. No luck."

She shook her head. "I'm sorry I can't help."

Thunder clapped outside and a slice of lightning cracked near the house.

"My word," Cricket said, "that sounded close! If you'll excuse me, I'll take my measurements and let you get on with your search. I hope you find him, I really do."

Jack let her go. She didn't know where Pop was. Nobody had the faintest idea; no one even knew where all the properties he owned were. He could be anywhere in the United States. Pete had mentioned that he thought Pop had sold the knight's templary in France, but Jack supposed Pop could just as well have left the country. "He is the most difficult man on the planet," he muttered, along with a well-chosen expletive or three.

"Did you say something?" Cricket asked, madly scribbling numbers on her notepad.

"Nothing fit for the ears of present company."

She turned back to what she was doing. "I can't blame him, you know."

"Blame him about what?"

"He didn't want your kidney. He didn't want anything from you at all. I polished your résumé, tried to make it seem like you were the kind of son who—"

"I heard the polishing." Jack threw himself into his father's recliner. "Pop didn't believe any of that crap."

Cricket sniffed, went back to ignoring him.

"Where'd you stay last night?"

"With Pete and Priscilla and the four babies."

He watched her stretch to measure the length of the current rod, admiring her lean body as she moved. "Full house?"

"Yes," Cricket said. "I love being there. They can use the extra pair of hands, and I enjoy the fun." She stopped to look at him. "Have you even seen any of your nieces and nephews?"

"Deacon, look," Jack said, "I haven't seen my brothers or my father in years. Why on earth would I have seen their offspring, which, by the way, only became part of the family in the past few months?"

She stared at him. "Some people like to make up for lost time."

Her words needled him. She knew nothing about his family, knew nothing about him. He really didn't feel like he needed judgment from someone who was supposed to be fairly non-judgmental.

"Nothing short of a wedding will bring your father back here," Cricket said, and Jack blinked.

"You don't have any children?" he asked.

"I most certainly do not." She bent down to examine the bottom of the windowsill and he didn't bother to avert his gaze from taking in a scrumptious eyeful of forbidden booty. "Anyway, what matters is whether *you* have any children. Your father lives for family."

"Jeez, don't rub it in." Darn Pop for being so difficult. He was almost tired of being lectured by Cricket, yet the instrument of his conscience-picking was at least attractive. Rain suddenly slashed the windows, and Jack noted the room had gotten darker. "When you plan for drapes, maybe something heavy enough to keep out the cold in winter and the heat in summer would be nice," he said, watching the rain run in rivulets down the wall of windows. "No sheer lacy things that just look pretty and serve little purpose."

"Oh?" Cricket straightened, much to his disappointment. "Planning on living here?"

"I don't think so," he said softly. "I haven't stayed in the same place for more than three nights in many, many years. That's not likely to ever change for me."

She looked at him, her gaze widening. It seemed to Jack that she reconsidered whatever she was about to say. Then she put away her things, allowing them to be swallowed by the enormous gypsy bag she carried, and said, "I'll be going now. It was good to see you again."

He laughed. "You are a gifted fibber."

"Just because I have good manners does not make me a liar."

"Whatever."

"I'll see myself to the front door."

He nodded amiably. "You do that."

She slipped past him, her carriage straight as a schoolteacher's. Because she was tall and lean, she moved gracefully, a sight he'd probably always enjoy watching. He really liked the way her dark hair fell around her shoulders, lustrous and probably softer than…hell, he didn't know what would be as soft as that woman's hair must be. It just looked silky, and it probably smelled good, too.

This train of thought was taking him nowhere fast. He was behaving like an ass to Cricket, and Pop's disappearance wasn't her fault. Jack got up and followed her to the door, where she stood staring out at the rain-whipped blackness.

"You probably don't have a raincoat in that suitcase-sized purse of yours."

"I'll be fine," Cricket said. "You have enough to worry about without concerning yourself about me."

"I didn't say I was worried. But it didn't escape my notice that your tires are fairly bald, and your car is a tad past old, and the roads will be a mess getting up to the highway. In other words, drive safely."

She looked up at him. "My, aren't we the gentleman suddenly?"

He scratched his head. "Tell me again which church you serve as a deacon?"

"I never told you at all."

"That's true. I'm just curious what congregation would put up with such a—"

"Jack," Cricket said, "the only thing on your mind right now should be Josiah."

"I suspect he's not driving in this weather. Nor is he out in it," Jack said.

Cricket hesitated.

"This isn't going to be a popular theory," Jack said, "but I'm betting that little Beetle of yours with the gummy tires doesn't make it to the main road. You'll be calling someone to hitch you out of the mud in less than five minutes. I'm sure my father would suggest you stay put until the rain passes."

Cricket closed the door. "I'll accept your father's kind invitation."

He nodded. "I bet if we poke around in the kitchen we'll find something to eat."

"I'm not hungry, thank you."

That was too bad. He'd been hoping she'd be eager to show off some of her culinary skills. "You don't like me very much, do you?"

"Let's not make this personal," Cricket said, making herself at home at the kitchen table while Jack checked out the contents of the fridge.

"Not me," Jack said. "I'm Mr. Impersonal."

"Wonder where he is, anyway?"

"You'd know better than me." There was fresh turkey and cheese in the meat drawer, and Jack felt the evening was improving already.

"There's a guesthouse on the ranch, right? A few barns?"

"I've searched everywhere." Jack closed the door, leaving the food behind, suddenly lacking an appetite. He felt a confession coming on, and those were never very good for his gut.

Cricket watched him. "What are you doing?"

Jack took a deep breath, slid into the seat opposite Cricket's. "See, here's the deal. The old man was rough on us, me in particular. He wasn't the kind of father who'd play ball with you, he wasn't around much, he wore us out with his criticism. If I had a penny for every mean thing he said to me, I'd be a wealthy man, I promise. Me, more than any of my brothers, never measured up. And he hated what I loved most, which probably just made me love rodeo more. I didn't have to be good enough for

Pop when I was riding—it was just me and the bull and hanging on for the sake of winning."

"So what happened?"

"He blamed me for a car accident my kid brothers had when they sneaked out to see me ride one night." He looked at Cricket, the old, painful memories rushing over him. "The thing that ticked me off the most was that I was crazy about my brothers. We felt like all we had was each other, and I basically got to be the father, in a way. I loved them. I would never have hurt them. I had no idea they were sneaking out to watch me that night." Still, the painful accusations cut. Remembering the beating his old man tried to give him hurt, too, but even more painful was the fact that he'd fought back. The two of them had gone at each other like prize-fighters, and Jack wasn't proud of it. "I suppose in the end I let him beat me," Jack said, "but I took skin from him before he did."

"I am so sorry," Cricket said, reaching across the table to pat his hands, which he noticed were splayed in front of him as if he needed the comfort. He moved his hands to his knees under the table, not wanting to appear as if he needed sympathy.

"I don't even know why I'm here," he murmured. But he did know, he knew he still loved his brothers, and Pop wanted those grandchildren, and if all it cost to make everybody happy—buy forgiveness—was a kidney, then that was cheap.

"Maybe you are a good man," Cricket said. "Maybe you really *want* to do the right thing."

He looked at her, then slowly shook his head. "I don't think so." He would never be good enough to live in her world. Repairing the cracks of his relationship with his family would take more than anything he had in his soul. Thunder and lightning cracked and boomed over the house, snapping the lights off. The refrigerator stopped humming. He thought he heard one of the many pecan trees that bordered the property give a tired groan, a warning that much more wind would drive it to split. "The lights'll come back on," Jack said to soothe Cricket.

"I'm not afraid of the dark."

Of course, she wouldn't be. She'd probably produce a glow-in-the-dark Bible from her purse, lead a few prayers, invoke the heavenly spirits for safety, and it would never cross her mind that the thing she should be afraid of was *him*.

Chapter 4

"I remember there was a flashlight somewhere in the kitchen." Cricket felt along the walls, wishing she could recall where she'd seen a plug-in flashlight. While she had to admit to a sneaky bit of excitement at being in total darkness with Jack, this was the type of thrill she didn't need in her life. "Aha!" Pulling it from the wall, she turned it on, flashing the light right at Jack's face. He was smiling, she saw, a sort of catlike grin.

"Feel better?" Jack asked.

"Since I don't see in the dark, yes, I do." How dare he pull on her heartstrings and then go alpha-jerk on her? He'd almost had her believing that he wasn't the prodigal his father claimed he was. She set the flashlight on the kitchen table. "Find another one and we'll each go our own way. I'll take Suzy's old room for the time being."

"Suzy's old room is where Pop was staying before he took off," Jack said.

Cricket replied, "Just tell me where you want me. I'll be up bright and early, as soon as the rains quit, and gone before you know it." She wasn't certain she'd actually sleep under the same roof with Jack, in fact, wouldn't even consider it if the roads were better. "And this is a secret to be kept between you and me, if you don't mind."

He grinned. "Do I look like the kind of man who kisses and tells?"

She grabbed the flashlight. "If you have kissed me, it must not have been memorable. I'll take one of the rooms that hasn't been in use."

He followed her as she went up the stairs. "I'll sleep on the sofa downstairs. Feel free to yell out if you get scared. I'll be close by enough—"

She stopped and turned on the staircase, not a hairsbreadth away from him since he'd been following her, his eyes on her rump, if she had Jack Morgan figured correctly. "I can't see myself calling for you to rescue me from anything."

"Not even a mouse?" he asked, his eyes dancing with mischief.

"Mice?" she repeated faintly. "Do you have them?"

He shrugged. "I can't speak to the quality of the upkeep at the ranch. There were many months when no one was here, so I suppose there could be some furry residents."

"You're horrible," she told him. "You're trying to give me the shivers."

"You wouldn't be afraid of a tiny furry rodent, would you, Deacon?"

She snapped back around and marched up the last couple of stairs, heading into the first room she saw. It was empty except for a dresser and a bed, it had its own bathroom, and best of all, the door locked with a satisfying click when she shut it in Jack's face. "Jerk," she muttered. "What woman loves a mouse?"

"Good night," he called through the door.

"Good riddance," she replied, hugging the flashlight.

Jack went downstairs, moving around skillfully in the darkness, and clicked on the TV as he tossed himself into his father's recliner. Then he realized the TV didn't work at the moment. There was nothing for him to do, and that made him miss Cricket's lively banter, even if she was a bit vinegary for his taste. He liked his women a bit more sweet and willing, and if they threw in a little hero worship, that was even better. Yet Cricket didn't seem to feel any inclination to adore him, in spite of the fact he was willing to give his father a lifesaving kidney.

Cricket probably wouldn't be easy to seduce at all. He could spend months wooing her and she'd likely remain cold to his advances.

Why was he even thinking about sex with the deacon? He had as much chance of that as…well, as finding Pop tonight.

He was forced to admit that he was worried about his father. The crusty old man was going to die for his independence. Secretly, Jack admired that. He understood the desire to go down fighting.

Suddenly there was a flashlight beam at his elbow and a tap on his shoulder. "Holy smokes!" he exclaimed, jumping to his feet. "Cricket! I didn't hear you leave your room!" How she'd made it down the stairs without even a creak, he couldn't imagine, but maybe thin frames like hers didn't put pressure on the floorboards like four rowdy boys could.

"I didn't mean to startle you," she said.

He took a deep breath to calm his racing heartbeat and sat down in the chair again. "Is there something you need? If there are no towels in the bath, you can probably—"

"I want to apologize for my behavior," Cricket said. "I've not been very nice to you, and you have a lot on your mind. I should be more considerate of your feelings."

Great. Now he was a pansy. "I'm fine."

"I think… I think I'd feel better if I sat down here with you for a while."

"I was just kidding about the mouse," Jack said, feeling bad for taunting her.

"I know. But if you wouldn't mind company—"

"Oh, sure, sure." Jack waved at the sofa. "Help yourself. Nothing good on TV, anyway." He winced at his weak joke.

She hesitated, and then to his great surprise—astonishment—Cricket reached out a hand toward him, the hand not holding the flashlight. Was she going to conk him with it? Jack stared up at her, perplexed by her actions.

She didn't say anything, just looked at him.

Then he got it.

Cricket wanted him. Or at least she didn't seem to want to sleep alone.

He took half a second to consider whether he should do this to the deacon—perhaps she was afraid of the dark, lonely, having a bad-girl fantasy, whatever—then threw any guilt out of his mind. Pulling her down into his lap, Jack kissed her the way he rode bulls, full out and with every intention of staying in the saddle for as long as he possibly could.

When Cricket awakened the next morning, she blushed at the memory of the wild night she'd shared with Jack. If anyone had ever told her that lovemaking was such a fabulous, heart-pounding, please-don't-stop experience, maybe she wouldn't have waited so long. But she had, she'd always been waiting for Mr. Right. Last night, although she knew Jack was no Mr. Right, she'd decided she was tired of waiting for the prince who might never ride into her life.

It had been worth it. It could even be addictive, which was not a healthy thought. She slipped away from the sleeping cowboy on the floor in front of the fireplace. The fire had burned low now, mostly just embers, but outside, the sky was dawning clear and crisp. The roads, though still muddy, would be passable.

She tried to figure out how to escape without waking Jack. The last thing he would want was a girlfriend, and most people who made love together might assume there could be some kind of ongoing relationship. She didn't relish him thinking that's what she wanted from him. At least she'd accomplished her goal, which was to understand what other women who fell in love were so happy about. It was hard to understand the giddy excitement over men and sensual pleasures when she'd never experienced it. Now she had, and she totally understood why women could fall so hard for the wrong man, and also why they could love one man all their lives. If she could enjoy the giggling, the excitement, the tears of joy and rapture, the feeling of living outside of her body that she'd experienced with Jack, she'd love the man she married with devotion all her life, too.

So if she never saw Jack Morgan again, she'd be okay with that. A practical girl understood the cards she was dealt. She'd counseled plenty of women who'd had their hearts broken by Mr. Wrong, all the while hoping he was Mr. Right. Cricket would never fall victim to a lack of common sense.

Today it was back to her church for her, and no more mooning over the dashing cowboy who'd no doubt broken a hundred hearts. She gathered her clothes and crept into the hall to quickly dress, glancing back over her shoulder at Jack partially wrapped in the blanket. She prayed the front door would open and close without him hearing—it did—and ran to her VW. The car vroomed to life, and she headed toward Fort Wylie with only a slight regret that she wouldn't see Jack again, at least not the way she'd seen him last night.

Last night's indiscretion was the only time she was going to allow herself to live outside the bounds of good moral direction, she promised herself firmly.

Jack had slept with enough women to know that it was a good thing if they didn't stick around for the difficult details of goodbye. Still, he was disappointed, and even ego-bruised, when he found Cricket had departed. Had she regretted last night? Wasn't he the lover she'd wanted? Doubts assailed him, a rare occurrence. He didn't like wondering about his performance. It was much more fun when women made him feel as if he was the greatest stud on earth.

In fact, Jack almost felt as if he'd been dumped. Dumped by the deacon, and refused by his father.

His father was understandable. They'd never been close, even though it was a reasonable assumption that a man who had so much to live for would be grateful for a kidney. After all, Josiah had given him life; Jack felt that returning the favor was good for his heavenly record. But no, neither Josiah nor Cricket seemed to feel the need to give Jack a little reciprocal gratitude.

He didn't feel it would have been too much to ask of Cricket to hang around, make him some eggs, act appreciative, maybe even slightly worshipful. She was very difficult to understand, and he didn't like that. Women shouldn't make a man think too long and too hard; otherwise it took all the fun out of the pursuit.

Her hair had been every bit as soft as he'd imagined, and her skin had smelled sweet, like roses and strawberries. It had been a gentle, clean fragrance that made him burrow his face against her neck, her breasts. Her touch had driven him completely insane.

He had never, ever, had a woman leave him without saying goodbye. He had always been the one who'd left. There was something final about a woman who departed of her own accord; it left the other player no moves on the chessboard.

At least the electricity had come back on this morning. Jack grabbed the blanket off the floor, where they'd made love in front of the cheery—and romantic, if he did say so himself— fire he'd built in the fireplace. A strange spot on the blanket caught his eye; dumbly he stared at the stain. And that's when he realized that Cricket Jasper had been keeping secrets. She hadn't offered him the slightest clue that she'd been a virgin, which felt somehow as if she'd cheated.

She wasn't a virgin anymore. Now it stung like crazy that she hadn't hung around for a goodbye kiss. Jack felt worse than at any time in his life, even when he'd been thrown flat on his backside—and maybe even stomped— by an assorted collection of ill-tempered bulls, as he tossed the blanket into the washing machine.

Cricket's desertion served as a reminder of the other people in his life who seemed to move on without saying goodbye. He didn't have to put up with this crap. After he'd tidied up the place so that no one would ever know he'd been there, Jack grabbed his stuff and headed back to the one place he knew was a safe harbor—the rodeo circuit.

Chapter 5

"Marry me," Josiah Morgan said to Sara Corkindale, the kind social worker who'd helped his son Pete and his daughter-in-law Priscilla adopt quadruplets last month. "Marry me and put me out of my misery."

Sara laughed. "I'm not willing to be a secret bride, Josiah. And if you *are* at death's door—as you've claimed you are, I suspect, to get sympathy from your family—why should I make myself a widow again? I've already done that once, and it's very hard to say goodbye to a good friend and husband. Why would I marry you knowing you're ready to hang up your spurs?"

He shook his head. "I like you," he said simply.

"And I like you."

She patted his arm affectionately in a way that was not at all condescending. Josiah hated everybody tiptoeing around him and treating him like an invalid. Sara made him feel as if he still had something to offer a woman.

"You'd like being my wife even better." She didn't seem inclined to bend to his way of thinking, so Josiah considered his other options. As he had moved himself into her house, where he knew none of his sons or their wives would think to look for him, he didn't have many options. He was rather at his hostess's mercy.

"You're going to have to tell your children where you are eventually." Sara looked at him with a gentle smile as she put a fresh-baked pound cake on the table, and then picked up her knitting. "If I marry you, they'll say I took advantage of you."

"No one has ever taken advantage of Josiah Morgan!" This was a fact; his sons wouldn't dare suggest it because it would be ludicrous. "I'll marry when and who I want."

"You can't hide behind my skirts, Josiah," Sara said, and his jaw went slack.

"Sara Corkindale, I should take you over my knee and spank you for suggesting I'm a coward." He thought about doing it and decided he didn't dare. Hide behind her skirts, indeed! No one had ever suggested he might be a bit thin-skinned and he rather admired her spunk.

She held up her work. "This is a baby blanket. It's going to be blue and white, and warm enough for winter's chill."

"It better not be for me," he said darkly. "Sara, I'm a man, not beholden to anyone."

"This blanket is for one of the babies at the orphanage. There are never enough warm things. And I know you're a man, Josiah, but you know you're hiding here when you should just express your opinion to your sons. If you don't want to have the kidney operation, then say so." She went on with her knitting serenely. "In the meantime, you can't stay here forever."

"I can't?" Josiah had gotten used to the comfort and peace of Sara's home in the past few days. He'd gotten used to the calm way she went about her business. In his mind, he'd envisioned himself living here until the end of his days.

She shook her head. "No, you can't. Not until you straighten your life out with your children."

She was still worried someone would think he'd been coerced into marrying her. She didn't understand that no one had ever made him do a thing he didn't want to. When Gisella had left him, there hadn't been a durn thing he could do about that, but still, that had been Gisella's choice. He'd always respected her decision, knowing he'd been at fault. But that hadn't been coercion; he'd become a single father because he'd been a bit of a ham-handed dunce. "Are you saying that once I tell everyone I don't want the surgery, that what I want is to get married, you'll marry me?"

She stopped knitting and looked at him. "Josiah, I would marry you if you were going to be around a while."

"Nothing's certain in life."

"I know that. But you seem determined to have an expiration date stamped on you, and it's hard for me to want to get married knowing that." She swallowed, chose her words carefully. "Don't ask me to care about you and then say goodbye to you in less than a year."

She had a point. Suddenly, he didn't want that, either. It would be horrible, holding her at night, watching the stars with her, seeing the sun come up in the morning with Sara, and knowing each sunrise might be his last.

"I still don't want to do it," he said quietly. "My son is reckless. He'll always be a hell-raiser. Sara, you don't know my boy, but Jack… Jack deserves the chance at the kind of full life I've had. And nothing's ever going to stop him from rodeoing, not even being minus a kidney."

"You'll have to stop trying to live everyone's lives for them, Josiah," she said, pulling her chair close to him. She put her head on his shoulder. "Our children have to make their own choices."

"So you're saying I should accept one of his body parts and then just sit around and wait for the phone call that he…he's gone to the great rodeo in the sky?" He didn't think he could do that. Some things were too awful to contemplate.

"Or you could accept his gift, and then go watch him ride as often as you can," she said.

"Watch him ride!" Josiah exclaimed. "Not durn likely!"

"Have you ever seen him ride?"

"No, and I ain't gonna start now!" Josiah felt an urge to yell, but knew he better keep his voice down. This was a lady's home, and he respected Sara too much to yell. But for pity's sake, the woman asked a lot of a man.

"I'll go with you," she said softly, and he melted like a pile of snow in August. "And I'll take you back to the hospital, too, so that they can finish looking you over. I think you'd want to do that. I'm sure you've scared your kids half to death."

"All right," he said, surrendering. "That's the first time in my life I've ever been sweet-talked into anything, you know."

She kissed his cheek. "Didn't it feel good?"

He felt like warm dough under her benevolent, cheerful gaze. "Yes," he said, "it felt mighty good."

In the last two months Jack had been to South Dakota, North Dakota and a few other states, chasing buckles and trying to forget Cricket. He hadn't heard from her, not that he'd expected to. It was crazy how he couldn't get the deacon off his mind.

He hadn't heard from stubborn old Pop, either. He had a new cell-phone number, so his brothers hadn't been able to reach him. Now that it was May and he'd ridden off a lot of angst, he'd had time to think about everything.

He wondered if Pop was still as opinionated as the devil. His brothers would have gotten word to him through the circuit if Pop had passed. Still, a strange itch tickled at him, telling him it was time to call home.

He called Pete. "It's Jack," he said.

"Jack," Pete said, "are you all right?"

"I'm fine. Just checking in."

His brother hesitated. "Where are you?"

Jack squinted at a sign he was parked under. "Somewhere in the Dakotas."

"Coming home anytime soon?"

"Not sure." Jack scratched his head. "Should I?"

"I don't know," Pete said, "but I think Pop wants to get married."

"He does?" Jack blinked. "How?"

"By a minister of some sort, I imagine."

"But last time I saw him, he was in a hospital."

"Yeah, and he maybe should still be in one. But Sara Corkindale, his lady friend, keeps him perked up."

"That's good news." Jack really didn't know what more to say. "When's the wedding?"

"I believe after he has the kidney operation."

Jack's eyes went wide. "You mean he's changed his mind?"

"She's changed his mind, more to the point. But I think the window of opportunity is closing."

Jack got the point. "I can be home in two days. Maybe less."

"I'll tell Pop."

"Hey," Jack said before Pete could get off the phone, "you haven't happened to talk to that preacher woman lately? Has she been by to visit the quads?"

Pete cleared his throat. "You haven't. Why should she?"

Damn. He hadn't seen them since he'd visited Pete at the hospital. Never held them, never touched them. "Man, I'm sorry. I'm an ass of an uncle."

"I won't tell them that," Pete said, "but I bet they'd like having an uncle around who can teach them how to ride a horse."

"That's a few years away, isn't it?" Jack frowned. Would they even be walking by now? He had no frame of reference for how fast children developed. They'd been in bassinets at the hospital when he'd seen them three months ago—had it been that long already?

"Time flies," Pete said.

Jack replied, "Okay, what are you hinting around about?"

"Not me," Pete said. "I'm not hinting about a thing. Would never spill any beans. Know how to keep my mouth shut. You just get home, and everything will take care of itself."

Jack grunted as the phone line clicked dead. What the heck had that been all about? Starting his truck, he turned due south and headed home to Texas.

Cricket couldn't believe how ill she felt. Pregnancy was supposed to make a woman glow; all she wanted to do was gag. She couldn't seem to catch her strength. Priscilla Perkins had sold her house to Cricket when Priscilla married Pete Morgan and Cricket felt at home in her new sanctuary, but she hadn't felt well enough to enjoy it in the past month. She'd hoped one day to reopen the cute little tea shop that was part of the house, but now she realized her hands were full for the moment. Her life was changing fast, and nothing was ever going to be the same.

She was scared. Questions tormented her. She loved the idea of being a mom, but at the same time she dreaded having to tell Jack. Before too much time passed, sharing their news was a fact she was going to have to face. There was no reason to feel too guilty right now about avoiding her confession; she'd talked recently to Suzy and Priscilla on the phone and each of them had mentioned that Josiah never had his operation, and Jack had taken off for parts unknown. No one knew where he was—he'd never even visited any of their homes or seen their children before he left.

They'd pretty much given up on him. As for Josiah, he'd made it plain he was going to live his life his way.

Cricket had another confession to consider—she'd also have to tell her church. While she didn't dread that as much as telling Jack—Jack was in for a life change he didn't want—the congregation was sure to be shocked. She hoped they wouldn't think worse of her, but her behavior would certainly strike everyone as embarrassing. They would want her to resign, of course. Her parents might be ashamed, and her brother was sure to be disappointed.

The bright spot in her life was that, like Laura, Suzy and Priscilla, she would have her own child. She'd told her friends, swearing them to secrecy, and they'd assured her they wouldn't breathe a word to Jack. Motherhood was the most wonderful thing to imagine, if she wasn't so worried about telling Jack. There was no way of knowing how he'd react, but she had a feeling it wouldn't be the best news he'd ever gotten.

It was time for her prenatal checkup, so Cricket locked up her lovely new house and left. Cricket wanted to ask the doctor if there was anything she could do about the nausea—eat better, drink something more healthy, anything to make her more comfortable. Fortunately, there was a wonderful selection of teas still in the cupboards of the shop. She was eating holistically, when she had an appetite—organic fruits, some yogurt, whole grains and chicken that was free of hormones and preservatives. Nothing helped.

An hour later, Cricket knew the nausea wouldn't be passing any time soon.

"Triplets!" Dr. Suzanne exclaimed with delight.

"Triplets?" Cricket's heart sank, her skin turning cold and clammy. "Do you mean three babies?"

"That's what I mean." The doctor smiled. "You've always been an efficient person, Cricket. You'll have a whole family all at once."

Cricket endured the gentle teasing silently. She couldn't talk. "Are you certain?" Nothing on the monitor looked like triplets to her.

"Three tiny heartbeats," the technician confirmed.

"It'll be quite a lot to ask of your thin frame," Dr. Suzanne said. "Bed rest will be required at some point, so you need to prepare for that. Get what you want done accomplished soon. And be thinking about some type of help while you're housebound."

Cricket closed her eyes, blinked, stared again at the monitor. She couldn't tell anything by looking at the screen, but the technician and doctor seemed quite convinced they were looking at triplets.

It was the craziest thing she'd ever heard. There was no way, it just couldn't possibly be true. She wanted to laugh, she wanted to cry, she had to lie on the table for a few long moments, shocked beyond anything she could have imagined.

If Jack had been the slow one among his brothers to start a family, he was about to make up for lost time in rapid fashion.

"I don't know how to tell the father," she said to the doctor, and her doctor smiled sympathetically.

"He'll be thrilled, Cricket, after the shock wears off."

Cricket wasn't sure this kind of shock was something that would wear off. Jack had never wanted to be a father. "Can you tell if they're boys or girls?" Cricket asked. She didn't know which Jack would think was worse.

"He'll love babies of either sex," Dr. Suzanne assured her. "We might be able to tell at a later sonogram, but it's still a little soon. For now, though, everything looks just right."

Cricket dressed and left, not completely comforted. Jack Morgan lived for rodeo; he wouldn't be planning diapers into his cowboy lifestyle.

And then a big smile lit her face. "I'm having triplets," she murmured. Never mind what everyone else might think about her condition. It was the most wonderful thing that had ever happened to her. "Thank you, Lord," she murmured, trying to decide who to give the good news to first.

Chapter 6

"This is not good news," Jack said, staring at his father. "You haven't been doing anything the doctor asked of you."

"I took a small sabbatical from good advice from doctors," Josiah said. "It's good to see you, though."

Josiah knew he was supposed to stop drinking whiskey. Sara had made him quit. But four days before the newly scheduled surgery, Josiah had started again. Jack suspected his father was nervous though he'd never admit it. "How the hell do you expect to get through this in the best possible shape while you're doing that?" Jack demanded.

Josiah raised a brow. "Since when did you become the parent, and I the child?"

"Since you started behaving irrationally. Let's have the bottle, Pop."

Josiah handed it over. "It wasn't any good, anyway. I've lost my taste for it, which is aggravating. And I think it's all Sara's fault."

Jack looked at his father. He half believed him. Josiah didn't exactly look like a shiny new penny, rather one that had seen its fair share of pockets and hard wear. "What's the matter, Pop?"

"Ah, hell if I know." Josiah scratched his head. "Don't like feeling like a baby."

"Babies have a good life." Jack tossed the bottle in the trash. "Enjoy the attention for a while."

"All right." Josiah sighed. "I'll give up the bottle, and you give up the rodeo, and we'll both suffer loudly together."

Jack considered his father's words as he stared out the hospital window. Life was tricky and weird. He really didn't feel like riding anymore, though he wasn't about to say so. Like Pop with his booze, rodeo just didn't have the same taste to him anymore. "We'll get through this, Pop," he said.

"See, that's the thing," Josiah said. "What if we don't? What if I let you do this, and something goes wrong?"

"Like what?" Jack glanced at his father.

"Like maybe the damn surgeon doesn't know what he's doing and he doesn't do you a good surgery. Maybe your body doesn't like having one functioning kidney and decides to go off. What if the one kidney you have left isn't a good one, and they gave me your best one?"

Jack shrugged. "Let's not borrow a lot of trouble, Pop."

"We need that praying friend of yours," Josiah said. "Deacon Cricket. She could sit at our bedside and bend the good Lord's ear on our behalf."

Jack sighed. "We can take care of ourselves."

"Speak for yourself. I like the way she coddles me. Give her a call."

He'd like to, but he wouldn't. She'd call him if she wanted to talk to him. After all, she'd left without so much as a "thanks, muffin." He'd replayed their time together over and over, and he couldn't think of a way he'd gone wrong. He'd finally consigned Cricket's silence to regret. She simply wished she hadn't made love with him, probably felt she'd done something wrong.

As many times as he'd replayed that night, all it got him was restlessness and cold showers. His skin was going to permanently prune if he didn't stop thinking about her. "I'm not calling her," he said.

"I'll do it," Josiah offered, "if you're too chicken."

"Pop," he said. "I'm so chicken I could be plucked of feathers. But don't call her."

"I won't," Josiah said, "but I will confess to making a different phone call that I think will surprise you."

Jack looked at his father, waiting.

"I called your mother the other day," Josiah told him.

Jack didn't want to go there. "That was a long time ago, Pop. No need to open that wound."

"She's still your mother."

Jack sighed.

Josiah didn't say anything else, which was a sign he wasn't pleased with Jack's reaction. "I guess the obvious question is, why did you feel the need to call her?"

"Sara suggested I should," Josiah said.

Jack looked out the window again, wishing the surgery was over already. He didn't want to be here. He wanted his father well because it was the right thing to think. And then he wanted to be gone again. Anywhere, nowhere, just not here.

"Sara said it was time to put the past to rest. Gisella probably misses you boys. And Sara and I talked about how bitterness breaks families in strange ways. Since we're having life-altering surgeries, it's best not to go into them with negative memories." Josiah smiled when Jack turned back to study him. "Sara works for child welfare services, you know. She knows a lot about what makes families tick."

"I'm glad you're happy, Pop." As far as Jack was concerned, his mother had chosen to leave and never come back. Never sent gifts, never wrote. He wasn't going to worry about what made families tick when the maternal clock had been broken for years.

"There's such a thing as forgiveness being good for the soul," Josiah said.

Jack frowned. "If I'm going to forgive someone, I'd start with you."

Pop's eyes bugged. "You wouldn't give me a kidney and hold a grudge, would you?"

Jack shrugged. "Holding grudges is part of our family identity. I learned it from you."

"I don't know if I want you giving me a kidney that's full of grudge," Josiah said.

"Quit trying to weasel," Jack told his father. "We're going to have the surgery this time, we're going to do it together, and we're both going to be happy about it."

"Not so much," Josiah said. "You boys ride me terribly, but I wasn't that lousy of a father."

"Don't sell yourself short." Jack sighed. "Hell, it doesn't matter anymore. Let's just live for the future."

"Glad you suggest it. Your mother said she'll be here soon enough."

"Why? There's nothing she can do."

"She wants to see all the grandchildren. She wants to see her boys. Said she wanted to meet the wonderful woman who talked me into getting off my high horse and calling her." Josiah's eyes grew misty. "Funny thing about your mother, she has a heart of gold. I wish I'd appreciated that when I was younger. It's something you miss out on about your wife when you're busy trying to make a living."

Jack blinked. "Are you going to marry Sara?"

"Yep," Josiah said, "just as soon as I'm well."

"Our family tree is odd," Jack said. "There's a lot of twists among the branches."

Josiah shrugged. "Every family has its twists and unique branches, son. The fact that we keep fertilizing the roots is what makes our tree strong."

"Oh, hell," Jack said. "Next you're going to be after me to do some fertilizing. Pop, kids is one thing you're never going to get out of me, so don't even start the chorus."

"Excuse me," the doctor said as he came into the room, "I'm Dr. Goodlaw."

Jack stood, shook the doctor's hand. "Jack Morgan."

"Ah, Mr. Morgan's eldest son."

Jack nodded.

"Well, I have an unusual bit of news," Dr. Goodlaw said. "We just had a kidney come up that is a match for you, Mr. Morgan."

"What does that mean, exactly?" Josiah's brows furrowed.

"It means that this particular kidney is from a young accident victim whose parents want his organs donated. He was healthy and active, and his family would like to know that his organs are helping other people to live healthy, active lives. I know you have a family match who has offered, but I recall you didn't elect for surgery under those conditions."

"No, I did not," Josiah said with a stern glance at Jack. "I don't elect, not one bit."

"It's up to you, Mr. Morgan, although a decision will need to be reached fairly quickly. There are other recipients in the registry, of course."

Jack and his father looked at each other. Then Josiah shrugged. "I don't need any time to think it over. I'll take the kidney."

Dr. Goodlaw nodded. "I'll go make the arrangements." He shook Jack's hand, then Josiah's. "This will move fairly quickly."

"Good," Josiah shot back. "I'm tired of feeling like I'm at everyone's mercy."

The doctor smiled and left the room. Josiah refused to meet Jack's gaze. Jack knew exactly what his father was thinking: *I owe nobody nothing.* Jack couldn't say whether he felt any particular relief that he wouldn't be giving up a part of his body. "Are you all right, Pop?"

"I'm fine," Josiah said. "As fine as anyone can be who just had a miracle thrust upon them."

"What do you mean?" Jack went and sat by his father.

"I prayed I wouldn't have to take your kidney. I couldn't stand the thought of you rodeoing with one kidney. I just don't want to outlive my kids," Josiah said. "Now that I've got my boys all around, I'd like to get to know you."

Jack felt honest emotion jump inside him. He looked away, cleared his throat. "I almost like you better when you're being a jackass."

"That's because I'm an enemy you can keep fighting against. You like holding grudges. But you won't get any fight out of me, son. I'm getting a young person's kidney, and I'm going to take full advantage of the spark it gives me. You're off the hook."

Jack shook his head. "You just didn't want anything from me."

"True." Josiah closed his eyes. "I don't want you doing anything for me that you don't really want to do."

"I didn't mind, Pop."

"I know you didn't mind the surgery, and I thank you for being willing to make the sacrifice. But I think it's better this way."

"Okay, Pop."

Josiah took a deep breath. "And since I'm wiping slates clean here, I guess you'll be wanting your million dollars."

"Not if it comes with a wife."

"It doesn't. But you do have to reside at the ranch, same as the other boys did."

"They didn't stay a year!"

"No, but they did get married, have families. They fulfilled what I wanted, which was to get along with each other, bring some harmony into our family."

"Pop, I was going to give you my kidney. I've visited you often in the hospital. That's pretty harmonious for us."

"Yes," Josiah said, "but it's your brothers I want you visiting."

"I will, Pop, I will."

"It won't hurt you to hold some babies, get to know your nieces and nephews," Pop nagged.

Jack held up his hands. "Pop, you're about to have surgery. We can talk about this later."

"We can talk about it now. Is it a deal or not?" Pop demanded, and Jack looked at his father.

"Why are you so hopped up about this all of a sudden?"

"Because I'm about to have complicated surgery! It's not like getting a hangnail removed. I need to make a phone call to my lawyer. I have to make sure all the family matters are tended to just in case my old body doesn't like young, healthy kidneys!"

Jack held up his hands. "Hang on, Pop, relax. Don't give yourself high blood pressure or they won't operate. What exactly is it that you want from me? Where do I sign on the dotted line so that you can cool down?"

"You have to stay at the ranch for a year, get to know your brothers, be a family. Same deal they got."

"And if, just if, a wife and family comes into the picture? Does that abbreviate the deal?"

Josiah sniffed. "I make those decisions when they occur. Depends on many factors. Do I like your choice of bride? Am I really getting grandkids? Are you improving your life? Being a good uncle? I don't want you loafing around the ranch for a year, biding your time just to get my million bucks. I don't want you forwarding your mail to the ranch and saying you live there. In other words, I wait and see what I'm buying before I pay."

"I don't really need a million dollars, Pop," Jack said. "I'm pretty happy being free."

"Yeah," Josiah said, "you're my hardheaded son."

Jack grinned. "I'll do this on one condition."

"I'm living with Sara," Josiah said. "I'm not insisting upon this because I need you to be my nursemaid."

Jack shook his head. Pop was the most stubborn human he'd ever met. "You don't start sending a bunch of women to the ranch to try to settle me, thinking I'll give up rodeo just because you find me a wife."

Josiah shook his head. "I would never do such a thing."

"You're fairly relentless in your pursuit of the perfect family tree."

"Not me," Josiah said. "I don't believe there are perfect family trees. But I do think wives are a durn good thing. Bring a man a lot of good stuff he never knew he was missing."

Jack shook his head. He tried to decide if he could stomach a year of family, and then he thought about Cricket.

Maybe it wouldn't be so bad to live in Union Junction for a year. "Where do I sign with my blood?"

Josiah rubbed his hands. "It's a gentleman's verbal agreement. Now get out so I can call my lawyer. I have to hurry because Dr. Moneybags may be here soon to take his pound of flesh from me."

"I guess I'll go check out the cafeteria."

"Good," Josiah said, reaching for the phone. "Find a cute nurse while you're in there. There's lots of them around here."

Jack headed to the cafeteria with no intention of taking that advice. He had one woman on his mind—and that was plenty.

He dialed up his brothers and let them know Pop's news. Then he drummed his fingers on the table, watching people move around with trays. He couldn't say he wasn't relieved not to be tied by an organ to his father. It felt as if they were coming to some kind of agreement between them, something almost resembling respect.

Since he was going to be a resident of Union Junction for a while, maybe it wouldn't hurt to call a certain deacon and let her know that he'd be living close by, just in case she was interested.

But what would he say? *I heard you bought Priscilla's house and tea shop in Fort Wylie, but I wish you lived in Union Junction so I could see you occasionally.*

There was no point.

Chapter 7

There were many details Josiah needed to wrap up before he went under the knife. Nothing was going smoothly with Jack, as it had with his other sons. They'd fallen in with his plans after a hiccup or two, but Jack was no closer to finding his way home to family than before. He was really worried about how Jack would accept Gisella. Josiah understood that his eldest son had always been a sincere loner, and if anything, anything at all got ticklish between he and his mother, Jack would disappear. No million dollars would bring him back. Jack lived in a world of his own creation.

Josiah knew why this was. As soon as Josiah got out of the military, he'd begun his lifelong goal of acquiring business and property. He was determined to deserve Gisella, give her everything she didn't have.

But Josiah was moody, struggling with start-up businesses. He and his wife fought a lot. Gisella hated being left alone on the ranch; she was afraid of the dark. Their few cattle started disappearing and Gisella was always edgy, afraid the boys would have a run-in with some dangerous rustlers. Gisella was from

France, and English was not her first language. She had no female friends where they lived out in the country to make her feel less isolated.

He was gone on a business trip to Dallas when he got the worried call from Jack. All of eight years old, Jack tried manfully to tell him his mother was gone—in the end, he dissolved into tears that Josiah would never forget hearing him cry.

His eldest son would never forgive his mother for deserting him. Jack had barely forgiven Josiah for the rough treatment Josiah had felt Jack needed to handle the hard knocks life was sure to mete out. Josiah wasn't sure he'd made the right decision with Jack. His eldest was almost too tough now, emotionally locked up. Nothing really penetrated his stoic approach to life.

Jack was likely to find a reason to skip Gisella's visit altogether. Josiah had pondered this, giving it great thought, and hatched a plan. There weren't many second chances in life, but he really wanted mother and son to have one with each other. He suspected that if this bond wasn't recreated, Jack would never be able to maintain a loving, giving relationship with a woman. Josiah hated that he cost Jack something in life that gave a man great pleasure.

Josiah hoped Gisella and Jack would both forgive him for what he was about to do—but it had to be done, for the sake of the family.

Two hours later, Gisella walked into the room unannounced. Grouped around Josiah's bedside were Gabe, Dane, Pete, their wives and Jack. Sara Corkindale was there as well, giving Josiah the comfort he had learned to expect from her calm presence. No one recognized Gisella except Josiah, and he felt the familiar flash of joy at her beauty and bearing. Time had not changed her cruelly by etching wrinkles on her face. He saw that she was smiling at him as one did at a long-lost friend. He hoped they could be friends after she learned what he had done.

He was about to be prepped for surgery and there was little time for fretting about the past. "My sons," he said, "this is your mother."

It was as if a stone dropped from the ceiling and landed in the room. No one went to hug her. The brothers stared at her so finally Gisella moved forward, giving Josiah a gentle kiss on the forehead. "You look well, Josiah, for what you have been through."

"I hope I look as well tomorrow," Josiah said.

Gisella looked at Sara. "You must be the wonderful woman who convinced Josiah to call me."

Sara smiled, and the women shook hands. "I'm sure you know that no one can convince Josiah of anything unless he is already convinced of it himself."

Gisella laughed, a full-throated sound Jack remembered from his childhood. It came upon him with a wild, stinging sensation that he'd never gotten over missing that laugh. He had never gotten over missing her. As a boy, he couldn't understand why she'd left him, what he'd done wrong.

Gabe went and hugged Gisella. Dane followed and then Pete. Jack scowled, wanting to hang back, but after the wives had been introduced, Jack realized the time had come. "Mother," he said, barely kissing her cheek.

She smelled fresh, like spring roses, and it occurred to him he'd missed that smell. Painful memories rushed over him.

"I can see my little man has grown into a big man," Gisella said. "I've thought about you often, Jack."

"Yes, yes," Josiah said, interrupting the homecoming, to Jack's infinite relief. "And now that your mother's here, there's some tidying up to do. Best to get these things done in case I croak under Dr. Moneybag's good care."

"Pop, there's no point in getting worked up about things that can wait. We're all shell-shocked to see Mom. Let us enjoy her for a moment," Pete pointed out, but Josiah waved an impatient hand at him.

"A man doesn't go to his grave with a messy conscience,"

he said, "not unless he's an idiot or run out of time, neither of which applies to me. Sara, may I have the box, please."

Sara produced a shoe box from her handbag and handed it to Josiah.

Josiah sniffed, then looked at Gisella. "Gisella, on many counts I was not a good husband."

"On many counts, you were," Gisella returned. "I was not the perfect wife. There is no such thing as perfection in a marriage."

"I like her," Sara said. "She understands family."

"I pick good women," Josiah said gruffly. "Sara, you might as well know this about me along with everybody else. Boys, in this box are all the letters your mother sent you over the years." Josiah pulled the top off the box. "You can see that none of them have been opened. I could have read them to you since I speak and read French, but I chose not to out of a stubborn sense of pride and misplaced pain. For this egregious misdeed, I apologize to you all and humbly ask for forgiveness."

Gisella's eyes sparkled with tears. For the first time, a little forgiveness toward his mother seeped into Jack's heart. "Pop," he said, "that's kind of brutal, don't you think?"

Dr. Moneybags came into the room to make certain his patient was being prepped and to give his soothing pre-surgery talk. "Doc," Josiah said, "I need ten more minutes before you roll me to the gallows."

"Mr. Morgan," Dr. Goodlaw replied, not sure whether to be offended or not, "I assure you we have an excellent team to perform this surgery. It is not a gallows situation."

"Ten minutes is all I need, please, Doctor. And I meant no offence to your skills."

The doctor nodded. "The next time I see you, you'll be asleep. Do you have any questions?"

Josiah looked around the room at his sons, their wives and the two women in his life. "Do I need much more reason to wake up after surgery with a grin on my face?"

The doctor smiled and left. Josiah let out a sigh. "Gisella, I owe you an apology. Many actually. I was mad when you left. It doesn't excuse what I did. It doesn't save me from the damage I inflicted upon our children. I hope you can forgive me."

Gisella started to say something, but Josiah waved her quiet. "Hang on a minute, there's more," he said. "The Christmas and birthday presents she sent you for many years were given to charity. I'm sorry. It was a selfish thing to do, more than selfish."

Jack stared at his father, looked at his mother, who seemed fairly upset but not necessarily destroyed by his father's confession. Then Gisella went over and kissed him again on the forehead.

"You are too hard on yourself, Josiah," she said. "You are a good man. Let's not think about the past anymore."

"Well." Josiah sniffed. "I was still an ass."

"I knew that about you when I married you. I didn't want a man who wasn't strong." Gisella smiled. "It takes a very strong man to ask forgiveness."

"Yeah. I guess. I have a lot to ask." Josiah looked around the room. "So, I have one more thing to tell the assembled family. By the way, I would like to see everybody together again and not necessarily on my deathbed next time—"

A general groan broke out in the room.

Josiah nodded. "Jack's going to reside at the ranch for a year."

"I'll *try* to," Jack interrupted.

"In order to earn his million dollars, he'll do it," Josiah said, ignoring his son's words. "However, I have begun the paperwork to cede the ranch to Gisella. It is now hers to do with as she sees fit, although it cannot be sold until after Jack completes his quest. Gisella, one year from today, you may sell it if you wish. I'm sorry I didn't give you the home and the love you needed when we were married, but now I hope to make up for that." Josiah looked at all his children, his gaze stern. "And I expect everyone to remember that my driving force is family. Visit your mother often."

He sat up and looked at Sara. "Get the nurses. I'm ready to be split open like a turkey at Thanksgiving."

She smiled at him. "Your family members may do it for you," she said sweetly.

"And that reminds me, no lawsuits over the land or ranch," he said, wagging a finger at all of them. "Or you forfeit your portion of my will, little as it may be after Dr. Moneybags takes his chunk. Is that understood?"

Everyone murmured a shocked assent except Jack, because he didn't need anything, money or land, from his father. Thankfully, he was tied to no one.

"Jack?" his father said. "This means more to me than a kidney."

Jack looked at his father a long time. Then he glanced at his mother, whose gentle smile beamed on him so warmly that it was difficult to continue being a hard case. "Sure, Pop, whatever."

Laura, Suzy and Priscilla went to hug Gisella and welcome her to the family. After a moment, the brothers did, too. Except Jack, who decided not to get caught up in the sentimental moment. It wasn't the time for him to live in the Hallmark-card family moment, no matter how much Pop wanted it.

Nurses entered the room to wheel Pop out. Jack's throat closed up. The feel of family, of being hemmed in, of life being out of his control, threatened to overwhelm him. He needed some separation.

He needed to ride. It was the only thing that would make him sane right now, feel in control. "Be well, Pop," he said, gritting his teeth as his father was wheeled down the hall to presurgery. They all watched as a suddenly silent Josiah was taken away. Gisella and Sara wiped away surreptitious tears, sitting down together side by side. Jack cleared his throat, realizing he, too, was tearing up with nervous emotion. This was awkward. He looked at the box of old, unopened letters on the table, a silent testament to Josiah's stubbornness. A ranch had been given to his mother with the proviso that Jack could live there with her for a year. What the hell was that if it wasn't a trap laid by Pop? But Pop didn't understand that the past couldn't be laid to rest with a quick apology and a confession.

"I'll be back," Jack stated, and left the room.

Maybe he would, maybe he wouldn't.

Chapter 8

Jack didn't get far. He bumped into Cricket, who was hurrying into Josiah's hospital room.

"Oh, my," Cricket said, glancing around. "I missed him, didn't I?"

Laura, Suzy and Priscilla came over to hug her.

"Josiah just left," Priscilla said. "But you'll be here when he wakes up, and that will make him happy."

Jack stared at Cricket. She looked different. For one thing, she was wearing a dress that brushed her calves, and boots. Since it was chilly today, he understood the need for warmth. But she also looked different somehow, in a way he couldn't explain. Glowing. Was she glowing? Perhaps it was the nippy air that had put the sparkle in her eyes.

"This is Gisella, mother of the Morgan brothers," Priscilla said, and Jack realized he'd forgotten his manners. He just couldn't seem to catch up to the speed of events in the room.

He joined the group. "Gisella, this is Cricket Jasper from Fort Wylie."

"Hello," Cricket said. "It's so nice to meet you. I've heard a lot of wonderful things about you."

Gisella smiled at her. "Thank you."

Cricket glanced around, her gaze settling on Jack. "I'm sorry I wasn't here in time to pray for Josiah."

Jack shrugged. "No problem."

"Your father called me yesterday," Cricket said, "but I'm a slow starter these days. I meant to be here earlier."

Suzy smiled at her, then patted Cricket's stomach. "You look beautiful."

Jack hesitated. No woman patted another woman's stomach, then told her she was beautiful unless she wanted her hand chewed off. Women and weight was a personal thing...unless... Jack stared at Cricket, shock spreading over him. Belatedly, he realized Laura, Suzy and Priscilla were smiling at him, watching his reaction. Cricket simply looked worried.

She *couldn't* be pregnant. Jack shook his head to clear his brain. His brothers shifted uncomfortably and Jack felt faint, as if he'd been thrown off a bull and hadn't landed quite right. "Cricket, you're not...is there something I should know?"

Cricket hesitated. "I was going to tell you, but—"

"Oh, jeez." Now that he looked at Cricket's waist and stomach more closely, he could see the obvious.

"We're having a baby," Cricket said, her face red. "I meant to tell you sooner, but—"

"Pete, scoot that chair behind Jack before he falls," Gabe said. "I remember when I found out I was having a baby. I felt like my boots weren't attached to the floor for a minute."

"I hope that meant you were happy," Laura said.

Gabe eyed Laura's enormous pregnant stomach. "Every day," he said. "It feels like I'm waiting for Christmas."

Jack sat in the chair Pete moved behind him. Then he jumped out of it, too stunned to sit. He couldn't take his eyes off Cricket. Was she really having a baby? *His* baby?

"This is so exciting," Gisella said, clapping her hands. "I'm going to be a grandmother again, and this time, I'll be here for the big event. Two," she said, with a proud smile at Laura, who looked as though she might give birth any day.

This could not be happening. Jack inhaled deep breaths to brace himself. "I'm going to be a father?"

Everyone laughed. Cricket smiled at him for the first time since she'd entered the room.

"Yes," she said softly, "to triplets, actually."

Jack couldn't move, he couldn't speak. Never had his life rushed so fast, not even the eight seconds he rode to the buzzer. This was different.

This was a crazy ride.

His brothers congratulated him, pounded him on the back, shook his hand. One of his brothers mentioned something about "nice shooting, bro," and general guffaws broke out. Gisella kissed Cricket on the cheek, and Sara smiled.

"Josiah's going to have such a gift when he comes out of surgery," Sara said. "He'll be so excited he'll probably recover twice as fast."

Jack tried to say that he was excited, too, but all that came out of his mouth was a rusty croak no one heard over all the sudden hugging and kissing of Cricket. Jack knew he needed to say something to her, act pleased, brag like an expectant father—but all he could do was try to keep his knees from knocking together and suck air into his lungs.

He'd never been so scared.

How could he—a man who spends all his time on the rodeo circuit—be a father? To triplets?

He had no home. He basically lived out of his truck. The rodeo circuit was his family. He had no steady employment, no way of caring for a wife and three children.

The obvious smote him—he was going to have to live on the damn ranch, prey to his father's manipulations, in order to earn the million dollars Josiah had set out as bribe money. It was fast dough, and he'd need it pronto if he meant to be something other than a loser father and shiftless husband. He stared at Cricket, realizing his whole life was changing, and he'd have to change with it.

"I'm thrilled," he said. "This is great."

Cricket knew Jack was anything but "thrilled." He looked pale, maybe even sick. It was a lot for him to take in on the day his father was having surgery. She wondered if he'd known Gisella was coming home and decided he had enough to bear without finding out he was a father. She forgave him for his lack of real enthusiasm, remembering that she'd had a few moments of shocked doubt before genuine happiness washed over her.

Still, she wished she and Jack knew each other well enough to be truly excited about being parents together. She wouldn't have come today had Josiah not called her, asking her to be there before he was taken into surgery. As it was, she'd missed him leaving and felt bad about that.

She'd known her secret might be out when Jack saw her, and tried to camouflage her pregnancy with a dress. He might not have figured it out had her good friends Laura, Suzy and Priscilla not given him a broad hint even Jack couldn't miss. She would have preferred to tell him herself, when they weren't surrounded by people, and when Jack wasn't worried about his father.

But now he knew.

"A wedding," Gisella said with delight. "Josiah didn't tell me the good news. When's the date?"

Cricket glanced at Jack, stricken. She didn't know what to say. She understood why Gisella might have misunderstood that there was to be a wedding, but—

"As soon as Pop's well," Jack said, shocking Cricket. "I imagine he'll be on his feet fairly quickly, don't you? He's a fighter."

"Indeed," Cricket said as Jack walked over and planted a kiss on her lips. "Can I talk to you a moment— outside?" she asked as everyone in the room was celebrating the idea of another Morgan wedding.

"Sure," Jack said, putting his arm around her. "Keep playing along with me. You're doing great."

She didn't like the sound of that. She'd heard that sneaky tone used before, but always from Josiah. "What are you up to?" she demanded when they were safely in the hospital hallway.

"You've got to save me," Jack said. "Pop's trying to trap me."

"Look here," Cricket said, already feeling heat run under her good sense. "I refuse to be regarded as a trap, Jack Morgan. You are not a rabbit that I set out to snare, for your information."

"Oh, hell, no, I didn't mean that." He held her against him, kissing her as Pete glanced out in the hall.

"Just checking to make certain you lovebirds hadn't flown the coop," Pete teased. "Mom's planning a huge wedding, just so you know. At the Château Morgan, which is to say the ranch. She has visions of you in a formal suit," he whispered to Jack so their mother wouldn't hear. "All the weddings she missed is making her want a doozy."

"Thanks for the warning," Jack said, waving his brother away. "Look, you can see what's happening here, can't you?"

"Not exactly," Cricket said. "I have a lot on my mind these days and haven't been focusing on the Morgan family, at least not the ones in Union Junction."

"Precisely my point," Jack said. "Pop's moved Mom onto the ranch. He's turning over ownership to her. I'm supposed to live there for a year with her to get my million dollars."

"What million dollars?" Cricket asked.

"All my brothers got a million for coming home to Pop. It was bribe money," Jack explained. "Now he's brought Mom into the picture because of his guilty conscience. None of my brothers had to live with her, though, and put up with Pop, and learn how to be a father all at once. The deck is stacked against me. I'm going to need your help, Deacon."

"I'm not a deacon anymore," Cricket said, detaching herself

from Jack's arms. She was reluctant to part from him but she didn't want to be part of a cover-up. "I wasn't really deacon material considering my unwed, pregnant state."

"Oh," Jack said, "a little too rebellious for the church, huh?"

"I consider myself to be, at the moment, and turned in my resignation to spare them having to ask me to leave." Cricket was terribly embarrassed by this. "Anyway, I'm not the person you need to talk to about any type of help. My days are spent warding off morning sickness."

"Marry me," Jack said. "We'll ward off a lot of things together."

She looked at him, wishing the proposal was offered seriously. He was so big and tall, handsome in a devil-may-care way. She knew this man was too much of a rogue to ever be tamed by a deacon and three babies—she wouldn't dream of getting involved in his scheme. "I can't, Jack. Don't ask it of me."

"Sure you can," he said. "Save me, I'll save you."

"But I don't want to live at the ranch. I mean, I like Gisella, she seems like a woman who's eager for a second chance. You need to spend some time developing that relationship," Cricket said, sort of realizing the wonderful madness behind Josiah's scheme. "You should obey your father, you know."

"You mean for the money."

"No," Cricket said. "Although that's definitely a plus. But your father knows what he's doing, he almost always has."

"Oh, you weren't here for the fireworks," Jack told her. "There's a box sitting in there full of letters Mom sent us over the years that Pop never opened. He's a stubborn old fart, and he let her suffer, and us. The only reason he's springing all this now is he's genuinely afraid of pushing up daisies after this surgery. I don't think I ever saw Pop take anything stronger than an aspirin."

"He had his own medicine," Cricket reminded him, and Jack nodded.

"True, but you get my point. Pop was scared silly of giving over the control of his body and his life to a surgeon. He felt like he had a lot of cleansing of his conscience to do. I'm okay with that," Jack said, "but I don't want him running my life so that his conscience is clear."

"What exactly are you proposing?" She looked up at him, wondering if Jack realized just how much like his father he was turning out to be.

"I don't exactly know," Jack said. "I'm working the details out on the fly, but it goes something like this. I have no prospects—some money put away, no job. No debt. No house. Am not especially close to my family. Not quite sure what I'm doing in life other than pleasing myself."

"So, as potential marriage material, you're not exactly a shiny catch."

He grinned. "That's a fair statement."

"Okay," Cricket said. "Again, you have to live at the ranch to earn your keep. I don't want to live there."

"We can live in the guesthouse," Jack offered. "It's big enough to raise a family in, and be private, while sticking to Pop's rules."

"This is going to sound crazy," Cricket said, "but I'm not marrying you for money."

"I wasn't exactly suggesting you should," Jack said, but Cricket shook her head.

"That's what it comes down to. You need money, so you want to marry me. The only reason you're proposing to me, Jack Morgan, is that I've got the three magic tokens that will push you into doing what your father wants. Otherwise, you'd just as soon walk away from any amount of money."

"This is true," Jack said. "Being a father does change my perspective. I don't want them growing up without a parent like I did."

"Oh, gosh," Cricket said, "you are a tangled web of insecurities and emotional angst."

"Yep," Jack said with a grin. "Part of my appeal."

"I wouldn't exactly agree, but I shouldn't have let you sweet-talk me into bed," Cricket said, knowing she was fibbing like mad. She didn't regret a moment of their time together.

"Ahem," Jack said, politely catching her in her retelling of who had instigated their lovemaking.

"Here's the deal—I just bought Priscilla's house and tea shop. I was always enchanted by her house and the business. I admired her ability to make a business out of almost nothing. So when she wanted to sell it to come live in Union Junction with Pete, I jumped at the chance to buy it from her. I suppose maybe I knew somewhere in my heart that I wouldn't be a deacon for-ever." She looked up at him, hoping he'd understand. "My life's changing pretty fast, Jack. A tea shop is something I can do as a single mom and still be at home with my children. Do you see why I don't want to leave Fort Wylie?"

Jack stared down at her, nodding. "Yes, I do," he said. "It's crazy, but it just might work."

"What?" Cricket demanded. "What just might work?"

"I'll be a tea-shop cowboy," he said with a wink and a grin, "Coffee, tea or me?"

That would cause a stir. There'd be more women hanging around the tea shop and her cowboy than she could bear. Cricket raised a cool brow in response to his deliberate teasing. "I don't think you could handle the heat in this kitchen, Jack Morgan."

Chapter 9

Jack knew the moment Cricket said she didn't want to leave Fort Wylie that he had to convince her to let him live in her world. It was the only practical solution that solved everything except money.

"A million dollars is a lot to give up, anyway," Cricket told him, all teasing spirit fleeing. "You'll resent me later for missing the opportunity of a lot of wealth."

Jack shrugged. "Don't try to understand me and we'll both be fine."

"It's not a matter of understanding you," she shot back. "It's a simple matter of understanding human nature. I don't see you being happy passing out cookies and cakes to moms with school-age children."

"It was your idea," he said, and Cricket blinked.

"How so?"

"You're the one who said it was the perfect way to be a stay-at-home parent, and that's what I'd like to do." Jack kissed her on the nose. "Two can live as cheaply as one. Surely five will be a snap."

"You haven't done much grocery shopping lately." Cricket shook her head. "Jack, do not use me and the babies as an excuse to get out from under your father's thumb."

"A thumb is a terrible thing to be under," he said.

"You're just exchanging his thumb for mine. Eventually, that's the conclusion you'll come to."

"You make me sound shiftless," Jack said. "I'll have you know, I'm responsible to a fault."

"This is a bad idea," Cricket said. "Even in my less-wild dreams, I thought my marriage would be more about love and less about business."

"You wanted to be an excellent businesswoman," Jack reminded her. "I'm just offering a partnership since we've already started parenthood together."

He had a point. The blue-ribbon prize she barely allowed herself to contemplate was that she'd win the rodeo man she wanted if she went along with Jack's proposal—and wasn't that worth doing for her children?

She looked at Jack's long, lean body and wondered if she was really thinking about her children or herself.

"So you'll marry me, Cricket?" Jack asked.

"Perhaps," she said, still worrying about the wisdom of marrying a man who'd never wanted to be married. "Something tells me nothing good can come of this. No tea-shop cowboy for me."

Jack grinned. "You make getting married sound so dangerous."

She looked at him—and wondered.

In his sleep Josiah was visited by ghosts. Or maybe they were angels, he couldn't be certain. They floated into his subconscious, three strong, lean, well-muscled Templar knights dressed in armor, looking very much like pictures he'd seen. Only these knights were serious, annoyed and bored, clearly out of sorts to be on this particular quest. He hoped they were angels coming to rescue him from his plight, but the possibility that he deserved disheveled, disheartened ghosts more than angels couldn't be overlooked.

"You abandoned us," the one he named Serious complained. The man could use a good shave and a respectable haircut. "You left us in the templary without so much as a kind word."

"Sorry," Josiah said. "I wasn't aware you were there."

"You wouldn't have said goodbye anyway," Bored said. "You don't like to say goodbye."

"It's a bad habit," Josiah agreed. "Why are you here?"

Annoyed looked at him. "For moral support. You asked for guidance and comfort, so here we are."

"I don't remember that," Josiah said. Maybe he had. He'd been terribly nervous about the surgery, a fact he hadn't wanted to share with his family since he felt he always had to keep the tough-old-lion face on.

"We wish you hadn't sold the templary," Serious said. "You didn't even give us a quest."

"Aren't you on one now?"

Bored waved a chalice at him. "This is a snap of the fingers. We need something important to do."

"But I'm pretty sure you're a figment of my drug-induced fears. Dr. Moneybags loaded me up pretty good on antianxiety dope, though I told the nurse I wasn't anxious. I'm more pissed than anything." Josiah felt that was a waste of his hospital bill. An aspirin was likely to cost fifteen bucks, never mind the amount of tranquilizers it would take to "antianxiety" him.

"We think we'll move onto the ranch with you," Annoyed said.

Josiah said, "I won't be there. Only my eldest son and his mother will live there."

Bored scrabbled around in his tunic for something, booze Josiah figured, to fill his chalice. "I'd help you out with that but they took my whiskey from me," Josiah said.

"Listen," Bored said, "a knight has to fight. It's what we do.

You never gave us anything to fight for. We need you to figure that out now."

Josiah blinked, shaking his shaggy head. "I don't have anything to fight for."

"Aha!" Serious exclaimed. "But you do. You wanted this
family. Now you have to stick around to raise it."

"I'm trying to," Josiah said. "Can't you see I'm getting a
new kidney?"

Bored scrunched his face. "Good to hear that you have no
plans to chicken out just because your son is."

"What does that mean?" Josiah demanded.

"It means Jack plans to be married at cock-crow in a faraway
town," Annoyed said, "to a woman of prayer."

"Cricket," Josiah said. "That's a good thing."

"Nay," the annoyed Templar said. "He plans to move away,
thereby thwarting your wishes."

"Has he no respect for his mother?" Josiah demanded, and
Bored hunched his shoulders, probably depressed about his
empty chalice.

"He is farther away from her than ever, and therefore you—"
Bored said "—you forced him to go away."

"Look," Josiah said, "I'm just trying to keep my family together."

Serious nodded. "Follow us," he commanded.

"Where?" Josiah asked, feeling a twinge of fear. Should he
be journeying with ghostly knights while he was being oper-
ated on? It didn't seem to bode well. They appeared as real as
Dr. Moneybags and just as unpleasant, as far as Josiah was
concerned. Why would he conjure up imaginary companions
at this late stage of his life, when he had everything he wanted?

"Follow us," Serious repeated, and Josiah left his body and
followed his trio of knights.

"This is the Cave of Fears," Serious told him as they stood
inside a strange cavern of many colors. "You have to face fears
or they become your reality."

"Shoot," Josiah said, "I'm not worried about my fears. They work themselves out in time."

"Because you avoid them," Bored said. "You can't avoid the fear of your son leaving you for good."

"Oh, hell," Josiah said, "I'm too tired to face that fear. Can't I beg off?"

"Knights don't beg," Annoyed intoned, "and you were born to be a knight. You raised your sons to be stronger men than you had been."

"I was born to be a knight?" Josiah asked, suddenly feeling stronger.

"What did your father and mother tell you?" Annoyed asked, his face etched by a scowl.

"That big boys don't cry," Josiah said, remembering. "But I cried often."

"Why?" Annoyed asked him.

"Because I hated being alone. I wanted brothers and sisters." It was painful remembering living alone in the country with no siblings. He'd never gotten over the loneliness, never.

"Face your fears in order to finally live the life you want. You have to change, not change your sons," Serious told him, and the three knights disappeared.

"Mr. Morgan," a faraway voice said. "Mr. Morgan?"

He blinked his eyes. His eyelids were almost too heavy to open. "I'll just nap awhile longer," he told the insistent voice, "if you'll be kind enough not to pester me."

"Mr. Morgan, you came through the surgery just fine," the voice told him, but Josiah knew he was really on the brink of his last chance at being the father he'd always dreamed of.

Jack wasn't sure how his mother could forgive his father for secreting her letters over the years—he wasn't sure he forgave Josiah for that. It would have made a huge difference in how Jack had perceived himself. He'd always thought it was his fault his mother had left, though later on in life he'd known that was not the case. Still, as a child, he'd only known she'd left, and he hadn't been able to keep her from going. He watched his siblings file in one at a time to visit Josiah and wished he was off in a bedroom with Cricket somewhere. The strangest itch had come over him to feel her stomach. He wanted to touch the soft mound where his children were. When would they kick? Were their hearts beating yet? He had no idea about babies. He supposed they did whatever they liked, whenever they liked. Cricket sat beside him anxiously watching the doorway, completely unaware of his proudly possessive paternal thoughts that soon turned to a more lustful nature.

He was in trouble. Maybe she didn't want to make love with him anymore. He had gotten her into quite the jam. Though his brothers congratulated him for his "good shooting," the fact was, she wouldn't be sitting there contemplating the hugeness of triplets if he'd obeyed the simple rule: *No love without a glove.* Among his friends on the rodeo circuit, everyone promised themselves they could touch, but not without proper protection.

He wondered if she would have ever come to him on her own to tell him about the pregnancy. Cricket was pretty independent. She had her life all set up without him.

Now that he knew, he had no intention of missing a moment, not one expanding pound, of her pregnancy. Naked, as much as possible. "Cricket," he said suddenly, "let's go."

She turned, staring at him with astonished eyes. "We haven't seen your father yet."

"He's going to be fine," Jack said, but Cricket shook her head.

"Relax, Jack, this family stuff isn't going to kill you." She patted his arm and turned back to staring at the hallway, waiting for one of his brothers to come out and share some news about Josiah. Laura, Suzy and Priscilla sat nearby her, clearly already counting her into their circle. He was the only one who was antsy.

It was probably because his mother sat with the women. Her

boys were waiting their select turns to see Pop. Sara sat near Gisella, but Jack hung back.

"Hey," Pete said suddenly, sticking his head through the doorway, "Pop wants to see you, Jack."

Jack blinked, startled. Cricket squeezed his arm to comfort him. "Sure thing, Pete," he said, not wanting to seem like a wuss, and walked into Pop's recovery room.

He wasn't really prepared for the sight of Pop so still, so groggy. His father barely opened his eyes, but when he saw Jack, he made more effort.

"Jack," he murmured.

"Take it easy, Pop," Jack said, trying to ignore all the emotions suddenly swimming around inside him. "You need to rest."

"Don't leave," Josiah said.

Jack hesitated. "I'm right here."

Josiah barely shook his head. "Don't leave Union Junction. Don't leave the ranch. We need you here."

Oh, boy. Pop had no idea what he was asking. Maybe it was the drugs, or the new kidney talking. "Hey, Pop," he said, "you go back to sleep, okay?" He backed away from the bedside, wondering how his father had known he planned to forfeit his million dollars. He had to marry Cricket; he needed to be in Fort Wylie with her. Pop would just have to understand.

Josiah watched Jack's retreat through half-lidded eyes. "Please," Josiah said, and Jack didn't think he'd ever heard his father use that word to him in all his life.

Chapter 10

Cricket saw the change in Jack the moment he left his father's hospital room. Jack made a beeline for her, grabbed her by the hand, barely said goodbye to his siblings and mother and Sara and left as if his heels were on fire.

"What's going on?" Cricket asked. "We need to stay here with Josiah."

"We need to go home and let you rest," Jack said.

"What happened in there? Is your father all right?"

"He's all right," Jack said. "He's not going to be any different because there's a young kidney inside him."

"Then why are we leaving? It feels like we're ditching the family when they need us the most."

"No." Jack looked both ways before he dragged her across the street. "Visiting hours are over, I promise."

"Then I need to head back to Fort Wylie. I have a lot to do."

"Great. Where are you parked?"

"Right here." Cricket stopped, looked up at him. "Are you all right?"

"I've never been better." Jack gestured at the car. "I think it's best if I drive you home."

"No," Cricket said. "I'm fully capable of driving myself. And you can drive your truck home to your ranch and do what your father asked of you."

"I'm going with you," Jack said.

"No," Cricket said, her tone as stubborn as his, "you're not dealing with your mother being here."

Jack shook his head. "What does that mean?"

"It means that you only want to marry me to get out of what you need to do. It's the big excuse, Jack."

"I'm going to be a father. I don't think there's anything disingenuous about marrying the mother of my children."

"Maybe not with anybody else, but with you, it is." Cricket looked at him. "Prove that you're not just running off with me like I'm your new rodeo gig."

"That's not fair," Jack protested. "And besides, how would I prove that I'm not avoiding something?"

"Tell me what your father said to you in his hospital room," Cricket said.

Jack's eyes hooded. "He said he felt fine."

"And?" Cricket was positive she was onto something because he was acting like a snake, coiled and waiting for danger to pass him by.

"I don't remember."

"I believe that," Cricket said. "And I believe that there'll be a lot of things you conveniently forget when we're married."

"You don't have a very high opinion of me," Jack said.

"On the contrary. I admire a man who constantly backs down."

His gaze narrowed. "No, you don't."

She raised her brows. "Tell me what happened in there, and don't tell me nothing did, because it was obvious by the way you flew out of there that something had."

Jack sighed. "This isn't going to work if you keep trying to read my mind."

She tapped a toe, waiting.

"Pop said," Jack told her reluctantly, "that he wanted me to hang around. He said he needed me here."

Cricket gasped. "And you're trying to hoodwink me into giving you a ride out of town! Shame on you, Jack Morgan! Your father said he needed you!"

"Yeah, but that's Pop," Jack tried to explain. "In the last year, he decided he needed all of us. He doesn't really *need* us. He's just—"

"A man who wants his family around," Cricket said. "Jack Morgan, how could you desert your father?" She stared at him. "It doesn't bode well for our future, that's plain to see."

"It has nothing to do with our future," Jack said, grabbing her and kissing her until Cricket thought her breath was going to give out. It was a wonderful kiss, a soul-stealing kiss, and Cricket very much wanted to fall in with his plans and let him hitch a ride in her Bug to Fort Wylie.

But she knew this was a pattern with Jack.

"That's what bodes well for our future," Jack told her. "I'm going to kiss you every day of your life, there's not going to be a day of our married life when I don't."

Cricket shook her head. "I'm not marrying you. You can't desert him in his darkest hour."

"Pop always has dark hours when he's trying to get what he wants!"

"We just can't do this while he's recuperating." Cricket got into her car, rolled down the driver's-side window. "You stay here and take care of family business. I'll be back in a few days to hang drapes."

He noted her change of subject and sighed. "Pop gave the ranch and land to Gisella. You probably better check with her about curtains and stuff."

Cricket nodded. "I will. It'll give us a chance to get to know each other, which will be a pleasure."

"I want you to get to know *me*," Jack said.

Cricket started the engine. "Marry in haste, regret at leisure," she told him. "Bye, Jack."

Jack stared after Cricket as she drove off in the little Volkswagen. She thought he wanted to be with her to get away from Pop. And his mother. His family, in general.

She was right.

He got in his truck and followed her.

Cricket was completely aware that Jack was following her down the highway. In a way, she hadn't expected anything less from him. Jack lived by his own rules. This time, however, he was going to have to bend, although she had to admit to a tingle of excitement that the man was so persistent in his pursuit of her. She had never been the object of a man's focus before, and the fact that the man was Jack would be enough to make her pulse pound with giddy pleasure under normal dating circumstances.

Yet they weren't dating. They were rushing down the road toward parenthood, which for Cricket took some of the romance and giddiness out of the equation.

By the time she got to her house in Fort Wylie, she'd figured out what she was going to say to him. *Go home, Jack, we need some time apart.*

"Hey," he said, pulling up next to her and getting out of his truck, "if you invite me in, I'll buy you the biggest diamond I can find in Fort Wylie."

Cricket shook her head. "I don't need a big diamond."

"For triplets, you do. I'd say you deserve a medal of honor."

She put her hands on her hips. "Jack Morgan, sweet-talking me isn't going to get you in my house. I need to be alone for a while."

"Why? I can be good company, sometimes."

"While that may be true, I suffer terribly from morning sickness. You do not want to be around for that."

"I'll watch TV. Don't worry about it." Jack grinned. "You think I've never seen a sickly woman before?"

"I'm not sickly!" Cricket frowned at him. "I'm pregnant. This phase will pass eventually, according to the doctor."

"Let me carry you over the threshold," Jack offered. "I need practice for carrying you over when we get married."

Cricket opened her front door and waved him in. "I don't want to be carried."

"You're not the most romantic girl," Jack told her as he scooped her up anyway and set her gently down in the foyer. "I'm a romantic guy, however."

"It can't all be your way," Cricket told him.

Jack sighed. "True, otherwise you'd be a lot easier to get along with. I never thought that the woman I asked to marry me would turn me down. It's a blow to my ego, I don't mind saying."

Cricket turned on a few lamps, filling the room with soft light. "Make yourself at home on the sofa in front of the TV, keeping your hands to yourself and your thoughts fairly pure."

"Wow," Jack said, "did that come out of the *How To Scare a Guy To Death* dating guide or something that deacons keep on hand for couple's counseling?"

Cricket sighed. "I'm going to change into something more comfortable."

"That sounds more promising." Jack sat on the sofa.

"If you think baggy kimono robes are promising, you may be in for a surprise. It's hardly Victoria's Secret."

"Next time," Jack said. "Anyway, I could romance you if you were wearing a paper bag. As a matter of fact, I'd find that really sexy."

Cricket shook her head and slipped into her bedroom to change. All the talk of marriage was making her nervous. "Was your father in a lot of pain?" she called to him from the bedroom.

"No, he's just a pain," Jack said. "It'll take more than surgery to slow him down."

Cricket wrapped the silky kimono robe around her, found some cozy slippers—not the high-heeled mules a woman who had a hot cowboy in her living room might prefer—and put her hair up in a ponytail. She walked back into the living room, finding Jack lounging on the sofa, staring at the ceiling. "Cowboy, what are you doing?"

"Thinking about how strange life is. Did you ever think when we met that we'd end up together?"

"Absolutely not. You weren't in my car twenty seconds and I knew you were bad news." She went into the kitchen, fishing around for some tea and crackers. "You should have stayed with your father," she said as Jack followed her into the kitchen.

"I should be with you," Jack said. "You're having my children. My father is merely having fun planning my future."

"Was he?"

"He never takes a break from plotting." Jack ran a hand through his hair and seated himself on a kitchen bar stool. "I need to meet your parents, you know. I'm very behind in my duties as a father."

"Oh," Cricket said, "I guess."

"Hey," he said, "I'm going to get my feelings hurt if I continue perceiving a decided lack of enthusiasm on your part toward my courtship."

"I'm sorry." She set a glass of tea on the counter that separated them. "I've got motherhood on the mind, not matrimony."

Jack drank some of the tea. "If you were counseling us as a deacon, what would your advice be?"

She looked at him. *I'd want to say, "Girlfriend, you better hang on to that sexy cowboy with all your might."* "I'd advise that rushing into things is a bad idea when two people don't know each other very well."

He shook his head. "Terrible advice."

"What would you say?"

He hopped over the counter, landing in front of her, and took her in his arms. "I'd say get me in bed as often as you possibly can, you lucky woman. Life's too short to miss out on the good stuff, and I am definitely good stuff."

Chapter 11

Cricket awakened the next morning with a deliciously warm, strong cowboy wrapped around her. Jack's arm was tucked around her waist, keeping her tightly against him. She could feel muscles, hairy legs, a strong chest up against her, and then something moving in the bed, jutting up against her backside insistently.

"Good morning," Jack said, and Cricket hopped out of bed with a gasp, running for the bathroom.

"Was it something I said?" he called after her.

Cricket slammed the bathroom door, locking it before getting into the familiar position she assumed every morning. She would have been humiliated, but she was too sick to care.

Ten minutes later, she dragged herself out of the shower and slipped back between the sheets. Jack placed a ginger ale beside her bed, along with a rose. "Where did you get all that?" she asked, reaching gratefully for the ginger ale.

"I moseyed over to the store while you were showering," he said tactfully. "I remember Mom giving us ginger ale when we had upset stomachs."

She studied him as he lounged on her bed with a newspaper, completely unconcerned about her performance in the bathroom. She'd probably been making horrible noises in there, and he didn't seem to care. Some of the awkwardness she felt about being pregnant slipped away from her. "I'd offer you breakfast—"

"Don't even think about it." Jack waved a hand at her. "I grabbed a doughnut while I was out."

"Ew," Cricket said. "If I was in a different place in my life, I'd make you an omelette."

"If you were at a different place in your life, I hope you'd offer me seconds of what I had last night." Jack grinned at her. "You're a lusty woman, Deacon, a very positive side of you that I never would have anticipated."

She blushed. "Lusty may be too strong a word."

"Enthusiastic, then." Jack put away the newspaper.

"I have to go," Cricket said.

"Where?"

"I have things to do."

He stared at her, waiting for more information. She sighed. "I have a doctor's appointment this morning. Then I plan on driving back out to visit your father."

"You can't keep doing that," Jack said. "You need to rest my children."

"They like the busy schedule. And soon enough I won't have that much time to visit Josiah, anyway. The doctor says I'll be confined to lying around in the not-too-distant future."

Jack thought about that. "Cricket," he said, "we need to pick a home. This dual-town thing is going to get old quickly. We need to be settled for the sake of the children."

She waved her hand at him. "I mustn't be late. Let me show you the door."

"Okay," he said. But he waited until she was ready to leave herself, then followed her to her car.

"No," she said, "you are not coming with me."

"I need to start learning about this pregnancy stuff. It'll be good for me to ask the doctor some questions."

Cricket shook her head. "Jack, I don't need any help just yet, thank you. Your father is the one who needs your help."

It was obvious he didn't like that answer, but neither could he argue with the truth. "At least let me wait outside, and then drive you to Union Junction," Jack said.

"No," she said firmly. "Jack, go your own way like you always have."

It felt mean to leave him standing there, because he was so convinced he was trying to do the right thing by her. She didn't want the "right" thing—she wanted something else from him, though she hadn't quite figured out what that was. The man had a lot on his plate right now, and she was pretty certain he was using her pregnancy as an excuse to get out of facing family matters at home.

"Cricket!" he called after her. "You're the most sexy, beautiful woman I've ever had the pleasure of arguing with!"

Cricket watched Jack through her rearview mirror. The man had made love to her last night so gently, so sweetly, that she knew she'd never be able to keep him out of her bed if he wanted in it, which was quite the dilemma for a woman who knew she had no business loving a man who possessed a wild heart.

Twenty seconds later, Jack turned, shocked that Cricket was pulling alongside him as he walked to his truck. He looked at her in her little Bug, wondering if she'd ever let him buy her a truck. There was no way she was going to be able to haul all the children he intended to have in that tiny, bubble-shaped vehicle. She didn't know it, but she was a big truck girl.

"Hey," she said.

"Hey, you," he replied.

"If you really want to come to the doctor with me, I guess that will be all right."

He grinned. "Couldn't live without me for a second, huh?"

Jogging around the vehicle, he hopped in. "I knew you'd find me irresistible."

She drove off. "Fathers should participate."

"Glad you came to that conclusion." He really was.

"And on that topic," she continued, and he waited for the real reason she'd come back to pick him up, "it sort of comes to me that I might not like rodeo any better than your father does."

"That's not true," Jack said. "I met you at a rodeo. You must have some fondness for it."

"I met you when I picked you up hitchhiking," Cricket reminded him, "something I hope you're giving up."

"You're so cute when you're possessive," he teased.

"Let's not digress," she said, and he sighed.

"I don't see myself giving up riding," he admitted. Yet he sensed this was a test, a crossroads that Cricket might hold against him. He'd have to tread very lightly.

"This is why I always recommend couples counseling," Cricket said. "It's important to discover differences between people that can put stress on their marriage later."

"Sometimes people just look for differences," he said. "This is one of those times."

"No, really," Cricket said. "I don't imagine raising three children is going to be any easier than what Priscilla and Pete are going through right now with their four."

"This isn't a romantic topic," Jack said. "Let's talk about how much fun last night was."

"Jack!" Cricket exclaimed, beginning to see a chink in the sexy cowboy's armor she wasn't certain she particularly liked. "This is a serious topic to me."

"Me, too. Rodeo is part of who I am. I can take a sabbatical for a few months, if you want, but—"

"And I might never stand at an altar with you," Cricket said stubbornly. "If my husband is going to be footloose and fancy free, I'd be better off learning to cope by myself."

He cheered up. "That might make you better off in Union Junction where you'd have plenty of help."

"I have parents and a brother here," she reminded him.

"That's right. I need to swing by and introduce myself to them."

"Not yet," Cricket said. "I'll let you know when I'm ready."

He didn't like the sound of that. "Cricket, while you claim that I'm the footloose one, you're awfully hard to tie down for a woman. You're supposed to jump at the chance to be a Mrs. All women do."

She winced. "Jack, sometimes you sound remarkably like your father."

"I'll take that as a compliment. Now," Jack said, "I can make you a solemn vow that I'll be very, very careful when I ride."

"Did I ever tell you that one of my favorite sports is parachuting?" Cricket asked.

"I doubt that," Jack said. "You're more a feet-on-the-ground kind of girl." How cute of her to try to rattle his cage.

"I'm most serious."

"Cricket, you don't have to try to show me how you feel. I understand that Pop has probably scared you silly about rodeo. But I assure you that the stories you hear about cowboys getting hurt, and cowboys getting nursed back to health by beautiful, sexy, willing women, are just legends we spin to each other."

She turned to stare at him. "Jack Morgan!"

He laughed. "Just kidding."

She shook her head. "I'm not."

"I know." He sighed. "Let's chalk this up as a loaded topic in our marriage."

"No," Cricket said. "I'm not kidding about parachuting. My brother is a professional parachutist. I've jumped ten times."

Something lurched inside Jack. Maybe she wasn't bluffing. Did preacher women fib like other women sometimes did, tell little white lies to get their way? He wasn't certain if he should try to call her bluff or not. She had a look in her eyes that made him wary—something that looked like calm truthfulness. He'd met a lot of fibbers in his life, and he was pretty certain Cricket wasn't bluffing. Could he have the bad fortune to fall for the one woman who liked jumping out of planes but wouldn't jump at a wedding ring? "Does Pop know this?"

"No."

"Does anyone know this about you?"

"Priscilla does."

"Well, it has to stop," Jack said, "if you're being one hundred percent honest. I don't need to be married to a parachuting preacher."

Cricket laughed. "That's what Priscilla calls me. I was a deacon, Jack, not a preacher. It's different."

He frowned. "Not to me. It means I'd be the one praying, and waiting for you to splat on the ground. Let's have no more of that silly talk."

She stopped the car in front of the doctor's office and got out. He followed, realizing she hadn't said she would obey his wishes. "Cricket, if you're pulling my leg, I don't like it."

"Okay," she said airily, and went inside the doctor's office to check herself in.

He felt himself getting a bit hot under the proverbial collar. "I'm sure your parents would never allow their only daughter to do such a thing."

"Daughter and son," Cricket said. "And we all jump together, rodeo man."

"This does not bode well for family gatherings."

"Parachuting is a lot safer than rodeo, I'll bet." Nodding to everyone in the waiting room, Cricket sat down and picked up a magazine. He glanced around at all the other pregnant women, realizing with some discomfort that he looked a lot like the other husbands in attendance. *We all look as if we'd rather be in a bar drinking a beer,* Jack thought wildly. *But I bet none of their wives jump out of planes!*

That was the problem—Cricket wasn't his wife yet, so she

didn't have to obey him. He tried to reassure himself that getting married would change things. Plus, surely being a mother would give her the perspective that she needed to be safe for the sake of his children. "I'd just like to say that parachuting is from several thousand feet up," Jack said, staying on his point, "and riding a bull only takes you about eight feet off the ground, approximately."

"It's still probably safer," Cricket said serenely, apparently determined to ignore his good advice.

Jack thought the conversation had gotten way out of control. He was not happy with his pregnant fiancée at the moment. She was trying to be the one who wore the pants in their marriage, and he needed to make certain she knew right here and now that he wasn't going to put up with that. "Do any of your wives parachute?" he asked the men in the room.

Five of six masculine hands went up. Jack's jaw sagged. "Why?" he asked.

"It's fun," one of the wives told him. "Hello, Deacon Cricket," she said. "Is this the hot cowboy you've told us so much about?"

Hot cowboy? Did Cricket really think he was hot? He sneaked a peek at her to get her reaction, noting Cricket's blush. He practically puffed out his chest, recognizing guilt written all over the pretty deacon's face.

"This is Jack Morgan of Union Junction," Cricket said, ignoring the "hot cowboy" comment. "He's having a wee chicken moment about jumping."

"Oh, Mr. Morgan," another wife said, "we have quite the parachuting club in Fort Wylie. There's a small airport here. It's great fun. You'll be ever so proud when Cricket starts taking your little ones out for their first jumps."

Jack felt strange wind whirring around his ears and the next time thing he knew, he was staring up into the face of a worried nurse. Cricket was peering down at him, as well. Considering he was flat on his back, he didn't feel very soothed. "I'm afraid of heights. Nothing higher than the back of a bull for me," he told the nurse, and she nodded.

"It's okay," she said. "You'll get over that fear the first time you jump, Mr. Morgan."

Chapter 12

Jack wasn't feeling any better by the time Cricket went in for her appointment. The physician seemed competent, but he had a hundred questions and felt silly asking everything he felt he needed to know. So he abstained, assigning himself the role of interested listener.

"I assume it's still okay to have sexual relations?" Cricket asked, and Jack perked up. This was a question to which he very much wanted to hear a positive response.

"As long as you feel like it," Dr. Suzanne said, music to Jack's grateful ears. "At least to a certain point," the doctor qualified. She measured Cricket's stomach, the same tummy that Jack had taken his time kissing last night. He noted that it was a very shapely tummy, almost enough to give him sexual thoughts he didn't need to have at the moment. He shifted in his chair, and the doctor smiled at him.

"Don't worry," she told him, "a lot of fathers have fears about hurting their partners during intercourse. And some worry that the baby will grab them," she said, laughing. "So please feel free to ask any questions you want to, Mr. Morgan."

Grab him? He blinked. What a horrible thing to say to a man! It was almost guaranteed to make a man anxious about things that weren't worth worrying about. "I don't have any questions," he said firmly.

She looked at Cricket. "Are you tired?"

"Just a little."

"Taking your prenatal vitamins?"

Cricket nodded. He made a mental note to make certain she was getting enough rest and taking her vitamins.

"Still nauseated?"

"It's getting better," Cricket said. "I think."

The doctor smiled. "Good." She rubbed some clear stuff on Cricket's stomach and touched a wand there. "Mr. Morgan, say hello to your children."

Like magic, he saw waves and curves on the screen. He saw a lot of black and white but nothing that looked as much like babies. Still, he fancied he could see something. "Are there really three?"

"It's quite a jumble in there," the doctor explained. "But they seem content for the moment."

"Can you tell how big they are? Can you estimate how long I have before I'll need full bed rest?" Cricket asked.

"Considering your size, I don't expect you to go past October, Maybe November. We'll do what we can to keep them inside you and growing healthfully as long as possible."

Jack blinked. October! That didn't give him a lot of time to get Cricket to the altar. He needed to get his father out of the hospital and on his feet. Laura was due with her baby any day. He swallowed, realizing that if he was going to convince Cricket to marry him, he needed to do it quickly, because she wasn't likely to feel the same need after the babies were born. He'd seen the slight embarrassment on her face in the waiting room; he'd known what she was thinking: *Here sits Deacon Cricket, local good girl gone bad.*

Those were *his* babies in her belly—he had to help her see the urgency of the matter. There was a lot that needed to be settled between them. The whole parachuting thing had thrown him. Frankly, he and Cricket needed to start developing a relationship where he would have some say in her life. If they weren't married, Cricket might begrudgingly label him a friend and nothing more.

"You're very quiet over there, Mr. Morgan," the doctor said, and Jack swallowed. Cricket looked at him with big brown eyes.

He needed to say something appropriate to the moment. But he was so lost.

"I'm gonna be a dad," he said slowly, wondering if he'd be any better at it than his father.

Could he be?

"Cricket, I need to meet your parents. And your brother. Soon, like today."

"Don't you think you should go home and see your father? He's recuperating from major surgery."

"Pop's got an army of people taking care of him. He'll appreciate my desire to introduce myself to your family."

"They're still digesting the fact of my pregnancy," she said. "I was slow to confess my situation." Truthfully she hadn't confessed it at all—yet. In fact, she was still deciding how to best tell them. She didn't have a lot of time before the Fort Wylie grapevine got to them, but still, Cricket didn't want Jack to know she was reluctant to disappoint her parents.

"I'd really like to meet them," he said, and Cricket sighed.

"I should warn you that they may not welcome you with open arms."

"I suppose that's fair," he said. "They looked forward to better for their daughter?" He wanted to know what he was in for, felt some determination to make things right in his life, at least do a better job with her family than he'd done with his own. "Did they feel that you'd been swept off your feet by a man who had no potential and no intention of settling down?"

"Well, I wouldn't—"

"Then they were right." Jack took her keys, opened the passenger-side door for her. "No more driving for you, Deacon. It's rest from now on. I don't want you lifting your littlest finger. I will take care of everything, just like Dr. Suzanne said."

"Jack!" Cricket hung back, refusing to sit down. "The doctor didn't say I was on bed rest yet."

"*I* say you're on bed rest. I intend to carry you and my babies around on a pillow."

"No," Cricket said stubbornly. "I don't want that. I'm used to being independent."

"Me, too," Jack said, "but I'm changing."

"No, you're not. You're exactly the same person who jumped into my car in January. You're avoiding your own family by focusing on me and mine."

"You need me more than they do," he pointed out. "Call your parents and ask them if they feel like meeting your Prince Charming."

Cricket shook her head. "Prince Charmings aren't supposed to be so bossy. And can you let the clutch out gently? This is a vintage Bug and I intend to keep it forever."

He looked at the floorboard and then the long stick shift. "Cricket," he said, "I hate this car."

She smiled and shrugged. "You don't like a lot about me, cowboy."

"No, I'm serious. This isn't a car, it's a tin can. I feel like I'm in the Flintstonemobile."

She looked at him, one eyebrow raised knowingly. "Can't drive a stick?"

No man liked to be caught looking inadequate, especially when he was applying for the role of chief protector in his lady's life. "Only in an emergency, and only if the vehicle isn't ancient. Where did you get this 'vintage' car?"

"My father won it years ago in a raffle." She gave him an airy glance. "My brother, Thad, keeps my car running for me. I can teach you how to drive it."

He wasn't sure he wanted to be taught anything by a woman who was pregnant with his triplets. Shouldn't he be taking care of her? "I'm going to buy you a minivan. That will solve everything. Where's the nearest dealership?"

He meant it. Today he was going to buy her the safest, biggest minivan on the market, complete with OnStar in case she got lost between here and Union Junction.

Cricket's lips pinched. Her pretty, brown eyes narrowed. With some trepidation, Jack recognized a storm brewing. "Is there a problem, little mama?"

"Yes," she said. "You. Get out of my car, you stubborn ape."

Cricket left Jack standing on the pavement in front of the doctor's office. The man could just find his own way home. He had plenty to deal with in his own house—he could just quit worrying about her. "My children, my car, my family," she muttered, motoring away from the cowboy. "My hobbies, my business, my pregnancy."

That was the problem. He wanted to worry about everything about her—he wanted to take over her life.

She liked her life just the way it was, thank you.

He said she was stubborn.

What she was was a shade dishonest.

She hadn't told her parents about the babies, and she hadn't mentioned she'd quit her job. In short, she couldn't take Jack home to her parents. Ultimately, she was worse about dealing with family matters than he was.

All the time she'd been trying to get him to tend to Josiah, she'd really been avoiding him getting to know her own family. "Where's an unmarried and pregnant gal's fairy godmother when she needs one?" she asked, and decided it was time to face life without one.

Cricket pressed in the numbers on the electronic keypad, and drove through when the massive wrought-iron gates parted. She rang the doorbell, her heartbeat suddenly racing. This visit was long past due.

"Cricket," her mother said, "how nice to see you."

"Hello, Mother."

She stepped into the highly polished marble foyer, waiting for her father to appear.

"Reed, Cricket's come to pay us a visit."

"Excellent, Eileen," her father said. "Cricket, dear, we've been expecting you."

Of course they were. By now they'd probably had fifty phone calls updating them on her downfall. Cricket sighed. "I've been trying to work things out on my own."

"I suspected as much," her mother said. "We wish you didn't have such an independent streak, dear. Your father and I hate standing on the sidelines when we wish we could help you."

Cricket followed her parents into the palatial living room, taking a seat near the huge bay window. "Everyone wants to help me," she said. "I feel a great need to stand on my own two feet."

Eileen blinked. "We know. That's why we didn't call."

Cricket glanced around. "Where's Thad?"

"Your brother is playing polo at the club. He told us you resigned from the church." Eileen looked sorry about that. "Cricket, dear, we know that working in the church was your dream."

"I've had a lot of dreams that haven't worked out," Cricket said. "I seem to be a bit unfocused these days."

"Well," Reed said, "entrepreneurs don't always hit the right note the first time out."

"That's the problem," Cricket said. "I'm not an entrepreneur. I was a deacon. But then, I fell for an inappropriate man, a man I knew wasn't right for me, who is the furthest thing from stable that he could ever be. The only thing I ever did that was stable was the Lord's work," Cricket said. "And now I'm pregnant and unmarried. How's that for not exactly practicing what I preach?"

"Oh, dear," Eileen said. "Reed, did Cricket just say we're going to be grandparents?" She fanned herself, looking faint.

Reed patted his wife's hand. "We hadn't heard *that* piece of news, Cricket." He looked as if he didn't know what to say.

"I just told the father and his family yesterday." Cricket felt small and selfish for visiting this shock on her parents. "I've really made a mess of things."

"Now, listen," her mother said, sitting up and accepting a glass of whiskey from her husband, "babies are not messy."

"No, but the parents are. At least these babies' parents are."

"Babies?" Eileen repeated, her voice very faint.

Cricket nodded. "I'm having triplets."

Eileen and Reed stared at their only daughter, their faces frozen.

"My goodness," Eileen said after a moment, "your cowboy must be in shock."

"I'll say," Reed said. "Three children and a wife will certainly cut into his winnings."

Cricket's mind was made up for her with that comment. "I'm not about to be a burden."

"What do you mean?" Eileen asked.

"I'm going to raise these children on my own." Cricket nodded, feeling all the pressure fall away from her. "Single motherhood, the most independent thing a woman can do."

"I'll say," her father said. "Ever changed a diaper?"

"Some," Cricket said, but now that she'd made her decision, she knew she was right. With the power of prayer and maybe a dozen child-rearing books, she could give being a mother her very best effort.

Independence was the only reason she hadn't accepted Jack's offer of marriage. Otherwise she'd always wonder if that footloose cowboy had proposed because he'd had to; she'd always wonder if she'd said yes because she was too afraid of standing on her own two feet when faced with three pairs of tiny eyes trusting her to do everything right.

Chapter 13

Jack wanted to stay in Fort Wylie and wait for Cricket to return—he was hanging out in his truck parked at her house/tea shop—but the call he got from Pete changed his mind.

"Laura's gone into labor," Pete said.

"I'll be right there."

It didn't feel right leaving Cricket, even though she'd been annoyed with him when she'd driven off. Petty annoyances passed, didn't they? Hopefully she wasn't the kind of girl who stayed mad. The only way he knew to work the kink out of an angry female was by making love to her, whispering soft apologies. Cricket didn't strike him as the kind of woman who'd settle for that.

But he could hope.

He scribbled a note and left it on her door so she'd know Laura and Gabe's baby was on the way.

By the time he got to Union Junction and the hospital, the baby had been born. "Go on in and see her," Dane told him with a grin. "Gabe's got him a cute little girl."

"A girl?" A girl to go with Penny and Perrin.

"Perrin'll be caught between two girls," Gabe said.

"That could be a good thing or a bad thing," Jack replied.

Gabe laughed. "Only time will tell."

Jack had grabbed some flowers and a pink giraffe in the hospital's gift shop. He walked into Laura's room holding the flowers aloft like an awkward prize. "How's the new mother?" he asked, handing the flowers to Laura as he gave her a kiss on the cheek and Gabe a slap on the back.

"Fine." Laura looked tired but happy. "This is Gabriella Michele. Gabriella, meet your uncle Jack."

Jack glanced at the baby with some fear, not daring to touch her. She seemed so tiny and peaceful snuggling in the crook of her mother's arm. "She's beautiful."

Laura smiled. "Gabe and I are hoping you'll be her godfather."

Jack glanced up, stunned. "Godfather?" His only recollection of a godfather was from the movies. What was expected of a real-life godfather?

Gabe laughed. "Yes. Laura and I decided it was time to tie you into the family."

Jack glanced again at the small, pink-wrapped bundle. "Are you sure?"

"Yes. Godfather Jack," Laura said, teasing. "You'll be the best. And it will give you practice."

He looked up at his brother and his wife. "I'll need lots of it."

Gabe laughed. "You'll get up to speed on babies very quickly."

Jack shook his head. "Life's moving very quickly on me, almost conspiracy-like."

"Have you told Pop about the triplets?" Gabe asked.

"I haven't even seen him. I came right here."

Laura smiled. "I think he wants to talk to you."

Jack felt guilty he hadn't hung around to see his father come out of surgery. "How's he doing?"

"Really, really well," Laura said. "But he's been asking for you. Bellowing for you, actually."

"Guess I'll step around to see him." Jack didn't feel particularly excited at the thought, but he also knew he couldn't put it off any longer.

"Are you going to do it?" Gabe asked curiously.

Jack knew exactly what his brother was asking. "What, move to the ranch?"

Gabe shrugged. "Just a warning, Pop's sure he's been warned by spirits that you have no intention of moving to the ranch because Mom's there."

Well, that was certainly odd. But Gabe could have no idea how correct Pop's "spirits" were. The old man was eerily prescient. "Hey, let me just celebrate being Godfather Jack for now, okay?"

"And Papa Jack," Laura said.

"That, too. Later on I'll worry about being Good Son Jack."

"And Millionaire Jack," Gabe reminded him. "The only way to the grail is through Mom this time."

"Yeah, well, who needs money, anyway?" Jack asked, and Gabe and Laura laughed.

"A man who's having triplets," Gabe called after him. "College educations and weddings are expensive."

Jack headed down the hall. "Hey, Pop," he said, entering his father's room.

Suzy and Dane were keeping Josiah company, but they got up and quietly exited when Jack walked in. "He's been asking for you," Dane said as he walked by.

Pop's eyes opened. "Jack?"

"Yeah, Pop. It's me. How are you feeling?"

"Probably the best I can feel after Dr. Moneybags has poked around inside me." He glanced up. "Where the hell did you go?"

Jack sat down next to his father. "I had to go see Cricket."

"Why isn't she here?" Josiah demanded.

"She had some things to do back in Fort Wylie." Jack patted his father's arm. "She's going to be busy now that's she's having triplets."

"Triplets?" Josiah's eyebrows raised. "Whoa," he said, "you knocked that ball out of the park, son!"

Jack shook his head. "When do you get out of here?"

"I don't know." Pop glanced around him weakly. "But when I do, I'm marrying Sara."

"Good for you." Jack was genuinely glad for his father.

"Let's make it a double," Pop suggested.

"My lady won't have me. Yet." Jack leaned back in the chair. "She's got a lot on her mind."

"Hmm." Josiah grinned. *"Triplets.* They'll sure keep you busy. Better get Cricket convinced to marry you before they're born, because she'll think of a hundred excuses afterward not to do it. She's still got pregnancy weight and won't look good in a wedding gown, that's one excuse. Or she'll say that she can't leave the children to go on a honeymoon. Or if you wait just a few years, the kids can be in the wedding." Pop looked at him. "Believe me, if the babies come before the ring, you're in for what is known as a prolonged engagement."

Jack's throat went dry. Pop's words seemed like good advice. "It does sound like something Cricket would do," he said slowly, realizing that if she was reluctant now, she wasn't going to become any more eager. "She's not the most conventional woman."

Josiah chuckled. "You wouldn't have wanted a conventional woman."

"I suppose not," Jack said, uncertain. He would have at least liked the woman he chose to be more excited about being his wife. "Hey, congratulations, Pop, on finding a good woman."

"I found two good women," Josiah said, "and I don't intend to make the same mistakes with the second one that I made with the first. Fortunately for me, the first one has forgiven me. Which reminds me, when are you going to do some forgiving of your own?"

Jack winced. "I've forgiven you, Pop."

"I don't need your forgiveness!" Josiah stated. "I meant your mother!"

Jack shrugged. "I'm not sure what to forgive."

"Well, you better figure it out," Pop said, "because as far as I can tell, you've got three babies on the way and a woman who doesn't want to marry you—two strikes against you—and you don't seem to have moved your things to the ranch." Josiah sniffed. "If I were a betting man—and I am—I'd bet your million dollars is going to stay safely in my wallet."

Jack wondered how much more a man had to be willing to give of himself besides a kidney to get a little peace. But with Josiah Morgan, Jack knew peace was a long way off.

Jack had a weighty decision to make. He was a godfather now, and that gave him a new look into the life of a man responsible for a child. He wanted to be a good godfather and a good parent, and the one thing that was staring him in the face was his lifestyle and lack of a secure income.

As his brothers were quick to point out, babies were expensive.

He knew Cricket well enough to know that she was going to try to raise three children and run the tea shop to pay her bills. Maybe she'd meant to purchase the tea shop and have someone else run it as an investment, but he doubted that. Cricket was an independent woman; she'd want to be involved in everything. She said she'd quit her job because of her unwed-and-pregnant status, but the ladies in the waiting room of Dr. Suzanne's office hadn't seemed cool to her at all. In fact, they'd seemed quite warm and friendly. He wondered if Cricket had made a decision she'd regret by resigning from her deacon's position, then decided it was none of his business for the moment.

What he had to decide was how he intended to convince her that he had the ability to take care of her.

The easiest way to financial stability was to do as Pop asked, blast him, which was exactly what had hung up his brothers.

However, they hadn't wanted to get married—not at first—and he did, pronto.

It was a weird thought. He was begging to be a family man, and he couldn't get his lady to have him.

His cell phone rang, and to his surprise he saw it was Cricket. His heartbeat sped up. "Hello?"

"Jack, it's Cricket."

"How are you?"

"I'm fine. Listen," she said, "I apologize for ditching you this morning."

"I know you've got a lot on your mind. I shouldn't have teased you about your car." He mentally slapped himself, thinking it was a subject best left alone, like the parachuting. She'd come to her senses about jumping out of high-flying vehicles when the babies were born. Three small infants would settle her down.

"Jack," Cricket said, "I just want you to know that I think it's best if we don't see each other for a while."

His heart crashed. "Why?"

"I… I'm just not comfortable," she explained. "I need to figure some things out on my own. When you're around, I catch myself falling into a pattern of convenience."

He frowned. "What the hell is a pattern of convenience?"

"Something I don't want. When you're around, you take over. And I seem to let you."

"Yeah, well," Jack said, not sure that he agreed that she let him do anything, "I think you should just marry me and be an independent wife."

"Jack, I can't marry you. It would be a mistake. The fundamental differences in our lifestyles would eventually catch up with us."

She meant rodeo. She envisioned herself as a rodeo widow. He shook his head. If that's what this all came down to, he supposed he'd have to concede the point. "I've got to make a living."

"I understand."

He didn't think she did, especially when he couldn't say,

"Hey, let's compromise, no rodeo for me, no parachuting for you," because he knew very well she'd blast his ears for trying to tie her down. It stunk being the one who was trying to do the tying down. "Cricket," he said, "I'm trying really hard to change."

"I don't want you to change," Cricket said. "I think things that are wild should be left to the wild."

"Well, I'm getting tamer all the time, Deacon. I'm a godfather now."

"To Laura's baby? Did she have her baby?"

"Yes. A healthy baby girl named Gabriella Michele. And I'm pretty darn excited about being a god-pop."

"That's great, Jack."

She didn't sound like she much cared. "Hey, Pop was asking about you."

"I hope he's doing well," she said quickly. "Will you please tell him I won't be able to do those drapes like I promised? I'm sure your mother would probably prefer to select her own, anyway."

Curtains were just the cover for what she was really trying to say. He sensed her slipping away from him. He knew the sound of someone escaping—he'd done it often enough to know. "Cricket—"

"I have to go, Jack," she said, and he heard the inevitable *thanks for the memories* in her voice.

"Cricket, dammit," he began, but the phone went dead. "That conversation went nowhere," he muttered. Didn't she care that she was shredding his heart? He wanted to be with her—he was darn sure they belonged together!

She didn't think so. And she was holding all the aces.

He had no choice but to try to convince that stubborn woman he was serious about being a family man.

His phone buzzed, alerting him that he had a text.

Just heard that you're expecting some ankle-biters, he read. Congratulations, you ol' dog.

He snorted at the words from a good rodeo buddy.

Another buzz.

Three children for the man who always said he'd never be a father? Way to ride!

Jack sighed. It was true—he'd certainly won the prize for fastest ride to fatherhood.

The texts kept rolling in. His spirits sank a bit as he received blessings and well wishes from his rodeo family. His worlds were colliding, shifting.

Which was exactly what he knew was bugging Cricket—she didn't want to change him. She didn't want to be responsible for him having to change.

Change was going to happen to both of them eventually. On whose terms, he wasn't certain.

For now, he turned his truck toward the Morgan ranch.

Chapter 14

Jack walked inside the house on the Morgan ranch, stunned to find his mother in the kitchen making cookies. He cleared his throat. "Hi."

She turned, smiling when she saw him. *"Bonjour!"*

He was uncomfortable with finding her in the house, much more than he'd thought he'd be.

"Moving in?" Gisella asked.

"I guess so."

She began rolling dough. "I'm glad you're here. Your father needs to lose his bet."

He blinked. Was that a friendly comment, or was she being antagonistic toward Josiah? "Why do you say that?"

She shrugged. "He wants to. He likes to think he's moving all of us around. Josiah is a stubborn man."

He sat at the kitchen table, deciding that maybe it was time they had this conversation. "What's in it for you?"

"Me?" She glanced at him. "My kids." She bobbed her head up and down. "And I'll have to admit, I've long wanted a second chance with Josiah."

Jack frowned. "He's planning to marry Sara, you know."

"Oh, I didn't mean that kind of second chance. I like Sara. I'm glad they're getting married!" She washed her hands as she finished placing dough balls on the cookie sheet. "But I never felt good about leaving Josiah the way I did. So I jumped at the chance to come back on different terms than we had before."

He was starting to get the picture. "You want redemption."

"Of course I do. Don't you?" She looked at him curiously.

He didn't know if he could forgive this stranger standing in the kitchen enough to forget all the years he'd wondered why she left. "I'm sure I do," he said carefully, knowing he was in much the same position as his mother, "but it goes both ways."

"I can do no more than hope for reconciliation. I can't change the past."

He didn't say anything, his silence an acknowledgment of her hopes. She was being very brave about returning home to a family she didn't know, and he realized he couldn't quite say the same about himself.

"I'm going to make the guesthouse my home," she said. "You'll be able to live here, if you want to."

"You don't have to do that," he said quickly. "In fact, Cricket's leaving the draperies and doodads to you. This is your home."

She shook her head. "The guesthouse is more space than I need. You, on the other hand, have a growing family. Unless you're planning on living in Fort Wylie."

"I don't know what I'm planning." Would Cricket move into this house with him when she had the babies? He didn't think she'd want to leave her mother, father, brother. Her tea shop. Her friends. He'd move there in a snap, but he didn't think Cricket would welcome that. Hadn't she just told him to shove off, in so many words? "I'm not planning anything," he said, "because the mother of my children seems to think she should raise our children on her own."

Gisella looked at him curiously. "I doubt she intends to keep you from your children."

"No, but she doesn't intend for me to live under a roof with her, either." Why was he telling his mother this? He hadn't planned to. It felt strange, out of place. And yet somehow comforting.

"It's a difficult thing you're both trying to do." Gisella put some baked cookies onto a plate, then took some flour out of the cupboard. "Let me make you a crepe."

"A crepe?" Was that the French version of comfort food? "You don't have to do that," he said, stiffening against the idea of her trying to mother him. The time for that was long past. "Thanks, though."

"A little powdered sugar," she murmured, looking around in the cupboard. "Simple food, you know. When you were a boy, you loved my crepes."

He frowned. "I don't remember."

"Of course you do not. It was a very long time ago. Still, I remember."

He suddenly realized how hard it had been on his mother to live with the memories of them growing up. She alone had held her memories, knowing that her children would not remember her, not much about her, anyway. He remembered some vague things, a flash of memory here, a sliver of laughter there.

"Look," she said with delight, "my old crepe pan!"

She held up a small copper pan, her face joyful. It wasn't gleaming—he doubted anyone had polished—or used it—in years. A slight smile twisted his lips. He watched her look at the pan with delight, as if she remembered all the times she'd used it fondly, and sudden bittersweet nostalgia overwhelmed him. He had loved his mother. He had missed her fiercely.

He got up and enveloped her in his arms, giving her the embrace he should have given her when she'd returned. "I've missed you," he said suddenly against the ache, and she laid her head against his chest for just a moment.

"When I left, I was taller than you," she said. "You were a little boy, only eight years old. Now you are so much taller than me."

"It's all right," he said, feeling her pained sadness in her thin shoulders, even the bones in her back, as she seemed resigned to the dark-shadowed memories. "You're home now."

"But I'm not forgiven," she murmured.

He said, "You are by me, Mother," and then he held her as she wept the same tears he knew he would one day if he wasn't there every moment for his babies' tears, their laughter, their falls and their eventual flights from his own nest.

Settling at the ranch was part of the bargain, and now that Jack had chosen his course, he was determined to do it well. He moved into the main house as his mother had suggested, then arranged a meeting with his brothers to discuss the best options for making a living.

"I don't have a whole lot of time," he said to Dane, Pete and Gabe as they all sat in the den of the home Josiah had envisioned as the place where the brothers would one day forge familial bonds. It hadn't happened, not the way their father had hoped, anyway, and yet still Jack felt closer to his brothers than he had in years.

"Hell, you'll think you have no time once those babies of yours are born," Pete told him. "You're still a bachelor right now with time to spare. We're the ones with no time."

"Sorry," Jack said gruffly, handing out beers. "I didn't mean my time was short today. I meant that Cricket's going to give birth, and I need to make some viable plans for the old bank account."

Dane grinned. "It's kind of funny to hear you talking like a family man."

Jack grunted. "Laugh all you like. The gods are laughing, too. But I still need to figure out my finances. I didn't know if you guys were interested in doing anything around here."

"Gisella owns the place now," Gabe reminded him.

Jack nodded. "She gave us the free and clear to make the property our own. She said she'd like to see it become a useful and lively place. Apparently, her parents baked pies and grew vines for homemade wine, so she believes land should stay busy and productive."

Pete looked at him. "We never met our grandparents. Are they still alive?"

"I don't know." Nobody knew much about Gisella's family. "Guess you could ask her. And I suppose one day we should open up Pandora's box and read the letters she sent us over the years." Jack frowned. "Not that I'm eager, but I sort of feel like we owe it to her."

He felt a little sadder than he expected to over his father's confession about the letters. All the years he'd believed his mother hadn't cared enough to write, cared enough to remember them…him.

"I'm sort of surprised she'd care to return after what he did to her. It takes an awful lot of forgiveness to love someone who sabotages your relationship with your children," Gabe said.

They digested that silently. Her return was too new for any of them to start examining the family tree. Jack certainly didn't want to stir up anything that might be painful to her. "Maybe she came back here because she had no one left in France."

Dane shrugged. "Possibly. Anyway, baking's not a bad idea, but none of us bake anything anybody would want, and vines take time and water and real experience that none of us have. We should probably stick to livestock, which we do know something about, if we're going to pick a family brand."

"I heard some of you were thinking about breeding horses," Jack said.

Gabe said, "I assume you need fast income."

"True," Jack said. "My window of opportunity is somewhat shorter than it used to be."

"There's all those pecan trees," Dane said thoughtfully.

"Yeah," Jack said. "That's right."

They sat silently, sipping their beers.

"The obvious answer might be to open a dude ranch, or even a bed-and-breakfast," Pete said. "But I don't know if I've got the stomach for strangers."

"Or the time," Gabe said.

"Cricket parachutes," Jack said, feeling the sudden need to have some sympathy from his brothers.

"No," Pete said. "If we bring a business like that out here, the liability would be insane."

Jack blinked. His brothers didn't seem surprised by his announcement at all. Why did he have to be the only one bothered by his woman's penchant for danger? "All I know is rodeo."

"Here's a stupid idea," Gabe said. "What about a haunted house?"

His brothers stared at him, their jaws slack for an instant.

"Why don't we just go all the way and open up an alien-sighting tourist attraction?" Pete asked, his tone ironic. "Or a circus. We've got enough sideshows in this family."

"Go ahead," Dane said crossly, "we'll just finally confirm to everyone in Union Junction that we're all crazy as goats around here."

"I *said* it was a crazy idea," Gabe said, "but at least I threw out a suggestion. What have you guys got?"

"Okay," Jack said, deciding to intervene before tempers flared. "Brainstorming's good. We need something that's—"

"Making money hand over fist doesn't seem to come easy to us," Gabe said. "Maybe Pop didn't pass his golden touch along to us."

They sat silently, considering the fact that maybe Pop was the only one among them who knew how to turn dirt into gold. "We haven't had any practice," Jack said. "This is the first time we've ever tried to come up with a creative plan for fiscal benefit."

"Which is scary when you consider that there are four of us trying to figure it out, and Pop did it on his own with four kids,"

Dane said, not pleased. "Pete, you have an excuse if your brain is mush with four infants keeping you up at night, but the rest of us should be pretty sharp."

Jack thought about his three on the way. He had to prove to Cricket that he was more than capable of being a good provider. "Who wants another beer?"

Without waiting for an answer, Jack got up and grabbed three more cans from the fridge, and another Coke for himself, and passed them around to his brothers. "Hell, I don't even know where I'm going to live. No wonder I can't figure out what business I should run."

Pete raised his brows. "You haven't talked Cricket into moving to Union Junction?"

"She doesn't want to leave her tea shop," Jack told him. "She plans to open it soon, and said one of us needs to have steady employment."

"Ouch," Dane said.

"Yeah," Jack said. "And she's got her family and friends there. She quit her church post, but I'm not sure if that will stick. Her doctor is there. All in all, I haven't been able to figure out a compelling reason to ask her to leave Fort Wylie."

"You're not compelling enough?" Gabe asked, and his brothers grinned.

"And she hasn't invited you to move in with her," Dane said, to which Jack shrugged.

"She's more practical than I, and pointed out that I'd forfeit a million dollars if I did move there. I'm only now beginning to process calling Pop on his bet. He thinks I have no plans to move to the ranch because of Mom. It's important to prove the old badger wrong." He leaned back in the chair, letting the leather of his father's recliner suck him into its comfort. "Mom and I have been talking, so on that front improvement's being made. The four of us are sitting here together, so improvement's happening family-wise, just like Pop wanted. But Cricket says she doesn't want to see me for a while," he admitted, his body sagging with defeat. "So I'm back to square one there. I'm just trying to make something of myself so she'll want me."

"It's not your finances holding you back," Pete said. "Cricket's not that shallow. It has to be something else."

"She says I overwhelm her," Jack told his brothers. "She says she's not as independent when I'm around. I think she's annoyed that I won't quit rodeo when I insisted she give up jumping out of planes. We're sort of at an impasse."

Silence met his words. Jack wondered what Cricket was doing right now. "I think I'll head to Fort Wylie. Maybe a bright idea will hit me on the way there."

"Thought you said Cricket doesn't want to see you for a while," Dane said.

Jack stood. "Simple miscommunication," he said. "If I can fix things around here with Pop, Mom and you guys, surely I can fix my relationship with a deacon."

"Forgiveness is easier to give than to get," Gabe said.

"What dummy said that? It's terrible advice," Jack told him, and Gabe shrugged. "If we all believed that," Jack continued, "we'd all be in a sinking boat. Anyway, I can't think about Pop right now. I need to meet Cricket's family. I need to figure out my woman, whether she likes it or not. Then I'll come up with a big idea for employment."

"That's the man," Pete said jovially. "Action instead of moping."

"Moping?" Jack repeated.

"I meant sitting around thinking," Pete explained hurriedly. He raised his beer can in Jack's direction. "Good luck and Godspeed. Let us know how it goes."

Jack stood, well aware his brothers were enjoying his dilemma with empathy and a little humor. That was okay. He knew they supported him, and it was a good feeling after all the years apart. "Hey," he said suddenly, "I never thanked you for sneaking out to see me ride. And then trying to come to the hospital. I never said it, but it scared the hell out of me when your car got hit."

Pete cleared his throat. Dane shrugged. Gabe grinned. "It was a wild night," Gabe said. "We made Pop a tougher man than he ever dreamed he'd need to be."

They all laughed, remembering how blazing mad Pop had been. But he'd been upset that his boys were sneaking out, frightened that they'd nearly gotten killed in a car accident. Jack understood that now. Parents didn't always show their emotions the way they felt them. He hoped he'd be able to tell his kids how much he loved them, then figured he'd better give himself a pass on being the perfect parent. "It was great knowing you were there," Jack said. "I liked having the coolest cheering section around."

"You better figure out a way to get Cricket to cheer for you," Pete said, and Jack headed toward Fort Wylie.

Chapter 15

This time Jack skipped Cricket's house altogether and went straight to her family home. Most likely, Cricket wouldn't be happy with this decision, but if he waited on her to introduce him, he'd be a father already. He had no intention of letting her be a single mom—he needed to get her safely to the altar without further delay. The wait was beginning to wear on him, and one thing he'd learned about the deacon. She could drag her feet like no other woman he'd ever known.

He managed to get himself buzzed through the massive wrought-iron gate by giving only his name and the nature of his call, which surprised him. He was greeted at the door of a large home—about the size of the Morgan home at the ranch, but built in a Grecian style—by an elegant, older version of Cricket, tall and dark-haired and manicured. "Mrs. Jasper?"

"Yes?" she said, giving his jeans, boots and cowboy hat a quick once-over, before her gaze peered past him to his truck for the briefest of moments.

He removed his hat. "My name is Jack Morgan."

"I've heard the name." She showed him in to a white room

that was air-conditioned—or just cold from the marble—and smiled at him. "You've come about my daughter, Cricket."

He resisted the nervous feeling settling into the pit of his stomach. This was a first for him, and being on the receiving end of a mother's scrutiny was unsettling. He made a mental note to remember when his daughters—surely he would have at least one daughter in Cricket's and his batch of triplets—had sweethearts over, he would keep the air-conditioning low and his demeanor antiseptic. No sense in encouraging every Tom, Dick and Harry to date his pink-ribboned darlings—but he was no average Tom, Dick or Harry. "Yes, ma'am, I have come about Cricket."

She looked him over again, then seemed to make a decision. "Please seat yourself in the den. I will let my husband, Reed, know that you are calling." She looked down at his boots, then at her white rug—he could almost feel her suppressing a mental shiver—then seemed relieved when he said, "I'll just wait right here, ma'am."

"Please call me Eileen," she said, then drifted down the hall.

"Whoa," he murmured to himself as he watched Mrs. Jasper depart. No wonder Cricket loved her tea shop and gingerbread house. It had life and warmth—this house was a displaced part of the Arctic Circle. He was shocked when Cricket and two men came down the hall, followed by her mother.

"Jack! What are you doing here?" Cricket asked, not sounding as thrilled as he might have hoped. Still, he hadn't told her that he was coming, and she was one of those independent women who thought they had to be in control of everything. This time, he was going to be in control, he thought, right before he found himself lying on the floor, staring up at the ceiling. *This seems to happen a lot around Cricket,* he thought, noting the blue frescoes on the ceiling surrounding the chandelier and the throbbing in his jaw.

"Thad!" Cricket hurried to help Jack up. "Why did you do that?"

Jack wondered the same, but he also knew. In fact, he completely understood her brother's reaction. "It's all right," he said gamely, sitting up. "I'm fine." He pushed Cricket's hands away from him and got to his feet. "You only get one shot at me, buster, and I figure I had that one coming." He glared at Cricket's brother and father. "Be warned, next time I will send your ass into the next county."

"Oh, dear," Eileen said. "Gentlemen, let's not fight. I'm sure we can solve this problem without violence."

"Mother!" Cricket exclaimed. "There is no problem! Thad, if you do anything like that again, you'll not be an uncle to my babies! Come on, Jack," she said, pulling him into the white room despite his boots. "Sit down."

"Don't coddle me," he said impatiently. "I've been thrown from small bulls that did more damage than your brother did." He raised his chin at the other males in the room, deciding to simply skip the niceties altogether. "I came to introduce myself. We've met, and clearly we won't be sharing a table at the holidays, which is fine by me." He stared at each of them before placing his hat back on his head. "Thank you for your hospitality. I'll see myself out."

"Jack!" Cricket said, following him down the hall. "Be reasonable."

He didn't answer, just kept walking. He'd been through a lot for this woman, but he wasn't going to be told to be reasonable or any other silliness. She'd put him on hold, she'd run off on him, she'd given him the silent treatment, all of which he'd been very patient with.

If Cricket wanted him, she knew where to find him.

Time had never crept so slowly for Jack. By mid-June, Jack knew Cricket wasn't going to look him up. By July, he knew she had no plans at all to even spare him a phone call. By August, he was hanging on to hope only by his bare knuckles.

Even Josiah didn't ask him anymore about Cricket, nor did

his brothers. Occasionally, he knew that Suzy, Laura or Priscilla went to see her in Fort Wylie, but they shared no news with him or their spouses. He wasn't sure why, but the deacon had deemed herself totally off limits, and he had to tell himself every day that he could lead a horse to water but for darn sure he couldn't make it drink, and right now, Cricket was in no mood to be led anywhere. He'd just dig himself into a deep hole with her, and that was no way to start off a parenting relationship. But waiting was the hardest thing he'd ever done by far. It was agonizing.

He worked on getting the barns pulled together. He inspected the pecan trees, wondering about harvesting them into some sort of crop. Only a few of them really needed spraying; most of them were healthy. He went and watched a rodeo in Lonely Hearts Station but didn't participate, all the will gone out of him. A man needed fire to compete, and he knew he was on a low burn for something else.

He kept Josiah company and got to know his brothers' children, the most fun he could remember having in a long time. The years seemed to melt away, for all of them. He thought he hadn't realized how much he missed them, but he knew in his heart his brothers were the only humans on earth who knew him better than he knew himself. Sometimes he wondered about all the years they'd lost, but then, he knew that everything had a purpose. So he didn't let himself think about the lost years and focused instead on the found ones.

He went down to the guesthouse every few nights and ate dinner with Gisella. The part of him that was sad that she'd left began to blossom with good thoughts and new memories. He grilled on her patio, and they sat on the wicker love seat chatting about things that mattered to no one but them. Gisella talked about her life in France, and how she'd known she would one day return home to Texas. He learned that her parents had passed away, but she still had many cousins, aunts and uncles. She treasured the years she'd spent with her mother and father but had sorely missed her boys. She'd known Josiah would never let her take the boys with her to France, and she'd known she could not stay with Josiah.

Jack knew all too well how his father could force a person between a rock and a hard place, with nowhere to turn but away. The anger he'd kept burning for so long inside him slowly banked, the fire out for good.

The only advice his mother had for him about Cricket was to let her come to him, which is what his father must have done concerning Gisella. Only, years later, when Gisella had come home, they were simply friends and nothing more, which suited everyone. Jack had no intention of being just friends with Cricket. He had fallen too hard for her, too much in love, to let her turn their relationship into friendship. He'd wait— but he also knew his waiting had a shelf life. Sooner or later, his babies would make her call him. So he waited, enjoying his nieces and nephews, planning a business with his brothers, watching his father heal under Sara's ministrations with some amazement. Josiah married Sara one Sunday under a canopy of pecan trees, with the setting sun behind them for decoration, and everyone threw birdseed at them and ate cake baked by Sara herself. Cricket didn't come to the wedding, but she sent a basket of teas and kitchen goodies, which Sara loved because she was always baking.

Jack gritted his teeth and told himself his waiting wasn't for-ever, even if it seemed as if it was.

And then suddenly, on a Monday night in late September, his cell phone rang and he saw it was Cricket. He felt his heart rate skid and then escalate like no bull riding had ever jacked his blood. "Hello?"

"Jack, it's Cricket."

"Hi," he said, putting down the sponge he'd been oiling a saddle with. "What's up?"

"I wondered if…you'd like to come visit."

Would he? This was the invitation he'd waited months to receive! "If that's what you want," he said, heading toward the barn sink to wash his hands.

"I do," she said. "And you might want to bring a change of clothes."

"Oh?" His brows raised, but he masked his surprise.

"Yes," she said, "I'm having a Cesarean section tomorrow, and I know you'll probably want to be around for the birth of your children."

He jogged toward his house. "All right," he said. "Will you be at your house or your parents'?"

"I'll be at my house," she said. "Come as soon as you can, please."

She hung up. He stared at his silent phone for a second, then snapped it off. "Holy smokes!" he exclaimed. "I'm about to be a dad!"

Cricket was huge. She knew she looked quite unlike anything Jack might remember about her. It felt as if babies were popping out all over, taking up residence inside her thin frame, squeezing her out of shape from every side. This was not the way she wanted him to see her—but she had no choice. If they were to have any future together, she knew she couldn't keep him from the birth of his children.

She'd thought long and hard about when she felt safe enough to allow him back into her life. The time had never been right. She missed him, but she had also worried that nothing about their worlds could ever be right together. She'd procrastinated long enough that suddenly, she found herself on bed rest.

Then she hadn't wanted to call him, hadn't wanted him to see her in a vulnerable state. She grew like a snowball going downhill, picking up size and girth as it rolled, and her vanity wouldn't allow her to surrender her figure to his eyes.

Then, today, Dr. Suzanne said she could wait no longer. The babies were as big as they could be inside her small frame; everything was straining. She'd held them inside her as long as she possibly could.

Cricket had no choice but to call Jack and let him know he was about to be a father. He'd sounded so shocked—and delighted.

She folded the last of her things for the hospital, smiled at the three white bassinets lined up in the nursery and jumped when the doorbell rang. Her heart zipped nervously inside her—she recognized Jack's impatient call through the door.

"Cricket! It's Jack!"

Slowly, she opened the door. It was hard to meet his gaze. Shyness swept her. Time apart had made her memory of him sharper, and yet somehow seeing him again brought home hard how handsome, how magnetic he was in person.

"Wow," he said, his gaze dropping to her stomach. His eyes were wide. "I—you're beautiful, Cricket." He handed her a bouquet of pink roses he'd been holding, blooms down, by his side, an afterthought he'd completely forgotten about in the shock of seeing her.

"I'm huge," she said shyly, not meaning to sound apologetic, but that's how her words sounded.

"Yeah," he agreed. "How do you feel?"

"Just huge. Come on in." She led him inside, feeling fat, fat, fat. The thin figure he'd once admired had certainly disappeared under several pounds of babies, and yet she wouldn't change a thing.

"You sit down," he said. "I'll take care of everything. Should you even be walking around?"

"Jack, I sent Mother home for acting just like that. And she needed some rest. I want you here, but I don't want to be hovered over. All right?"

He seemed to hesitate. "I don't know if I can promise you not to hover. It just seems like you need to be resting. I almost feel bad, Cricket, for what I've done to you."

She couldn't help a smile. "Believe it or not, this is the most amazing thing that's ever happened to me. I couldn't be happier."

"You couldn't be more beautiful," he said, "unless you were sitting or lying down, at which point I could relax."

It was a large hint and she realized how nervous he was. "If I sit, will you not pace?"

"Was it that obvious?"

"You're like a tightly wound jack-in-the-box." She grimaced. "I didn't mean to make a play on your name. Sorry about that."

"It's pretty much true. Suddenly I feel as if I have springs attached to my muscles, making me jumpy." He sat, his gaze searching her face. "You seem calm, though."

"I am." Somehow she felt better just by his presence. Her mother had been such a huge help, but as the big day neared, Eileen had begun to get nervous, antsy. They'd started to get on each other's nerves, which Cricket hated, because she could tell her mother was trying so hard to be helpful. Finally realizing that she, too, was tight and feeling guilty about Jack, she sent her mother home. It had been the right thing to do. "I would have called you sooner," she said, "but there was so much I needed to do on my own."

"As long as I'm here for the big show," he said, "I'm content. Excited, even. Scared. Lots of emotions."

"There's some wine in the cabinet," Cricket said, but Jack shook his head.

"No, thanks. I intend to share every emotion with you."

"Jack," she said suddenly, "I should have called to tell you how sorry I was that Thad punched you."

"Forget about it. I already have."

She so much wanted him to give her family a second chance, and yet they had treated him rather dreadfully. Looking into Jack's warm gaze, Cricket wondered if they could ever start over on new ground. She really wanted that.

"Hey, I'm serious," he said. "It wasn't important."

"You never called," she said.

"I understood you were going through a lot."

"Yes, but my family should have been more courteous."

"Nah," he said. "You're their only little girl."

"Well, Thad wants to make it up to you."

He looked at her, his brows raising, a little suspicion in his gaze. "Yeah?"

She nodded. "He wants to take you up for a jump."

"Ah. And does he want to pack my parachute for me?"

She looked at him. "I don't blame you for feeling that way."

He sighed. "I'm sorry. I know your brother doesn't want to push me out of a high-flying plane with a malfunctioning parachute. He's honest enough to at least try to kill me in person."

"Jack!" She knew he was teasing, but she couldn't help feeling protective of her brother. "You don't know Thad. He's a sweetie, really. He was so sorry about punching you."

He shrugged. "I'll pass on the jump, if it's all the same. Unless Thad wants to do some bonding over bull riding," he said, perking up. "That'd be a great way for us to celebrate those brother-in-law bonds."

"Maybe we'll wait on the bonding," she said.

"That's probably a good idea for now," he replied. "I'm going to be very busy for the next few years. I don't suppose you'd allow me to touch your stomach?" he asked, his voice wistful. "I'm awfully curious to meet my new children."

"Go ahead," she said, not having the heart to refuse him. But when his hands closed over her stomach, Cricket's heart jumped into her throat. These wonderfully large, masculine hands had gotten her into trouble in the first place...and she still remembered the magic they could play on her oh-too-willing body. Every time Jack touched her, she felt the sweet temptation run hotly through her veins, and Cricket knew she'd never be able to tell this call-of-the-wild cowboy no—except about becoming his wife, except about moving to Union Junction, except about ever getting into his bed again.

Chapter 16

Jack tried not to wince when Cricket said, "I'll sleep on the recliner tonight."

He hadn't expected an invitation into her bed, but to have her distance herself from him by sleeping in a recliner sort of hurt his feelings. "You're safe," he said, his tone brisk. "I'll take the recliner."

She looked at him, a heartbreakingly sweet face that had only grown more beautiful to him since her pregnancy. "I always sleep on the recliner," she said softly, "even when my mother helps me. Anyway, there are five bedrooms in this house. There's plenty of places to sleep."

"Why do you sleep in the recliner?" he asked, glad that she wasn't trying to avoid contact with him.

"The babies are restless at night. There are three fighting for space, and so when they start doing their gymnastics, as I call it, it's challenging for my body if I'm lying down. It's also hard to get up."

She was quite a bit larger than he'd expected her to be. He thought about how his father had warned him that if he didn't get Cricket to the altar before the babies were born, he might never get her there. "You look lovely," he said, his voice hoarse. He got all choked up just thinking about the fact that this wonderful woman was having his babies—how much luckier could a man get?

"You wouldn't think I was attractive if you saw me undressed," she told him matter-of-factly. "You should see the support system Mom and I rigged underneath this kimono so that I can stand up."

He looked at the flowing, shapeless dress she wore. "You look like you're ready for a luau or a garden party. I would never guess you're carrying three children in there if I didn't know better. Are you sure our babies are big enough to survive?"

"I worry about that, too," she said softly. "But the doctor thinks they each will weigh around five pounds. In my mother's generation, a five to six-pound baby was considered healthy. I try not to scare myself to death over things I can't control."

"No, no," he said hastily. "And I don't know the first thing about pregnancies, anyway."

"Well, we'll know more tomorrow. I'm glad you're here," she said with a gentle smile at him.

He didn't know what to say to that. Why hadn't she called him sooner? Why hadn't she agreed to marry him?

It hit him that this woman had changed his life, changed him. And he had never seen it coming. Like a strong wind, she'd blown him over. "So you'll sleep out here," he said, "because it's more comfortable and not because you're worried about me—"

"I've slept in this recliner for the past month," Cricket told him.

"And you'll call me if you need anything in the night, even just getting up to use the, you know, go into the powder room," he said delicately.

She nodded. "I'm in your hands. Completely."

He took a deep breath. "I won't let you down."

She looked at him. "I know. That's why I called you. You're the one person I want by my side when I go through this."

He felt better knowing that she trusted him. "Good night," he said, and though he didn't kiss her good night, he wanted to more than anything.

"Jack?"

"Hmm?" He paused in the act of checking out the sofa. Could he sleep there? It didn't seem right to go sleep in a comfy room in the back while she was stuck in the recliner. Shouldn't he keep vigil with her tonight? What if she needed something suddenly and he didn't hear her?

"How's your mother?"

He looked at Cricket. "She's fine. Why do you ask?"

"I just wondered."

He looked in her eyes, sensing a deeper question. "You're asking if we're getting along."

She hesitated. "I suppose so."

"And you're wondering if I'm living at the ranch, getting along with Mom and making my father happy."

"I haven't heard much about you," she said, her gaze direct. "I do wonder if the black sheep is making its way back home."

"Mom's fitting in to Union Junction just fine."

She smiled. "You know I meant you, Jack."

"I never really considered myself a black sheep," he said, settling onto the sofa. "And I'd appreciate your not referring to me as such in front of the children. They can hear everything you say, you know." He slipped off his boots, arranged himself among the pretty flowered pillows, slid his hat down over his eyes.

"You're avoiding the question about your mother," she prompted.

"Not so much," he said, "but I'm still working on my million, if you're wondering about that."

"I see," she said, and he removed his hat to turn and stare at her.

"Why? Thinking about moving to the ranch?"

She shrugged. "I consider all our options."

"Hey," he said, "are you having second thoughts about being the wild girl of Fort Wylie?"

Her chin lifted. "Maybe, cowboy, maybe I am."

He sat up, his heart suddenly beating very quickly. "I don't suppose you'd be offering me any kind of proposal, would you?"

"Not marriage," she said hastily, "just…parenting together."

"Oh." He sank back into his reclining position. "Give a guy false hope, why don't you. Sheesh."

"I know it would be best for the children if we raised them together, I just haven't figured out how we'd manage it."

"Glad you're slowly coming around to my side," he said, feeling grumpy.

"I'm just trying not to tie you down," Cricket said.

"You're the one avoiding the rope."

She sighed. "I know you have a lot of family things to attend to. I don't want to be a distraction."

"You *are* a distraction, whether you want to be or not. You're carrying my children. Where else do you think my mind is most of the time?" He sighed, wishing it were tomorrow already, wishing he knew whether his children would be born with all their tiny fingers and toes intact, whether they would be as pretty as their mother, wishing he knew something about being a father. "Listen, Pop's fine. He married Sara and they're the happiest couple you ever saw. She makes him lots of salads and other things she calls cleansing foods for his kidneys. Pop complains that all he wants in life is a cookie and maybe a double-fudge cake, and Sara smiles and gives him a different variation of something healthy and they're both happy. Mom seems to like living at the ranch. She gets lots of visits from grandchildren, and this time I think she'll stay. She prefers the guesthouse, and I stay in the main house, but still, I come across her from time to time. She's gardening in a huge way and has been studying herbs. Says she's going to plant a bigger garden next year. Wants you to pick out drapes when you have time, maybe also next year," he said begrudgingly. "I swear that's what she said. But no pressure. We've survived without new drapes for many years, we may never get them." He felt pretty glum about that, just because he knew it was something his father had felt was important to the house. Actually, he knew his father only kept the ranch house because he had some mysterious connection to it, one that seemed to be growing even on Jack. "Weirdly, Pop claims there's ghosts in the house."

"What kind of ghosts?"

"Friendly ghosts. Misplaced ones who decided to take up residence there. They're from France," he explained. "It's not a reaction from the kidney surgery, as far as I can tell—he really believes there are ghosts there."

Cricket smiled. "Your father is awesome."

"No, really," Jack said, certain that Cricket thought he was just spinning a tale. "Pop swears they came from France to pull him through the surgery."

"Why aren't they living with him and Sara, then?"

"Because they need a grail. They're on a quest," he explained. "And Pop says they're in a snit because he left them in his templary, so they chose to follow him." He wondered how much he could share with her about the ghosts and decided to go all the way with this one. "Cricket, every once in a while, I could almost believe they're there, which I feel pretty weird saying to a deacon, because I'm pretty sure you don't believe in ghosts. Maybe angels, but not ghosts."

Cricket giggled. "I believe anything you tell me."

"You don't." He closed his eyes again. "If you did, you'd believe that you and I need to get married for the sake of the children."

"Ugh," Cricket said. "Let's stay on the subject of ghosts. It's safer. How many are there?"

"Three," Jack said. "The house definitely feels fuller with them around."

"Eek," Cricket said. "I'm not staying at the ranch house anytime soon."

"Oh, a little ghost or three wouldn't chase you off," Jack said, feeling grumpy again. "You've got other reasons you won't come live with me."

"True," Cricket said. "I don't see myself anywhere but here."

He didn't, either. The old house with its quaint gingerbread trim suited her. There were baby presents along one wall, waiting to be opened, cards expressing well wishes for Cricket's pregnancy lined a sideboard. "I'd move here but I'm determined to outlast the old man's stubbornness. He thinks I can't stay in one place for more than a few moments. Mom says she thinks I should lighten Dad's wallet of a million dollars if for no other reason than to show him I can stick to one place. Be a family man."

"I agree with your mother," Cricket said. "Most people never see that much money. And a job is a job. Although I heard that the Lonely Hearts Station rodeo is coming up soon." She considered him for a moment. "I'm sure you miss your old life, Jack."

He turned to look at her again. "Who told you about the rodeo? Laura? Suzy? Priscilla?"

"They stopped by the other day," she said, her gaze innocent.

"And filled you in on things you shouldn't be troubling your pretty little head about," Jack said.

"Maybe not, but my pretty little head likes to know what the father of my two girls and one boy is doing."

He sat up. "Two girls and one boy?"

She nodded. "Yes, cowboy. I wasn't going to tell you, I was going to let you be surprised during the delivery, but I can't keep the news to myself any longer."

"Man," he said. "That's like hitting the lottery!" He jumped off the sofa, paced around the room for a moment. "Cricket, you *have* to marry me."

She shook her head. "'Have to' is something I opted out of when I gave up my church position."

He caught his breath. "Is that why you did it? Because you didn't want to feel forced to marry me?" He'd sensed that the women in the waiting room at Dr. Suzanne's hadn't felt anything but caring toward their deacon.

"Yes," she said. "I knew I wasn't going to get married, and I felt that they deserved a deacon who was living a bit more holy than I was."

His heart sank. "Still feel that way?"

She nodded. "To be honest, I've received a number of visits to reassure me that my position is waiting for me whenever I want it. But I know I'm doing the right thing."

Which meant she had no intention of ever marrying him. Jack realized he was walking in a supersize patch of trouble. "Why did you tell me all this after you mentioned the rodeo? Is there a connection?"

"Sort of," Cricket said. "It's my way of letting you know that I understand about rodeo. I know you understand about my love of parachuting. And that we'll have to figure out a way to be parents while understanding that we had a miracle of three babies, but we'll have to agree to be partners."

He frowned. "Partners? That sounds like new-age labeling for 'Cricket and Jack will be single parents'."

She didn't reply.

"Okay," he said, "I think I get it. You're telling me that you'll let me hang around and help you raise the babies from afar. I'll live in Union Junction and you'll live in Fort Wylie. You jump and I'll ride, and somehow in there, while we're living completely separate lives, we'll raise kids who somehow miraculously understand that Mommy and Daddy are too weird to be committed to each other." He paused. "Maybe the word I'm looking for is *selfish*. That's how it seems to me, anyway."

Cricket's brown eyes flashed at him. "Do you have a better suggestion?"

"No," he said, "because talking about this is going to make us both crazy. The obvious answer from a less involved person is that we should have used a condom or never gone to bed together, but frankly, Cricket, that would be like saying I don't want these children, and I darn well do. I also want you." He let out a deep breath and wondered why he wanted her right now, this minute, in the worst way. If nothing else, he'd like to be able to hold her, reassure her that everything was going to be all right, and "they" were going to be all right, but he couldn't hold her, she was ensconced in that recliner. All she needed was a moat around her and she'd be completely protected from him. Never had he known a woman with as much resistance as she gave him. "Let's get some sleep. Tomorrow's going to be a busy day, and the coaching tape I've been watching says the coach needs his rest the night before his children come into the world. Supposedly, birthing day is just like Christmas, only about a thousand times better."

He pushed his hat down low over his eyes. It hurt to know that his children wouldn't have a traditional family. Though his parents hadn't stayed together, they'd started out as a family and he remembered that it was later, when his mother had left, that his father had changed, turning into a sour, angry man.

It was important to have both parents around. He didn't like Cricket's plan, not one bit, but she was a stubborn girl, and he had lots of experience with stubborn. He had a father who was, and a mother who was, and brothers who knew something about stubborn and Templar knights living in his ranch house who'd stubbornly decided they were part and parcel of Josiah's legacy. Truly, Jack wasn't afraid of stubborn.

He'd just wait his deacon out. He would out-stubborn them all.

A father had to be strong. Now he understood Josiah, and loved him more for what he'd taught him about being a real father. Over the years, people—even Jack—had said that Josiah Morgan was a jackass. But now Jack knew that Josiah had simply been strong.

Chapter 17

Cricket knew that she loved Jack. She always had. But right now, while she was being prepped for surgery, she wished she hadn't asked him to come.

She had never seen him nervous. She'd seen him hanging on to a wildly charging bull with a grin on his face. She'd seen him face down an angry father, a possible kidney operation, all with not a trace of fear or anxiety.

Right now, Jack Morgan was more nervous than she was. He was trying hard not to be; he was working hard at being a good coach, a soothing presence.

But she could feel how tense he was. He kept swallowing, his Adam's apple jerking uncomfortably. An active man, Jack never liked to be still, but the kindest description of what he was trying hard not to do was pace. The very fact that he was trying to stay in one place was unsettling—she would far rather he pace and let loose some of his nerves.

He gave her a weak smile and Cricket sighed. "It's going to be fine, Jack," she told him.

"Darn tootin' it's going to be fine," he said. "I've already given the doctor her pep talk."

"Pep talk?"

"Yes." He nodded adamantly. "She is not to hurt you. You are not to feel any pain. She's not to drop my children, nor traumatize them in any way. I want everything soft and comforting for everyone." He took a deep breath, passed a handkerchief over his brow. "This is hard work."

She smiled. "Why don't you go get a cup of coffee." She thought something more fortifying would be even better but didn't dare suggest that to him. Perhaps if he just left for a bit, the surgery would be over and he'd be a new father.

"No," Jack said. "The doctor says I'm doing fine."

Cricket smiled. "Dr. Suzanne has the patience of Job."

"Yes, well, she said that if I get any more nervous, she's going to have a pretty nurse give me a sedative in my riding cushions and I'll miss all the fun." He looked aggrieved. "I'm not nervous. I can't understand what she's referring to."

Cricket couldn't help her broad smile. "I like you like this."

"Like what?"

"With emotions." She looked at him. "You always seemed so coldhearted before."

"I was never coldhearted to you, Deacon."

"I don't know," she said softly. "I never felt like you could give your heart completely to anyone or anything. Then I saw you trying to help Josiah, and I began to think there was more to you than just pride."

"I think I'm about to break a sweat, and all this talk of being coldhearted makes me want to show you just how hot I am for you."

"Oh," she said, "not with me wearing this silly hair covering and big as a house."

"Especially with you wearing that green hair covering and even bigger than a house."

"Jack!"

Dr. Suzanne laughed as she came to stand beside them. "I heard that, Mr. Morgan. You're supposed to reassure my patient, not give her a complex."

"I can't give her a complex," Jack grumbled. "She had plenty of those before I came along. I'm just trying to work them out of her."

"Is that true, Cricket?" Dr. Suzanne asked with a smile.

"It's a strange form of seduction, Dr. Suzanne, but I suppose I had to choose a wild one to father my children."

"All right, Dad," Dr. Suzanne said, "stand to the side of Cricket, please. Let's find out if you're as good at birth coaching as you are at rodeo."

"Yeesh," Jack said, grabbing Cricket's hand, determined to be supportive. "I heard you tell my father that I was only fair at rodeo."

"It was best he know the truth," Cricket said sweetly.

"I see how this relationship goes," Dr. Suzanne said. "You two are in the early 'in-love' phase. It's a fun time. My husband and I remember it fondly." She smiled as she teased them.

Jack raised a brow. "Early love? Cricket's never said she loved me. Do you know something I don't?"

Dr. Suzanne laughed. "Not me. I'm just the obstetrician. Okay, Cricket, are you ready for the biggest moment of your life?"

Cricket glanced at Jack for the quickest fraction of a second and thought, *He's the biggest moment of my life.*

Of course, she would never tell him that. She was pretty certain that the key to a heart as wild as Jack's was to always be free to ride off into the sunset, wherever the sun set next. What would he say if she said, *Yes, Jack, I'll marry you*?

He'd be happy at first—that was the nature of a competitor. After a while, the bonds of matrimony would begin to chafe. And then what? Would they end up like Gisella and Josiah, who were only now learning to be friends?

* * *

The most wonderful moment of Jack's life, absolutely awe-inspiring and scary as hell, was when Dr. Suzanne placed his first-born child in his arms. It was a girl with a perfectly round head and sweet lips, crying like nobody's business, and he couldn't believe anything so tiny could contain such a set of lungs. "Hey," he told the baby, "simmer down now. I've got you, little thing."

A nurse standing near him chuckled. "Babies cry when they're born. We grade them on it."

"Oh," he told the baby. "I think you're passing with flying colors."

The nurse took the baby from him, though he wasn't ready to let go of his daughter. Another nurse placed a second baby in his arms, this one also a daughter. Her head wasn't quite so round, but she had a light dusting of hair and a softer cry. "This one's not yelling as much," he told the nurse. "Didn't you say you were grading them?"

"Yes," the nurse said. "All babies are assigned a number."

"Hey," he told the baby. "Don't be a B student. Give us a good wail."

"No," the nurse said, laughing. "She's fine. Just fine."

"Whew," Dr. Suzanne said. "Mr. Morgan, you have two healthy infants."

"Two?" His head reared up. "I'm supposed to have three healthy infants."

"And so you do." The last baby was handed to him a few moments later, a nice, barrel-chested son, who was louder than both his sisters. Jack grinned. "This one's an A student," he said, his heart full to bursting. "Cricket, all these children take after you."

"I doubt anyone has ever told the deacon she's loud," Dr. Suzanne said. She looked at Cricket. "You did fine. How are you feeling?"

"I feel excited. Happy. Tired," Cricket said. "But mostly, I feel like holding my children."

Jack watched as each baby was given to Cricket. He watched

mother and children bond in that special way that mothers can with their babies, and he realized that good mothers just simply had that connection. His heart full of understanding now for the pain that Gisella must have felt during her long years away, he resolved to be more understanding of his mother.

"Cricket," he said, going to her side, "you really are the most beautiful woman I've ever known. It's just in you, all the beauty a man looks for in a woman."

"Why, Jack," Cricket said, "whatever has gotten into you?"

He looked at his children squalling red-faced and adorable around their mother. "You," he said, "I think it's you."

"Are there names for the children?" a nurse asked.

Jack looked at Cricket. "Are there names for the children?"

Cricket said, "We haven't discussed names yet, but I have suggestions."

"Good," Jack said, "because they're not leaving this room as Baby Morgan A, B and C."

Cricket hesitated, frowned at Jack. He sensed he'd stepped in trouble again. "What?"

"Jasper," she said.

He blinked. "Jasper?"

"That's my last name."

He got it. "Oh, no," he said. "No, see, I'm a traditional guy. We may not be married, but we will be. And those children will bear the name of their father from day one. They're not going to be asked embarrassing questions on the playground like, *Where's your father?* and *Who's your daddy?* and *Why didn't your father love your mother enough to marry her?* No!" he said loudly, shaking his head. "Deacon, here's where I draw the line with my size-eleven boot. I've been asking for months. You're the one who's stubborn as a mule, but you're not going to saddle our babies with a lifetime of laughter and finger-pointing. Trust me, I know all about the questions kids ask other kids, and I'm very sensitive to this. You can pick the first names and the middle names—hell, pick all the names you want, but I've picked the last name and these children are all Morgans. Write it on the charts, Nurse. M-O-R-G-A-N, just like the horses."

Everyone, including Dr. Suzanne, stopped to stare at Jack. Cricket studied him for a long moment, then sighed. "All right," she said. "Gisella Eileen, Jonathan Josiah and Katie Rose."

"Morgan," Jack said.

"Morgan," Cricket echoed.

"Where does the Katie Rose come in?" Jack asked.

"My name is Katherine. Cricket is a nickname."

"I never knew that." Jack looked at her. "I like Katie. What about Rose?"

"I just like it," she said, lifting her chin.

"I don't know if I want my son named after me," Jack said. "And Pop's already got one namesake, thanks to Pete and Priscilla."

"If we're going traditional, let's do it all the way," Cricket said.

"The kids will call him JJ," Jack said.

"They didn't call you that."

He looked at her. "No, I've always been Jack."

Cricket closed her eyes, looking tired for the first time. Dr. Suzanne finished examining her stitches and said, "Now that we've got that solved, let's let everyone get some rest."

"That sounds good to me," Jack said, "Cricket, can I get you something?"

"Yes," she said, sounding sleepy, "a wedding ring."

Jack glanced at Dr. Suzanne. "Did she say what I thought she said?"

A nurse checked Cricket's pulse. Dr. Suzanne stepped close to the bed. The babies were taken away, wheeled down to the nursery in their plastic bassinets. Jack had been relieved that they hadn't seemed to require any type of serious extra care.

"Cricket," Dr. Suzanne said, "did you say you needed something?"

Cricket opened her eyes for a second. "I think sleep will do me just fine, Doctor, thank you."

Dr. Suzanne shrugged at Jack. "We'll take her to her room now."

Jack nodded, let down like all get out.

"Congratulations, Mr. Morgan," Dr. Suzanne said. "Three healthy babies is a lot to be thankful for."

"Yes," he said, wishing that Cricket really did want the one thing he didn't seem to be able to give her.

Chapter 18

When Cricket awakened, Jack wasn't in the hospital room like she thought he'd be. The nurse saw her anxious look.

"Dad's down at the nursery," she said with a smile, and Cricket relaxed. She couldn't explain it, but his face was the one she'd wanted to see when she woke up. She wanted to see her babies, too, but she had an overwhelming need to see Jack.

It was almost as if she was afraid that he might leave and not come back to see her. She knew he would always want to see his children. He talked a lot about wanting to marry her and she'd always pushed that suggestion away, fearing that he'd tire of her once his wanderlust took over again—and then something had told her that she was the one doing the damage by being nervous about the same thing his father had been nervous about. There was no reason to put distance between herself and Jack because of rodeo. Rodeo was the symbol of a way of life Jack loved—he'd never said he planned to give it up, and he'd never said he loved her. Not in so many words, but he had offered her a commitment. And one thing she'd realized someplace between the amazing birth of her children and the joy that they had all come through the experience just fine was that Morgan men stayed committed to their women. Even now, though years had passed between Josiah and Gisella's marriage, Josiah was still committed to Gisella's well-being.

She had nothing to fear from Jack. No matter what happened between them, he was never going to ride off into the sunset and forget about her.

Perhaps she'd worried knowing about the animosity between father and son. But that had been smoothed over, perhaps even more than just a leveling of old anger. Sometimes she thought she sensed genuine affection growing between the two. Even with his mother, Jack seemed to be making an effort to reestablish their relationship, something that had to be hard after so many years apart.

He didn't even seem that concerned that her brother had taken a shot at him. She was more angry with Thad than Jack. Jack had shrugged it off. Her parents had given him a rather reserved welcome, and Jack hadn't opposed her naming one of the children after her mother.

Contrary to everything she'd ever known or heard about Jack, he didn't seem to hold a grudge past the point of necessity. Affection and responsibility for his family appeared to come more easily to him than anyone—and maybe even Jack—had ever thought it would.

Time would tell.

Of course, she didn't have much time. She hadn't told Jack this yet, but her parents and Thad had offered to take over her tea shop and run it themselves. They had a hankering for a family business, and a sweet tooth that wanted to see the tea shop stay operating. With three newborns in Cricket's life, they worried she wouldn't have the time or energy to run the shop. This solution would keep her business in the family, and it would allow her to move to Union Junction, which, as they pointed out, she might have to do at some point for the sake of the children. Cricket would even make money monthly, as her family intended to divide the business in quarters. It was a sound idea, and it left Cricket with no financial reason to stay in Fort Wylie.

But she knew she couldn't pack up and follow a certain rodeo man without a plan, either.

Jack knew the cavalry had arrived by the sound of many voices raised with anxious delight. Voices that he recognized, knew and loved well, made his heart expand. His family was on the premises, heading straight for the nursery. A large group of people rounded the corner, every member accounted for except Josiah.

"Jack!" Laura, Priscilla and Suzy exclaimed, rushing to hug him.

"Show us our new family members," Laura told him, and with the proudest grin he'd ever worn, Jack pointed through the glass.

"Ah," Gisella said, "two girls and a boy!"

"One named after you, Gisella," Sara said. "If Josiah could see them, he'd be so proud." She began taking pictures on her camera phone, despite the glass. "Josiah's on pins and needles to see pictures," she told Jack. "It was all I could do to make him stay home and rest."

"How's Pop doing?"

Sara and Gisella smiled. "He's antsy," Sara said. "But when the children come to visit, he's much better."

Pete, Gabe and Dane came to shake his hand. "Good going," Dane said as Pete helped lift some of the Morgan brood to the window to see their new cousins.

"Thanks," Jack said. "But I didn't do any of the work."

Gabe laughed. "You did *something*."

"Three babies," Gabe said. "Who would have ever thought Jack Morgan would be a father to three?"

"Not me," Jack said. "I'm still in shock."

"But they're the most beautiful babies you ever saw, right?" Pete asked.

Jack grinned. "How did you know?"

"I just did," Pete said. "How's Cricket? And when are you going to get her to Union Junction?"

"That I don't know," Jack said. "Maybe never. But she was amazing. She made the whole thing look easy." Jack was pretty sure he could never carry children and then birth them—it was pretty good being the dad and watching everything from a few feet away. "The doctor says Cricket can go home in a few days."

"Home to Fort Wylie?" Gabe asked, and Jack nodded.

"I think that's going to be our home."

"Well," Pete said. "It'll only cost you a million dollars. Pop will say you were always the black sheep or some nonsense. He did mutter that you were the only one of his children who had his babies born outside of Union Junction."

Jack scratched his head as he listened to the women coo over the babies. He stared through the window at his progeny, loving the sight of tiny fingers and faces. He'd never planned this moment in his life; never thought he'd have kids. "Baby steps," he murmured. "Tell Pop to relax. I'm just taking baby steps."

Pete clapped him on the back. "That's right. Just enjoy the moment. Being a dad is the best."

Jack nodded, agreeing. But being a dad and a husband would be better. He intended not to let Josiah's warning about never getting a woman to the altar after the babies were born come true.

"Hello!" Jack heard, turning to see Thad and Cricket's parents arriving for their first peek at the babies.

"Aren't they beautiful—" Eileen exclaimed, giving Jack a brief hug. Reed shook his hand more awkwardly, and Thad hung back just a split second before offering his hand as well. Jack performed the niceties, introducing Cricket's parents to his huge family, and then some strained silence ensued.

Then Gisella said, "These babies are so lucky to have so many people who want to hold them!" and that seemed to melt the ice a little. Although Jack wondered if it would have thawed at all if Josiah had been there.

Josiah wasn't going to think much about Cricket and Jack living in Fort Wylie, and Jack began to wonder if he could spend much time with these frosty in-laws who clearly wondered what their daughter saw in him.

The next few days were spent learning how to bathe the babies, breast-feed the babies and letting Cricket get her strength back. Cricket seemed to take to mothering like a bird to the air, and Jack felt his role was pretty much being a support system.

In fact, he was beginning to feel oddly as if he wasn't of much importance to the parenthood equation. He fetched tasty snacks to tempt Cricket and he held babies, but mostly he was beginning to feel like the human equation of the car hood ornament—just there for show.

Flowers arrived in a steady stream for Cricket and Jack—many from his rodeo friends. His cell phone buzzed with texts keeping him up-to-date on circuit happenings—and on the morning of their last day in the hospital, Jack received a text that caught his interest.

The committee has obtained a new sponsorship. This year's top rodeo prize in Lonely Hearts Station will be worth a million dollars!

Jack's jaw dropped. That was a lot of dough.

He'd won at the last rodeo in Lonely Hearts Station.

A *million*-dollar purse. The same amount Pop was offering for something Jack wasn't sure he could give. But rodeo was what Jack did best. Bull riding was a piece of cake compared to living with family angst.

"Jack?" Cricket said. "You look like you're deep in thought."

The babies had been wheeled to the nursery for baths after their feeding. Cricket gazed at him, her pretty eyes sleepy now. She wasn't taking a lot of pain medication, but Dr. Suzanne had warned him that Cricket needed lots of rest.

And he needed to think. "You go to sleep," Jack told her. "I'm going to head out for a bit. I'll shower at your house, and you get some sleep."

"All right." She smiled at him, then closed her eyes.

He looked at Cricket for a long moment before he left, his mind racing.

Chapter 19

"What do you mean, Jack's entered the Lonely Hearts Station rodeo?" Josiah demanded, staring at his three sons who'd come to visit him. He felt fine, he was tired of everybody coddling him, and he could tell by the expression on Gabe's, Dane's and Pete's faces that they'd debated the wisdom of telling him. *They didn't want to upset me*, Josiah thought to himself, annoyed that everybody seemed to think he needed protection from the bumps and bruises of life. "Tell me everything and quit holding out on me."

Pete sighed. "He entered. He rides tomorrow."

Josiah's eyes bugged. "He didn't tell you, did he?"

"No." Gabe shook his head. "We found out about it completely by accident. I saw Mimi and Mason Jefferson in town and they mentioned it." He shrugged. "My best guess is that Jack doesn't want us to know. Doesn't feel he needs a cheering section."

"Hell's bells," Josiah said. "You can bet Cricket doesn't know, either. She would have mentioned it to Priscilla, at least."

Dane nodded. "That's a pretty safe assumption."

"So why's he doing it? The rascal!" Josiah shook his head. "His babies are only two weeks old! He needs to stay home with Cricket and the children. He can't spend his life on the road anymore." Josiah's white brows quivered above suddenly bright eyes. "There better be a durn good reason."

"A million dollars," Pete said, and Josiah blinked.

"All he has to do for that is live at the ranch for a year. Same deal you boys got."

"Yeah," Gabe said, "but Jack's always done things his way."

Josiah sniffed. "He should be at home helping Cricket, not running after a fool's dream that may only net him some broken bones."

Dane shrugged. "Don't think he wants our opinions or he would have told us and we wouldn't have heard about it through the grapevine."

"True," Josiah said, reaching for one of Pete's small babies when it started to cry. He held the child against his chest, looked at Sara. "I'm sure you have a pearl of wisdom to toss out here."

"No," Sara said, lifting the crust on a cherry pie. "This is done to a turn. Who wants a piece?"

"I do," the four men said, and Sara laughed.

"Good." She started to cut the pie, noticed the frown on Josiah's face. "Whipped cream on top?" she asked.

"I trust you for your honesty," Josiah said, and Sara sighed.

"Once upon a time you asked me what you should do if Jack were to give you his kidney and then still want to ride rodeo. I said that you should go watch him. After all, you'd be well, and this is Jack being Jack. Why waste time keeping distance?" She handed out plates to appreciative men. "Life is short. I say we all go, and we all applaud, no matter the outcome."

"What if Cricket doesn't know?" Josiah asked gruffly. "Won't it seem as if we withheld information from her?"

"That's not my affair," Sara said. "Nor is it yours. All we can do is support Jack in his efforts. For all you know, he wants to win that million dollars so he can tell you he's moving to Fort Wylie."

"That's what I'm afraid of! He just wants to tell me to shove off!" Josiah exclaimed, and Sara dropped a kiss on his forehead.

"I know, you old fussbudget," she said fondly. "This time, you're going to have to tough it out. You can't control your kids anymore—this one may earn his way right out of your control and into Cricket's world."

"I'll pick out my clothes for tomorrow," Josiah said. "let's at least caravan out there and show that the Morgans are backing one of their own. I swear, I may need a new ticker if Jack gets stomped."

"You'll need a new ticker if you keep eating this pie," Pete said appreciatively. "Sara, you should enter this pie in the state fair."

Josiah sighed to himself and kept his fretting silent. All the money in the world couldn't tame Jack. His eldest son was going to do things *his* way—he always had—and this time, Josiah was going to show him how proud he was.

Cricket was worried about Jack. She knew enough about her man to know that he was quiet. Too quiet. It wasn't just that he was tired from helping her with the babies. He was a huge help—even her mother had commented on how devoted Jack was to making sure she and the babies had everything they needed. Her heart had been warmed by her mother's slow-won approval.

She wondered if he regretted making love to her, then knew she was being silly, suffering some type of postpartum blues. Jack had never once complained. In fact, he seemed to adore the babies. One day she'd gotten up, surprised by how rested she felt and walked out to the den to find all three infants sleeping on a nice soft pallet, their father asleep not two feet away on the sofa.

Now that she was formula-feeding—she hadn't had much luck with breast-feeding, though Jack had been endlessly encouraging—he'd taken over the making of the bottles with relentless precision. He made notes about each baby's feeding in a notebook. And diapering, he said, was no different than roping—you just had to be fast while the little buggers did their best to get away.

That had made her laugh.

But for the past two days, Jack had been so preoccupied that she was beginning to get nervous. Probably he needed a break from the schedule of three newborns. "No doubt Jack must feel housebound," she confided to Thad when he came over to visit one afternoon.

"Absolutely," Thad said. "I'd be going stir-crazy."

"I know I am," Cricket said, and Thad looked at her.

"Take a jump," he suggested.

"I would love to," she murmured, knowing full well what Jack's response to that would be.

"A couples jump is good for closeness," Thad said, and Cricket's heart leaped inside her.

It would be wonderful. That's exactly what they needed. But Jack would never agree. "I don't think he'd go for it."

"Maybe not right away," Thad said. "It may take a little more time to get used to the idea. He'll come around."

"Maybe," she said, not sure about that.

"I'm a little surprised you're not at the rodeo," Thad said. "I actually came over to see if you needed a babysitter."

She looked at Thad. "Babysitter? You?"

He shrugged. "You don't think I can take care of my nieces and nephew?"

"Well, I—what rodeo?"

"The Lonely Hearts Station rodeo."

She shook her head. "Why would I?"

"You went last year," Thad pointed out. "And the father of your children is a bull rider, right? I just thought it made sense that you would."

"Oh." Cricket slowly got up to rearrange some toys. Some

days her stitches still hurt. Her body didn't feel quite itself just yet, but she was secretly delighted with her progress. She'd lost a healthy amount of weight and felt good. Jack had helped with that. Every once in a while, when he thought she didn't know he was doing it, she'd catch him checking out her legs or her breasts. In general, he seemed to keep his gaze on her often, which made her feel attractive. "Jack hadn't mentioned he wanted to go this year."

Thad didn't reply. Cricket had assumed Jack had gone to visit his father today—when he'd left the house, he'd merely said he'd be back later tonight. She glanced over at her brother, hesitating as she saw him watching her, his face concerned. "What?"

"Nothing," he said quickly.

"Something," she said, an old routine between them. "Something's on your mind."

"Not so much. Just these little babies," he said, getting down on the floor to watch them as they lay on the thick pallet Jack had fixed for them.

Cricket liked the pallet better than the bassinet because the babies seemed to like lying together, cuddled up next to each other. They looked like peas in a pod, and she had taken tons of pictures of them. *Angels*, she thought. *These babies are angels. Funny how Josiah thought he had ghosts at the ranch house.* And then it hit her.

"Jack's riding today, isn't he?" she demanded.

Thad cleared his throat.

"Thad!" she exclaimed, sensing her brother's reluctance to be the bearer of bad news.

"Oh, come on," he said. "Don't make me be the rat fink."

She was going to kill both the men in her life, her brother because he was being a wienie, and Jack for not telling her about his plans. Of course, she wasn't his wife, he could do as he pleased, but... "I don't understand why he didn't tell me."

"Fear of failure." Thad shook a rattle for the babies, who

seemed more interested in their toes. "Fear of disappointing you? I don't know."

"Why are men so complex?" Cricket demanded. *Particularly mine?*

"Fears," Thad said. "Men have a lot of them."

"Oh, baloney. I spent years counseling couples and I never—" Cricket paused, thinking about all the couples she'd talked to, learning their private stories. Usually, couples felt that their partner wasn't listening to them, and that lay at the root of their problems. It was all about miscommunication, and clearly she and Jack were also misfiring on that front. "I changed for him," she said, "he didn't change for me."

Thad blinked. "That doesn't sound right, but I can't quite put my finger on the improper logic."

"Probably not." Cricket took a deep breath. "But he just can't decide he's going to slip off without telling me."

"Wait," Thad said. "Rodeo is how the man makes a living, isn't it? Do you think he just went to work, like any other man would? Jack probably didn't think it was earth-shattering news that he was going to try to make a buck."

"Why are you taking his side?" Cricket asked.

"I'm not. I'm trying to dig my way out of trouble. I don't like to cause trouble," Thad said, "and I don't want Jack to think I'm a weasel for telling on him."

"I gave up jumping because of him," Cricket said, starting to steam, "and he had no intention of giving up rodeo!"

"Wait," Thad said, holding up the rattle. "You didn't give up parachuting because of the cowboy. You were pregnant, Cricket! Be reasonable."

She was trying to be. But she was hurt Jack wouldn't confide in her. She'd been worrying about him feeling tied down when obviously he was just going on with his life, while she... she had decided to give up an activity she loved, knowing he didn't want her doing it.

"Have you guys talked about this giving-up thing?" Thad asked.

Cricket shook her head.

"Well, I wouldn't get myself in a knot, then."

Cricket knew her brother was right. "I'll take you up on that babysitting offer."

He looked at her. "I'm happy to do it, but do you think this is wise? Are you cleared to drive yet? Maybe you should just talk to him when he gets home."

"I want to see Jack ride," Cricket said.

"For support?"

She wasn't sure. But this was who Jack was, and Cricket knew that. Rodeo was so much a part of him that even Josiah hadn't been able to threaten, bluster or buy it out of Jack's life. "Not just support," Cricket said, "but because I'm not going to live the next fifty years of my life with a man who's afraid to tell me what he loves in life."

"Okay," Thad said, "that sounds healthy."

She intended for their relationship to be very healthy. "And schedule a jump for me," Cricket said, "one month from today."

"Shouldn't you talk to Jack first?"

Cricket headed to her room to change. "You just worry about being Uncle Thad today and put away your counselor's hat." The truth was, she wasn't sure what to tell Jack. All she knew was that this rodeo was a defining moment in their relationship. She planned to make certain she and Jack didn't repeat history, drifting apart like Gisella and Josiah had when their marriage was young. She and Jack weren't even married, and that put them on shakier ground even than Gisella and Josiah's relationship had been.

She kissed each baby on the head and went out the door, anxious to catch Jack before he rode. Who knew what could happen?

Chapter 20

Cricket remembered the first time she'd ever seen Jack on the back of a thrashing bull—she remembered because that's when she'd fallen in love with him. It had been love at first sight. She'd known it; there'd been no escaping her unruly heart's longings for the cowboy.

This time was no different. She got to the rodeo just in time to see Jack's first ride, her breath nearly stopping in her chest as she watched him stick to the back of the bull the best he could. Arm held up high above his head trying for more points, Jack made it to the buzzer before being thrown to the ground.

She gasped, and knew better than to dash to the rail to check on him. In fact, she didn't want him to know she was there at all.

There was no point in making him nervous or unhappy, taking his mind off of his ride. She wanted him to do whatever it was he had set out to do.

She seated herself high up in the stands, away from where anyone she knew might see her. Jack's scores were announced and she proudly noted he had earned a respectable score. Surely he'd be pleased with that.

But she knew he wouldn't be completely pleased unless he won.

"Got a sweetie riding?" a nearby middle-aged woman asked her. She threw some peanut shells down and smiled warmly at Cricket.

"Um, just a friend," Cricket said. "You?"

"A son." The woman's smile turned a little rueful. "You know how it goes. Rodeo gets into their blood at a young age."

Cricket swallowed, thinking about her own baby boy. In six years or less, he'd be old enough for snatching the bow off the calf's tail games. Jack would probably want to buy him a tiny pony to practice riding on—of course he would. One step always led to another—

"I don't think he's got a shot at the million," her seatmate said. "There's too many cowboys in there with a lot more experience. Still, I'm hoping he does all right."

Cricket's blood went cold. "I'm sorry. What do you mean, a million?"

Her new friend's penciled brows nearly reached her hairline. She tossed down a few more peanut shells, munching happily. "The million-dollar purse," she said. "Guess anybody could use that much good luck, huh?"

Cricket's breath caught. Now she knew exactly why Jack was riding. It wasn't because he couldn't be tamed. She had said she wouldn't move to the Morgan ranch. Jack had always said he wanted to be with her and the children. He fully intended to stay forever at her tea-shop home. A million dollars would replace the money he would give up by not fulfilling his father's wishes. And contrary to what she'd told his father when he was in the hospital, Jack had ridden very well at the last rodeo here. He had to figure his chances were just as good as the next cowboy's. Sudden anxious nerves assailed her. There was probably nothing worse to start out a relationship on than making someone feel that they had to change everything in their life because of you. Thad was right—Jack had made lots of changes for her.

And lots of sacrifices. "Yes," she murmured, "anyone could use that much good luck."

She stood, giving the woman a smile. "Best of luck to you."

"You're not staying?"

Cricket shook her head. "I saw what I came to see."

She left, slipping out so that no one would be the wiser to her presence. She got into her vintage VW and drove home, saying a silent prayer that Jack's every ride would be safe and long.

But mostly safe.

Jack was happy with his first ride, but the key was making all his rides good ones. He'd felt a strange pop in his knee as he'd landed on the ground and could tell his knee was aggravated, enough to swell a bit. When the round of rides finished, he checked the scores, seeing that he was in third place going into the next round tomorrow. Good enough. He had a chance. A million dollars was enough money to keep him in the game. He thought about Cricket and his tiny, fairly bald, sweeter-than-he-thought-they'd-be children, and knew he had to ride on.

He went to secretly ice his knee.

"That was pretty good," Josiah said reluctantly. "But I still wish he'd just live at the ranch, Gisella."

Gisella and Sara smiled at him. Josiah shrugged. "Okay, I'm proud. He's a little bit better of a rider than I expected him to be."

Pete, Dane and Gabe looked at each other. Laura, Priscilla and Suzy had stayed home to watch the children, deciding to make a barbecue celebration for everyone when they returned.

"I thought he got up a bit slow," Pete commented.

"I did, too," Dane agreed.

"I thought Jack was just staying low, trying to see which way the bull was going to go," Gabe said, waving at his brothers to be quiet around Josiah.

Josiah turned his head to stare at his sons seated behind him. "What are you boys talking about?"

"Nothing, Pop," Pete said.

"I didn't see anything slow," Josiah said, "except maybe that clown."

"Yeah," Gabe said. "It's fine, Pop. No worries."

Josiah sniffed and turned back around. "You boys would know better than me what Jack normally looks like on a ride. But I thought he looked good."

"Had a new sponsor, too," Pete said.

"Probably got that because he's the rider with the most children," Gabe said, and they laughed.

"That's not funny," Josiah said. "You boys are too hard on your brother."

"We're just picking at you, Pop," Dane told him. "We can see your hair turning whiter by the second."

Josiah sighed. "You see how they treat me, ladies. I suffer."

Sara patted his arm. Gisella handed him some popcorn. They watched the next round begin and Josiah wondered how much stress one father could take. He, too, had seen Jack get up slow, and he was nervous. In fact, it was his worst nightmare. Jack wouldn't turn in his number over a little bump or bruise—or much else, either. Not with him sitting within a shot of the big prize. Josiah held in a groan and tried to focus on the fact that he was supposed to be having a great time sitting around with his family, watching Jack do what he loved, something he'd never been able to do before. He was a father, and sometimes, being a father was a really tough job. "Well, show's over for us for today," he said. "Let's head home and eat some barbecue. Tomorrow's a big day, and I want to be back bright and early."

Cricket had just put the triplets down for their three-hour nighttime nap—they weren't sleeping through the night, nowhere close, of course—when Jack walked in. Limped in, she realized.

She didn't ask him about his injury. If he wanted to talk about it, he would.

"Hey," he said to her.

"Hi to you, too."

"How are the babies?"

She smiled. "They had a big day. They were a little hard to get down, but they're sleeping now."

He limped over to the sofa. She bit her lip, wanting desperately to ask him, knowing he wasn't about to share. He was so much like Josiah, after all.

"Can I help you get your boots off?"

He shook his head. "I got it. Thanks."

She watched him struggle with his boots, then turned away. Tea was what she did best, she decided, tea and prayer. "I was just about to make a nice soothing cup of tea. Can I get you one? And maybe some chocolate cookies? I like chocolate cookies when I'm not... I mean, at night."

He glanced at her. "Cricket, you don't have to wait on me. I'm living here to help you with the children. So how about you sit down, and I'll make the tea and cookies?" Getting up, he took her hand, gently guiding her toward the place where he'd been seated. "Tea and chocolate. I can handle that."

She closed her eyes as she sat, listening to him rifle through the kitchen. He was stubborn—had she ever realized how much?—and the best thing she could do was let him be himself. It hurt; she desperately wanted to take care of him. But by opposing his livelihood, she had put a distance between them that only time would breach. Casting about for a safe subject, she finally said, "I got an offer from a church today. It was on my message machine when I got home."

He set tea and cookies in front of her, like an offering from a prince. "Congratulations. I'd like to hear all about that after you tell me where you went today."

She'd slipped. Jack's eyes were on her, intent and interested.

She could fib, but she wasn't going to. He would find out soon enough. "I went to watch you ride."

The tea cooled between them, the cookies sat untouched. Cricket had no appetite.

"I should have told you," Jack finally said, leaning into the seat across from her. "And may I just make the observation that you're not supposed to be driving yet."

"We should tell each other a lot of things," Cricket said. "Later on. When we have time. Right now, why don't you let me cut those jeans off of you and see what we can do about your knee."

He sighed. "I would actually appreciate that."

She carefully cut off his jeans, iced his knee with a bag of frozen peas and elevated it, grateful when he fell asleep on the sofa.

He looked exhausted. *This is what I signed on for when I fell for Jack Morgan,* she thought, gazing at him, dark and tired and incredibly handsome on her flowered sofa. *Thank God he came home to me and the children tonight.*

This was the starting point for everything to come, she decided. If Jack was going to be a road warrior, then she wanted him to know that he was always welcome to come back home to her.

Having him in her life was worth the agony of separation, worry, loneliness. Yes, Jack Morgan was worth it.

Chapter 21

Early the next morning, Thad, Eileen and Reed came over to watch the babies while Cricket drove a protesting Jack to Lonely Hearts Station.

"You're not supposed to be driving," Jack insisted.

To that, Cricket just said, "Hush."

"At least drive my truck. I know you're killing yourself driving that ancient Bug-thing." If he won the rodeo, Jack determined right then and there that he was buying Cricket a minivan. Something like a tank, with all-around air bags. The babies were due to visit the doctor any day now for their first checkup, and little Miss Independent would probably insist on driving herself. If his woman and his babies were going to be on the road constantly, especially if she accepted whatever job she'd been offered, then they were going to be as safe as he could make them. He filed her job offer under the Next Emergencies to Deal With in his brain, took a brief moment to consider whether he wanted a working wife, decided that if he interjected an opinion on that at this moment he'd probably get his head handed to him. Cricket had already taken his rodeoing without protest; he'd best keep his mouth shut while he was ahead.

Besides, until he got her to the altar, he had very little to zero say in her decisions, anyway. "My truck is newer," he said, fighting one small battle at a time. And Cricket finally said, "All right. You just lie back there and visualize winning."

He honestly didn't need to lie down; the swelling was almost gone. The knee felt a bit stiff but it wasn't enough to keep him from riding. "Why do I have the feeling that you're being very understanding, even for a deacon?"

"I have no idea," Cricket said, backing out of the driveway.

He gazed at the tea-shop side of the house as she drove away. It was quaint; he knew she loved it. But there was little yard for kids to play in and no place to keep ponies. Teaching the kids to ride was still a few years away; still, he dreamed about riding with his children. He thought about serving tea and cookies in their family tea shop, considered the fact that Cricket's parents had offered to buy the place and run it. She hadn't said anything lately about their offer; there was too much happening in her life for her to move now. Maybe if he won the million-dollar purse, he'd start a business, keep his wife at home.

She'd never said a word about the prize money, just offered silent support. "You're planning a jump, aren't you?"

Her eyes met his in the rearview mirror. "I did mention it to Thad. It's too soon right now, obviously, but it's been a long time. I'm ready to get back to my life."

Just like he was getting back to his were the unspoken words. "My dangerous love earns a living," he pointed out.

She said, "Let's have this debate later."

"Nah," he said. "Just go ahead and tell Thad that if the mother of my children jumps out of a plane, I'll return the punch he welcomed me to the family with."

They spent the rest of the trip to Lonely Hearts Station in silence.

* * *

Jack Morgan was a pain in the patoot, Cricket thought, censoring her thoughts. Bossy, domineering...domineering...bossy. She grit her teeth, not about to fuss with him before he rode. With her luck, her stubborn cowboy would break his neck and the last words he would have heard from her would be *Punching my brother would be a mistake on your part, you bigheaded creep.* Cricket sighed. She loved Jack, even when he was annoying. Maybe attitude was part of his game-day preparation. She'd smooth that out of him later.

She parked outside the arena and he got out. There was no reason to say anything; she didn't know what he needed to hear before he rode, anyway. Did one say *Good luck* or *Break a leg?* Was he superstitious? She didn't know.

She squealed when he jerked the driver's-side door open, shocked when he melted her with a steamy, heart-stealing kiss. His eyes blazed down at her when he finished, and then he walked away.

"Okay," she said after she'd recovered, "I think that was how we say good luck in Jack Morgan's world."

She liked it. Her heart was racing, she was nervous as all get out, but she wasn't about to not witness her man's two rides today, win, lose or fall.

Josiah had never been as anxious as he was today. "There's nothing worse than watching your son deliberately try to kill himself," he said, carping to everyone in the double-cab truck.

"Pop, it's going to be fine," Pete said, who was driving the brothers and Pop to Lonely Hearts Station. "Jack's been doing this for years."

"And as I recall, getting stomped a few times, too. I seem to remember a few—"

"Pop," Dane said, "don't get agitated. There's nothing you can do about it."

"There never was," Josiah said on a sigh.

"That's right," Sara said. "Now, just be proud."

"And be glad only one of our sons did this," Gisella said. "I don't think you could have survived the agony of more of them riding."

"Actually," Josiah said, reflecting back over the years, "want to know what scared me the worst?"

"Not really," Gabe said, and everybody laughed.

"What scared me the most was my other three sons going into the military. Now *that* made for some sleepless nights." Josiah looked out the window, watched the landscape rush by. He'd been proud of their service to country, durn proud, knew they needed to do it. But he'd spent a lot of worried nights around the world, wondering if he'd stayed home more, if his boys would have known him better, wanted to be with him.

"You never said that before," Dane said.

Josiah snorted. "What do you think? I had a Texas Ranger, a spy, a soldier and a bull rider for sons. Did you think I had a heart made of iron?"

"Yes!" everybody in the truck exclaimed at once, then laughed. Josiah knew they were teasing him, but they were wrong. It was a wonder he hadn't needed a new heart instead of a kidney.

"Well, I did," he said, okay with playing Tough Pop for the occasion. "I had to be strong to survive the lot of you."

"We know, we know," Gabe said, chuckling, but Josiah didn't care that they were teasing him. Almost all of his boys had come home—he figured he'd gotten everything he wanted, and then some.

Cricket put her hands over her eyes when the bull charged from the gate, accompanied by the announcer yelling, "Mighty Jack Morgan, riding Hell-Beast! Come on, come on, Morgan!" She peeked through her fingers, her heart completely arrested in her chest. Up and down Jack went, mimicking the rolling, thrashing motions of the bull. Never had time passed so slowly.

Never had she been so afraid. This was nothing like jumping out of a plane; watching your man at the mercy of a bull with nothing but his wits was horrible. She was so proud, she didn't know what to do except hang on.

When the buzzer sounded, Jack flung off hard; he hit the ground, jumped up out of the way of the whirling bull. Cricket leaped to her feet, her hands clasped, as everyone in the arena clapped wildly—when the announcer called out Jack's score of ninety-three and a half, the applause was earsplitting.

"We thought we saw you down here," Pete said, startling her.

"Did you see that?" Cricket cried, throwing her arms around Pete's neck.

"Yeah," he said, chuckling, "he's about to give Pop a coronary. Come sit up here with the family."

She scurried up after him, and hugged all the Morgans one by one. "Aren't you proud?" she asked Josiah, who wiped his brow.

"I'm just glad to be here," he said, "durn glad I am."

"Me, too," Cricket said. "*Me,* too."

Jack leaned his head against the boards of a stall, held his breath against the pain. *I can do this. I'm so close. I win, I have college education funds paid for, I can stay at home with my children the way my father never could. I can figure out a business that I can run from a tea shop. I can be with Cricket for as long as she'll put up with me.*

He'd read his mother's letters and he knew family was everything. Family was his dream. That's why he rode.

"Bro," Jack heard.

He raised his head. "Hey, Pete. What are you doing here?"

"Same thing we were doing here yesterday. Pop wanted to see you ride."

Jack perked up. "He did?"

"Oh, yeah. Wild horses couldn't have kept him away. Let's take a look at that knee." Pete squatted next to him. How Pete had found him, Jack wasn't sure. He'd found the most private place he could find to rest, hide, disguise the fact that his knee was killing him. He didn't want anyone telling him he couldn't ride.

"What do you mean, my knee?" Jack asked.

Pete shrugged. "You got a couple hours before you ride. There's a place down the street where we can put you in a bathtub and ice your knee."

Jack knew Pete's suggestion was wise. He still chafed at it, cursed his injury. "I'd really rather stay here."

Pete looked at him sideways. "Ice bath and a shot at a million, or pride and a knee that won't let you stay on."

"Have you seen the draw?" Jack asked.

"Man-O'-War," Pete said, needing no further elaboration.

A registered bounty bull. He was in a great place for the ride of his life—or the stomping of his life. "Ice," he said, "and an ibuprofen Big Gulp, durn it."

"Durn it" was Pop's favorite expression. Pete grinned.

"Now you're talking like a champ," Pete said, helping his brother up.

Actually he was *thinking* like Pop, Jack realized. Jack felt Pop's steely stubbornness strengthening him, and he was thankful.

Cricket called her family to check on the babies, reassured by her parents' calm words.

"Don't worry, Cricket," Eileen said, "I've raised a few children, you know. Anyway, we're delighted to have them all to ourselves. Three of them, three of us—we're equally matched, I'd say."

Cricket smiled. "Thank you."

"So, I'm almost too excited to ask, but how is Jack doing?"

"Fine, as far as I can tell," Cricket said. "He had a great ride this morning."

"Good," Eileen said. "Tell him we said 'bust a move' or whatever young people say these days. I heard that on TV. We've been watching kids' shows when we're feeding the children. Reed and I have decided we're going to order them some good old-fashioned sitcoms, like *The Honeymooners*. These kids aren't going to know about some of the best things in life if they have to grow up on what serves for family programming today."

Cricket smiled at the thought of her mother and father perusing old TV-show catalogs for her babies. "Thanks, Mom."

Eileen giggled. "You should see your father kowtow to these babies," she said on a whisper. "They don't wave a finger that he's not completely immersed in the moment."

"I'll call you later, Mom," Cricket said. "I hear the announcer saying something and I don't to miss anything."

"Good luck!" Eileen said, hanging up.

Cricket hurried back to her seat. "Did I miss anything?" She glanced around. "Where's Pete?"

"He went to do something," Gabe said. He handed her a bag of popcorn. "He should be back soon."

Cricket turned around, scanned the arena. Clowns moved barrels, workers began to take their positions where there were either open gates for departing bulls or help cowboys out of the arena. Cricket put the popcorn on the seat, suddenly lacking appetite. She whipped back around, staring at Dane and Gabe. "Pete went to see Jack, didn't he?"

"I believe so," Dane said, his voice calm.

Cricket realized he was trying to comfort her. "Because of his knee?"

"Because everybody needs a coach," Gabe said. "Don't worry, Cricket. Jack's ridden a ton of times, he's good at what he does."

"Okay." Cricket turned around, determined not to be the kind of woman who made everybody worry about her. Gisella briefly patted her on the back; Sara came and sat next to her. She took a deep breath, warmed by the support.

Before she realized it, the first bull of this round shot from the gate, accompanied by the announcer's voice excitedly calling his name. Cricket didn't hear a thing; it all blocked out. She heard Gabe say that Jack would ride last and consigned herself to sitting in a stonelike trance.

But this day wasn't about her, Cricket remembered, so silently she reached her hand over to Josiah, slipping her fingers between his. He didn't look at her, kept his gaze locked onto the arena, but he held her hand tightly.

"Jack Morgan!" the announcer called suddenly, "in second place, and needing a score of ninety-four to win! Ride, Man-O'-War, *Go-o-o-o-o-o*!"

Cricket and Josiah clutched each other's fingers; Pete, Gabe and Dane jumped to their feet. Gisella and Sara clung to each other as the bull threw itself in the air time and again, Jack hanging on with every ounce of his strength. Cricket could feel him straining; understood exactly what he was riding for, could even feel his focus. She'd never felt so close to him, almost reading his soul. In a flash, he went by, punishing leaps from the bull absorbed into his body. Cricket had no breath; she almost thought she saw a vision of three knights riding beside him, part of him, glorying in his quest.

The buzzer buzzed and with one mighty leap, the bull threw off Jack. He landed on the ground and Cricket was so dizzy she thought she saw the three knights help him to his feet. She and Josiah and all the family jumped up, cheering wildly.

"Did you see that, folks?" the announcer shouted with glee. "A bounty ride! A quicker-picker-upper if we ever saw one! Mighty Jack Morgan, folks, with a score of...ninety-five and a half! We have a winner of the Lonely Hearts Station Rodeo! Jumping Jack Flash!"

Someone shoved a microphone in front of Jack's face as he rose from the ground. "Words from the winner!" the reporter demanded, and Jack took the microphone.

His chest was heaving, his face stuck with bits of sawdust, but he was grinning. "I do have something I want to say. I want to thank my sponsor, Lonely Hearts Station Rodeo, my fam-

ily, the good Lord and his angels. But more than anything, I
want to say to Cricket Jasper, deacon from Fort Wylie and the
most amazing woman I have ever had the pleasure to meet—"
he dropped onto his good knee "—Cricket Jasper, I love you
like crazy, I'm in love with you the way I never thought I'd love
anyone. To paraphrase an old movie, *The Music Man,* somewhere along the line I got my foot stuck on my way out the door
when I met you. It's been the best thing that ever happened to
me. Do me the honor of marrying me and I promise I'll be the
husband you deserve."

The audience went wild, applauding and whistling. Cricket
shot to her feet, but Jack didn't know where she was in the audience. She was blocked by cheering spectators.

Suddenly she felt lifted by strong hands, nearly helping her
off her feet to the rail. She climbed over to rush across the saw-
dust-covered arena into Jack's arms. "I love you," she told him.
"Of course I'll marry you. You're the prince I always dreamed
of, my rodeo man."

He kissed her and the audience clapped louder, loving a
happy ending and a good show, and Jack looked down at his
deacon, then waved his cowboy hat to his family cheering in
the stands.

Epilogue

Josiah loved having all his family around. Gisella adored living at the ranch, where it was always active, always filled with love. It was family, the way the Morgans had always dreamed it would be.

Jack turned, smiling at the huge ranch house he'd never thought he'd call home, where he now found sanctuary and peace. He went inside and found his wife in the den, putting the babies down for naps in the bassinets in front of the huge new windows she'd had installed. Streaming sun illuminated the room, which looked very much like a photograph straight out of *Southern Living*. The drapes Cricket had created were full, elegant swaths of rich fabric, framing the windows with perfect grace.

Cricket said she loved living in Union Junction, loved the Morgan ranch. Their lives had changed when Jack won the rodeo, but it had nothing to do with the money and everything to do with Jack's delight with being a father. He and Cricket had married in a lovely ceremony at the ranch. She'd taken a position as a deacon at a church in Union Junction, thrilled to be doing what she was good at once again. Her parents took over the tea shop, along with Thad, and they were enjoying their new position in the community. They spent a great deal of time running out to see the babies, who seemed to grow by leaps and bounds, and who never lacked loving arms to hold them and adoring hands to guide them. Jack bought Cricket the minivan he'd promised her, but his favorite gift was a three-stone engagement ring, one diamond for each baby she'd blessed him with.

Josiah gave his son the promised million dollars, which Jack decided to put toward his real dream of endowing a community college in Union Junction. Many times he'd pondered what Cricket had told Josiah that day in the hospital, when she'd told his father Jack was a huge believer in education. The thought had turned into a dream for children of Union Junction to have a college where they could expand their educations without leaving the town, if they wished. Pete, Dane and Gabe helped fund the college, and Josiah was chest-pounding proud. As far as building worlds went, he thought Jack had gotten the hang of it very well.

Cricket never did parachute again—she said one of them living dangerously was more than enough—but Jack did. He took Gisella up, with Thad's guidance. The experience was crazy, Gisella and Jack agreed, and it reconstructed a cherished bond that they had both always missed.

Jack admired his wife's handiwork for a few more moments, knowing how pleased his father would be with Cricket's choice of drapes, then gathered his wife into his arms and whispered something to her, soft words not even the babies could have heard.

But Cricket heard every word her husband spoke to her. She smiled at her rodeo man, and kissed him. "It's good to be home," Cricket said, and Jack nodded.

It had been said before, but there really was no place like home—and Jack's home was with Cricket and his triplets.

The true grail for the Morgans had been family.

* * * * *

The Bull Rider's Baby Bombshell

Amanda Renee

Books by Amanda Renee

Harlequin Western

Saddle Ridge, Montana

The Lawman's Rebel Bride
A Snowbound Cowboy Christmas
Wrangling Cupid's Cowboy
The Bull Rider's Baby Bombshell

Welcome to Ramblewood

Betting on Texas
Home to the Cowboy
Blame It on the Rodeo
A Texan for Hire
Back to Texas
Mistletoe Rodeo
The Trouble with Cowgirls
A Bull Rider's Pride
Twins for Christmas

Visit the Author Profile page at
millsandboon.com.au for more titles.

Amanda Renee was raised in the northeast and now wiggles her toes in the warm coastal Carolina sands. Her career began when she was discovered through Harlequin's So You Think You Can Write contest. When not creating stories about love and laughter, she enjoys the company of her schnoodle, Duffy, as well as camping, playing guitar and piano, photography, and anything involving animals. You can visit her at amandarenee.com.

For Brad,
Thank you for the inspiration.

Chapter 1

Call Jade.

I can't do this.

Please forgive me.

Jade Scott read her sister's note for the tenth time since arriving in Saddle Ridge. Almost an entire day had passed since Liv had vanished, leaving behind her month-and-a-half-old triplets. Jade would've arrived sooner if there had been more flights out of Los Angeles to the middle-of-nowhere Montana. She'd ditched the godforsaken town eleven years ago and had sworn never to return. But her sister's children had annihilated that plan. Especially since Jade had been partially responsible for their existence.

"I didn't call the police like you asked, but now that you're here, I think we should."

"No!" Jade spun to face Maddie Winters, her sister's best friend and the woman who had taken care of the children for the past twenty hours. "As soon as we do, Liv's labeled a bad parent and those girls go in the system."

"Nobody will take them away with you here." Maddie

checked to see if there were any new messages on her phone. "I'm really worried about her."

Jade scanned the small living room. A month ago, it looked like a baby—or three—lived there. Today it looked cold and sterile, devoid of any signs of the triplets. The crocheted baby blankets and baskets of pastel yarn were gone from the corner. Once covered with stacks of photo albums her sister couldn't wait to fill, the coffee table now sat bare. Embroidered pillows with their cute mommy and baby sayings no longer littered the couch. Her sister had even removed the framed pictures of the girls along with their plaster hand- and footprints from the mantel. Except for the video baby monitor, nothing baby related remained in sight. Why? She knew Liv's desire for order was strong thanks to their chaotic upbringing, but she'd never thought her sister would wipe away all visible traces of her children.

"I'm worried too. We don't need to involve the police though. She wasn't kidnapped." Liv was a chronic planner and everything about the situation felt deliberate. "She made a conscious decision to walk away. She wrote a note, she called you to babysit and then left on her own accord. If we call the police, the girls go into the system. Hell will freeze over before I let that happen."

Jade knew all about the system. She and Liv had spent fourteen years in foster care, bounced from place to place until Liv had been old enough to become her guardian. Being two teenage girls on their own had forced them to grow up fast. Too fast.

Jade's phone rang inside her bag jarring her back to the present. It wasn't her sister's ringtone, but she reached for it to be safe. It was her office in Los Angeles. She answered, praying Liv had called there by mistake instead of her cell and they were patching the call over to her. "Yes."

"I'm sorry to bother you," Tomás, her British assistant, began. "I just wanted to let you know the Wittingfords have finally decided on their venue for their summer opener."

Jade's heart sank. Tomás's call was great news, just not the news she wanted to hear at that moment. The Wittingfords were the most extravagant clients her event planning company had seen to date. And their showstopping party guaranteed to outshine all the celebrity weddings she'd produced this year.

"I'm glad to hear it. I just wish I was there to oversee it." Jade tugged her laptop out of her bag and opened it on the dining room table. "Email me the contract and I'll review it. I want you to look it over first. Flag anything you question. I need you to be my extra set of eyes while I'm away. And please call my clients and tell them I've had a family emergency. Give them your contact info and make sure they understand I haven't abandoned them. But they need to phone you with any issues or changes and you can fill me in later."

"I'll get on it, straightaway. Any news about your sister?"

"Nothing yet." Jade lifted her gaze to see Maddie glaring at her from the living room. "I need to go. We'll talk later."

"I can't believe you're putting work first." Maddie picked up the baby monitor from the coffee table and checked the screen.

"I'm sorry you don't approve of my multitasking." Jade turned on the computer. "I know my sister. She doesn't do crazy. Wherever she is, I'm sure she's safe. While I try to figure out what's going on with her and where she ran off to, I still have a business to maintain."

"And walking out on your newborn triplets isn't crazy?"

Not unless you knew the whole situation. "All right, tell me again. What time did you come over yesterday afternoon?"

"A little after three. Liv sounded frazzled when she called. I asked what was wrong, but she kept doing that answer a question with a question thing that drives me up a wall. I got nothing out of her." Maddie ran both hands through her hair, on the verge of tears. "I tried to talk to her, but she took off the second I walked in. I found the note taped to the nursery room door a few minutes after that."

"When did she remove the baby things from in here?"

"I don't know." Maddie shook her head wildly. "I'm trying to remember the last time I came over."

"What do you mean? You're her best friend and you didn't check on her? When I left, you assured me you would. You only live next door."

"She insisted on space so she could learn how to take care of the girls on her own. I guess it's been a little over a week since I've been here. I'll be honest, her abrupt dismissal hurt. I had been staying in the guest room after you left. I should have noticed something was wrong."

Uneasiness grew deep within Jade's chest. "I keep thinking the same thing. I missed our video chat on Sunday night because I was too busy with work." Many of Jade's ex-boyfriends had accused her of putting her career before anyone else. Had she selfishly done the same with her sister? Jade scanned her inbox, hoping to find an email from Liv. Nothing. "I'll check her office. Are you able to stay for a little while longer?"

"For however long you need."

Jade continued to walk around the old farmhouse. Her sister had set up three bassinets in the room next to her office in addition to an equal number of cribs in the former master bedroom, now the nursery. Liv had been prepared. Some may even say overprepared. She'd read every parenting book and magazine she found. Took infant care classes and had insisted Jade learn infant CPR too. From researching the best laundry detergents and baby shampoos to memorizing the symptoms of childhood illnesses and diseases, she'd planned for every contingency. It didn't make sense why she left. Outside of neither of them not knowing what good parenting was.

Their father had been a drifter and their mother had been behind bars on and off since Jade was two. They'd seen the inside of more foster homes than they could count. Some good, some bad. Whenever they had made it into a decent one, their mother had gotten out of jail, claimed to be ready to raise them again after completing her therapy and halfway house program only to fail miserably weeks later and wind up right back in jail. Her mother had always wanted what she couldn't have. That included Liv and Jade. Once in her care, she'd discovered they were too much work to support. Besides, her drugs were more important. She wanted those more than anything. More than her children.

The court system had reached a point where they said no more, and Jade and Liv had mixed emotions the day they learned they wouldn't have to live with their mother ever again. Liv had handled it better than she had. Jade had been angry. All the time. It hadn't helped that kids had picked on her constantly at school. One kid had been the ringleader. The one she had trusted, and then he betrayed her. And she had never forgotten him. Wes Slade.

Jade opened the bottom filing cabinet drawer and scanned the hanging folder tabs. The last one had *BABY* scrawled on it. The generic word surprised her. At the very least, she'd expected all three girls' names to be written on the label, if not three separate files. She removed the thick folder, laid it on the desk and began looking through it. On top was the first ultrasound picture of the triplets. Jade ran her fingers over the black-and-white image. She could still see her sister holding up the photo to the screen during their video chat. Liv had been shocked, but thrilled just the same. She was finally getting the family she had always wanted. And it had been a long time coming.

Liv had battled fertility issues for years. Married at twenty-three, she and her husband had tried everything to get pregnant. There was just enough wrong with each of them to prevent a successful pregnancy. Kevin had wanted to adopt, but it had been important to Liv to carry her children and have a physical connection to them. He'd refused the donor idea and their constant baby battles wound up destroying their marriage.

Jade sat in Liv's ultralux, oversize perfect-for-pregnancy office chair and glanced around the room. Her sister had always been neat and organized. Not a pen or paperclip out of place.

She peered inside Liv's desk drawers hoping to find a clue to her whereabouts. Everything related to her job as a financial planner. Liv still had another two months of maternity leave until she had to return to work full-time. Working from home would help the transition although Liv had considered hiring a nanny during the day so she could talk to clients without interruption.

Her sister had a plan. A definitive plan on how her life would run smoothly as a single mom of three children. Walking away was completely out of character.

Jade continued to flip through the contents of the folder. The only item left was Jade's egg donation contract giving her sister the biological link to the babies she wanted. She just hadn't expected Liv to use all the embryos at once. Because of her sister's long infertility battle, the doctor had believed her best chance for a successful pregnancy was to implant them all in hopes one would survive. The surprise had been universal.

"Dammit, Liv, where are you?"

She stood to put the folder back in the drawer when she noticed another one lying on the bottom of the cabinet. Sliding the other files forward, she removed the thin, unmarked and probably empty folder. She flipped it open to double-check and saw another donor contract. Why? Jade had been the only donor. Liv had used a fertility clinic for the father.

She began to read the document:

This agreement is made this 22 day of July 2017, by and between Olivia Scott, hereafter RECIPIENT, and Weston Slade, hereafter DONOR.

"No, no, no!" Jade's heart pounded in her chest. "Liv couldn't have." She continued to read the contract. But she had. Wes Slade was the donor and the father of Jade's biological children. Her sister had fertilized Jade's eggs with the man she despised more than anyone.

* * *

A few hours later, Jade stood in front of the check-in clerk at the Silver Bells Ranch lodge. The woman whispered into the phone. "One of Wes's fans is here to see him."

"Excuse me. I am no fan of his."

The clerk cupped the mouthpiece and whispered, "She may be an ex-girlfriend."

"Are you kidding me?" Jade reached over the counter and snatched the phone. "This is Jade Scott. I need to speak to Wes concerning my sister, Liv. It's…um…an emergency of sorts."

Still reeling from her discovery, Jade needed absolute confirmation Wes was the triplets' father. She prayed he had backed out or that Liv had changed her mind at the last second. Anything…just not this.

"Oh hey, Jade. It's Garrett, Wes's brother. It's been what, ten years or more? I saw your sister and the triplets last week. They sure are beautiful. Reminded me of my two when they were born."

You have no idea. Jade swallowed hard. "I'm staying with the kids for a few days while Liv is—is away on business. She's unreachable today and I have a problem at the house. Since she and Wes are friends, I'm thinking he might have some ideas." At least Jade assumed they were friends. Who would ask a casual acquaintance to father their children?

"He's out with our guests on a trail ride. He should be back soon. You're welcome to wait or maybe I can help you."

"Uh, um. No. I appreciate the offer, but I need Wes. I don't mind waiting." Yeah, she did. The longer she waited, the more questions churned in her brain. "Where's the best place I can catch him?"

"The stables." Garrett paused. "Do you have the girls with you? I'm sure my daughter would love to me—"

"They're with the sitter." The last thing Jade needed was to introduce the triplets to their cousin.

The entire time Liv had been pregnant, Jade kept her part in the process tucked neatly away in the dark recesses of her brain. Surprisingly, Liv had carried to almost thirty-seven weeks. The day of her sister's scheduled cesarean, Jade had been by her side in the operating room, cheering her on. But the moment Jade had held those tiny bundles of perfection and stared into their blue eyes, reality hit. She was the biological mother of three little girls and she had wrestled with it during the rest of her stay in town. They were Liv's children. Not hers. It wasn't until she was on a plane flying back to LA three weeks later that she finally breathed easier. Once she had returned to her normal routine, any lingering thoughts of being their mother faded and she gladly slipped into the role of auntie.

Until today.

She needed to find Liv...fast.

Garrett took the reins as Wes dismounted. "Thanks for helping out."

"No problem." Wes didn't mind filling in for other employees while he was visiting the ranch, considering they had covered for him plenty during his last few months of employment on Silver Bells. It had been an unbearable period in his life and he'd wanted nothing more than to get away from Saddle Ridge. And he had. He'd moved to Texas and escaped the drama he once called home.

"Oh, I almost forgot." Garrett snapped his fingers. "You have a visitor. Do you remember Jade Scott?"

Wes damn near tripped at the mention of her name. Even though he couldn't think of one person he despised more than Jade, it was her sister he didn't want to think about.

"What is she doing here?"

"I guess she's babysitting the triplets while her sister's away on business. She has some emergency at Liv's house. I offered to help, but she insisted on talking to you."

"Keep your distance from the Scotts." Wes swallowed hard. This was exactly why he hadn't wanted to come home for his brother Dylan's wedding and his niece and nephew's christenings. "They can call someone else. I have no business with Liv or Jade."

"What's with the attitude?" Garrett asked. "I thought you and Liv were good friends. Besides, it's too late. Jade's about ten steps behind you."

Wes turned to see her weaving through the ranch guests walking back to the lodge. His stomach somersaulted at the sight of her and he wasn't sure if it was because of their past or how much she had transformed since high school. The mean girl who had once made his life miserable had gone from a rough, chip-on-her-shoulder teen to a California knockout.

Sleek, rich mahogany waves replaced the frizzy curls she used to have. But that body and those curves...good Lord Almighty! Her black polka-dot chiffon blouse revealed just enough of her ample cleavage to make any man look twice, and her tailored black pants hugged her hips in perfection. She exuded an edginess combined with old Hollywood glamour and if she had been any other woman on the planet, he would have moved in for the kill. Their past made her off-limits and his connection to her sister sealed that deal.

"Wes." Deep blue eyes held his gaze before traveling the length of him and back.

Transfixed upon her matte ruby-red lips, it took every ounce of strength he had left to respond. "Jade."

"Hey, kids. A conversation requires more than that." Garrett laughed. "Try hello, how are you." He nudged his brother in Jade's direction before walking away.

"What do you want?" Wes hadn't meant his tone to be as harsh as it sounded.

"It's about Liv. Is there someplace private we can talk?"

Wes stiffened. "I have work to do." He turned to tend to his horse, but it wasn't there. Silently, he cursed his brother.

"I thought you were on vacation from your job in Texas."

He reeled to face her. "Who told you that?"

"The rodeo school where you work." She stepped toward him and wobbled in her ranch-inappropriate four-inch heels. He reached for her arm to steady her and instantly regretted the contact. "I looked you up online. I need your help."

Wes released her and rubbed his palm, wanting to erase all traces of her from his body. "On second thought, I don't care what your reasons are. I'm asking you as politely as possible to leave."

"Wes, please." A half-foot shorter, even in those ridiculous heels, she stared up at him.

"What could you possibly need my help with?"

"Tell me I can trust you first."

"No. You can't trust me, so let's end this now. Goodbye, Jade." The intoxicating scent of her perfume wasn't enough to entice him to hear more.

"I know."

It wasn't so much the words, but the firm way she said them that stopped him in his tracks. "Do you care to expand on that?" He prayed it wasn't what he thought.

"I found the contract today at my sister's house," Jade whispered. "Before I go into details, promise me everything I tell you will stay between us."

Wes wanted to argue and deny his role in Liv's daughters' paternity, but the worry etched into Jade's face gave him pause. "Okay, you have my attention. And yes, you can trust me."

Jade assessed him sharply, making him more uncomfortable than he already was. She had no reason to take him at his word considering their past had thrived on a mutual loathing of one another after their brief high school romance. Her shoulders sagged as she closed her eyes momentarily, shielding him from the pain that reflected in them.

"Liv left the triplets with Maddie yesterday and hasn't returned."

"That doesn't sound like Liv." Wes's heart dropped into his stomach. "Have you called the police? Or checked the hospitals?"

"I called every hospital within a two-hundred-mile radius while I waited for my flight last night. I don't want to involve the police. This isn't a case of her getting in a car accident. She left a note saying she was leaving. Do you have any idea where she might've gone? Has she ever mentioned a place she enjoyed going to when she was under a lot of stress or anywhere she always wanted to visit?"

"Not offhand. I can't believe she left the girls." Wes propped a booted foot up on the fence rail and stared into the corral. "I was afraid this would be too much for her."

"Wait a minute." Jade grabbed him by the arm and forced him to look at her. "You suspected she was in trouble?"

"That's not what I'm saying." Wes checked over his shoulder to make sure they were still alone. "I was long gone before those babies were born. And for the record, this wasn't an easy decision on my part. There was never anything romantic or sexual between your sister and me. We were good friends. She was there for me during the darkest time of my life."

"So how did you get from point A to point B?" Her face soured. "She told me she used an anonymous donor."

"Liv hated the thought of a stranger fathering her children. I had initially said no, then I realized she wanted this more than anything and relented. I felt I owed her for being there for me over the years. But that's where it ended. I couldn't continue our friendship, knowing she was carrying my—" Wes shook his head. "They are not my children. I refuse to say they are."

"I'm not asking you to raise them." Thick sarcasm laced her assurance. "Just tell me what happened."

Wes hesitated before answering, not wanting to sound callous. "Liv and I went our separate ways. She called me once I was in Texas and told me she was having triplets. I'll admit, I had my concerns and asked if she could handle that many babies. She said she was a little overwhelmed by the news, but even more excited. I could hear it in her voice. She also had you and her friends. So, I continued on with my life."

"Turns out she was more overwhelmed than we both thought." Jade's phone rang. She removed it from her bag, checked the screen and then rejected the call. "No matter how long it takes to find her, I'm not abandoning those babies. You can't, either."

"I am not getting involved. I did my part and then got out of town for a reason. Many reasons. They are not my responsibility. She should have gone with an anonymous donor like she had with the eggs."

"She didn't use an anonymous egg donor."

"Then whose were they?"

"Mine. You and I are those girls' biological parents."

Chapter 2

Jade never saw a person pale so fast. "Don't you dare faint on me."

"For God's sake, I've never fainted a day in my life. A bull has knocked me unconscious a time or two in the rodeo ring, but I've never fainted." Wes's hazel eyes narrowed. "You're the biological mother of those children?"

"Believe me, when I saw your name on the donor contract I was none too thrilled. It's like the universe was playing some cruel joke on me."

"On you?" Wes snapped. "You're the last person I would have chosen." His abhorrence for her darkened his features. Features she probably would've found attractive under normal circumstances.

"At least I provided a biological link. You, on the other hand—"

"Go on. Finish what you were going to say." The muscles along his jawline pulsated.

"No, because regardless of our feelings toward each other, we created three beautiful lives. I will not insult them by insulting you."

Wes tilted his hat back, revealing an errant lock of dark blond hair. He folded his arms across his chest, causing his formfitting gray T-shirt sleeve to ride up and expose the hint of a colorful tattoo on his biceps. Biceps that were much larger than she remembered from high school.

"As much as I want to argue with you, that's a very mature attitude and one I should adopt myself." Wes stepped away from the fence, giving her his full attention. "When I agreed to do this, I did so under one condition. Total anonymity."

"I have no intention of saying anything." Jade had wanted the same condition, but she and Liv had discussed the possibility of one day telling the children. Especially if a medical reason arose. That was most likely why she wanted the father to be somebody she knew. Just in case. "The truth may come out, regardless."

"It can't." Wes's eyes widened. "I had second thoughts shortly after I did it. First of all, I never wanted kids of my own. And second, my family would never forgive me for not being involved in their lives. Even though that's what Liv wanted."

"Yeah, I'm not so sure about that." Jade wondered if her sister's feelings for Wes ran deeper than she'd admitted. "Had you already planned to move away when she asked you to be the donor?"

"No. I mean, we discussed how unhappy I was living in Saddle Ridge for reasons I won't get into right now. My bull riding schedule keeps me on the road a lot too, so she knew I wouldn't be around much."

"How did she react when you told her you were moving to Texas?"

Wes winced and rubbed the back of his neck. "I told her over the phone after I had already left. It was all of a two-minute conversation. One I purposely kept short because I couldn't handle being involved in her pregnancy or the baby's life. Then she called and told me she was having triplets."

"You had to have been as shocked as I was." The thought of

Liv carrying and raising one of Jade's children had been surreal enough. And even though she'd been fully aware they'd
harvested three of her eggs, Jade never saw beyond one child.
She'd automatically assumed it was a one-time deal. At the very
least she'd expected her sister to have told her they'd used all
three the day of the procedure.

"That's an understatement. Look, I just came off a full week
of competition and I'm only here for another week and a half
before I head back to Texas. My family has two baby christenings this weekend and Dylan's wedding is the next. And I'm
competing midweek in South Dakota. I'll help you in whatever
way I can, but I'm not going anywhere near those babies. I can't
do it. Despite what you think Liv's intentions may have been,
she stressed I was to be a donor only. Nothing more. I can't get
emotionally involved."

"I don't know what to do. Maddie said Liv had been adamant
about caring for the babies on her own, so she sent her home.
Aside from some brief text messages over the last two weeks,
I haven't really spoken to her. Based on the little information I
have, Liv may be suffering from postpartum depression."

"Oh man." Wes shoved his hands in his pockets. "That's
pretty serious."

"I don't think she'd harm herself, but Liv doesn't do well with
failure." They'd grown up with failure in every way imaginable
and they both worked hard to avoid it now. "I'm wondering if
she recognized what was happening to her and removed herself
from the girls to protect them. Possibly to get help."

"Would she have had that much clarity?"

"She called Maddie and asked her to come over and babysit. And then there was the note she left telling Maddie to call
me. When I checked her room, her luggage was missing. Her
closet and quite a few drawers were partially empty leading me
to assume she packed for a trip of some sort. She planned every
step. It's not erratic behavior. She's either on a long vacation or
she checked herself in somewhere."

"What did the note say?" Jade withdrew the folded slip of paper from her bag and handed it to him. He read it, then turned it over as if expecting to find more. "This is all she wrote?"

Jade nodded. "That's it."

Wes scrubbed the day-old scruff on his chin. "This sounds permanent. I'll talk to Harlan and see what he can find out."

"Your brother? Why? What can he do?"

"He's a deputy sheriff."

"Then keep him out of it." Jade snatched the note back from him, suddenly wishing she hadn't come to see Wes. "The police and social workers always believe they're doing what's best for the children when they don't see or understand the whole picture. I'll handle this."

He stared at her as if she had two heads. "Look, I don't like the idea of involving my brother, either, but you can't do it alone. Triplets are hard enough for a conventional family, let alone a single parent. Your sister's a prime example of that. Do you have help at the house?"

"Maddie said she'd be willing to stay for however long I need her."

"Unless Maddie quit her job since I left in January, she works full-time."

"Are you offering your help?"

"As in physically be there with you?" Wes held up his hands and stepped back. "Oh no. I don't want to see them and please don't force them on me."

"I would never force a child on anyone. They deserve better than that. I only came here because I thought you might have an idea where she went. My mistake."

Jade trudged back to her car, almost twisting her ankle in the process. What the hell had possessed her to wear high heels to a ranch? Stupidity along with vanity. She'd wanted to show Wes that despite the horrible rumors he'd spread about her in school, she had made something of herself. Eleven years later and she was still letting his opinion matter.

* * *

For a small town, the drive back to Liv's house felt like an eternity. Except for a handful of neighbors, her sister lived fairly isolated on the outskirts of Saddle Ridge. Maddie greeted her at the door, tense in anticipation of good news.

"How are the girls?"

"Still asleep. I expect them up soon. Once one's awake, the rest follow. Did you hear anything?"

"No." Jade slipped off her shoes and kicked them aside. "I ran into a friend of hers, though. Wes Slade."

"He must be home for the wedding and christenings."

"You know about them?"

"They only invited the entire town."

Of course, they had. There was nothing like living in a small town. "So, they were good friends?"

"Until he moved to Texas. His leaving really upset Liv since he hadn't even bothered to say goodbye. He's a hottie and a half, but the two of them never hooked up. Probably because he was hooking up with everyone else in the county." Maddie's face turned pink. "Present company excluded."

Jade was all too familiar with Wes's libido.

"My sister never mentioned him. When did they become friends?"

"I'm not really sure since I didn't live here then, but based on different things she's said, I've always assumed it was around the time Wes's father was killed."

"I remember Liv mentioning that, but I didn't realize they knew each other that well." Jade had never discussed Wes or the rumors he had started. The rumors that led to one of his friends assaulting her. Liv had had enough going on between school and working whenever she could to save for college. Regardless, Liv had to have heard the rumors from her friends. Saddle Ridge was too small of a town not to. Was that why she kept her friendship with Wes from her? Or had Wes said something?

"I tried calling Liv again, and it went straight to voice mail.

I left a message telling her you were here and that the girls were fine."

"Nothing about them missing her?" Jade asked.

"I—I don't remember exactly what I said. Should I have?"

Jade dropped her bag on the antique hall table in the foyer. "If she's suffering from some form of postpartum depression I'd like to believe hearing the children miss her would prove how much they need her. That's just speculation on my part." She wondered if her sister would interpret their being fine as confirmation she'd done the right thing. But Maddie blamed herself enough already. Jade didn't need to add to it. "Why don't you head home, take a shower and relax for the night. I appreciate you going above and beyond like you have."

"Are you sure?" Maddie gnawed on her bottom lip. "I realize you were here when the girls were born, but do you know how to take care of an infant? Let alone three?"

"I'm sure I can handle feeding them, changing a few diapers and putting them to bed." Jade's hands flew to her chest. "Oh my God! Liv was breast-feeding."

Maddie shook her head. "No, it didn't work out. She wasn't producing enough milk and was unbelievably sore. They started on formula pretty early."

Jade had headed back to LA eight days after the girls were released from the hospital. "She never told me."

"She probably wouldn't have told me if I hadn't been staying here. It really upset her."

"I bet." Jade imagined her sister thought not being able to breast-feed as the ultimate failure.

"Have you ever mixed formula before?"

"Can't say that I have." Jade sighed.

"Come on." Maddie motioned for her to follow. "There's kind of a formula to making formula and it all starts with boiling water."

By the time Maddie walked her through the steps, Jade understood why women opted to breast-feed. Even though the can came with directions, she took detailed notes, not wanting to risk a mistake.

"Just remember to toss out any mixed formula after twenty-four hours. You can make a large batch of it, but it's not like milk. You can't keep a gallon in the fridge for a week. If any of them don't finish their bottle, toss it because their saliva can contaminate the formula."

"Got it. I'm assuming this is the bottle sterilizer?" Jade pointed to a large dome-shaped appliance sitting on the counter.

"Yes. You can also run their pacifiers through there. But—" Maddie opened the cabinet next to the sink and removed three bottomless bottles and a box "—it's more convenient to use these with the liners. That way the nipples are the only thing you'll need to clean. Just toss the liners in the trash."

After a crash course in infant feeding, Maddie left for the night. Jade peeked in at the girls before heading to the guest room to change. She stood in the doorway as she'd done earlier, almost afraid to get any closer to the children who were biologically hers. She still had a tough time wrapping her brain around it. If she intended to take care of them until Liv returned, she needed to remember Liv was their real mother, not her.

She tiptoed across the room to their cribs, choking back tears. They were beautiful, and she'd help create them. The inexplicable desire to hold them overwhelmed her. She wanted to tell them how much she loved them and that she'd never abandon them. How bad had things gotten for her sister to walk away from her children?

She reached over the side of the crib and lightly ran her hand over one of their matching white-and-pink cotton bunny onesies. *Matching!* How would she tell the girls apart? They were fraternal triplets, but they looked alike to her. Especially at this age. Liv and Maddie could tell them apart, but Jade hadn't spent enough time around them yet. If it wasn't for the large *A*, *H* and *M* stenciled on the wall above their respective cribs she wouldn't have known who was Audra, Hadley or Mackenzie.

"What if I mix them up?"

Hadley stirred at the sound of her voice but didn't wake up. Jade scanned the room. She needed something to distinguish them from each other. Nail polish came to mind, but she feared they'd chew it off. She ran back downstairs to Liv's office and dug a black permanent marker out of the drawer. She'd have to write their first initial on the sole of their foot until she researched a better solution online. Maybe the pediatrician could offer a suggestion. She had to call there anyway to find out when the babies' next appointment was. First, she had to fabricate a plausible excuse as to why she was calling and not her sister. She didn't want to arouse suspicion about Liv.

One triplet began to cry as she reached the top step. She ran into the room, pulled off the marker cap with her teeth and wrote a large *H* on the bottom of Hadley's foot when the odor of a full diaper smacked her square in the jaw.

"Good heavens. For a tiny little thing, that is one big stink." Jade lifted Hadley into her arms as Audra began crying. Within seconds, the room was full of shrieks and smelly diapers. She couldn't pacify or change the girls fast enough. She wasn't even sure how to get them downstairs to feed them. Maddie would. Jade went to pull her phone from her pocket before remembering she left it in her bag. "Okay, I guess we're going down one at a time."

Mackenzie started crying louder than the other two before she reached the hallway. "What is it, sweetheart?" She cradled her against her chest, afraid to put her down. "You have a clean diaper and I will feed you in a few minutes." Mackenzie's tear streaked face turned red while her tiny arms flailed in the air. Jade adjusted the baby's position and sat in the rocking chair. "Shh, I've got you. I know you miss your mommy, but I'm here."

Mackenzie's cries continued along with her two sisters and Jade wondered if Liv had postpartum depression or if she'd needed a sanity break. She easily saw how this could try even a saint's patience after a while. Jade couldn't do this alone. She needed help.

Wes sat in Liv's driveway for ten minutes before he got the nerve to walk up the porch stairs and knock on the door. Once he did, he heard a baby cry from inside. He hadn't even considered he might wake them up. He hadn't considered much on the drive over except that he hadn't given Jade his phone number and he didn't have hers. His concern for Liv was worth the risk of seeing the girls.

Wes's heart pounded in his chest as a cold sweat formed across his brow. His biological daughters were inside that house. It was the closest he'd ever been to them and all he wanted to do was run. Why hadn't he called Liv's house and left a message on the answering machine if Jade didn't answer? Because he hadn't thought this through. The reality he'd created three children with the bully responsible for the beatings he'd received in the high school locker room struck him harder than a runaway Mack truck.

"Maddie, I need you!"

A chill ran down Wes's spine at the sound of Jade's desperate plea. He grabbed the knob and flung the door open, causing it to bang against the interior wall. "Jade!" He ran toward the baby cries, uncertain what he might find. He stuck his head in the numerous rooms that branched off the center hall of the old farmhouse. "Jade, where are you?" he asked as he reached the kitchen, only to find Jade, barefoot and disheveled holding one screaming infant in her arms while the other two wailed from bouncy chairs perched on top of the table.

His heart stopped beating at the sight of them. His daughters. His. They had his DNA, his genes, his— Wes grabbed the doorjamb.

"Thank God you're here." She took a step toward him.

He shook his head, trying not to break eye contact with her

for fear he'd look into the eyes of one of his daughters. "Why are they crying?"

"Wes, meet Audra." She held the infant out to him. "Please help me."

His arms rose automatically to take her without hesitation as his body betrayed his will. He closed his eyes, not wanting to see the life he'd helped create. The weight of Audra in his arms made her all that more real. Her cries stopped as a soft mew emanated from the tiny bundle. He didn't want to look. But he couldn't not look. He needed to see his daughter.

"Oh my God." His heart sprang back to life.

"What is it?" Jade frantically asked.

"She's beautiful," he whispered.

"They all are. We made quite the heartbreakers."

He lifted his gaze to hers. The edginess had faded to a gentle softness. Even with her stained blouse and what appeared to be a black marker streak across her left cheek, she exuded beauty. "I guess we did." He lowered his eyes to the other two girls contentedly sucking on the bottles Jade held for them. And then he saw more black marker. "Did you write on their feet?"

"I had to. I couldn't tell them apart. They're not identical, but they sure look that way to me."

Wes cautiously stepped forward as if walking on ice. He'd held a baby before. He'd been around plenty of children in his twenty-nine years. Somehow, these three seemed more fragile than any of the others combined.

"The nose on that one is a little more upturned." Wes glanced at the infant's foot. "What does the *M* stand for?"

"Liv never told you their names?"

"She sent me a birth announcement, or what I assumed was one. I never opened it."

"Wow, you really haven't spoken to her in months because she chose those names in January."

"I stopped taking her calls when she told me she was having triplets." He reached for the third bottle sitting on the table and held it up. "May I?"

"Be my guest. She refused to eat for me."

Wes sat in the chair across from her and held the bottle to Audra's tiny lips. She hesitated for a second before eagerly drawing on the nipple. Her eyes reminded him of Jade's…big, blue and the color of the Montana sky on a bright summer day. He wished somebody would pinch him because feeding his daughter was the most surreal experience of his life.

"I hate that I didn't call. It bothered me then, but it bothers me more now. I can't help wondering if my abandonment contributed to her leaving."

"I won't criticize you for walking away because if Liv and I weren't sisters, I may have done the same thing."

Jade's candor surprised him. "So, you still haven't told me what the *M* stands for."

"Mackenzie and the other is Hadley."

"Audra, Mackenzie and Hadley." His cheeks hurt from smiling. "It's a pleasure to meet you. I'm—" He wasn't sure how to introduce himself.

"You're a friend of their mother. That's all we can ever be."

Ten minutes ago, Wes didn't even want to be a friend to anyone connected to the children, now it hardly seemed enough.

"How is this supposed to work? You can't even feed the three of them on your own."

"That's not fair." Jade held a bottle up to the light to see how much formula remained in the liner. "This was my first try. Although I'm not sure what my sister was thinking when she told Maddie to call me. I'm not exactly mother material. My job's super demanding and consumes most of my time."

"What do you do?"

"I own a high-end event management company in Los Angeles. You could say I'm a party planner to the stars. I'm surprised my sister didn't tell you."

He would never have guessed she'd chosen that career path.

He figured she would have chosen… Wes stared at her, not recognizing the woman she was today. He'd never given much thought to what she did after high school. Once she'd moved away, he had been thrilled to have her out of his life. Even though her cruelty still stuck with him.

"Your sister rarely mentioned you."

Jade recoiled at his comment. "Well, that's nice. At least you didn't tell her how much you hated me."

Just as much as you hated me. "I met your sister the day of my father's funeral. We were both at the Iron Horse, saddled up to the bar. She recognized me and offered her condolences. At the time, I was too lost in my grief to realize who she was. That was the night she and her husband called it quits. She was hurting and I couldn't see past my anger over my father's death."

"I'm so sorry you had to go through that, but I'm glad you two found comfort in each other."

Wes nodded. "That old saying about misery loving company is true. We were two lonely souls drowning our sorrows. The next day I didn't even remember her name, but we kept meeting there night after night and as time went on, we met less at the bar and more in a booth with coffee and a bite to eat. It was only then I realized she was your sister. I couldn't have gotten through those days without her."

"I tried talking her into moving out to LA when Kevin left. She refused to leave this place. We'd bounced around so much in foster care that once she had this house, hell would freeze over before she left it."

"She didn't really discuss where you two had lived while growing up, but I got a real sense that home meant everything to her." Liv had sidestepped most references to her childhood, and he'd assumed she'd wanted to keep that door closed forever. He understood where she'd been coming from and never pressed further. "Our friendship started out consoling each other over what we'd lost. My father and her husband. Once we got that out of our systems, our conversations shifted to the future and what we wanted out of life. She talked a lot about wanting a family of her own."

"Liv's not one to dwell in the past." Jade sat both bottles on the table and lifted Mackenzie into her arms.

"No, she's not." Wes waited for Jade to grab a burp towel, but she didn't. "You need to hold her a little more upright and against your shoulder. And you should have something to protect your shirt because she will spit up." He stood, still cradling Audra in one arm while he opened and closed drawers until he found what he was looking for. He draped a towel over Jade's shoulder, noticing the softness of her hair against his hand as he did so. "Watch me." Audra had finished her bottle. He set it on the counter and shifted her in his arms. "Hold her like this and lightly pat her back."

"How did you get so good at this?" Jade mirrored him.

"I've had practice. More than a man who never wants kids should." Wes had seen enough dysfunction in his own family to kill any desire he'd ever had of settling down. His father's death had fractured the final fragments that had held the Slades together. Getting tossed off a bull hurt a lot less than losing someone you love. Three of his four siblings had maintained a close relationship to each other, but their mom had taken off for sunny California. Much like Jade had. Nevertheless, he'd learned to keep an emotional distance ever since. "Any more thoughts where your sister might be?"

"Tomorrow I'll call every postpartum depression treatment center I can find, including over the border in Canada just to be on the safe side. She's an adult, so I'm not sure if anyone can legally tell me if she's there, but I at least have to try."

"Well, the reason I came here tonight was to give you my phone number and to get yours."

"You could've called the house and given it to me seeing as you didn't want to meet the girls."

"That dawned on me while I was knocking on the front door." Wes sniffed the top of Audra's head. She smelled like new car smell for humans. "From the looks and sounds of things, it's a good thing I did. Where's Maddie?"

"I sent her home. She'd been here for over twenty-four hours. The woman hadn't even had a shower or change of clothes."

"It looks like you could use the same."

"Thanks a lot." Jade attempted to smooth the front of her shirt.

Wes laughed as he settled Audra into the empty bouncy seat and lifted Hadley into his arms. "I didn't mean that to sound as insulting as it did. It was a poorly worded offer to watch the girls while you take a few moments for yourself."

"Are you sure?"

"Considering I made a commitment to help bring these three into the world, I think I can commit to babysitting while you shower."

"Thank you."

"But…this is a onetime deal, Jade." He didn't want to delude her into thinking he'd changed his mind about being involved in their lives. "I'm here now, but once I walk out that door, I'm not coming back."

He couldn't—wouldn't—risk his heart. It was already on the verge of shattering into a thousand pieces.

Chapter 3

Jade awoke with the worst backache of her life. She eased her body out of the rocking chair she had tried to sleep in last night. Staying in the guest bedroom down the hall proved futile after hours of tossing and turning. It didn't help that she kept getting up and checking on the girls every few minutes. The video baby monitor was great during the day, but it was difficult to see at night when the only light in the room was an elephant lamp on the dresser against the far wall.

How had her sister done it alone in a house this size? It was the middle of summer and the place creaked whenever the wind blew. She could only imagine how loud it was during the blustery Montana winter. There was too much house, too much baby and not enough time to breathe.

Liv had surprised Jade when she'd first mentioned in vitro. It had been one thing to want a baby with her husband, but as a single parent? Their mom had failed at single parenting ten times over. And she couldn't help wondering if their mother was part of the problem. She had never bonded with them and vice versa.

Jade tried to remember the days after the girls were born. Liv had stayed in the hospital for three days and the girls had been in the neonatal intensive care unit for almost two weeks. It had been so hectic that she hadn't noticed if Liv had bonded with the girls. Could she have missed the signs? Even though she'd been sore, Liv had been determined to get up and move around when she needed to. In hindsight, Jade shouldn't have left so soon. Work had beckoned and despite her connection to the girls, she should have sucked it up and stayed an extra couple of weeks with her sister.

Jade quietly slipped out of the nursery and grabbed her phone off the charger in the guest room. It was a few minutes after five in the morning. Los Angeles was an hour behind them, but knowing Tomás, her assistant was probably awake. The man had been her shadow for the last five years. His attention to the finest of details and endless amount of energy kept her business running smoothly. He was the only person she would ever trust to handle any given situation the way she would.

The hardwood floors groaned as she made her way to the narrow staircase leading to the kitchen. She hesitated on the top step and listened for any sign that she'd woken the girls. Confident they were still asleep, she continued downstairs and beelined for the coffeemaker. Once the caffeine began coursing through her veins, she dialed her assistant.

"Good morning, gorgeous." Tomás's chipper voice boomed through the phone. "And how is our temporary *mummy* holding up this morning?"

"Let's just say I made it through the night in one piece." For the next fifteen minutes, she sipped coffee and filled Tomás in on yesterday's events, including Wes. Tomás had been the one person she had completely confided in about her past. He knew the good, the bad and the ugly.

"Oh, darling. You've been holding out on me." He lowered his voice to a whisper so not to wake his husband. "I just pulled up your cowboy online, and that's the finest male specimen I've seen in forever. He just oozes testosterone and ruggedness."

"Tomás!" Jade nearly knocked over her mug. "Do I need to remind you what he did to me?"

"No, but I think I need to remind you he was only a teenager back then. Now..." Tomás clucked his tongue. "He's a hundred percent man."

"I don't care when it was. Cowboys never did it for me."

"Your cowboy is a champion bull rider and his earnings last year were almost four times more than what I made."

Jade straightened in her chair. "You can see how much he made?"

"I sure can." He gave her the web address and she pulled up his stats.

"I had no idea bull riders made so much money." Jade continued to scan the page. Turned out Wes was one of the top bull riders in the country and fifth in the standings this year.

"It also seems your boy is active in social media. That's quite a good morning."

"What are you talking about? How did you find that out?"

"I went to his website, westonslade.com."

Website? "I didn't realize he was that popular."

"I thought you said you looked him up online."

"I did. But I used one of those people directories, so it showed me his place of employment first. And that's where I stopped."

She typed in the address. Okay, the website was impressive. Professionally done and sexy, yet unreservedly masculine. She clicked on the first social media account and wondered if he had a team posting for him as she did. Nope. A selfie of him lying in bed with the caption Good Morning had posted a few minutes earlier and it already had close to a thousand likes. The hair on the back of her neck rose as she read one erotic reply after another. Most from women although there were a handful of men on there too.

"I swear, Tomás," she warned. "I better not see your name pop up."

Tomás cleared his throat and the sound of him rapidly hitting a key on his computer reverberated through the phone.

"I can't believe you."

"It's not like I hit Send."

She continued to read the posts and noticed Wes hadn't responded to any of the comments. "Okay, so maybe he's just a narcissist."

"If I didn't know any better, I'd say your kitten claws have come out."

A flicker of movement on the baby monitor caught her attention. Hadley's legs were beginning to kick. Judging by last night's diaper changes, that was the sign another was coming.

"I'll have to call you back. The little ones are waking up."

"Okay, love. You take care of those beauties and I'll touch base with you sometime this afternoon."

An hour later, Jade was either on the verge of tears or a nervous breakdown. She couldn't do this full-time. And she was used to dealing with difficult. But Hollywood bridezillas were easier to handle. And potty trained.

When Maddie stopped by around six thirty, Jade almost threw herself at her feet and begged for mercy.

"Oh, Jade." Maddie's eyes trailed up and down the length of her. "What have they done to you?"

Jade thrust Mackenzie into her arms. "How can anyone in their right mind think having a baby is a good idea?"

Maddie laughed. "You must've had some night if you're swearing off kids altogether."

"I've never wanted children. Never. I'm too busy and too active to be tied down. And so was my sister up until she decided to do this. She and Kevin were always off backpacking or flying to Europe for the weekend. It was constantly go, go, go. And even after they split up, she would tell me about the spontaneous weekend trips she would take to Texas or Wyoming or— I'll be damned."

"What?"

"She was following Wes on the road, wasn't she?" Jade couldn't for the life of her figure out why her sister hadn't mentioned his name or at the very least, that she was going to rodeos.

"I wouldn't say she was following him. She met up with him if his competitions fell on the weekend."

"And there wasn't anything between them?"

"No. I can honestly say I don't believe they ever even kissed."

She didn't think Wes was capable of having a platonic relationship with a woman. She thought she knew her sister better than anyone did. She couldn't have been more wrong. It didn't make sense.

"I take it you haven't heard from Liv?"

"No." Maddie smiled down at Mackenzie in her arms. "I wanted to call, but I don't want to drive her further away."

Jade had fought the same urge throughout the night. "I didn't, either. Once the kids fell asleep, I called a bunch of treatment centers specializing in postpartum depression. They were all in-patient facilities within a day's drive from here."

"And nothing?"

"It was an exercise in futility. No matter how much I pleaded, privacy laws prevented them from releasing any information. I left the same message for Liv at each place in case she's there, 'Just let us know you're safe.' I'll call out-patient facilities today and do the same thing. Other than that, I'm at a loss. This can't go on indefinitely." Jade hated to involve the police, but the more time passed, the more concerned she became. She honestly thought Liv would have reached out by now. "One day, okay, I get it. There's a lot of stress involved with caring for triplets. But we're going on two days and postpartum depression or not, a text message would have been nice."

"What happens if she doesn't come back? Can you legally take them with you to California?"

"I'm not sure." The same scenario had played through Jade's head earlier. "If I just leave with them and she returns in a frazzled state, she could accuse me of kidnapping."

"You don't think she'd do that, do you?"

"Yesterday, I didn't. Today, I'm realizing there's a lot I didn't know about my sister. Before I can leave with them, I would have to report Liv missing and the kids would go in the system. They'll probably have to evaluate me and my home in LA before releasing them to me. I'm Liv's only relative so I hope that counts for something, but I can't be a hundred percent certain the girls won't go in foster care. I need to contact an attorney."

"I can put together some names, if you'd like." Maddie eased Mackenzie into her bouncy chair.

"Thanks, but I'll call the one Liv used to set up the donor paperwork."

"You know who she used?"

"Ah." Jade froze. Her brain short-circuited as she tried to cover her slip. Liv had wanted everyone to believe she used two anonymous donors. "She mentioned someone a few times. I'm assuming she has the name and number in her office. I'm sure I'll recognize it when I see it."

Maddie nodded, seemingly unconcerned. "Before I forget, today's garbage day. Monday, as well."

"That was on my list of questions to ask you." She'd made many lists in between phone calls, ranging from to-dos to how-tos. There was satisfaction in checking off a task as she went about her day. "Would you mind watching the girls for a few minutes while I get it together?"

"Sure, I don't have to be to work until nine o'clock so I have time. Take a shower and get yourself cleaned up, including whatever that black mark is on your cheek."

"Black mark?" Jade walked into the small half bath off the kitchen and flipped on the light. "Are you kidding me?" She had a three-inch-long black permanent marker streak starting at the corner of her mouth going toward her ear. "I can't believe he didn't tell me."

Jade had taken such a quick shower last night while Wes had watched the girls, she hadn't bothered to look in the mirror.

"He was here for quite a while." Maddie's voice lilted with implication.

Jade rolled her eyes. Maddie must have seen his truck in the driveway. "We were just comparing notes, and he watched the kids long enough for me to shower and change."

"Apparently it wasn't long enough. You have some time, go do what you have to do."

Jade ran upstairs and grabbed the bathroom garbage along with the bag from the Diaper Genie.

"I never thought to ask what you do for a living," Jade said as she returned to the kitchen and lifted the lid off the trash can alongside the counter.

"I'm a court reporter. It's nowhere near as glamorous as your job. I can only imagine what it's like meeting all those celebrities."

Jade inwardly laughed. Her job was far from glamorous. "I don't just have celebrity clients, but they are the majority of my business. And let me tell you, those happy smiles you see plastered on the pages of magazines aren't always real. Underneath they have the same fears and concerns as the rest of us. Sometimes I feel sorry for them. Every move they make, especially when it comes to their wedding, gets photographed and scrutinized. I can't even begin to tell you the lengths we have to go to sometimes just to get a client to a venue. It can be a logistical nightmare. Some days seem like they'll never end, but I wouldn't trade it in for the world."

How was she going to run a business and care for Mackenzie, Hadley and Audra? She never wanted kids and now she had three. No. She squared her shoulders and tied the garbage bag closed. She had to stay positive. Liv would come back and everything would be fine. Jade opened the back door off the mudroom and almost tripped over three car seats sitting on the top step.

"Okay, we need to find a better place for these."

"Oh my God!" Maddie jumped up. "Those are from Liv's car. When did she put them there?"

"I have no idea." Jade moved one aside and ran down the steps into the yard, hoping to find her sister.

"They are a little damp from the morning dew," Maddie said. "They've been out here for a while."

Jade wanted to collapse in the grass and cry. *Where are you, Liv?* She took a deep breath and plodded back up the stairs to the mudroom. "I don't think I opened this door yesterday. Did you?"

"I did when I put the garbage in the can. That was sometime in the early afternoon. It had to have been after that."

"Then she came back." Jade's heart rose to her throat. "But when?"

Jade closed her eyes and hoped it wasn't when she and Wes had fed the girls in the kitchen last night. Liv would have had a clear view of them from the steps. Seeing the biological parents together with their children was the last thing her sister needed. She just prayed it hadn't pushed Liv further over the edge.

Wes had thought the worst mistake of his life had been the day he miscalculated Crazy Town's spin direction and damn near died when the bull tossed and trampled him. He'd changed his mind when Liv told him the embryo transfer had been a success. It still hadn't compared to the mistake he made last night.

There had been an uncontrollable force driving him to Liv's house. He'd gone and done the one thing he'd sworn he never would. And now that he'd met his daughters, he couldn't get their tiny cherub faces out of his head. His heart couldn't handle seeing them again knowing they weren't his to keep. Not that he wanted to keep them. Just the opposite. The sooner he got out of town, the better.

He'd spent most of the night down at the stables to avoid

Garrett's countless questions about Jade and her emergency. He wished Jade had just called and left a message instead of talking to his brother. Then again, if she hadn't stalked him at the ranch, he never would have spoken with her and she knew it.

His phone rang, and he was almost afraid to check the display. It was half past nine and it could be anyone, from his management team to one of his friends. But his gut told him it was Jade. The thought alone both frightened and excited him.

He braved a glance at the screen. Her name flashed at him like a rodeo clown waving a red flag. He froze long enough for the call to go to voice mail. He couldn't talk to her. Talking would lead to seeing his daughters again. His daughters. They were no longer a concept. Even after their due date had passed, Wes had refused to think of them as tiny humans almost two thousand miles away from his new home in Ramblewood, Texas. Now he had no choice.

He had held them in his arms and they had imprinted themselves on his heart. How could he walk away and go back to life as usual? Especially when they were growing up in his hometown where every time he visited his brothers and their growing families he ran the risk of running into them. And what would happen when they got older and started driving or playing sports? He was bound to see their names in the newspaper or mentioned by a neighbor or friend. Saddle Ridge was a small town and nothing escaped anyone.

Wes stormed to the tack room. He needed to go for a ride and clear his head. The voice mail notification chimed from his back pocket. As much as he wanted to ignore it, he couldn't. His finger hovered over the play button, praying Jade had called to say she had found Liv and everything was fine.

"Wes, it's Jade. I know you have your phone in your hand because you posted a pic online less than five minutes ago. At least it was better than the tacky one of you in bed. Anyway, I'm calling to tell you Liv came back to the house sometime yesterday or during the night. I don't know when or how long she stayed, but it may have been when you were here. Please call me as soon as you get this. I'm scared of how she may have reacted if she saw us together with the girls."

Wes took the front porch steps of Liv's house two at a time. Jade opened the door and pulled him inside before he had a chance to knock. He told himself repeatedly on the drive over he was there only for Liv's well-being. Any attachment to the girls was off-limits.

"Thank you for coming. I know this is the last place you want to be."

Wes followed her into the small living room off the main hall-way. He'd half expected to see Audra, Hadley and McKenzie when he turned the corner, instead the room looked exactly as it always had.

"It doesn't even look like a baby, let alone three babies, lives here."

"Exactly." Jade paced the length of the small off-white area rug. "We were so busy feeding the girls yesterday I didn't get a chance to show you this." She grabbed his hand and led him down the hall to a narrow closet. The gesture was innocent enough, but her palm against his felt more intimate than a kiss. Within seconds she released him, and damned if he didn't miss her touch already. He balled his fist, refusing to feel anything for the woman. "This is what I mean when I say Liv knew what she was doing."

She swung the closet open and flipped on the overhead light. There were numerous neatly stacked, transparent lidded bins with index cards taped to the front of them listing each one's contents. Baby toys, baby blankets, baby photo albums…all generically labeled.

"Why is everything in the closet?"

"These had all been in various rooms when I left a little over a month ago. Sometime between now and then, she ordered storage containers and packed everything away."

Wes wandered around the first floor of the house, peering into each room. "I've never been upstairs, but nothing down here looks any different from before she got pregnant. The place was always spotless. Is it possible she took the bins out when she needed them?"

Jade shook her head. "It doesn't make sense. Those photo albums used to be on the coffee table. She couldn't wait to fill them. I looked inside and there are three, possibly four pages' worth of photos. And the baby blankets...she was so proud that she'd learned how to crochet for her daughters. Those are shoved in a box too."

"What about the nursery? Did she change anything in there?"

"No." Jade started up the stairs, but Wes's feet refused to follow. "Are you coming?"

"Aren't the girls up there?"

Her shoulders sagged at the question. "So that's it? Last night was a onetime deal and you're never going to see them again."

"I thought I already made that clear." What part of not wanting to be a parent didn't she understand? He had to set boundaries before she expected more from him. "I'm not here for them. I'm here because you said Liv came back to the house and you're afraid she saw us together. I'm here because I'm worried about her. I'm not worried about the girls. I trust you with them."

"How very big of you." She closed the distance between them, her eyes blazing with anger and fear. "Hell, I'm surprised you haven't snapped a picture of them and posted it all over the internet to see how many likes and follows you can get."

Wes put a hand on her arm. "I know you're upset, and I meant what I said yesterday. I'll do whatever I can to help you find Liv. But please, don't take it out on me. This isn't my fault just like it isn't your fault."

Jade dropped her gaze. "It is our fault. We missed the signs. You taking off to Texas is no different from me flying back to LA as fast as I could. We both abandoned her."

"We were only donors." Wes bit back the bile he now associated with the word. "Those kids aren't ours. And you didn't abandon Liv. You were there when the babies were born. You helped bring them home. You're caring for them night and day. You're living in the same house with them. They're the first thing you see in the morning and they're the last thing you see at night. I don't even have to be here to recognize you're getting attached to them."

"Of course I am." Tears filled her eyes. "I never wanted to feel this way, but they're our daughters. How can you not get attached?"

"They are your nieces, but they can't ever be anything to me. That's how Liv wanted it."

Jade tried to pull from his grip, but he refused to let go. Not when she was in so much pain. Her heart beat wildly against him as he held her tight to his chest. Despite the past or the resentment he still felt toward her, he wanted nothing more than to ease the guilt she carried.

"It's okay." He smoothed her hair and rested his cheek against the top of her head. "It's going to be okay. We'll find Liv, make sure she gets the help she needs and bring her home to her children."

"I'm scared she's not going to be okay or that she'll do this again." Jade sobbed against him. "She came back, Wes. She was here, and she left. She walked away twice. How could she do that?"

Wes eased her onto the couch, summoning every ounce of strength he had not to panic. Between the abandoned triplets he'd never wanted to be involved with and Liv's fragile emotional state, he felt the overwhelming need to protect the Scott women, even if that included Jade...the woman who had made his life pure hell.

"Tell me what happened."

After Jade explained about the car seats she'd found earlier, he figured there was a fifty-fifty chance Liv had seen them together. Since she'd purposely kept their identities from the other, he understood how watching him and Jade with the girls might upset her.

"I'm not trying to belittle your concerns in any way, but why do you think seeing us together would push her over the edge?"

Jade shifted on the couch to face him and tucked her bare legs underneath her jean-short-covered bottom. Coupled with her deep V-neck white cotton T-shirt, she wore ultracasual extremely well. A little too well since his jeans felt snugger than they had a minute ago.

"I think my sister had a thing for you and maybe still does."

Wes threw his head back and laughed, knocking his hat on the back of the couch. He removed it and set it brim side up on the coffee table while running his other hand through his hair.

"Trust me, your sister was not interested in me romantically."

"How can you be so sure?"

"Because she's still in love with Kevin. That's one broken heart I don't think she'll ever get past."

"She divorced him years ago."

"He divorced her," Wes corrected, surprised she didn't know. "I was with her the night she was served. And she was served very publicly in the middle of the Iron Horse."

Jade's mouth hung open in disbelief. "Is she so afraid of failure that she has to hide her pain from me? Or am I that cold of a person she didn't think I would understand?"

Wes couldn't believe the words coming out of her mouth. "Get over yourself. It isn't about you. From the little she told me about both of your pasts, she was the one taking care of you while you did whatever you wanted."

"That was hardly the case."

"Really, because the Jade I remember was constantly getting into trouble. You were an angry kid. And mean. God, you were mean."

"I'll own up to having an attitude, but I was mean to only you and that's because you said I'd slept with you. Your lie almost got me raped by your friend."

"What?" His fists clenched. Wes couldn't imagine any of his friends forcing themselves on a girl. "Who are you talking about?"

"Oh, come on. You know damn well I'm talking about your buddy Burke. Every time I saw you two together afterward you were laughing at me."

"Burke tried to rape you?" A slow rage began to build in his chest. Burke had been more of a rival than a friend. They'd competed against each other in all aspects of their lives. From bull riding to girls. "When?"

"Our ninth-grade fall harvest dance. How can you not remember?" Jade jumped up from the couch as if it was on fire and faced him. "You two were sitting on the gym bleachers laughing and pointing at me. I'd had enough and decided to leave. Burke followed me into the hallway, threw me against the lockers and reached under my skirt. He tore off my underwear!" Her eyes filled with tears. "He told me he wanted what I gave you. I physically had to fight him to break free. He had his zipper down and was ready to go."

Wes's stomach churned. "He said you two had hooked up. He even showed me your underwear. I was crushed you chose him over me. Jade, I had no idea what really happened."

"It wasn't consensual! Torn underwear should have been your clue?" Jade shook her head in disgust. "It happened because you told everyone we had slept together. You told everyone I was easy. He assumed I was shareable when you and I had only kissed."

"Yeah and we had dated for almost a month." The words came out of his mouth before he could stop them.

"So that meant I owed you sex?" Jade's face reddened. "We started dating, like, my second week of ninth grade. Liv and I had just come out of another group home and had moved in with a new foster family. I hadn't even told my sister about you. I was trying to learn everyone's name and get acclimated to a new town. I was fourteen years old and you kept pushing me to go further than I was ready. And then you broke up with me because I wouldn't. Do you have any idea how that made me feel?"

"I'm sorry," Wes whispered. He lifted his gaze to hers. "Everything was a competition to me back then. I was hurt that you didn't like me as much as I liked you. I didn't even know what sex was. I mean I did, but I hadn't done it yet. Burke had. So I lied and said I had too. He was the only one I told." He rose from the couch, torn between wanting to comfort her and beating the crap out of Burke. His old rival had moved to New Mexico after high school, but the next time they crossed paths on the rodeo circuit, he'd be damn sure to teach him a lesson.

"Burke taunted me every chance he could, and you were right there next to him. We had just been placed with a really nice foster family, and Liv and I finally believed we had a place to call home. As nice as it was, it was never easy. At least not for me. I felt like I had a scarlet letter emblazoned on my chest, thanks to you. And two years later, on Christmas Eve when my foster mom's brother tried to force himself on me, I believed it was my fault, because it had happened to me once before."

"Please tell me he didn't—"

"Rape me?" Jade violently shook her head. "No. Liv walked in, saw what was happening and kicked his ass. But when the police came, they didn't care what I said. He claimed I had been the aggressor and they took his word over mine."

Wes felt sick. One of his brothers had recently dealt with a serious bullying issue involving his daughter and Wes had been so angry when he heard that, he had wanted to drive straight through from Texas to Montana to confront her attackers. He'd never considered himself one of those people. But he had been. And so had Jade. As much as he wanted to confront her about her bullying, he refused to turn his apology around on her. "I never intended to put you in physical danger or make you feel like any less of a person."

"That rumor followed me around until the day I graduated. I'm sure your brother is a great deputy sheriff, but any faith I had in the system disappeared that night. Instead of arresting my attacker, they sent me to a group home. Liv was eighteen then and she immediately petitioned the courts for guardianship. Within the month, the state had released me into her care." Jade began to pace the length of the small room. "We struggled to survive after that, but we did it. Liv worked two jobs and still managed to attend college full-time on the scholarship she'd won. I worked every day after school and on weekends to help pay the bills. I owe my sister for all she did back then, and I refuse to let her down." She stopped less than a foot in front of him and folded her arms tight across her chest. "And after what you did, I think you owe me too."

He'd call them even after what she'd done in retaliation all those years ago, but the determined set of her chin left him fearing where her next sentence would lead if he disagreed. "Fine."

"We created those three lives upstairs. And despite our donor contracts or how we feel about the situation, we have an obligation to Liv to make sure they're cared for. I can't do this alone. Outside of hiring a stranger, you're my only choice. Since you're in town, I'm asking you to help me. You can stay in one of the guest rooms."

"Whoa, you want me to move in here?" Wes may have been willing to handle the grocery shopping or running whatever errands or chores she needed done, but living under the same roof with her and the girls was out of the question. "That would send up all sorts of red flags to my family."

"I just told you I can't do this alone." She stared up at him. "I highly doubt you want to run the risk of the girls not getting what they need or heaven forbid, getting hurt because I only have two arms? What if there's a fire? I thought about that last night. I don't know what Liv would have done in that situation."

Guilt trip launched and on target. "Fine, but kindly keep my time with them to an absolute minimum. I'll take care of the laundry, run wherever you need me to go and clean the house. Once this is over, you'll still be around the girls. I won't. There's no room for me in their lives so let's not make this any harder than it needs to be."

One of Jade's perfectly arched brows rose. "Of course."

Frustration coursed through his veins. She was handling him just like she probably handled her troublesome clients and he didn't appreciate it. He couldn't leave her to deal with this mess on her own, either. He had a week and a half until Dylan's wedding, and then it was back to Texas. This time he had no intentions of ever returning to Saddle Ridge.

Chapter 4

Jade should probably have her head examined for asking Wes to move in with her and the girls. While she'd never forgive him for the past, their talk last night had lessened her anger about the situation. She doubted she'd ever have full closure over the event that had spiraled her teen years out of control, but at least she'd discovered his intentions hadn't been as malicious as she'd thought.

Wes stayed true to his word. Since yesterday morning, he'd helped her around the house, made sure all Liv's bills and utilities were up-to-date and even washed, folded and put away countless loads of laundry. But when it came to the girls, he slept downstairs on the couch and excused himself from the room whenever they were near. Like now...he was in Liv's office researching other treatment centers and contacting some of their mutual friends while she prepared another round of formula. Now that she had mastered feeding the girls with the help of a rolled-up towel to support the bottles, she didn't need Wes at mealtime. But, despite their history, some company would've been nice. Caring for triplets had quickly become an isolated job. He could have at least helped during diaper changes or bath time.

The house phone rang, and Jade almost broke her neck tripping over a chair when she ran to answer it.

"Hello?"

"May I please speak with Jade Scott?"

She shivered at the direct tone of the man's voice. "This is Jade."

"Ms. Scott, this is Jacob Meyer, Olivia's attorney. We met last year. Your sister asked me to contact you."

"Have you heard from Liv?" Her pulse began to beat erratically. "Is she all right?"

"Olivia asked me to call you and let you know she's safe."

"Thank heaven she's okay." Jade slumped against the counter, but her relief was short-lived. "If my sister is all right, why are you calling me? What happened?"

"Liv has checked into a recovery center and she'll be there for a minimum of thirty days, possibly longer."

Thirty days? She couldn't possibly stay in Montana for that long. "What kind of recovery center? What's wrong with her and how can I get in touch with her?"

"Contact is forbidden during the first week of treatment. She has authorized me to tell you she checked herself in for postpartum depression."

"I knew it. I should've seen the signs sooner." Jade looked up to see Wes standing in the kitchen doorway. She covered the phone with her hand. "It's Liv's attorney. He says she's in a treatment center."

"Where?" Wes asked, avoiding all eye contact with the three tiny faces fixated on him.

Jade shrugged and uncovered the phone. "Can you at least tell me where she is?"

"She asked me not to. I can tell you that I met with her yesterday and she has granted you temporary guardianship and power of attorney until she is able to return."

"Yesterday? That means she must be close. Unless she flew there. Then in that case—"

"Ms. Scott, please refrain from trying to contact your sister. Even if you called every PPD treatment center in the country, legally they are unable to acknowledge her residency. You'd be wasting your time and theirs."

"But she does plan on coming home." Wes crossed the room to her, every bit as eager for the answer as she was.

"Most definitely. Your guardianship is a temporary solution to an unfortunate situation. If it's any consolation, this isn't the first time I have had a client with PPD. They've all recovered, but the length of time in which that happens varies from person to person. Your sister's situation is more unique because of the donor aspect and the fact she's dealing with triplets. Considering the role you played in their births, I have to ask…are you prepared to be their guardian?"

Jade squeezed her eyes shut and exhaled slowly. "Without a doubt, but do those documents allow me to take them to California?"

"California? Part of your sister's recovery involves exposure therapy and a slow reintegration back into their lives. You and the children need to be available for all family sessions."

"That's further proof she's someplace relatively close."

Jacob cleared his throat. "Ms. Scott, you have to remain in Saddle Ridge. I hope you can make the necessary arrangements. Your sister's counting on you."

"I refuse to allow those children to go with anyone else." She wasn't sure how she'd make it work, but she didn't have a choice.

"I'll need you to stop by my office to go over these documents. Are you available around two this afternoon?"

"I'll be there."

Jade's body went numb as she hung up the phone. Her sister was safe, but unreachable. Now she was responsible for her biological children. Children she already felt too attached to.

"What did he say?"

"Not a lot except Liv is in an undisclosed postpartum depression—PPD as he called it—treatment facility and she'll be there for at least thirty days, if not more. He has guardianship and power of attorney papers waiting for me. Apparently, he met with Liv yesterday, so I'm assuming she came in to see him, although I guess he could have gone to wherever she is. He told me I have to stay in town so Liv can have visitation with the girls."

"That means she's close and this will be over soon." Relief swept across his face and it prickled her a bit, even though she felt the same way. They were both thinking too much about protecting themselves and not about what was best for the girls.

"I should do some shopping after the attorney's office." Jade slid onto the chair closest to Audra. She lightly squeezed the infant's chubby little toes. "I wasn't prepared to stay here for a week, let alone a month. I only packed a few things and most of Liv's prepregnancy clothes are too tight on me."

"I want to help in whatever way I can, but I can't stick around for the entire month. I have to get back to my job in Texas."

"And I have a job waiting for me in California. Correction… a business that I happen to own and June is our busiest month. Never mind all the planning that goes into each event or the millions of dollars we pay our vendors. Because you are so right, bouncing around on top of a bull for eight seconds is much more important. I don't expect anything from you past this upcoming week. And honestly, it doesn't even sound like you'll be around much anyway."

"Is this how it's going to be? Your job is more important than mine?" Wes kept his voice low. "We need to work together, not fight. I realize it's difficult to put the past aside. I also realize I need to remain a stranger in the girls' lives. Liv wanted you to be their aunt. She never wanted me to be a father beyond their creation. Once this is over, I don't plan on seeing them again. I won't be returning to Saddle Ridge."

"You're never coming back?" The thought alone sent her into a slight panic. "What about your family?"

"They are more than welcome to visit me in Texas. I have a small house down there with a guest room."

"That's it? You've already decided?"

He jammed his hands in his pockets. "I can't put myself or them through it. The more they see of me, the more questions they'll ask later."

Jade knew he was right, she'd just hated the thought of him walking away from his hometown forever. Not that she should care. But Wes had deep roots in Saddle Ridge. Something her damaged past never allowed her to have. He belonged near family. And Liv belonged near her. There was nothing tying her sister to Montana and Jade genuinely believed Liv would be happier in California. "I hate to ask you this, but since Maddie's at work, I really need you to babysit them this afternoon while I run into town. I promise not to be long."

Wes's cheeks puffed out and for a second she thought he'd give her an argument. "Do what you have to do." He strode across the kitchen and grabbed a bottle of pop from the fridge as his mini fan club watched from the table. Jade already saw little bits of him in Hadley. Especially her stubbornness. "Something's been bothering me all night. Didn't Liv have a baby shower?"

Jade nodded. "It wasn't that big though. I'm assuming you know her circle of friends. You, Maddie and Delta are the closest to her. Or at least you were until you moved away. And Delta's been battling cancer for the past few months. I don't even think she was at the shower. Liv has a few friends in town and some from her old job, but now that she works from home and her company is based out of Nebraska, she doesn't have the comradery she used to have. She made a lot of major life changes since she and Kevin divorced."

"Thanks for squeezing that subtle guilt trip in there." Wes braved a glance at the triplets, but his face showed zero emotion. How could he not smile when he looked at them? "What I was trying to get at, don't women usually receive baby swings and all sorts of big items at their showers? My sister-in-law had a huge baby registry. Aside from what you showed me in the closet, I don't see any other gifts in the house."

"I bought her the car seats and a triplet stroller along with a monthly diaper subscription. Her friends gave her gifts, but there was never a swing. Aren't they too small for them?"

"Are you kidding me?" Wes sat his drink on the counter. "I bought Belle this awesome Bluetooth infant seat that swings and rocks, mimicking the mother's movements. You can control it from your phone and adjusts in multiple positions so they can sleep, play, eat...you name it. I even gave one to Dylan's fiancée, Emma, for their new daughter. Here—" Wes tugged his phone out of the front pocket of his jeans and tapped the screen. "This is the video I took the other day of my nephew Travis—Belle and Harlan's kid—in his."

"Wow. He looks so much like the girls. Especially Mackenzie." Jade looked from the phone to the triplets who remained entranced by the man continuing to ignore them. Wes growled under his breath and Jade returned her attention to the large automated infant seat. "That looks really nice. The girls would love that. Where can I order one or three?"

Wes took the phone from her. "I got it covered." He tapped the screen again. "What's the address here? I can never remember the house number."

"You don't have to do that. They look expensive." For a man who claimed he didn't want kids, Wes certainly knew his way to an infant's heart.

"I can afford it." A hint of annoyance evident in his tone. "It's something I should have done months ago. Liv was my best friend and I never even bought her a baby gift. Regardless of my part in this, I shouldn't have shut her out the way I did."

"Seventy-five."

"Seventy-five what?"

"You asked the house number. Seventy-five Brookstone Lane."

"Oh." He entered the address into his phone. "I was expecting another guilt trip. My mistake."

"Let's just say I was silently agreeing with you and leave it at that."

"Fair enough. Unfortunately, I can't get next day air shipping since today is Friday, but they will be here on Monday."

"When do you go to South Dakota?" Not that she cared what he did. She hated to admit it, but last night she'd felt more comfortable with him there. A floor separated them and they had barely said a word to one another after he agreed to stay. Regardless, she'd worried a little less. Then again, she probably would have felt the same way if Maddie had stayed over. And since she had volunteered, maybe that was a better idea.

"Tuesday evening. I will be back sometime on Thursday. Don't forget I have two christenings tomorrow, a family celebration tomorrow night and a prewedding party on Sunday. I don't expect to be around much during the day."

"About that. I may have overreacted. You're home for such a short time and this is a special week for your family. You should be with them. Especially since you don't plan on coming back to Saddle Ridge. Maybe it is best if I hire someone."

Wes stared at her, causing her to shift uncomfortably. Sarcasm or some other retort would have been better than nothing. With Maddie around at night, she'd only need help during the day. Possibly even two people, since she needed time to work. There had to be a nanny service nearby where she could hire someone reliable and less…less Wes. She didn't want to like him, but after their talk last night and his infant seat gesture, she found herself doing just that. Although she owed him an apology of her own after what she did to him in school. "About last night—"

"I thought you didn't want a stranger around." Wes's tone bordered on accusatory.

"Only because I didn't want to explain Liv's absence. The guardianship papers make it legal and I don't have to worry what anyone else thinks. Not that I want my sister's personal problems broadcast around town." Although people might be more sympathetic to postpartum depression than Liv skipping out on her babies for a month because of a job.

"What are you going to say when someone asks where she is?"

"I don't want to lie. It makes things more complicated. I'm sure she assumed people would find out the truth. A thirty-day absence is hard to hide."

The girls finished their bottles, and she rinsed out each of the plastic liners before tossing them in the trash. She'd learned her lesson yesterday after the garbage can stunk to high heaven. The liners were more trouble than they were worth. She'd use regular bottles for their next feeding.

"I don't know how I'm supposed to feel about any of this."

Jade turned off the faucet and dried her hands before facing him. "You and me both. I think it was a mistake to involve you. I should've thought it through. Hell, I should've thought everything through." Jade prided herself on efficiently moving from one thing to another. That principle worked great in business, not so much in her personal life. "It bothers me that my sister was so emotionally distraught she had to abandon her kids in order to get help. You're telling me what you should've done for her and I'm thinking to myself how wonderful I thought I'd been by donating my eggs and enduring all the hormone injections and doctor visits. My body was bruised and my mood swings and hot flashes triggered by the hormones almost caused my entire team to quit. Never mind all the time I had to take off work."

"I had no idea it was that involved. My part was over in— well, you know." A tinge of pink creeped up his neck as he quickly reached for his drink.

"Despite my research, it had been more involved than I'd ever imagined. But she called me a hero for doing it and kept thanking me for the sacrifice." Jade lifted Hadley into her arms. "I thought I'd been this great sister by taking off even more time for the delivery, plus all the things I'd purchased for Liv and the girls. I was so busy congratulating myself, I missed the obvious. I should have been more aware of her needs and made sure she had the proper help. And I shouldn't have left so soon after the girls came home from the hospital."

"If she didn't want Maddie's help, what makes you think she would've welcomed someone else's?"

"Because Liv had talked about hiring a nanny once she went back to work, even though she was working from home. I can appreciate why she wouldn't want a nanny during those initial bonding months, but the point is I hadn't noticed a problem because I was too busy trying to escape."

Wes exhaled a slow breath and stared at Audra. She met his gaze and held the stare. And then smiled.

"Oh my God, did you see that?" Wes laughed. "She smiled. She actually smiled."

"Or she has gas. Either way, that's the first time I've seen any of them make that face. I think she likes you."

"Yeah, well." Wes cradled the back of Audra's head and scooped her into his arms. "Don't get attached to me, kid." He sat in the chair across from Jade and slowly rocked the infant. "I sympathize with your guilt. I'm sure Maddie does, too. But from what I've read on the postpartum depression websites, a lot of women try their hardest to cover up how they're really feeling because they don't want anyone to know they're not bonding with their children."

"And many times they are crying for help and nobody's listening." She had replayed every phone and video conversation over in her head last night and one thing stuck out more than anything else... Jade had purposely kept the calls short. She had made one work excuse after another to get off the phone, ignoring her sister's needs.

"You can analyze it to death, but it won't change anything.

All we can do is accept what's in front of us and take it day by day. As much as I want to walk away, I can't. Whether we like it or not, we're a temporary team."

Jade hated temporary. The first sixteen years of her life had been filled with temporary. Temporary meant loss. And nine times out of ten, loss brought pain along for the ride. Even if she left tomorrow, there would be pain. As unconventional as they were, sitting around the kitchen table and holding the daughters they'd created felt natural on some alternate plane. If her heart wasn't ready to let go now, how would it ever be ready in a month?

Wes had never been more terrified in his entire life. He thought he could handle being alone in the house with Hadley, Audra and Mackenzie, but he'd underestimated their cuteness factor. Jade had tried to put them down for a nap before she left, but they were having none of it. So Wes relented to baby play-time on the mat in the center of the living room. Thank God they were too young to roll over and crawl away giving him some semblance of control. Gripping his finger was one thing. Gripping his heart was altogether different.

He checked the wall clock. Jade had only been gone for fifteen minutes. That was barely enough time to get to the attorney's office. He groaned. And she was clothes shopping afterward…he was doomed.

Mackenzie intently watched the musical, plush butterfly mobile he had set up over their play mat. Jade hadn't been kidding when she said Travis and Mackenzie looked alike. They were cousins, born days apart from one another, yet they would never know it. Wes choked down the unfamiliar lump in his throat. The startling realization that Travis and the triplets would be in the same grade, possibly even the same class all through school sucker punched him in the gut.

"How did I miss that before?" If they looked alike now, he could only imagine the resemblance as they got older. People were sure to question it. Jade had already asked Liv to move to California. Somehow he needed to convince them both that was the best thing for all of them. Then maybe he could visit his family freely again. Although in the back of his mind, he already knew he would forever associate Saddle Ridge with the three girls he would never see after this week.

Wes's eyes began to tear. "How could you do this to me?" he asked the triplets. "You weren't supposed to be cute. You weren't even supposed to let me like you. How can I not like you? Have you looked in the mirror?" Audra smiled again as if she understood. "You're adorable. I see a lot of your mom in you. I guess I shouldn't call her your mom since Liv gave birth to you. She's your mom. But your aunt Jade, she's a special woman. She went through a lot to help bring you into this world. And your mom, she's going through a lot too. But when she comes home, she'll be better than ever." At least he hoped so.

He couldn't help but have the same fears Jade had. What if Liv relapsed? What if raising triplets on her own proved to be too much? Jade's lifestyle and work schedule didn't mesh well with raising children. She'd even admitted to not wanting kids of her own. And neither did he. But once he retired from bull riding next year wouldn't he have the time for a family?

Wes rocked back on his heels. What the hell was he thinking? He'd never planned on having kids and even if he had, his daughters weren't his to raise. Liv didn't want him parenting her children. She'd made that painfully clear when she proposed the idea. Up until that point, he had only casually mentioned not wanting kids. So when Liv became adamant about him not being in the girls' lives, it hurt. Not because he wanted to be a father. But because she thought so little of him. The fact she had been hurt and shocked when he moved away had surprised him. How could she have expected them to stay friends? In the back of his mind, he'd wondered if Liv would try to rekindle her relationship with Kevin once the babies were born. Even more reason for her to be happy he was gone. The Liv he knew had become a walking contradiction.

Wes ran his fingers lightly over the bottoms of Audra's feet. "Are you ticklish yet?" Her big blue eyes reflected innocence at its purest. "There's a big world out there waiting for you to conquer it." Her little legs kicked, and he noticed her foot was marker free. "Did your aunt Jade finally figure out how to tell you apart? I always knew. Yes, I did." He lifted her into his arms. "And I'll always remember you as being my first daughter to smile at me."

A tear rolled down his cheek, and he quickly wiped it away. Contrary to what his former ex-best friend thought, Wes enjoyed being around kids. He adored Harlan's eight-year-old daughter, Ivy, and a good 50 percent of his job at the rodeo school in Texas involved him training young children to compete.

Liv had insulted him when she'd assumed it wouldn't bother him to run into his own kids. If that hadn't screamed how she really saw him, he didn't know what would. In hindsight, that should have been his sign to turn Liv down. If she had used an anonymous donor, they could have stayed friends after he moved. Instead he chose to sacrifice it all to give his friend what she wanted most in this world. A known biological father to her children, even though he was technically unnamed.

None of what he did changed how much he hated the idea of marriage and settling down. That had more to do with his parents' dysfunctional marriage. A detail his brothers managed to leave out whenever they remembered the good times. A fight usually followed every one of those good times. Ironically, the only brother who understood was the one who had killed their father.

"You're going to have the best life. Even if I can't be here to see it, I'll make sure you're okay. Better than okay. Think of me as your fairy godfather. I'll always watch over you."

As the girls began to fall asleep, Wes attempted to figure out the logistical nightmare of getting three infants off the floor and down the hall into their bassinets. "How did Liv do this?"

He wished he had thought to bring the car seats in from the mudroom. It would have made baby transport much easier. That reminded him. He needed to install the car seat bases into Jade's rental car. Would they all fit side by side? Two yes, three…no way. Liv had talked about leasing a large SUV but he didn't know what she had eventually chosen.

He tugged out his phone and one-hand typed a quick text message to Jade.

Swing by rental car company after attorney. Need a larger vehicle to fit three infant seats in one row.

Since he wouldn't be around much this weekend, he wanted Jade prepared for any emergency. She and Maddie didn't need to fumble with fastening the seats into two cars if the unexpected happened. He'd take the vehicle down to the sheriff's department and have Harlan or one of the other deputies double-check he'd installed the seats properly. Besides, it would give him a chance to explain his disappearance to his brothers. By now they had probably assumed he was shacked up with one of his old girlfriends while he was in town. If it hadn't been for Jade, he would've been. Unfortunately, for the past two nights, she'd taken center stage in his dreams.

That wouldn't have been a bad thing if he hadn't still resented her for the pain she'd caused him in school. He understood her reason now, and he felt horrible for the role he had played, but it hadn't lessened the damage she'd done. He had been beaten up many times in the locker room after she'd spread around that he had used her as a front because he was gay. The rumor had followed him on the high school rodeo circuit and home. While his brothers only ribbed him about it in the beginning, his father had taken the rumor as gospel and had berated him daily. Her lie had made it impossible for a friend of his to come out because he feared the same treatment from their classmates. Her cruelty had affected far more than just his life. The sad part was, he had started their feud.

After opting to use the bouncy chairs, he successfully made it into the downstairs nursery. Then a whiff of something rotten almost caused him to gag. "What is that?" He covered his nose. "Did something crawl in here and die?" He quickly scanned the room and inspected each crib. "I can't leave you girls in here." He slid their bouncy chairs into the hallway and the odor followed them. Hadley kicked her little legs and made a sour face. "Is that smell coming from you?" He leaned closer and gave her the stiff test, almost passing out in the process. "Oh, that's just not right. How can someone so small and beautiful smell so rotten?"

After changing Hadley's diaper, he decided he'd be proactive and change the other two, just in case. By the time he'd settled them down for a nap, he needed one himself. He also needed to fumigate the room. Located in the back corner of the house, the nursery's open windows offered a nice cross breeze. Northwest Montana got hot in the summer, but most of the time they didn't need to run air-conditioning.

Unwilling to leave them alone in the room, Wes eased into the antique rocking chair in the corner. He ran his hands over the worn wood. He had been with Liv when she stumbled upon it at the county yard sale. He never imagined sitting in it and watching his children sleep. Now he didn't want the moment to end.

Chapter 5

Other than the few minutes he'd spent with Jade when she returned from the attorney's office yesterday, he hadn't seen her or the girls. Maddie had stepped in his place as soon as she'd gotten off work last night. He hadn't even been able to say goodbye when he dropped off Jade's new rental SUV after he had the car seats inspected at the sheriff's department. He'd phoned Jade twice, but she kept reiterating she had it covered and she didn't need him. Once again, he felt cut out of the triplets' lives. And while that had been the original plan, he didn't like it so much now.

Watching Harlan and Dylan stand up as godfather for each other's children left him a little sad and lonely. Three of his brothers had kids—five among them—yet they'd never asked him to be a godfather. Dylan and Garrett had done it twice. That just showed how his brothers saw him. He guessed he couldn't blame them. His reputation had been far from stellar and he had begun to distance himself from them after their father's death. They were always cordial to each other and even joked around some, but the closeness they had once shared continued to fade.

Harlan had made more of an effort recently, but now it was too late for Wes to stay in Saddle Ridge. Even if he wanted to be the girls' father, Liv didn't want that. And he couldn't risk his heart breaking every time he ran into them.

When he had stood in the church earlier, he envisioned Audra, Hadley and Mackenzie's christening. Who would be their godparents? He assumed Jade, but who else? And why was he jealous of a man he didn't even know. Did Liv even plan on having them christened? Maybe they had been already. As much as he wanted to know the answers, he knew he had no right to them. And that stung. His brain wanted him to admit that Jade was doing the right thing by keeping him away, but his heart told him otherwise.

"Okay." Harlan wrapped an arm around Wes's shoulder and steered him away from the other christening guests mingling around the Silver Bells Ranch. "It's time you tell me what's really going on."

"What are you talking about?" Wes attempted to shrug him off, but his brother refused to lessen his grip.

"For starters, you showed up without a date. You rarely come to dinner without one, let alone a big event. And something seemed off with that whole car seat situation yesterday."

And here Wes had thought his brother would commend him for putting the children's safety first. "I told you the truth. Liv's sister is here watching the kids."

"I get that. But why isn't Jade using Liv's car and where is Liv anyway?"

Wes faced his brother. "Look, if I tell you, I don't want it to go any further. Not that it won't be public knowledge at some point anyway. For now, I'd appreciate you keeping this quiet."

For the next half hour, Wes explained the circumstances surrounding Liv's disappearance, conveniently leaving out his role in the triplets' parentage. "And because of my friendship with Liv, Jade asked me for some help. Now that she knows her sister is safe, she's trying to make the best of a very difficult situation. I'm here, so I agreed to pitch in whenever she needs me."

"After Molly walked out on me and Ivy, I had questioned if she had postpartum depression and if I had missed it."

"Wasn't Ivy a year old?"

"If untreated, it can manifest into other disorders. When Molly finally returned, she told me how unhappy she had been in our marriage and that she hadn't been prepared to have a child. To this day I still wonder if PPD played a part in her disappearance. And she had disappeared just like Liv. Only Molly was gone for years. Liv had the sense of mind to get help."

"But Molly's fine now, right?" Ivy's mother had popped back into their lives last year shortly after Harlan and Belle's wedding. Liv's baby drama had just begun to grab hold of Wes at the time and he had selfishly ignored what was going on in everybody else's lives.

"Molly's great. Her relationship with Ivy is still strained, but she missed seven years of her daughter's life. It's a work in progress. And I can't say for sure that she had PPD. I don't think she could, either. But I can tell you Liv is not alone. I've gone on more than a few calls relating to the baby blues as some people ignorantly refer to them. The baby blues and postpartum depression are two different things."

"I saw that mentioned on a few websites too. I watched the girls alone for a few hours when Jade met with the attorney yesterday, and it was overwhelming to say the least."

"I think it's hard for people who've never carried a child—both men and women—to understand all the changes a woman's body goes through postpregnancy. Physical and emotional. Personally, I find the entire process fascinating and beautiful. Granted, I haven't always felt that way. I made a point to be home for a month after Travis was born so I have a better appreciation for it this time around. I can thank Molly for that."

"I didn't realize you and your ex had become such good friends." Wes hated the growing distance between him and his brothers. He and Harlan especially. Wes was a little less than a year older and they'd always been close. But ever since Ryder accidentally killed their father, he'd found it next to impossible to escape their family's dysfunctional past. His brothers' memories differed widely from his because they'd either chosen to ignore it or they'd been that oblivious. Ryder had understood. Until the night he'd made the Slade family the talk of the town. Now that distance seemed impossible to close.

"I don't think Molly and I will ever be good friends." Harlan laughed. "Let's just say we have a newfound respect for one another. She pointed out how absent I had been when she had Ivy. Liv carried triplets, almost to term if memory serves me correctly. Her body alone had a lot to recover from. It's too bad she didn't have a partner supporting her through all of this. Kevin would have made a great dad if he hadn't turned out to be such a jackass."

"She definitely loved him." Wes grabbed two beers from an ice-filled horse trough and handed Harlan one.

"He loved her, just not enough." Harlan twisted the cap off his beer. "He's getting married sometime next month."

"You're kidding." Wes had only been gone for six months and the Kevin he knew had been loving the single life when he ran into him on New Year's Eve. "To who?"

"Some woman from Kalispell. I haven't met her personally, but I hear she's nice. She has a couple kids from a previous marriage."

Wes froze, the bottle halfway to his mouth. "Wait a minute. That SOB divorced Liv because he didn't want to raise another man's kid and he's marrying someone with kids?" Wes had to tell Jade.

"Yep." Harlan took a long tug of his beer. "In all fairness to Kevin, I think there's a difference between watching your wife carry and give birth to a stranger's child versus coming into the picture years after the fact."

"Still, that had to have hit Liv hard. You wouldn't happen to know when they got engaged, do you?"

Harlan removed his hat and wiped his brow with the back of his arm. "Not sure, but I received the wedding invite probably a month ago. I'm surprised you didn't get one. They just about invited the entire town. I think it's still in the envelope it came in. I can check the postmark when I get home. You think this was a trigger, don't you?"

"Amongst other things." Wes had read the risk for postpartum depression increased when the woman had a weak support system, had difficulty in breast-feeding, relationship problems and stressful events in their life. Those are just the things Wes knew Liv had battled. He loved his friend dearly, but she wasn't ready to be a single parent. And certainly not a single parent of three children. He should have said no. "Excuse me for a second while I call Jade and fill her in."

"Fine, but don't run off somewhere tonight." Harlan clapped him on the back. "We have a lot of celebrating to do and you're a part of it. You've been gone for too long. It hasn't been the same around here without you."

Wes's head started to pound with guilt. He doubted Dylan or Garrett would take the time to visit him in Texas. He could already hear the excuses about how they were too busy running Silver Bells. Even though Harlan had stuck his head in the sand right beside their brothers, he desperately tried to keep what was left of their family together. Surely Harlan, Belle and the kids would spend the holidays with him in Texas. Of course, it wouldn't be every year, but maybe every other one. Despite the past, his chest ached, already longing for the family events he'd miss.

"I didn't want to say anything earlier in front of Dylan and Garrett because I was afraid it would start an argument, but where's Mom?" She hadn't visited after either of Holly's or Travis's birth and now she'd missed the christenings. "This is the first time in years that all of us are together and she can't drag herself away from her new family and precious California to see us. Ryder killed Dad. Why is she punishing us?"

Wes competed in the Golden State a few times a year, and during the rare times his mother made an appearance at one of his events, she brought along her new husband and his adult children. What should have been a nice visit always turned into Wes feeling like an outsider with his own mother.

"We asked her to come and Dylan sent her a wedding invite. She responded tentatively. Considering she missed this weekend, I'd wager a guess that she'll miss the wedding next Saturday." Harlan turned away and watched Belle sitting under one of the ranch's shade trees breast-feeding Travis. She caught his gaze and smiled. Their love for one another radiated across the pasture. Wes had been so hell-bent on never getting himself tied down, that he hadn't given much thought to the sweeter side of marriage. He'd never even come close to that level of commitment with anyone.

"You're a lucky man." Jade's face clouded his vision. No! Jade would not become the first, either. He took a swig of beer. "Let me make this call and I'll catch up with you in a minute."

"Sure thing." Harlan's eyes remained transfixed on Belle as he hopped the top fence rail and walked toward his wife and baby. A love like that was rare. Just because three of his brothers had stumbled upon it over the past year didn't mean anything. They were meant to be family men. He wasn't.

He pulled Jade's number up on his phone and tapped the Call button, praying she'd shoot him straight to voice mail.

"Hello?" Her voice, sultry and deep, reverberated in his ear. Good Lord! One word, two syllables and he was already a goner.

"It's Wes. I'm sure you're busy, but I had to tell you what I just heard about Kevin."

"Kevin? As in my sister's Kevin?"

"As in someone else's Kevin. He's getting remarried. The invites went out about a month ago."

Jade sighed through the phone. "That had to have stung. I wonder why Maddie didn't mention it."

"Maddie moved to town after the divorce. She doesn't know Kevin and I doubt Liv would have mentioned the wedding to her."

"I wish she had confided in me."

"If I hadn't left, I'm positive she'd have told me." Wes chose his next words carefully, not wanting Jade to feel bad about her strained relationship with Liv. "The circumstances surrounding my friendship with your sister leant itself to many all-night discussions about her ex and my family. I moved away, but I should have stayed in contact with her. I own that. That being said, I think this goes beyond Kevin getting married again. His fiancée has kids, so—"

"That jerk!" Jade shouted into the phone. "So he'll be their stepfather."

"You see where I'm going with this, right?"

"My poor sister. She battled everything silently. I shouldn't be surprised. She always has."

"What do you mean?" Once again, the Liv who'd been his friend for almost five years and Jade's version of the same woman were two very different people. She'd been raw and honest, and their talks had been extremely therapeutic and cathartic. If something had bothered her, she'd told him.

"We bounced around a lot when we were kids. Whenever our mom got out of jail and claimed us—" Jade snorted "—as if we were a piece of luggage, Liv became the parent. Constantly babysitting Mom and trying to keep us safe. Between cleaning up drug paraphernalia and hiding our mother's own money so she couldn't blow it all, she took the brunt of the abuse. But I never heard her complain. Not once."

"No child should ever be subjected to that."

"Just like no teenager should have endured the teasing you did because of me. I didn't want to do this over the phone, but I can't wait any longer to apologize to you. I'm sorry."

"That's it? That's all you have to say?" Wes turned away from prying eyes and walked toward the stables as he fought to keep his voice low despite the resentment bubbling beneath the surface. "I understand your grudge against me and I admit, I was wrong to do what I did. But, sweetheart, what you did was a lot more than teasing. You telling everyone I was gay not only got me beat up at school, it followed me on the rodeo circuit and home. Dammit!" Wes tripped and caught himself before he hit the ground. He couldn't walk as fast as he wanted to run. Hell, he wanted to fly far and fast. He unlatched the tack room door and swung it wide. Cradling his phone between his chin and shoulder, he grabbed a saddle and blanket off the wall racks.

"Wes, I—"

"My father looked at me with disgust." Wes interrupted whatever excuse she had in her arsenal. He had to finally tell her how she'd ruined his life. "I won't repeat some of the names he called me, but your little game incited fights at home. Not only between me and my dad. But between my parents because my mom defended me. My dad could be a loving man, but he could also be a bigot. You have no idea what that did to us. What *you* did to us."

"I didn't—" Jade swore under her breath. "I never told anyone you were gay."

"The hell you didn't."

"Wes, please hear me out," Jade pleaded.

Wes held the phone from his ear, tempted to hang up.

"Wes?"

"Fine." He had no idea what compelled him to give her a chance to explain, because there couldn't possibly be any justification for her cruelty. "Go for it."

Jade sighed heavily. "I was labeled a slut after you told everyone we had slept together. After everything I'd been through, that really hurt. Here I was the new kid and I already had a reputation for something I didn't do. One afternoon when I was changing for gym class a few girls started calling me names.

I wasn't going to take that, so I stood up for myself and I told them we never slept together, and that you had broken up with me because I wasn't your type."

Wes scoffed. He didn't even know what his type was back then. "That's not what I heard."

"I know. One of the girls had twisted my words and inferred that I was saying you were gay. All I wanted to do was get out of that damn locker room, so I didn't respond. By the end of class, the rumor had spread and instead of correcting it and telling everyone that wasn't what I'd meant, I said nothing." Her voice broke. "My silence perpetuated the rumor and for that I'm truly sorry. If I had known what was going on with you at home, I swear I would have been there telling your father it wasn't true."

Tension eased from his jaw as the anger began to slip away. "Even after what I had done to you?"

"Yes. No one deserves what you endured." Her voice soft, barely above a whisper. "My assistant and truly my best friend, Tomás, is gay. He's told me some horrific stories about how he'd been treated when people learned of his sexuality. I would never wish that on my worst enemy. I'm sorry. I realize that doesn't mean much today, but, Wes, I am so sorry for not setting the record straight from the beginning."

For years, he had wanted to rip into Jade and tell her exactly how he felt. To force her to see how bullying affects not only the person being bullied, but everyone around them. While she was wrong to let the rumor get out of hand, he was just as much to blame. He'd lied and told one person they'd slept together, and she'd paid a steep price. If he'd kept his mouth shut and his pride at bay, she'd never have been in the position to defend herself and the escalation wouldn't have happened. They'd both suffered greatly at the hands of the other.

"Wes, are you still there?"

He entered Bonsai's stall, and rested his head against the quarter horse's neck. The animal bobbed his head and nickered, welcoming the human contact.

"Honestly, Jade, I get it. I know all too well how easy it is to lose control of a situation. I also need to accept my part in this. What was it we learned in physics class? For every action there is an equal and opposite reaction. I don't know if you'll ever be able to forgive me. I certainly don't expect it, but I—" Wes swallowed hard at the words he never thought he'd say. "I forgive you. I think we need to put our resentment aside and end this here."

Silence echoed through the phone for a long moment before she spoke. "End this? You make it sound like we won't see you again."

"You made it very clear last night and earlier when I called that I'm not needed. The girls are in very capable hands. But I wish you had come to this realization before you involved me in their lives. I can't unsee what I've already seen. I can't unfeel what's already in my heart."

"You need to spend time with your family. I believe that even more now than I did before. And I'm sorry for getting you involved, but come on, Wes, we were already involved. Who else could I have turned to? You were the only person who knew everything."

"Almost everything. I didn't know about you."

"And your reaction to the news was justified. You told me your initial connection to my sister was misery loves company. I can relate. I didn't want to be alone. I wanted someone who understood. Someone in the same position I'm in. Maddie—" Jade lowered her voice to a whisper. "She's a great help, but she doesn't get it the way you do. I saw that you were struggling with this so I set you free. I don't know what the right thing to do is."

"The right thing is to say goodbye." Wes blinked away the moisture forming in his eyes as he smoothed the saddle blanket over Bonsai's back. "It's better this way."

"Wes—" Her voice was barely audible.

"Goodbye, Jade." Wes disconnected the call and turned off

his phone before shoving it in his pocket. He lifted the saddle on the horse and tightened the cinch straps. Nothing cleared a man's mind like being alone with his horse. And since his Tango was in Texas, his uncle's beloved horse was the perfect stand in.

He slid his boot in the stirrup and swung his other leg up over the saddle. He took the reins and exhaled, already feeling like he'd made the right decision to walk away.

A few days ago he'd been itching to jump on the next plane out of town. Now the thought left him empty. He wanted to see his brothers' children grow up. To be there for their birthdays, Thanksgiving, Christmas or whatever special event they had going on. But in doing so, he'd see Audra, Hadley and Mackenzie. He'd have to. He wouldn't be able to stay away and he didn't want to confuse them. He needed to stay anonymous, for their sake and his.

The house was quiet except for the sound of Jade's fingers tapping on her laptop keyboard. The girls had a 2:00 a.m. feeding a little over an hour ago and had fallen asleep shortly afterward. Even with Maddie's help, Jade struggled to get work done. Two days had passed since she'd last spoke with Wes, three days since she'd seen him. It felt more like a month. She'd promoted Tomás, giving him authority to run the office and hire two more employees. They'd lost a couple lucrative clients over the weekend because Jade wasn't personally there to oversee their event planning. No amount of video chats made up for one-on-one client relations. Tomás was good, probably even better than she was at the job. She had faith in him.

She'd confided in him about how she had severely affected Wes's life. And Tomás pulled no punches when he told Jade that her silence had been just as damaging as if she had actually said the words. He also told her to forgive herself. She laughed at the mere thought. Forgiveness had to be earned and she'd done nothing to deserve it.

Jade slammed her laptop closed and spun around in Liv's

übercomfortable office chair. Her purse and keys hung on the door handle, mocking her. She hadn't left the house since her trip to the attorney's office on Friday. Three days. Well, technically four since the night had already crossed into Tuesday. She'd never been that reclusive. Not even when she had the flu last year. She wanted to go for a ride. Not a long one. Just long enough to feel like she'd really gotten out of the house. What if Maddie woke up? What if the girls woke up? And what if they didn't?

Jade grabbed her bag and tiptoed to the back door before she realized Maddie's car blocked hers in the driveway. Crap! Normally she parked at her own house next door, but Maddie had gone grocery shopping after work and it had been easier to park closer and carry the bags into the house. She turned to head back into the office when she noticed Maddie's car keys on the counter. She could move the car, or…she could borrow it. It was borrowing, right? After all, it would be more responsible of her to leave behind the vehicle with the infant seats in case of an emergency.

Okay, logic aside, she was about to steal Maddie's car. The need for an escape—however brief—won out. Was this how Liv had felt? Walking out the door was simple when you were alone. She couldn't imagine doing it with three little ones in tow. She still hadn't taken the girls out of the house. That probably wasn't healthy. This was why she needed a nanny. Unfortunately, finding one qualified enough to care for multiples had been challenging. They were in high demand.

Jade removed a pad from the kitchen drawer, wrote Maddie a note and left it on the counter along with the keys to the SUV…just in case she woke up. Easing the door closed behind her, Jade practically skipped down the drive. She glanced up at the nursery window, guilt weighing heavy on her chest. Jade never felt guilty for anything. She was cutthroat in business and her personal life. Yet she'd been back in Saddle Ridge for less than a week and she'd worn guilt like a push-up bra. And it was every bit as restrictive and uncomfortable.

Five minutes into her escape, Jade realized she was on her way to the Silver Bells Ranch. It was the middle of the night—correction, it was the wee hours of the morning and she had no idea where Wes even stayed on the ranch. For all she knew, he could have left early for South Dakota.

Doubt aside, Jade pulled onto the main ranch road. Except for the other day when she'd first confronted Wes, she hadn't been there before. The full moon glinted off the roof of the picturesque three-story log lodge reminiscent of a Thomas Kinkade painting. Beautiful as it was, it didn't take her breath away like the cowboy walking out the front door did. Jade froze, framing Wes in her headlights. Broad shoulders, lean waist, long legs. No man should look that good. He approached the car and tapped on the passenger window.

"Are you looking for the Silver Bells Ranch lodge?" he asked as she reluctantly lowered the window. "Jade, what are you doing here?"

She groaned, uncertain of the answer herself.

"Is this Maddie's car?"

He leaned in the window, close enough for her to smell the sharp, clean scent of soap. Had he just showered? Maybe he was returning from a tryst with a ranch guest. She felt heat rise to her cheeks and thanked God the car's dark interior shrouded her embarrassment. Why couldn't she have taken a quick drive into town and back?

"Jade?"

She gripped the steering wheel tighter and braved a glance at him. Between his hat and the darkness, she could barely make out his features. "It was the last vehicle in the driveway, so I borrowed it. I have a lot of work ahead of me tonight and I needed to clear my head for a bit. I pulled in here to turn around. I hadn't expected to see you." *Good Lord, why was she ram-*

bling? "What about you? I'm surprised to see you wandering around this late."

"The ranch still isn't operating with a full staff and I'm trying to fill in wherever I can. It makes for long nights." He tried the door handle. "Can you let me in? I wouldn't mind a lift back to my cabin."

"Um, sure." Jade pressed the lock release and he slid in beside her. His bicep brushed against her arm as he set his hat on the dashboard. She now understood the meaning of *compact car*. Mistake number two…she should have flip-flopped vehicles and taken the SUV instead. At least he would've been an arm's length away. "You'll have to tell me where to go."

When he didn't respond, she lifted her gaze to his. The dashboard lights turned his warm hazel eyes a deep, dark chocolate brown, drawing her into their depths. The man was too much, on too many levels. They didn't even like each other, so why the sudden attraction?

Because it wasn't sudden. He had been her first crush fifteen years ago, before he screwed it up. Crush or not, she hadn't been ready for anything sexual back then. She'd spent years hating him, only now she wasn't sure how she felt. Knowing the truth had lessened that hate, if she could even call it hate anymore. That anger had been redirected toward Burke, where it should have been all along. She had no right to feel anything toward Wes except remorse. While she'd endured bullying and slut-shaming for four years, the physical attack had been swift. Wes had endured far more because of her silence.

"I wanted to call you."

Jade rested her head against the seat and laughed. "You're the one who said goodbye."

"That doesn't mean I don't still care."

Jade ignored the sincerity in his voice and shifted the car into Drive. "The girls are fine. I haven't found a nanny yet and there's been no word from Liv or the treatment center."

Wes covered her hand with his. "What about you? How are you doing?"

Jade gripped the gearshift tighter under the heat of his palm. "I, um, I've been busy trying to keep my company going. It's a bit tough to do this far from home."

"I can imagine." He gave her hand a light squeeze before releasing it. "That's quite an operation you have there. I hope you don't mind. I looked you up online."

Nervousness crept into her chest as she shifted the car back into Park. "Hey, it's fair. You already know I looked you up. I noticed you haven't posted any photos for the past few days."

"I haven't been in the mood. I haven't wanted to do much of anything since…since I last saw you." He hooked her chin with his finger, gently forcing her to turn toward him. "You've been on my mind. Constantly."

"We're enemies," she whispered.

"We were enemies." His breath, warm against her cheek, sent a shiver through her body. "We are so much more than that and as hard as I try, I can't forget the lives we've created together, however unknowingly. We will always have that connection and no one can take that from us."

"Wes." Jade choked back a sob. "There's nothing we can do about it. They aren't ours to keep. As much as I fear my sister won't get better, I have to believe she will. We can't acknowledge that they came from us. And nothing can ever come from that connection. Liv didn't want us to know about the other. It was her secret, and a friendship or whatever is impossible."

"Now we can't even be friends?"

Hurt reflected in his eyes and it took every ounce of restraint she had not to touch him and attempt to ease his pain.

"No. The risk is too high. And it would hurt Liv. I still need to find a way to tell her you've seen the girls and have spent time with them. I'll discuss it with her doctor when I visit her. I think it's a big enough problem to warrant a third party. I can't imagine her not being threatened by it."

"No chance of keeping it secret, huh?"

Jade shook her head. "If I never planned to see her again, then maybe. I can't look at my sister and lie though. The truth would come out eventually."

"Let me ask you something." Wes shifted in his seat and leaned against the door. "Twice now you've mentioned the truth coming out. Were you and Jade planning to tell the girls that you're their biological mother?"

"Possibly. It depends on the situation." It broke her heart knowing the girls might one day learn their mother and aunt had lied to them for years. Regardless of how well-intentioned the lie had been. "There are a number of factors I wish I had considered before agreeing to this. It's been a lot harder than I imagined. For all of us."

"I have an idea, but I want you to hear me out before you say no."

"Okay, should I be worried?" She laughed nervously.

"If you moved to the ranch—"

"Are you insane?" He must be to propose the one thing that would send her sister into orbit. "Absolutely not."

His brow furrowed. "It's a good idea if you'll let me finish."

"Okay." Jade bit back a retort and raised her hands in surrender. "Go ahead."

"You obviously feel isolated at Liv's house because you're driving around in the middle of the night. You don't have a nanny or any other help during the day. Now I may not know of any professional child caregivers, but I can personally vouch for many of the teenagers living on this ranch. I've known them their entire lives from when their parents worked on my father's ranch and then came here. They are home from school for the summer, looking to earn some extra cash. I'm sure one or two of them would be more than happy to give up cleaning guest quarters to help you with the girls. The few I have in mind helped raise their little brothers and sisters so they're not inexperienced."

Hiring them wasn't a bad idea. But move to the ranch? No. "Why can't they come out to the house?"

"Because they don't have cars. They would need someone to transport them back and forth. Their parents work, and it would be too much of a strain on you."

Okay, he had a point there. "Your idea has merit, but I think it's better if I wait and find a professional nanny. I'm flattered, but after the things you said the other day, I'm confused why you're asking me to move in with you?"

"You wouldn't be living with me because I won't be here. I head out to South Dakota tomorrow...well I guess it's already tomorrow, but I'll be back in time for the wedding on Saturday. Then I head home to my job and life in Texas."

Jade's stomach knotted at the thought of him leaving. "Do you have a girlfriend waiting for you there too?"

Wes's features softened as a slow smile eased across his face. "Aw, sweetheart." He ran the back of his fingers lightly down her cheek. "I'm flattered by your jealousy, but I am one hundred percent single."

"I am not jealous." She smacked him away.

"Ouch!" He rubbed his hand. "You're cute when you're riled up."

"You are so asking for it." The man infuriated her more than a bridezilla with a bathroom emergency. He also turned her insides to mush. Only he could make her feel like a lovesick teenager again. Not that she was lovesick. *Love* was *evil* spelled backward...okay...misspelled *evil*. Regardless, it was close enough and she wanted no part of it. Love came with attachments and commitments. She had enough of that at work. She was married to her job and that was all she needed. "You can't just install me in the lodge and leave me with a bunch of strangers."

"I was thinking more along the lines of one of the guesthouses that are not in use. My brothers are still rebuilding Silver Bells. Business is much better than it was a year ago, but we're still not fully booked." Wes ran his hands down his thighs and Jade wondered if he was as nervous as she was. "Of course, I would have to discuss it with them first, but I don't see it being a problem. If you're worried about people gossiping about Liv being in a PPD treatment center, I promise you, my family is not like that. Harlan understood and even enlightened me about a few things."

"You told him?" Jade closed her eyes, silently adding one more item to the list of things she had to tell her sister. "Why did you do that? Liv should have an opportunity to say what she does and doesn't want people to know."

"Harlan didn't give me a choice. He knew something was wrong when I showed up at the sheriff's department with your rental SUV instead of your sister's. I have a hard time lying to my brothers the same way you have a hard time lying to your sister."

"Fine, but I can't move cribs and whatever else I need to your family's ranch."

"We have cribs. Emma—the woman my brother Dylan is marrying on Saturday—wanted families to think of Silver Bells as a second home when they visited. She personally redecorated a few of the larger guest cabins with mothers in mind. We have five brand-new cribs at the ready. Those particular cabins have full kitchens with dishwashers, washing machines and dryers, guest bedrooms, rocking chairs and all the creature comforts of home."

"Wow." She planned events at guest ranches with similar amenities and they didn't come cheap. "Your brothers must have some budget to do all that."

Wes shook his head. "That was all Emma. She bought into the ranch as did many of our employees over the last six months. Silver Bells was on the verge of bankruptcy after my uncle died. Now it's a thriving family and employee-owned business. It still has a way to go, but it's getting great reviews and by next summer there will be a reservation waiting list."

"The way you speak so proudly of the ranch, I'm surprised you aren't a partner."

Wes rested his arm on the open window frame and stared out the windshield. "They asked me, but I think they felt obligated to. I had to say no anyway."

"Because of Mackenzie, Audra and Hadley?" Jade hated how three innocent children were the cause of so much misery. It wasn't fair.

"They were a part of it, but I had already planned to leave. I see my father wherever I go in this town. Some of those memories are really good and others not so much. I hate Ryder for what he did. And I hate my father for the way he treated me. For the way he treated my mom. I hate my mom for leaving and never coming back. She wasn't even at the christenings. Those are her grandchildren, but she couldn't do it."

Jade reached across the armrest and entwined her fingers with his. "Maybe the pain is too much for her to return. The same way you said it would be too painful for you to come back."

"I've told myself that a thousand times. She's remarried and I'm happy for her. I truly am. And please don't get me wrong, as much as I hate some of the things my family has done, they are still my family and I love them with all my heart. Just like I love Audra, Hadley and Mackenzie."

"I think it's impossible not to." Jade wanted to comfort him… to find comfort in him, but the barriers were too great for her to cross.

"I didn't want to. I tried not to. But the truth is, I loved them the minute Liv showed me the ultrasound. Something changed in me that day and I can't explain it." His fingers tightened around hers. "I realize I hurt your sister by severing all ties with her after that, but I was afraid to stay friends. If that was my reaction to a grainy black-and-white photo, I could only imagine what it would be like seeing them once they were born. Let alone in person. And I was right. They took my breath away. I may be heading back to Texas on Sunday, but I will never be the same after these two weeks."

"Neither will I." Jade released him and covered her face with her hands. The tears she had carefully held in check over the past few months finally broke the dam. "I feel so guilty for regretting my decision to do this. But I would never take it back. I would never trade their lives in for anything."

"I know, honey. I know." Wes wrapped his arm around her shoulders and pulled her to him. "Neither would I."

"How do I do this?" She sobbed against his chest. "And how am I supposed to do it alone?"

"Move in here."

"How can that possibly work? If you see a resemblance between the girls and your nephew, don't you think your family will? Never mind that my sister would freak over the arrangement."

"You're forgetting that one of your sister's best friends is engaged to my brother Garrett. She may notice a resemblance whether you're here or not. Granted your sister had started the process before Delta and Garrett got together so she couldn't have predicted that connection. But she knew about Harlan and Belle's baby because I told her. Harlan told me when Belle was only four weeks along."

"What did she say?" Jade asked against the softness of his shirt.

"She was thrilled for them. A few days later she had our embryos implanted. But she didn't think this through. I have a lot of respect for Liv, but I think she was so in love with the idea of having a baby, she didn't see the whole picture. Like what happens when Travis and her daughters are in the same class together? Someone's bound to comment on the resemblance. What happens if one of those girls wants to date him when they get older? They're cousins. What is she going to do? How will she explain that?"

"Oh my God! I hadn't thought of that." Jade pulled away from him.

"You shouldn't have to."

Wes brushed her hair away from her face, allowing it to fall behind her shoulder. His touch tender and kind, as if they'd actually been friends. She hadn't thought he was capable of so much compassion.

"You were a donor. I was a donor," he continued. "I can't tell you how many times I've replayed that scenario in my head these past couple days. Your sister either has to move out of town, or she needs to face the cold reality that people will discover the truth. As much as I don't want to reveal my role in this, I realize I can only control a part of it."

"That had to have weighed on Liv." People had babies every day without complication, yet Audra, Hadley and Mackenzie were surrounded by it. Any decision she, Wes and Liv made affected them.

"I'm sure it did. It's too big of a secret to bear. Up until five days ago, she was the only one who knew the entire truth."

"It's killing me not to be able to talk to her." Ironic since she had subconsciously avoided speaking with Liv for weeks. "I have so many questions."

"She may not have any answers."

"I got so mad at her this afternoon." Jade hugged her arms to herself. "I lost another major client because I'm not in LA. Tomás is wonderful and I trust him with my life, but I had contracts with people who expected me to handle their events personally. And to a large degree I had. There's a lot I can do remotely, but I can't hold someone's hand through a catering or cake testing or walk them through a venue. My face on Tomás's iPad just wasn't enough to convince them to stay. We had already invested quite a bit of money in this one. I took a big hit."

"That doesn't seem right. Can't you fight that?"

"Sure." Jade bitterly laughed. "And then that celebrity will tell their friends not to use us. LA may be a large city, but it's a small town at heart. Everyone knows everyone else and reputations can be destroyed with one phone call. I have to suck it up." She inhaled deeply. "I'm mad at my sister for putting me in this situation. I'm not mad she has postpartum depression. But let's be honest, she made some big mistakes. And let me tell you, I pass some of that blame on the fertility specialist she went to. Counseling should be mandatory, especially when implanting three embryos in a single mother. I find that irresponsible. So, yeah, I'm mad. And the guilt eats at me for feeling that way because Liv had to be a complete wreck over this."

Wes gathered her into his arms again and held her tightly. "You're human first. That's why I'm asking you to move in here." His voice smooth and insistent as he rested his head on hers. "By staying at Liv's you're doing exactly what she did. Let me and my family help you. And if they figure out the truth, we'll handle it then. Hopefully it won't come to that. Don't wait until you're so strung out, both emotionally and financially, to do something."

"What about Maddie? She's personally invested in this. She loves the children."

"She should come with you so you're not alone at night."

Because you'll be in Texas. Jade wanted to be selfish and ask him to stay. A small part of her loved the connection they shared. Wes Slade, of all people, was the one person who completely understood. The pretense had slipped away and she wanted nothing more than to lean on him for support.

She lifted her head from his chest and looked into his eyes. Could she really put the past aside and trust him?

"Maybe moving here isn't such a bad idea. But it's only temporary."

Wes cupped her chin, his mouth inches from hers. "It's going to be okay. I'll talk to my brothers and we'll figure this out. Together."

"Together?" Jade had never yearned to kiss a man so badly. "But you're leaving."

"I'll call you every day." He stroked her cheek, brushing away what remained of her tears. "You'll still have me."

If only she had him... Her sister would never forgive her. Jade sat up straight and gripped the steering wheel. "Okay, um, yeah, talk to your brothers and we'll take it from there. How about you show me where to drop you off."

Wes cleared his throat and adjusted his jeans. "Make a left at the stables and follow that road to the end."

Jade shifted the car into gear and stepped on the gas. The engine revved, but didn't move. "Please tell me I didn't break Maddie's car."

"Try putting it in Drive instead of Neutral." Wes laughed under his breath.

Jade stared down at the glowing *N* on the shifter. What was it about Wes? She took pride in always remaining in control, yet whenever she was around him, she made a fool of herself. He was charming, thoughtful, handsome—okay, downright sexy—but he was off-limits. A relationship, even a fleeting, one-night sexual one, was out of the question with the father of her children.

Damn.

She braked the car abruptly in front of his cabin. "Get out."

Wes laughed, making no move to open the door.

Jade flipped up the armrest and reached across his lap for the door handle, pushing it open. "Get out before I do something we'll both regret."

Before she could retreat to her side of the car, he gripped her waist and tugged her onto his lap, the full extent of his arousal evident against her hip. "What if we don't regret it?"

"We can't." She splayed her hands on his chest and pushed away from him, her back against the dashboard.

"Because you don't want to, or because of your sister?"

"Oh, I definitely want to." Her eyes wandered down his abs to his belt buckle as his thumb grazed the side of her breast. In seconds, she could have his jeans unzipped and end the tension between them. She closed her eyes, relishing the thought. She'd never understood that deep sexual yearning she'd heard her brides talk about...until now. A shrink once told her it had been because of her past. She'd always believed she just hadn't met the right man yet. But despite the unfamiliar desire raging deep within her, she couldn't betray her sister any more than she was already.

"We can't do this to Liv. It's not fair to her."

"Okay." He nodded silently and released her. "Just for the record, I don't think it's fair that your sister gets to dictate how we feel about each other." Wes reached for the door. "Before I say any more, I'm going to go take a cold shower."

Jade slid back to her side of the car. "You and me both."

"We could always take one together." Wes snatched his hat from the dashboard. "But then we'd get all steamy again. Good night, Jade. I'll call you after I speak to my brothers." He stepped out of the car and closed the door, giving her a pleasant view of his backside in the process. He leaned in the window before walking away. "Sweet dreams, sweetheart."

"You too."

"I do believe you're blushing."

"Good night, Wes."

Jade pulled away from the cabin before he tempted her further. If he could melt her resolve without even kissing her, she could only imagine what would happen to her if he did. Wes was right, he needed to go back to Texas. She was safer that way.

Chapter 6

Jade stepped outside the large log guest cabin and admired the rising sun over the Swan Range. Okay, maybe Wes was right, the view was photoworthy. She sipped her mug of coffee as Belgian horses grazed lush green grass in the corral twenty yards from the expansive wraparound porch. Dylan and Garrett had been gracious enough to offer her the place for free, but she refused. She could afford to pay their more than reasonable rate, although a part of her wondered if they had discounted the cost. Wes had been insistent on paying the entire bill, but Jade relented and allowed him to share half the expense.

Wes had only been gone a day, and she surprisingly missed him. The ranch, vast as it was, seemed empty without him there. Not that they had spent any time there together, except for the day she arrived and their heated exchange in Maddie's car.

She glanced over at the maroon Ford parked alongside the cabin. Her body began to tingle at the memory. She'd almost had sex with Wes Slade in the front seat of a car. What the hell was happening to her? They weren't in high school. Regardless, the man had already affected Jade and the girls. He hadn't been a part of their lives for very long, but the triplets seemed more content and settled when he was around. Nothing would replace their mother though.

For infants, they'd had so many changes in their little lives and Jade was grateful Maddie agreed to stay at the ranch with her. She had been their one constant. It also didn't hurt that the woman had a major crush on a ranch hand she met at the christenings who just happened to live on the other side of the property.

"Here you are," Maddie said from the open doorway. "Wow. That view's worth a million bucks and then some."

"Are the girls awake yet?"

"Not yet." She padded barefoot to the railing and inhaled the fresh scent of morning dew. "This has to be the first night they've slept more than four hours in a row."

"Maybe it's the country air." Jade had the best sleep of her life after feeding and putting the triplets to bed around two thirty. "I should brace myself for the dirty diaper onslaught while you get ready for work."

"I don't know." Maddie, still in her sleep shorts and T, flopped into one of the porch rocking chairs and closed her eyes. "I may play hooky today and just admire the landscape."

"You mean admire Jarrod."

Maddie glared at her and narrowed her eyes. "Do you see Jarrod anywhere, because I don't."

"No, but I'm sure you'll know his schedule by tonight. And if you get dressed fast enough, you can catch him at the breakfast buffet up at the main lodge."

"Really?" Maddie shot upward. "I mean, breakfast sounds like a good idea."

Jade stifled her laughter as Maddie ran back inside the cabin. She wished she had a friend like Maddie in LA. Tomás and his husband were always around for business or pleasure, but Jade felt like a third wheel whenever they went out together. Her social calendar was packed almost every night so she couldn't complain, but most of those events were business related in some way. She had to out-network the competition to remain relevant, which didn't leave much time for dating.

"Good morning!" A woman called out from an ATV as she drove up to the porch. "It's refreshing here, isn't it?"

The voice and the face were familiar, but Jade couldn't place the woman. Then the realization hit her. "Delta?"

"I know, I look different with a pixie cut, but I didn't have much say in that." She eased off the ATV and unfastened a large tote from the back before climbing the steps. "How are you? I'm sorry I wasn't around when the babies were born."

Jade gave the woman a hug, then held her at arm's length. "Wow! You look amazing." Delta had been stunning before, but her deep mahogany close-cropped hair accented her slender neck, perfect breasts and mile-long legs. "You look more like a supermodel than someone recovering from cancer."

"Well, thank you." Delta mock-strutted a mini catwalk and spun around. "Cancer forces you to take better care of yourself. Besides eating healthier, I'm working out more and kicking some major butt. Life's too short not to. I'm really sorry to hear about Liv. I wish I could have been around more during her pregnancy."

"No, no, please. You had your own struggles. I get it."

Delta nodded, her eyes brimming with tears.

"I have something for you." She held up the bag. "Belle—Harlan's wife—has been teaching me how to bake whole grain bread and muffins, so our kitchen is overflowing with all sorts of yumminess. I thought you and Maddie would like some."

"Absolutely. She's inside getting ready for work."

"Ready for work or ready for *Jarrod*?" She fanned herself as she said his name.

"Oh, you know, huh?"

"Honey, I had a ringside seat to the drool fest. And yes, dear Maddie was drooling."

"Why don't you come in and you can tell me about it over

coffee." Jade opened the screen door and held it for Delta. "We may actually get a chance to talk before the girls wake up."

Delta followed her to the large family-sized eat-in kitchen. Jade loved the cabin's thoughtful little details, like easy-to-sterilize solid core countertops and child safety latches on all the cabinets, top and bottom in case someone's child was a climber.

"Besides wanting to pawn my food off on you, I sort of have a favor to ask."

"Okay." Jade poured two mugs of hot coffee and set them on the table. "Do you take cream or sugar?"

"Just black, thank you."

Jade peered into the tote and pulled out a bag of blueberry muffins. "Oh, these look amazing," she said before taking a bite. "These are incredible. I love the addition of the orange zest. It really brightens the flavor."

"I thought so too. Normally you see lemon and blueberry paired together, but the orange is a nice citrus twist."

"I'm sorry. I guess I'm hungrier than I thought." Jade wiped her fingers on a napkin. "Please ask me the favor."

"Um, okay." Worry lines creased Delta's forehead as she death-gripped her mug. "I'm sure you can imagine the first half of the year was really rough for Garrett, me and the kids."

Jade reached across the table and covered her hands. "What is it? Did something else happen?"

"It's nothing bad at all." Delta's caramel-brown eyes met hers. "It's just a big favor to ask. June has been our turning point of sorts. I'm done with chemo, my scans look great and we can finally move on with our lives."

"I have an idea where this is going." Jade hoped she was correct.

Delta returned her enthusiasm. "Garrett and I have been talking and we really want to get married this summer. The problem is, the kids leave to visit their grandparents in Wyoming on Monday, and they won't be back for a month which would give us more than enough time to squeeze in a honeymoon. It's important his kids are in the ceremony, so eloping is out of the question."

"And you want to have the wedding this week."

Delta's smile widened. "After the christenings on last Saturday, we asked Dylan and Emma if they would mind us getting married this weekend too. We thought it would be the perfect time since many of the same people we'd invite are already in town. They loved the idea."

"I'm so happy for you!" Jade gave Delta another hug. "Dylan and Emma have their wedding planned and set for Saturday afternoon and the reception goes into the evening. We don't want to disrupt that, but we also realize that many people are flying or driving home on Sunday. We just want a simple ceremony, at sunrise Sunday morning and then a quick breakfast reception before everyone leaves."

"It sounds wonderful. I'm jealous I haven't thought of that idea before. I've planned a lot of double ceremonies, but yours is a much better idea. One wedding doesn't encroach on the other."

"Exactly. And we'd each have our own anniversary date."

"So." Jade folded her arms over her chest. "Are you going to ask me or what?"

"Okay." Delta beamed. "I know you're super busy with the triplets and your company in LA, but would you be willing to help plan our wedding? I realize it's only four days away, but—"

"But nothing. I would love to." This was the pick-me-up Jade needed. To physically get her hands on a project instead of doing it remotely. "I have a ton of ideas already."

"We're on a tight budget though." Delta winced. "I know you do big, lavish Hollywood ceremonies. That's just way out of our reach."

"You'd be surprised how many celebrities want small weddings. My assistant had an intimate ceremony last year, and it meant so much more than the bigger ones." Jade lowered her voice to a whisper. "But don't tell anyone I said that. It would kill my business."

"I promise I won't." Delta giggled. "I feel bad that Liv won't be here for it though."

"Liv's happy if you're happy. I won't even tell her when I see her. I'll leave that for you."

Delta nodded. "Thank you for doing this for us. One more thing, my dog Jake has to be in the ceremony. I can't get married without him."

"You're welcome and I've added many dogs to wed—" The sound of one baby, followed by another, rang out from down the hall. "They're playing my song. I think Emma had the right idea putting us so far away from the main lodge."

"It's loud when there's three of them, isn't it?" Delta stood with Jade. "Do you mind if I help? I haven't seen them in a month."

"Sure." Jade swallowed hard, hoping Delta didn't pick up on the similarities between the girls and Travis, especially Mackenzie. "Just be forewarned, they can pack an odoriferous punch."

"Oh!" Delta waved her hand in front of her face as they entered the bedroom. "That they do. Chemo annihilated my sense of smell and taste buds, but I'll tell ya, I can definitely smell that. Is that normal?"

"For Stinker One, Two and Three, yes. Wes said Travis's was slightly better, but not by much. I don't know if it's their formula or what. They have a two-month checkup at the pediatrician's next week, and it's at the top of my list."

"Oh hey, Delta." Maddie wrinkled her nose as she entered the room. "Welcome to the danger zone. Enter at your own risk."

"You think after working around horses and their manure for most of my life, a baby would smell like roses. Okay." Delta squared her shoulders. "Where do we begin?"

Jade bet if Delta had goggles and a hazmat suit, she'd have put it on. "Neither one of you need to help me. Go get some breakfast and ogle your men."

"Nonsense." Delta hip checked Jade out of the way. "Three babies, three of us. Let's do this before they claim a victim."

As if on cue, Audra, Hadley and Mackenzie stopped and stared up at the women laughing at them for a brief second before continuing to cry.

"Oh, did we insult you?" Maddie lifted Audra out of the crib. "We're sorry. Just like Aunt Jade is sorry she labeled you with a Sharpie when she first got here."

"You did what?" Delta's eyes widened at she lifted Mackenzie.

"Ah, I'll take her." Jade eased the infant out of Delta's arms. She didn't want her getting that up close and personal with the triplet that resembled Travis the most. "Mackenzie's the fussiest."

"She is?" Maddie asked. "Since when?"

Jade scrambled for an excuse. "Monday. You were at work when I noticed it. I've been double-checking to make sure she doesn't have a rash or anything. I should have mentioned it before." Jade hated having to lie to the one person who'd been the greatest and most unexpected help to her over the past week.

"I think all three of them have been a little more gassy than usual." Maddie grabbed a diaper blanket from the dresser and knelt on the floor to change Audra, giving Delta the changing table. "Definitely let Alyssa and Megan know when they come today."

Jade had met with two of the sweetest teenage girls after Wes had helped move her onto the ranch. His future sister-in-law, Emma, had personally used them many times and highly recommended them. At first Jade wondered if hiring two people was overkill, but she liked the idea of them having each other for companionship so they wouldn't get bored. Jade needed to devote her full attention to work, and she didn't want to feel compelled to entertain a babysitter.

"Someone please tell me the baby labeling story," Delta asked.

"Maddie will never let me live this down. I was afraid of

mixing up the babies so I wrote their first initial on the bottom of their feet."

"With a permanent black marker," Maddie added.

"It washed off...eventually." Jade rolled her eyes. "It's not like I had them tattooed."

"Why didn't you use nail polish?" Delta asked as she changed Hadley.

"Because I thought they'd chew it off."

"Not if you put it on their toes." Delta held her nose and shoved the offending package in the Diaper Genie. "They're not coordinated enough to reach them."

"In case my sister hasn't told you already...babies were never my thing. Liv wanted a big family. I wanted the big house in the Hollywood Hills."

"And now you have the kids and you're living in a log cabin on a ranch." Delta refastened Hadley's onesie and rubbed her belly. "There you go, little one. All clean and sweet smelling."

"I'm here temporarily," Jade quickly added. "I have a lot invested in my business. I can't be away from it forever. I'm already taking major financial hits after one week."

At least when she had visited Liv when the babies were born that had been planned. Her clients had known in advance she wouldn't be around during those dates, with the understanding Liv could have gone into labor early instead of getting induced. She'd had months to plan for her absence and some clients had even chosen to push their events out so Jade would be in town overseeing them. She couldn't blame them for being furious she was gone again.

"Do I hear someone's phone ringing?" Delta asked.

"That's mine." Her assistant's familiar ringtone beckoned from the kitchen. Jade glanced up at the wall clock. It was shortly after seven and she knew he was eager to go over today's schedule. "It's Tomás. We have a big event tonight."

"On a Wednesday?" Maddie lowered Audra into her crib,

then gently nudged Jade out of the way. "Go take your call. I can do this."

"Thanks." She stepped aside and walked toward the bathroom to wash her hands. "Hollywood doesn't care what day it is." The phone stopped ringing, and she envisioned Tomás huffing impatiently as he waited for her outgoing message to finish so he could leave a voice mail. Jade hesitated in the doorway, watching Delta's reaction to the triplets. If she detected any family resemblance, she didn't show it. Then again, don't a lot of babies look similar at that age? Maybe Wes had been overreacting. Maybe they both had been and everything would work out the way Liv had planned.

"What's wrong with you today?" Wes's agent asked as the medics wheeled him through the arena's corridors and outside to the mobile sports medicine trailer. "Your head clearly wasn't in it. I picked up on that before you ever entered the chute. You blew me off when I asked. I hate to say it, kid, but you seem a little soft this week."

Maybe if he could get the image of Jade sitting on his lap out of his head, he might be able to concentrate. He'd never been more attracted or infuriated by any other woman. And yeah, in a perfect world, he'd like to see where things might lead with her, but their lives were far from perfect. Once he'd explained to his brothers yesterday about Liv's disappearance and asked if Jade and the girls could move to the ranch, it had raised all sorts of questions. Adding Maddie to the mix had been the only reason they stopped. His brothers didn't even think he'd keep two girlfriends in the same house.

"I've been in Montana and I haven't had a chance to ride or work out for over a week." The multimillion-dollar rodeo training facility he taught at in Texas had a top-of-the-line fitness center and both real and mechanical bulls for training. The pay was great, but the perks were even better. He'd taken every advantage of it when he wasn't on the road.

"That's no excuse," Pete argued. "You lived in Montana up until you moved six months ago, and you were fine then."

He was right, and Wes couldn't fight the truth. "Look, man." Wes reached with his good arm and tapped the medic's leg. "I'm fine to walk. I dislocated my shoulder, not my feet."

"You know the rules," the man said without slowing down. "We can't do that in case you have other injuries. Just be glad we didn't take you out strapped to a stretcher."

"Very funny." The dig was a not-so-subtle reference to an injury he had last year during finals. He'd been furious at himself for miscalculating the bull's rotation and wound up unconscious on the arena floor after the animal headbutted him. He knew the second he'd awoken he'd been eliminated from the competition. He'd gone out kicking and screaming louder than Audra, Hadley and Mackenzie.

"What's got you all in knots. Is something going on with your family that I don't know about?"

"You could say that."

"As long as it doesn't involve a woman," Pete scoffed.

"Try four."

"Four what? Four women?" Pete almost tripped over his own feet.

"Right on!" The older medic walking alongside them tried to high-five Wes before realizing he was on his dislocated side. "Whoops, sorry. My bad."

"You've gotten in more trouble with women than anyone I know." Pete clucked his tongue. "Don't let them get in the way of your career."

Once they reached the trailer, Wes insisted on walking up the steps himself. He refused to be wheeled up a ramp despite the medical team surrounding him. After he stripped off his safety vest and shirt, Dr. Shelton began assessing his injuries.

"What's this…your third dislocation in two years?" he asked, reviewing his charts on a tablet. Deceiving from the outside, the forty-foot-long trailers housed state-of-the-art mobile medical centers that traveled nationwide treating sports injuries. Competitors no longer had to go to the emergency room since they could perform everything including X-rays, minor surgery and casting on-site. They were also his largest sponsor and trying to hide any injury was futile.

"Just pop it back in, Doc." Wes ground his back teeth from the pain.

Dr. Shelton handed his tablet to one of the nurses. "You know the drill. Sit up straight and shrug your shoulders." The man gripped Wes's wrist and eased his elbow into a 90-degree angle, keeping it close to his body and in line with his shoulder. He slowly began to rotate the arm outward until the pressure increased on the dislocation. "Now try to relax as much as you can."

"I'm feeling that, Doc." Wes exhaled slowly and looked up at his agent hovering nearby. Pete had helped him build his career from junior rodeo greenhorn to champion, and he hated disappointing the man even more than he hated disappointing himself.

"We're almost there." The doctor gripped his upper arm and slowly moved it out and upward. "Good. Now put your shoulders back, your chest out."

Wes closed his eyes trying to focus on anything other than the pain. He didn't remember any of his other dislocations hurting this bad. Then he heard a pop, and the pain began to subside.

"Keep your back straight. It's not quite all the way in yet," Dr. Shelton said as he rotated Wes's arm toward his chest.

"There we go, there we go." Wes tilted his head back at the release.

"And you're done." The man let go of his arm. "Let's get you into X-rays so we can see what's going on in there."

Wes stood, the tension draining from his shoulder. "I'm fine."

"Look," Pete said, stepping in front of him, "you didn't qual-ify, so it's not like you're riding again. Let the man do his job."

"I made eight."

"No, Wes. You didn't. Your time was 7.8, and it was a sloppy 7.8."

He missed it by two-tenths of a second. "Dammit." Wes kicked the chair behind him. "I thought I had it." He rarely missed qualifying. His sponsorships were coming up for re-newal and a few younger competitors had been slowly push-ing him down in the ranks. This was not the time to screw up.

"We'll talk about it later." Pete pulled out his phone and tapped at the screen.

"Come on, Wes. Chaps off, gown on," the doctor ordered.

"Fine."

"I'll be outside waiting." Pete's phone rang, and he was out the door before Wes had a chance to respond.

He unfastened his chaps and kicked off his boots. He sus-pected Pete was already looking to poach one of the younger riders from the lesser known agents. He may not like it, but he couldn't blame the man. Wes intended to retire at the end of next season, even though he hadn't told anyone of his plans yet. He wanted to have two solid final years and another champi-onship under his belt before then. The higher he went out, the more money he could earn training the next generation of com-petitors. He had nothing else to fall back on.

After two hours of tests and endless waiting, Dr. Shelton's grim expression told Wes all he needed to know. Controlling the argument building in his head, he sat patiently and listened.

"Three dislocations, extensive ligament damage and now a rotator cuff tear, the only thing I see in your immediate future is surgery."

"No." Wes shook his head. "Absolutely not. I'll just rehab it again. The Ride 'em High! Rodeo School where I work in Texas is connected to the Dance of Hope Hippotherapy Center.

They have the best physical therapists in the state. You know the place, Doc, and you know their reputation."

"Tell me something." Dr. Shelton clasped his hands. "On a scale of one to ten, what was your pain level when you rode today?"

"I don't know." Wes had thought the week off from teaching and competition would have given his arm and shoulder a rest. He didn't want to admit defeat. And he wouldn't. Not yet. Besides, it hadn't been bothering him this bad. "Maybe a five, possibly a six."

"Compare that to a year ago. What was your pain level then?"

"None." Wes snorted. "I don't get the question, Doc. I wasn't injured then, so of course it would be zero."

"Exactly. You weren't injured then, now you are."

Wes stood. He didn't appreciate games, let alone one at his expense. "I'm not having surgery."

"What's this about surgery?" Pete asked from the doorway.

Dr. Shelton's brows rose as he stared at Wes. His medical records were private and the man couldn't legally say a word to Pete. But his sponsorship contract stipulated they were to be informed of any and all injuries affecting his ability to compete. In the end, the sponsor would tell Pete and there was no sense in delaying it.

"The good doc is recommending surgery."

"What kind of surgery?"

"We haven't discussed that yet." Dr. Shelton removed his glasses and rubbed his eyes. "Your client refuses to hear what I have to say."

"Because I know you're talking rotator cuff surgery and that will take me out of competition for six months."

"Probably longer," Pete muttered.

"Not happening. At least not now. I choose rehab and at the end of the season, I will have it reevaluated and we'll take it from there."

"That's months away," Dr. Shelton said. "If you have surgery now, you'll have a strong chance of recovering and competing in a full season next year. I can pretty much guarantee that won't happen if you wait much longer. You can't ride without pain."

"I'm tough enough to ride through it."

"Thank you, Dr. Shelton." Pete clapped Wes on the back and gave him a gentle shove toward the door. "We will definitely consider all options."

Wes opened his mouth to argue and received another shove.

"Cool it," Pete growled under his breath. "Thank the man and let's be on our way."

Wes hated being corralled like a head of cattle, but Wes paid the man a hefty percentage to keep him from sticking his foot in his mouth so he might as well shut up.

"Thanks again, Doc. Seriously, I'll consider what you said." *Just not so much.*

Once outside, Wes thought Pete would strangle him. "What's the matter with you? You don't argue with the sponsor."

"I don't take orders from them, either. Besides, he only works for the sponsor."

"And now they know you're injured and you're refusing surgery." Pete pulled a pack of cigarettes out of his pocket and lit one. "If they don't pull your sponsorship now, they sure as hell won't renew it next year." He took a long drag and exhaled slowly. "We're talking a lot of money, Wes. And that's just from one sponsor. I know you don't like the idea of surgery, but Dr. Shelton's right. You get it done now, you're only out for part of the season and next year you'll be as good as new."

Wes snatched the cigarette from his mouth and snapped it in half. "Don't you dare badger me about my well-being while you're blowing smoke in my face."

"You're right, I'm sorry," Pete said sheepishly. "I just feel for you."

"Yeah, well, this is my career we're talking about, not yours. There's no guarantee I'll recover from surgery before next season just like there's no guarantee I'll be able to compete at all.

If I wait, I have a shot. I'll get through the pain." Pete opened his mouth to speak, but Wes cut him off before he had a chance. "You can walk back in that arena, snatch up one of the young kids you're so hot to get your hands on and they'll get my sponsorship because I'll be home while they're competing."

"You think I'd be that disloyal to you?"

"No, I think you'd be that smart. You have your own bottom line to watch out for and I can't blame you. I need some time. I need to finish the season and see what happens. I can't even teach after rotator cuff surgery. What am I supposed to do? Ride 'em High! didn't hire me for my good looks."

"Not with your ugly mug." He laughed.

"Do you want me to fire you now or wait till later?"

"Sorry." Pete cleared his throat.

"I need time." If this was his last season, then he needed to make plans. He had to discuss it with his boss in Texas and see what their doctors and physical therapists had to say. More than anything else, he had to keep his head clear and away from all things Jade and the girls.

He'd fly to Montana in the morning, get through Dylan's wedding on Saturday and then fly out that night. Three more days. He'd keep his word and check in on Jade. He'd make sure they had whatever they needed until Liv came home, and then that was it. The girls weren't his to raise and he couldn't get involved with Jade knowing what they'd created and couldn't have. He had to move on. He had too much riding on the next few months and the sooner he got into physical therapy, the better. Nothing had ever interfered with his career and he wasn't about to let anything or anyone start now.

Chapter 7

Emma and Dylan had been gracious enough to invite Jade to the rehearsal dinner Friday night at the lodge, but she declined. After handing Tomás every key to her queendom along with check-writing capabilities, she was on the verge of a mini-meltdown. She thrived on control, as did Liv. Even though she had promoted Tomás last week, it wasn't the same as giving him access to the business bank accounts to pay vendors and their employees along with the power to make both business and financial decisions in her absence. After a caterer almost bailed because she couldn't transfer funds into their account on time, she realized something had to give.

She trusted Tomás, she just didn't like relying on someone else to run her company or any other aspect of her life. Which must be driving Liv crazy, because that's exactly what Jade was doing for her. She wished her sister would call. They'd never gone this long without some form of communication. Whether it had been a brief text message or a voice mail, they'd kept in contact with each other. Every morning she reached for her phone and fought the disappointment of the deafening silence.

"How about we go for a walk?" Jade asked the girls, who were happily rocking in the new infant seats Wes had bought them. He was right, they really were a godsend. Emma showed her how she used hers with her six-month-old daughter, Holly, who Jade was relieved to see looked nothing like the triplets. Feeding and naps were much easier and she was sure Liv would appreciate that when she returned home.

Jade bundled the girls in their triplet stroller and set off on the paved path that wound around the ranch. "Your mommy would love it here." It was unfortunate Wes and Liv hadn't been a real couple. The girls would have enjoyed growing up on the ranch with family. It was ironic in a way. Liv wanted family so desperately, and even chose a man to father her children from Saddle Ridge's largest, yet they both wanted to keep the girls a secret from their cousins, aunts and uncles. Jade and Liv never had any of those people in their lives. Maybe if they had they would have grown up loved.

Her sister's poor decision making still bothered her. It had been one thing to ask Jade to be the egg donor. But Wes? Look-swise, there was no arguing he was a fine specimen of a man. But his attitude…maybe not so much considering she hadn't seen him since before he left for South Dakota on Tuesday. He'd come back last night, according to Maddie, who had seen him while she was locking lips with Jarrod behind the stables. He texted her and had even called twice, but she had been on the phone with Tomás and a client and couldn't answer. When she called back, it went straight to voice mail, as if he'd turned off his phone.

It didn't matter, anyway. Wes was leaving for good in a few days and so would she once Liv came home. Although she should probably stick around for a month—if not more—afterward to make sure Liv was truly okay alone with the girls. Jade still couldn't quite pocket the anger she had about that. It would be much easier if the four of them came back with her to California. With the exception of her ex-husband, her sister had no other ties to town. She worked remotely and could do the same job from Los Angeles. Jade didn't think it was selfish to point that fact out to both the doctor and Liv. Jade had been more than reasonable so far.

Up ahead in the distance, Jade saw Wes atop a beautiful black-and-white quarter horse giving a group of guests a riding lesson in a large, dirt-covered outdoor arena. *Damn, he looked good.* She checked her watch, surprised he wasn't at the rehearsal dinner. She set the brake on the stroller and crouched down beside the girls. "Look, that's your da— Oh dear!"

I can't believe I almost said daddy. Jade stood up and quickly released the brake. If she could slip up that easily now, what would happen if she made that kind of mistake when the girls were older. As she turned the stroller around, she noticed Wes watching them. Within seconds, he was at the fence and Jade noticed a sling around his neck and arm.

She tried to tell herself she didn't care, but the cold, hard fact was she did. "What happened to you?"

Wes smiled down at the girls who were intently looking up at his horse. "I had a run-in with a bull and dislocated my shoulder. This is just a precaution while it heals."

Jade's palms began to throb from gripping the stroller handle too tight. "I still don't understand all the fuss over eight seconds. It's so dangerous."

His expression hardened. "Those eight seconds require a lot of skill and athleticism."

"Don't get your boxers in a wad." Jade hated when men got touchy about sports. "I'm not saying anything to the contrary. I just don't get the attraction."

"I wear boxer briefs, thank you. I'm not going to lie…there's an adrenaline rush every time I compete. But it's also my job, and those mighty highs are sometimes accompanied by devastating lows." Wes nudged his mount closer to the fence. "Is this the first time they've seen a horse?"

Jade peered over the top of the stroller, trying desperately not to picture Wes wearing nothing but boxer briefs. "They've um—they've seen the Belgians from a distance. I think they may be more fascinated with you though. We—uh—they haven't seen you in a few days."

His mouth curved into a cocky grin. "You're cute when you're flustered."

He shifted in his saddle and Jade wondered if she affected him the same delicious way he affected her. His eyes perused her body before stopping at her breasts. She'd always been self-conscious of their generous size, but Wes's appreciative gaze made every nerve ending in her body prickle with desire. Definitely not thoughts she should be having about the man who defined *complicated*.

A muscle twitched along his jawline as he returned his gaze to hers. "I've been busy helping my family with the upcoming weddings this weekend. I heard you're planning Garrett and Delta's ceremony."

"It's going to be so sweet." Relieved by the subject change, Jade began to relax. "There really wasn't much to it since they stressed simplicity. But it will be uniquely different from Dylan and Emma's wedding."

"I've never seen your face light up so much before." Wes's devastating smile made her bite her bottom lip to prevent her jaw from hitting the ground.

"I love event planning. It brings people together and makes them happy. Speaking of which, why aren't you at the rehearsal dinner?"

"Because the ranch has guests and my brothers have their hands full. I went to the ceremony rehearsal and told Garrett I would take his evening lesson. I thought you'd be there."

"I guess Emma told you she invited me. Is that the real reason you didn't go?"

Wes averted his eyes, giving Jade her answer.

"Well, we'll be seeing you, then." She spun the stroller around and started back to the cabin.

"I told you the truth but that wasn't good enough. You had to dig deeper."

"Go away." Jade waved to him over her shoulder.

"Jade, stop. It's not like that." Wes paced her on his horse. "It's complicated."

"Seriously?" Jade continued down the path. "You're going to talk to me about complicated when I've uprooted my life more than you have. You get to go home in a few days." Jade stopped herself from adding, *while I'm stuck here.* She didn't want to think of Audra, Hadley and Mackenzie that way despite feeling like a prisoner of sorts.

"At least you still have your career."

"What?" Jade stopped and looked up at him. "What happened?"

"There are a lot of factors involved, but the short of it is, my competing days may be over before my planned retirement and I'm not sure what to do. Chirp on all you want about giving up more than me, but I may have just lost everything." He ran his hand down the horse's neck and gave him a scratch. "This is one of those days I wish Liv was here. She was the best sounding board."

Jade knew she should maintain a friendly distance from Wes, but couldn't fathom having to give up her career. Especially at such a young age. "I realize the girls and I are part of your problem, but if you're willing to join us for dinner, I'm willing to listen. I can't replace her advice, but I'm here."

"You're not a problem, Jade. I'm sorry I ever made you think that." He glanced over his shoulder at the guests. "Where's Maddie tonight?"

"On a date with Jarrod. And Alyssa and Megan are babysitting your brothers' kids." Jade still had work to finish, but she craved adult conversation more. "I wouldn't mind the company."

He nodded. "Give me an hour to finish here and clean up."

"Great." A giddy rush swept over her at the thought of cooking for him. "Do you like Italian?"

"Love it. I'll see you soon." He winked before riding away and she couldn't be sure if it had been at her or the girls. Probably the girls, although she secretly wished otherwise. There were a thousand reasons why she should stay away from Wes Slade, but they had suddenly escaped her brain. And she was okay with that. At least for one night.

"I didn't realize you could cook like that." Stuffed, Wes willed himself to stand and help Jade clear the kitchen table. "It definitely beats the pizza we ordered last week."

Jade had fed the girls before he arrived, giving them time to enjoy their meal. It hadn't been candlelight and champagne, but between her vintage yellow floral dress and the wine, it bordered on romantic to him. He tried to ignore the ever-increasing emotions churning in his gut, drawing him to her like a bear to honey. He was failing. Miserably.

"Chicken scaloppine is one of my specialties. A perk of working with some of LA's finest chefs and caterers is I get to learn how they prepare many of their signature dishes."

"I think I would gain ten pounds a week if I ate your cooking every day." His hand brushed hers as he handed her another plate, causing the hair on his arm to stand on end at the jolt of excitement she sent through him. If this was her effect on him without trying, he'd be a goner if they were an actual couple.

"No, you wouldn't," she said as she rinsed the silverware and dropped it in the dishwasher basket. "Half the time I skip dinner because I've been nibbling throughout the day and the other half of the time I order out because Tomás and I are working an event."

"How is he managing without you?"

"I guess I should say he's doing great. The problem is we're losing clients because I'm not there. He's overworked because he hasn't found a suitable replacement for his old position. It's going to take an extraordinary candidate to do what he does, which is why I told him to hire two people. While he's interviewing, he's also doing a large portion of my job. He has the mentality of 'I'd rather do it myself than delegate it' and he's quickly learning he has to let go of the smaller things. On the flip side, Tomás and the rest of my team have managed to bring in some lucrative last-minute clients like a movie wrap party the other night. Filming finished way ahead of schedule and they needed something large, lavish and fast. With my contacts and Tomás's vision, he pulled off a quarter-of–a-million-dollar party in under twelve hours."

"That's incredible." Wes couldn't imagine wasting that much money on a party. "Then why do you still seem nervous?"

"The company is my baby, my spouse, my everything. The day I graduated, I bought a one-way bus ticket to Los Angeles and the following week I got a job at an event planning company. The job itself sucked. The pay was horrible. But I loved seeing how we took nothing and turned it into something beautiful." Wes may not personally care for frivolous spending, but he enjoyed the way Jade's features grew more animated as she spoke. "At the end of the day, no matter how tired we were, we had something spectacular to show for it. I worked my way up until I was ready to start my own business."

"I didn't realize you left right after high school." Wes had an inclination she'd left because of the misery he'd unknowingly created for her.

"I couldn't get out of this town fast enough. It's not like I had good memories here. That's why I don't understand Liv's attraction to it. If it was all about Kevin, then maybe I can convince her to come back to California with me."

Jade poured two mugs of coffee and handed them to Wes. "Can you bring these into the living room while I move the girls' chairs?"

"Why don't you let me do that?" Wes watched their content faces as Jade lifted the first chair off the dining room floor.

"It's okay, I got it."

Audra and Hadley looked around the room and continued to

discover the taste of their own hands, while Mackenzie peacefully snoozed.

"They really love those things, don't they?" Not seeing any coasters, Wes set the hot cups on a parenting magazine on the end table.

"I think I may love them more than they do. I switch the chairs on and once they fall asleep, I put them in their cribs. Usually they're all asleep by now, but you're their favorite shiny new toy. I can't thank you enough. Liv will love them too."

"Shiny new toy, huh?" Wes laughed. "I can't say I've ever been described that way before. All kidding aside, maybe you shouldn't tell Liv they're from me."

"Why? Maddie said she was hurt when you ended your friendship. I would think she'd be happy you gave her this gift."

"Maybe, maybe not. I still wonder if she saw us with the kids that night."

"If she did, she's in the right place to deal with it." Jade shrugged her shoulders. "I don't mean that to sound as harsh as it does. The reality of the situation is, whether she did or didn't is out of our control. I can't keep dwelling on it and neither should you. I'm having a difficult enough time mentally preparing for the pediatrician on Tuesday."

"What's so scary about a pediatrician?"

"I'm afraid if she thinks I'm doing something wrong, they'll take the girls from me. I know it sounds irrational, but I can't shake the thought." Wes noticed a slight tremble in Jade's body as she spoke. "I've read my sister's books at the house, and I think I'm following every parenting blog on the internet, but I have nothing to compare it to. Even Maddie said the same thing. We've never done this before. At least she has a little more experience from helping Liv. Then again, Liv never did it before, either. What if the doctor feels I'm not qualified to care for them? And why are you laughing at me?" She swatted him.

Wes gently cupped her face in his hand. "Because it doesn't work that way and you're doing an amazing job. Look at them."

His hand slid down her shoulder, turning her body away from him. His chest pressed lightly against her back as he eased behind her. The fingers on his good arm lightly trailed down her waist and settled on her hip. "Those are three very blissful babies." He leaned into her, wishing he could pull her even closer and shield her from the pain of the past and erase her fears of tomorrow. "They are healthy, well-nourished children. They're clean. They have clean clothes and a small village of people willing to pitch in. Nobody is going to take them away."

"I want to believe you." Her voice broke as she whispered, "It's so hard."

Wes shifted behind her and lifted his sling over his head.

"Don't you need to wear that?"

"I'm supposed to keep my arm as close to my body as possible. Unless I'm—how did you put it?—bouncing on the back of a bull, I'm not really in any pain without it. The sling just makes me aware of what I shouldn't do with my arm until it heals. I think I can make a small exception."

Wes moved to the corner of the couch, softly tugging her to join him. Wordlessly she settled between his legs, her back still to him. He was pushing the boundaries of their relationship more than he should, but the overwhelming need to protect and care for the four females who'd interrupted and taken over his life won out.

"I know you went through hell growing up. But what your mom did and what you're doing are worlds apart from one another. You're not the same person she was. No one is going to compare you to her."

"Why not? I can't help comparing Liv to my mom." Jade's voice pitched. "I'm disgusted with myself for even thinking it. What if that's what happened to my mom?"

"Your mom was a drug addict." Wes wrapped his arms around her, inadvertently resting on top of her breasts. One lone part of his body twitched at the skin-on-skin contact and he prayed the reaction didn't become too evident.

"Maybe that's why. She got pregnant with me a year after Liv was born. What if she had PPD after me and didn't know how to handle it? I've read numerous reports citing a genetic link to postpartum depression. She said our dad wasn't around. That he was some loser drifter, but he had to have been around for at least two years because Liv and I have the same father. At least that's what she told us."

"Have you ever attempted to contact him?" Wes tried to imagine what life would have been like never knowing his father.

"I can't. Our mom never told us who he was, and we have no idea where she is or if she's still alive. There's no father listed on our birth certificates. I cringed when I had to show it to get my driver's license and passport. The woman at the post office had the nerve to argue with me over the blank field on my passport form. Everyone in line behind me heard me explain I didn't know who my father was. I was so embarrassed. Stuff like that happens, even in this day and age. That's another reason I'm surprised Liv chose the route she did. She hated that growing up."

"By the time the girls are old enough to know what a birth certificate is, I'd like to think people will be more educated to the changing family dynamic."

"I like that you get it." Jade tilted her head and looked up at him. His eyes trailed over her face, stopping on her full red lips. How did her lipstick manage to stay on through dinner? He wanted to kiss her to see if it would survive the heat between them. More than that, he wanted to kiss away her worries and promise her everything would be all right.

"I agreed to be a donor so the fact I accept a modern family shouldn't surprise you."

"Nothing should surprise me at this point, but every time I turn around something else does." Her sultry voice, whether intentional or not, only heightened his desire.

"Like what?" The selfish part of him secretly wished she'd

say her attraction to him, while the logical side of him hoped she didn't.

"Like your comment earlier about your career possibly being over."

Wes's heart thudded to a jarring stop. He had managed to forget the realities of his job for the past hour. "A bull rider has a short shelf life as do many other sport professionals. By the time you hit thirty, your body starts feeling every fall three and four times more than you did in your early twenties. Especially when the same injuries keep reoccurring."

"Is that what happened with your shoulder?" Concern etched deep in her features as she frowned up at him.

"Pretty much." Wes rested his head against the back of the couch and stared at the ceiling, not wanting to see the pity he was certain would follow. "Now I need to make the decision to either have surgery and sit out for the next six months, possibly longer, or try to finish this season, then rest for a few months and try it one more time."

"Six months?" Jade twisted sideways, draping her bare legs across his jeans as the hem of her dress rose, exposing her more to him. Her toned thighs begged to be caressed and his inner voice begged to comply. "I can't imagine not being able to work for that long."

Unable to tear his gaze from her body, he allowed himself the pleasure of studying it without physically touching her. He wanted to memorize every inch, every curve. And the woman had curves. Luscious Marilyn Monroe curves that tested the seams of the cotton dress's bodice. The tops of her full breasts rose with each breath. He silently thanked God the zipper was in the back because the urge to set them free quickly became a test of his willpower.

"I'm glad you see it that way." Wes wished he had kept on his sling. It would have given him a place to rest his arm. He lifted it to drape across the back of the couch and winced. Silently he cursed, at the pain and the effect Jade had on him. He patted the cushion next to him, hoping the steady beat would force his heartbeat back on track. "My doctor and my agent don't. It's not just a financial thing. I've made quite a bit competing and I've socked a lot of it away. Not being able to compete means not being able to teach. It also means someone younger can come in and take my place both in the arena and at the rodeo school. Big names attract spectators, sponsors and students."

"Humor me for a second and allow me to play devil's advocate. If you are planning to retire at the end of next season, what is so bad about retiring this year?"

"For starters, I wanted to retire on my own terms. To go out on top, with another championship win. I haven't had one since I was twenty-six. I've been chasing my own success for three years. If I retire with the championship, I'll have more options afterward."

"What kind of options?"

"Endorsement deals and collaborations with equipment manufacturers, my own bull riding clinics, TV analyst gigs." Everything his father said he could be if he worked hard enough. The man may have questioned teenage rumors and have been cruel with his words at times, but he believed in Wes's ability to win. "There are a lot of options when you're one of the best. And I was one of the best. And then I made mistakes."

"Mistakes as in your agreement with Liv?"

"If you had asked me that question a few weeks ago I would've answered yes." Wes still couldn't believe how attached he'd grown to the girls in a little over a week. "Liv, my uncle's death, moving to Texas and their birth…they were all distractions. But no, helping to bring Audra, Hadley and Mackenzie into this world definitely wasn't a mistake. Even with all the past issues between us and your sister's postpartum depression, I'm glad I did it. I just want them to grow up happy."

Jade laid her head on his shoulder as they watched the three beautiful lives they'd unknowingly created together. "So this is what normal feels like."

Wes started to laugh. "I'm not sure if I'd call our arrangement normal."

"No, I mean two adults at home on the couch while the little ones drift off to sleep. The closest I've ever gotten to the experience is on a TV show. It's nice."

"Yeah, it is." Wes buried his nose in her hair, never wanting to forget the scent of her shampoo. Contentment washed over him as he held her while watching their daughters. It was wrong for him to think of them that way, but he wanted that pleasure. Just for one night. He'd never be this close to having a family ever again. And that was okay, because this was the only family he wanted to remember. That realization welled in his chest. He didn't want to be a dad. He didn't want a wife or a family. His career and livelihood were collapsing around him and all he wanted to do was stay in this moment and not let go.

Chapter 8

Jade hated to miss a wedding or any party, for that matter. It went against every fiber of her being. More important, she hated not being able to see Wes amongst the groomsmen. She even bet he'd be the most handsome man there. The more time she spent with him, the more she liked him beyond the physical attraction. If they had reconnected for any other reason, they may have had a fighting chance at something real.

A cool Montana summer breeze fluttered the curtains on the open windows. It was perfect outdoor wedding weather and the forecasted clear night would make for a magical reception under a star-filled sky.

Technically she could attend the wedding. Emma had extended her an invite but, despite receiving many offers to baby-sit the triplets, Jade felt it was more important for the bride and groom's friends to attend instead of her. She just wished the ceremony wasn't happening on the most remote part of the ranch where she couldn't even catch a glimpse of it.

Jade stepped onto the porch. It was still surreal to her to walk out a front door and see wide-open spaces. Even when she lived in Saddle Ridge as a kid, there had always been other houses surrounding them.

The ranch was quiet this afternoon. At least where the cabin was. She envisioned the bustle of the bride and her attendants as she got ready, and the guests filing into the newly constructed wedding venue overlooking town and the Swan Range. Jarrod had picked up Maddie an hour ago, giving her a chance to give her friend her seal of approval. She'd spent fifteen minutes with them and she could already envision their wedding.

Jade had developed a sixth sense about relationship longevity years ago and she had a pretty good track record at picking the odds. She could also tell when her own relationships were doomed and had learned to eliminate the heartbreak by getting out early on. The problem with Wes was, if she removed Liv and the girls from the equation, she didn't see that heartbreak potential. She genuinely liked him and wanted to spend whatever time they had left together. But her sister and the triplets did exist and no amount of justification would make any relationship with Wes right.

It wasn't fair. She'd made a career of planning happily-everafters and her life was more of a lonely-ever-after. Los Angeles was the land of opportunity. Where big dreams were made and realized. For the most part, Jade lived that life and she'd been satisfied. Now that she'd had a taste of family, she wanted it. Only the family she wanted wasn't hers to keep.

Jade stormed back inside, annoyed for worrying about her love life instead of Liv's recovery. She wasn't in Montana for herself. She was there for her sister and no sacrifice should be too big. Then why did it already feel like it was?

"It's all temporary, Jade," she said to no one as she pulled out a kitchen chair and sat at the large round table covered in wedding paraphernalia. Any feelings she had for Wes were only in the here and now. In a few months, they would be a distant memory. She shook her head to clear him from her brain. "Okay... time to focus on Delta and Garrett's wedding tomorrow."

Jade checked and rechecked her lists. Even though the sunrise ceremony was much more casual than tonight's wedding, there was still a lot involved to pull it together before the guests arrived. Normally she'd schedule vendors to come in and do all the setup, but Delta and Garrett's budget left Jade doing much of the work herself. It had been a long time since she'd planned an old-school wedding, and she secretly loved every minute of it. Even with teams of people helping her back home, the intense stress to coordinate every event was exhausting. This wasn't. From assembling table centerpieces in mason jars, hand folding silverware napkin pouches and arranging a bridal bouquet from flowers grown on the ranch, Jade welcomed this new level of stress. She enjoyed her celebrity events in Los Angeles, but she loved the close family atmosphere of this more.

It's only temporary.

"Go away." Jade didn't need her inner voice reminding her none of it was hers to keep.

"How did you even know I was here?" a man said from the doorway. "I haven't knocked yet."

"Wes!" Jade shot out of her chair so fast she almost knocked it over. "You scared me half to death." She quickly grabbed the baby monitor to see if she woke the girls. "What are you doing here?"

Good heavens! Jade gripped the table for support. Wes's tall silhouette in the open door frame was a memory she never wanted to forget. His broad shoulders, lean waist and muscular long legs made her breath catch in her throat. But it was when he took a step forward and she saw him standing before her in his black cowboy hat, dress Wranglers and boots, white buttondown shirt and silver-gray vest that her tummy flip-flopped a thousand times over.

"You look great." Had she just said that out loud? *Get control, girl.*

"Thank you." He touched the brim of his hat and nodded.

Now, that was something she didn't see in LA. "What are you doing here and where's your sling?"

"I refuse to wear that thing today. I'll be fine if I don't over-use my shoulder or arm. And I'm here to escort you to the wedding."

"Did Emma or Maddie put you up to this?"

"Nobody puts me up to anything. Emma would like you to be there, though. Megan's mom is on her way over to babysit the girls and before you argue with me, she said she's happy to do it."

"I appreciate the offer, but I need to work on tomorrow's wedding. I have to start setting up as soon as the reception ends tonight. Delta and Garrett put together a group of volunteers for me."

"I know. I'm one of the volunteers."

"You?" Jade mentally kicked herself for not realizing Garrett would ask him for help. It was a given. Yet in the back of her mind, she couldn't wait to see Wes's appreciation for her contribution to his brother's wedding. Especially since she refused to accept any payment beyond the necessary supply and rental fees. This was her gift to Delta for being such a good friend to her sister. She would have preferred to cover all the expenses, but the bride and groom refused.

Wes crossed the room to her. "I won't take no for an answer." He placed both hands on her shoulders and turned her toward the hallway. "By the time you're ready, the sitter will be here. Just don't take too long, I have to be there in twenty minutes."

"Twenty minutes?" Jade tried to look at him over her shoulder as he continued to push her toward the bedroom. "Nothing like giving a girl short notice." Truth was, Jade had mastered the art of getting ready for a formal event in under ten minutes. It was a requirement in her industry, especially on the occasion she juggled multiple events in one day.

"I will spend the rest of the night helping you with whatever you need." He stopped and released her shoulders as they reached the girls' bedroom.

"Wes?" Jade whispered. The smile he'd worn only moments ago had faded to sadness. "What is it?"

"In twenty-four hours, I'll be on a plane to Texas. I'll never see them again."

Jade rested her hand lightly on his arm, uncertain how to console him. She couldn't even begin to comprehend the thought of walking away forever.

"Liv's original plan may have been to keep you out of their lives, but she may not feel that way now. There's still hope."

"That's a big if, and until I know for sure, I can't allow myself that hope. I made an agreement with your sister and I have to stand by that unless she says otherwise. I can't just watch from a distance, though. You should go get ready," Wes said before walking back to the dining area.

Jade didn't know which was harder...remaining in their lives and always wondering what could've been, or never having the opportunity to see them grow up. Either choice was a tremendous sacrifice and there was no alternative.

She sealed herself in her room and leaned against the door. The realization she may never see Wes again struck her heart like a lightning bolt splits an oak. Attending the wedding with him would be the only *date* they'd ever have. Not that dating Wes was ever a possibility. Then why did it hurt?

She quickly tugged her shirt over her head with one hand while opening the closet door with the other. She'd found the sweetest vintage clothing store in town the day she met with Liv's attorney. The shop owner had been setting out a display of '50s dresses and other outfits, all in her size. They'd fit as if they had been made for her and Jade couldn't resist buying the whole collection.

She removed a red-and-white rose dress from the hanger and slipped it on. The tailored bodice, nipped waist and full, flared skirt accentuated her curves and made her waist appear smaller. And she was all for anything that thinned her out a bit. The accompanying petticoat added a touch of extra volume and made her feel ultrafeminine and a little giddy about attending the wedding with Wes. Of course, he would be up front with his brothers during the ceremony, but a small part of her looked forward to a dance afterward. Jade hadn't allowed herself that pleasure in years because it was a rarity she was a guest at anything. Tonight, she'd make an exception. It was the last chance she'd have to enjoy Wes's company on a personal level and she wanted to savor it, because come tomorrow night, she'd miss him and what could never be. Tonight was theirs.

Wes strutted prouder than a peacock down the white pine walkway of the wedding venue with Jade on his arm. He heard a few gasps, a hint of a whisper here and there and quite a few "they look lovely together" from the older crowd as they made their way to the front of the outdoor ceremony site.

Dylan had designed and built the gazebo and surrounding venue seating as a wedding gift for Emma on the very spot they had fallen in love. It had been six months of hard labor to complete it on time, but the location overlooking Saddle Ridge with the majestic Swan Range before them was their declaration of love to one another in front of everyone and heaven above.

For a man who'd never cared about sentiment or long-term relationships, these past two weeks at home had forever altered Wes's sense of family. He wanted someone to look at him the way Emma looked at his brother. He wanted someone to plan the rest of his life with and children to watch grow up and raise families of their own. He wanted the woman who was ever so slightly pressed against him. The woman whose perfume tickled his nose in an "I can't get enough" kind of way. He wanted the chance to see where things could lead with Jade. Even an early retirement didn't look so bad with her in the picture. Only she wasn't in the picture. At least not past tomorrow.

Wes clenched his fist against the painful vise slowly squeezing the life out of his heart. Twenty-three hours and counting before he stepped on that plane. It would be all right once he was away from Jade and the girls. It had to be because he couldn't live with the agony of always wondering *what if.* He just needed some time to shake it off. And since he refused to retire early, he needed to focus all his attention on winning the championship.

"I'm so glad you decided to join us." Dylan hugged Jade. "Emma will be too."

"You did a beautiful job." Jade glanced around at the long, curved pine benches Dylan had permanently built into the ground. "It's absolutely breathtaking here. I never knew Saddle Ridge could be so beautiful."

Neither could Wes.

"Emma and I hope to one day see our children get married here. And maybe the rest of both our families will choose this place too." Dylan nudged Wes. "You're next, little bro."

"Yeah, that's not going to happen," Wes said, feeling as if his tie was suddenly about to choke him to death. As he adjusted it, he noticed Jade's shoulders sag as she turned away from him. *Crap!* Even though they both knew they had zero chance of a future together, he could've chosen his words a little more carefully. He looked up at Dylan, who stood there shaking his head. *Double crap!* "Why don't I show you to your seat?"

"I can manage, thank you." Jade hurried to her seat before he had a chance to stop her. He would've appreciated a private second alone to explain himself, although what explanation was needed? Neither one of them could possibly be that disillusioned to believe they had anything past tomorrow.

"Go after her." Dylan gave him a friendly shove.

"No." Wes took his place beside his brother. "It's not like that between us. We're just friends."

"I don't know who you're trying to convince, but there's a lot more between you and Jade than friendship."

"Are you ready?" Reverend Grady asked Dylan. "I just got word your bride is on her way."

"I've never been more ready." Dylan excitedly rubbed his hands together.

Garrett squeezed in between them. "Let's get you married."

Once again, neither of his brothers had chosen him to be best man at their weddings. It was such a petty thing, but considering they had been each other's best man at their first weddings, it would have been nice if they could have chosen him and Harlan to stand up for them this time around.

Harlan clapped him on the back. "Hey," he whispered. "The other day Belle and I decided to renew our vows and I want you to be my best man. I didn't have one last year and I'd really like you to do the honors."

Leave it to Harlan to pick up on his insecurities. "Are you sure you don't want to ask one of them?"

"Nope. I choose you and you better be there. August 1, no excuses. We're going to have a real wedding this time. Maybe Jade will still be here since it's only five weeks away."

"Not you, too." Wes smoothed the front of his vest as a white, antique horse-drawn carriage crested the horizon. "Jade and I can never be more than friends."

"Who knows, maybe she'll move here." Garrett chimed in on his right.

Wes tugged at the collar of his shirt. "She has a lucrative business in LA and I have no intentions of ever going Hollywood."

"She isn't going to want him after what he said earlier," Dylan added. "Poor guy doesn't know what he's missing." His smile widened as Delta's father helped her down from the coach. "Love, marriage, kids…it's everything."

"It sure is," his other two brothers said in unison before Harlan leaned over and whispered, "What did you say to Jade earlier?"

"Shh." Wes brushed him off. Getting ganged up on by his siblings was the last thing he needed. Especially with Jade watching him from three rows away.

She looked beautiful today and he hadn't even had the decency to tell her. Her retro glam made his heart race every time. A part of him longed to go back in time to the decade she wore so well. Where life was simpler and modern science didn't complicate matters. If they had been a couple, they wouldn't have had Hadley, Mackenzie and Audra at the same time, but Wes was a firm believer in destiny and the girls would've been born regardless. Of course, all the stars would have had to align in order for them to be together today.

Emma's best friend led Garrett's children down the aisle, followed by Belle and Delta pushing Travis and Holly in white strollers ahead of the bride. Every member of his family—both blood and extended—were a part of Dylan and Emma's wedding. Everyone except Audra, Hadley and Mackenzie. They could have been right beside their cousins in their own strollers and included in all the wedding photos the family would pose for later. Photos that would hang on walls for decades to come and grace the pages of albums for future generations to look through.

Liv had wanted a family, but in creating that family, the three of them had collectively and knowingly excluded the girls from their *true* family. That had always been the plan. Wes had never wanted anyone to know he'd fathered his best friend's children. Now that plan seemed so shortsighted.

At the time, he'd only factored in his own feelings and hadn't considered the bigger picture. That's not to say he would have changed his mind and done things any differently. But maybe, just maybe, he would've come up with a solution that included his family in the girls' lives. He was powerless to change the situation now. He'd made his decision a year ago and was legally bound to it. The law may prevent him from calling them his girls, but in his heart, they would forever be *his girls*. And Jade would always be the mother of his children.

"Friends, family and neighbors," Reverend Grady began. "We are gathered here today to celebrate the union of Dylan

Slade and Emma Sheridan. Over the past year, I've come to know the Slade family rather well. I've officiated over two of their weddings, two christenings and sadly one funeral. During that time, I've noticed one common thread interwoven throughout this family. The thread of love."

Love. All four of his brothers had fallen in love and had been married at least once. Three of those marriages had ended in devastating heartbreak. Love and heartbreak were two concepts that had eluded him for twenty-nine years. It was impossible to get your heart broken if you didn't fall in love. Yet somehow, in a few short weeks he'd learned the meaning of both words. The love he had for his daughters was like nothing he'd ever experienced before. And tomorrow he'd experience heartbreak for the first time when he walked away.

Jade sensed Wes's unease during the ceremony and she wondered if the same thing she'd been thinking ran through his head, as well. That a massive family celebration was missing three new members. She couldn't help questioning her sister's logic once again. She understood Liv's desire to personally know her children's father, but why Wes? Why did she choose the man with the largest family in town? And why did she choose the one man Jade couldn't get out of her head.

She'd only been around him for a week and a half and she found herself tempted by the forbidden fruit. Her sister had spent almost five years with him. Their friendship had lasted longer than Liv's marriage. Despite Wes believing Liv was still in love with Kevin, she couldn't picture her sister pining for anyone that long. They hadn't even missed their mom for more than a few months and she was the only family they had outside of each other.

As the reception began, Jade attempted to slip away unnoticed. The ceremony itself was the most important part of a wedding, although she hoped no one ever told her bridal clients that. The money was in the after party.

"Excuse me." A woman lightly tapped her shoulder. "Are you Jade Scott?"

Jade turned to see Molly Weaver, Harlan's ex-wife. "Wow, I wasn't expecting to see you here." The last she had heard, Molly had left town shortly after her divorce.

"I moved back to town last year. I'm sorry to hear about your sister."

Jade's hackles rose. "Um, okay what did you hear about Liv?"

Molly paled. "Oh, maybe Harlan shouldn't have told me."

Nice. Real nice. Wes had assured her that his family wouldn't broadcast Liv's illness around town and his brother had done just that. "Liv is a fighter and this time away will only make her stronger. She'll be back before we know it."

"I'm sure she will. And just so you know, the only reason Harlan told me is because I walked out on my daughter when she was only a year old. He asked me the other day if I'd felt the same despair postpartum depression women experience."

"Did you?"

"Possibly. It was seven years ago and I was very overwhelmed by the prospect of being a parent. My pregnancy wasn't planned like your sister's was. It happened, and nine months later I found myself married to a man I didn't love with a daughter I wasn't sure what to do with. And I tried. I did. But walking away was easier than trying harder. It took me six years to figure that out. Even if PPD had been a factor in the beginning, the rest was all on me and my selfishness."

"Why are you telling me this?"

"Because regardless of why you leave your children for someone else to raise, that guilt stays with you. Even after you do the right thing whether that be returning or staying away— and I firmly believe some parents should stay away—the guilt never leaves. I just wanted you to be aware of that when your sister eventually comes home. She'll have to live with that for the rest of her life. You'll understand that bond one day when you have children of your own."

Jade's stomach knotted. "I appreciate your candor. What is your relationship like now with your daughter?"

"We're still navigating the waters. I don't know if she'll ever forgive me completely. I've always heard kids are resilient, and they are to a certain extent. But you never forget your mother walking out on you."

"Oh, believe me, my sister and I understand that all too well."

Molly's hands flew to her mouth. "Jade, I'm so sorry. I totally forgot you and Liv had been orphaned."

Orphaned. The word irked her. Orphaned meant the child hadn't had a choice in their fate. Both Liv and Jade had decidedly concluded they were better off without their mother and had said as much in court. "No worries. Our mother didn't exactly walk out on us, she walked out on herself."

"I didn't mean to bring up any bad memories. I guess I just wanted to say I'm here if you want to talk. Maybe I can give you some perspective from the other side. Again, my situation differed from your sister's, but I'm sure a lot of the sentiment is the same." Molly looked past Jade. "I think someone wants your attention."

Jade turned around to see Wes walking toward them. So much for her slipping away unnoticed.

"Molly," Wes said through gritted teeth.

"Hi, Wes. I'll leave you two alone. Think about what I said."

"I will. Thank you."

"What did she want?" Wes asked as Molly walked away.

"She heard about Liv and said she could sympathize. She really has changed since high school. She's trying, Wes. If Harlan can give her a second chance, you can too."

His brow furrowed. "She really did a number on my niece and brother."

"And forgiveness is hard-won, but sometimes when you look deep within your heart, you realize you've already done it."

Wes's jaw hung slack. "Are you saying what I think you're saying?"

Jade exhaled slowly, relieved to finally release the last of her resentment. "I have forgiven you for the past."

"That means the world to me to hear you say that."

"Now, if you'll excuse me, I need to get back to work." Jade turned away, not wanting to spend any more time around Wes than necessary. While there was no denying his physical attraction to her, his earlier comment to his brother before the ceremony served as a not-so-subtle reminder they could never be anything more than what they were.

"Please don't leave." He touched her arm, sending an instant shiver through her body. "The reception is just starting."

"I have a lot to do for tomorrow."

"No, you don't. While you were getting dressed, I saw your numerous lists on the table and everything was checked off."

"Your brazenness aside, I have other lists for tomorrow morning I still haven't touched on top of the events I'm working on in LA."

"I told you I would help." Wes jammed his hands into his pockets. "This is not going how I planned. Let me start over and begin by apologizing for the way I acted earlier. I was also hoping you would sit with me and my family for the reception. You already know everyone."

"Thank you for the apology, but it isn't necessary. I know where we stand. And I appreciate your offer to help, but the only thing I'll need from you and the others is some assistance setting things up in the morning. Megan and Alyssa are coming over after the reception and spending the night. They'll help with whatever little things I have left."

"What about Maddie?"

"Since she's Delta's maid of honor, she decided to stay with the rest of the wedding party at the main lodge." Jade doubted anyone would sleep tonight with all the excitement of two weddings. "Could you meet me here at three sharp? That will give us three hours before the ceremony begins."

"Of course." Disappointment registered across his face and

Jade wasn't sure if it was because she asked him to meet her at the ungodly hour or if he'd hoped to go back to her place after the wedding. "If you plan on going all night long, you'll need to eat. You're already here and the lodge chefs have prepared an amazing menu. I snuck a taste of a few things this afternoon. Besides, you look amazing in that dress and it would be a shame if people didn't see you wearing it a little longer."

Jade couldn't help herself from smiling at the compliment. "By 'people,' do you mean you?"

"Yes." The stubborn set of his chin told her there was no getting out of dinner. "Shall we?"

Wes offered his arm and for the second time that night, she allowed him to lead her through the maze of familiar faces she hadn't seen since high school. Friends, not-so-friends, store owners and even a teacher or two. She'd known the entire town would be there, but she hadn't taken the time to process who all that would entail. After the thirtieth "it's been so long" over dinner, Jade began to enjoy catching up with people and hearing what they'd done with their lives. She'd even met the woman who'd originally owned the dress she wore and other outfits she'd bought at the vintage store. For the first time, she felt comfortable in Saddle Ridge. The bright lights of LA seemed so far in her past she almost couldn't imagine going back.

Midconversation with her old English teacher, Wes's palm settled on the small of her back. She leaned into the intimate gesture, luxuriating in the heat emanating from his body. Inhaling deeply, she allowed herself the pleasure of his touch. They'd never see each other again after tomorrow and she didn't want to deprive herself of their last moments together.

"Dance with me," he whispered.

His velvet-edged voice against her cheek sent a shiver of excitement straight to her core. Powerless to refuse him, she smiled at her former teacher. "Please excuse me."

Wes gathered her in his arms and elegantly guided her to the dance floor like a seasoned professional. She knew the man had mad skills in the rodeo arena, but she'd never expected him to know how to waltz.

"Are you enjoying yourself?" he asked. His hold firmed as his muscular chest flattened against her breasts and the length of his growing arousal pressed against her belly.

"Immensely," she purred, not meaning the word to sound as sultry as it had. "Are you?"

Wes twisted his face indecisively. "There's just one thing that can make this night better than it already is."

Without waiting for her to respond, he lowered his mouth to hers, branding her with his lips. His embrace tightened as her trembling limbs clung to him. His kiss, surprisingly gentle yet dangerously erotic, intensified with each stroke of his tongue. Her heart drummed against his chest in unison with his as the rest of the wedding guests slipped away. She had never wanted a man as much as she desired Wes. The ache so great it bordered on unbearable. The man she'd once despised shared a bond with her no one could ever break. In the safety of his arms, nothing could hurt her. If only it could last.

Jade broke their kiss and looked up at him. "We can't do this."

"Yes, we can." Wes dipped his head again and kissed the side of her neck.

She flattened her palms against his chest. "Wes, we are not alone. And I won't be alone all night."

Wes tilted his head back in frustration and groaned. He widened his stance to lower his height closer to hers and held her face between his hands. "Then allow me one more kiss before we say good-night."

His lips claimed hers once more. His kiss, surprisingly soft yet commanding, melted away what remained of her defenses. For once in her life, Jade wished she could hold time in the palm of her hand so this moment would never end.

Chapter 9

Sleep had alluded Wes in the handful of hours between their kiss and sunrise. A sense of renewed hope grew inside him as he once again stood alongside his brothers in front of their friends and family. He was leaving for the airport in less than twelve hours, and even though he'd sworn never to return to Saddle Ridge, he now looked forward to Harlan's recommitment ceremony in August. A part of him had even considered flying out to visit Jade in Los Angeles. He'd never been fond of the city before, but spending more time with her would be worth the sacrifice. And who knew? Maybe nothing would come out of it, but he wasn't ready to walk away without trying.

Just as the ceremony began, Jade removed her phone from her pocket and quickly walked toward the catering tent. Instinct told him it was about Liv or the girls. He couldn't see her walking away from the wedding she'd meticulously planned for any other reason.

"Do you, Garrett, take Delta to be your lawfully wedded wife, for better or for worse, for richer or for poorer, in sickness and in health, to love and to cherish, forsaking all others from this day forward?"

Wes wanted to follow her, but he couldn't leave midceremony. His insides twisted as a million thoughts ran through his mind. If the call had been about the girls, she would've run. She didn't run. It had to be about Liv. Maybe it was Liv.

"What is wrong with you?" Harlan whispered between clenched teeth beside him.

"Do you, Delta, take Garrett..." Reverend Grady's voice began to sound like the teacher on the *Peanuts* cartoon.

A trickle of sweat ran down his temple as Jade emerged from the tent and quickly made her way back to the ceremony. Her face tight and unreadable. Once seated, he fully expected her to look his way, but she remained focused on Delta and Garrett...as he should be.

"You may now kiss the bride."

The applause and celebratory shouts almost knocked him off balance. The ceremony was over and he'd missed a good part of it. Could he have been any more of an ass? He joined his brothers as they congratulated the couple, fighting the pain that rocketed through him when he gave them a hug. He'd pushed his shoulder to the limit last night on the dance floor with Jade and this morning when they were setting up for the breakfast reception. He was scheduled to compete in Oklahoma later in the week and he seriously doubted he'd be able to.

"Are you okay?" Harlan asked.

"My shoulder's really bothering me." Wes searched the faces in the crowd for Jade, but he didn't see her. "Excuse me."

Wes jumped off the side of the gazebo and beelined for the catering tent, almost running into Jade as he entered. "Was that call about Liv or the girls?"

"It was Liv's treatment center." Jade looked past him to the wedding guests before returning her attention to him. "It's less than an hour from here." Jade laughed sarcastically. "At the very first place I contacted. Actually, I contacted them a few times but my sister didn't feel the need to let me know where she was."

"Why did they call today? Especially so early."

"Sunday is family day, and Liv wants to see the girls." Jade's features clouded in a mix of joy and sadness. "I have to leave in a few minutes. They would like me to be there by eight so Liv can spend the day with them. Something about an assessment, cognitive therapy and reacclimation sessions. I didn't understand it all, but I'm sure I will once I get there."

"Okay, I'll go with you." Wes reached in his pocket for his phone realizing he'd left it in his cabin. "Let me borrow your phone so I can change my flight."

"What? No." Jade shook her head and walked away from him, checking each of the chafing dish burners. "You need to go home."

"I want to be there when you tell her about us."

Jade shushed him and tugged him to the corner of the tent away from the servers. "I'm not going to ambush my sister by telling her I know you're the girls' father, or that we've been playing house while..."

"While what? Falling for each other? After that kiss, you can't deny there's something between us."

"I can't devastate my sister like that. I don't want her to feel like it's two against one, especially when the two are her daughters' biological parents. I refuse to put her through any unnecessary hell. You need to get on that plane today, and return to your normal routine. Once things settle down, I will talk to her about allowing you to have a relationship with the girls. But this thing between you and me—" Jade swiped at a lone tear rolling down her cheek "—was temporary. We both knew that."

Wes wanted to argue. He wanted to tell her they still had each other, but he knew any involvement with Jade would be a constant reminder of their daughters. He didn't fit into their lives. He was never meant to. He didn't know how to walk away, either.

"Saying goodbye is harder than I thought it would be." He lifted her chin to him. "At least let me come back to the house with you to see the girls one last time." A tightness grew in his chest. "Please give me that much."

"What about the reception?" Jade peered around him. "They're headed this way now. This will be over in an hour, maybe two. A lot of people are traveling home today. You need to be here for your family."

"I need to say goodbye to my daughters," Wes demanded.

"Shh." Jade swatted him. "Keep your voice down."

"You involved me in their lives and as much as I fought against it, they grabbed hold of my heart. I refuse to leave here without saying goodbye, with or without you."

"Okay." Jade rested her hand on his chest. "I'm not trying to hurt you. I thought I would spare you the pain, but I understand your need to see them. Meet me at the cabin. I need to tell Delta and Garrett I'm leaving."

"Tell them I'll be back in a few." Wes stormed out the tent's back flap. He wanted time to say goodbye to the girls…alone. He jerked off his tie as he half walked, half ran to his truck. Safely in the confines of the cab, he smacked the steering wheel. Hard. He didn't know how to do this.

Within minutes he parked beside the cabin. Tugging his wallet from the pocket of his jeans, he removed a couple hundred-dollar bills. He had no idea if Jade had promised Megan and Alyssa more or less, but this would have to do for now. He needed them to leave.

He hopped down from the truck and took the porch stairs two at a time, startling the teens when he opened the screen door. "There's been a little change of plans." Wes held out a folded bill to each of them, his eyes settling on the three cherub faces happily rocking in their chairs. "I will settle up with you later if you're owed any more than that."

"Are you sure?" Megan asked. "We're supposed to stay until the wedding is over."

"I'm sure. In fact, why don't you go down to the reception

and have breakfast with everyone else. Jade's on her way here, so I have it covered."

Wes tried to stop fidgeting as he waited for the teens to gather their overnight bags and leave. He only had a few minutes left to spend with the girls. He closed the front door behind them and sat cross-legged on the floor in front of his daughters. Unable to hold back his tears any longer, he lifted Hadley into his arms and cradled her against his chest.

"What have you done to me, little one?" He kissed the top of her head, inhaling her familiar baby scent. "I never meant to fall in love with you, but I couldn't help myself." He brushed the back of his fingers against Mackenzie's cheek as her big sparkling blue eyes met his. "I have to go away for a little while, but I'll be back in August. I don't know if you'll still be here or not, so I have to say goodbye now." Wes heaved a sob. "Oh God, how do I do this? You three will always be a part of me. And I will always watch over you. I promise. You won't know it, but I'll be there. You are my three little gifts from heaven and I will love you forever."

Wes heard the sound of a car door outside the living room window. It wasn't enough time. He wanted more. He needed more. He settled Hadley back in her chair. "You're going to see your mommy today. And she loves you more than life itself." He leaned forward and kissed Audra on the head. "You'll grow up and rule the world. You can be whoever you want to be." Wes wiped at his eyes. "I love you, now and forever."

The front door opened behind him. How could his time be over already? It wasn't fair. He kissed Mackenzie on the forehead and rose, his back to Jade. "Will you call me later and tell me what happened with Liv?"

"Of course," she said softly. "And you can call me whenever you want."

"Yeah, not like that won't be too difficult." Wes reached for his phone to take a picture of them, but he realized he must have left it in his cabin and cursed. "I never got to take one photo of them. Not one. I have nothing to take with me."

"I'll send you all the photos you want." Jade's voice broke.

"No." He shook his head, incapable of saying anything more. He closed his eyes and turned away from the girls, his heart shattering into a million pieces. He forced himself to walk to the door, unable to look back. "Goodbye, Jade."

Wes stepped onto the porch, forever a changed man. A broken man. All the things he'd thought meant something in his life were inconsequential compared to the love for a child...and a woman. His life would never be the same.

A counselor named Millie carried Audra's car seat down the hall of the postpartum depression treatment center as Jade followed with Hadley and Mackenzie. "This is where most of Liv's initial reacclimation to her daughters will occur." Millie opened the door to a casual living room–type area and held it for Jade to enter. "The visits will increase, and at some point the children will join Liv here at the center so she can learn how to balance her emotions while caring for them."

"Wait, what? I haven't agreed to overnight visits here." Jade set Hadley's and Mackenzie's car seats on the beige carpeted floor. The place may resemble a warm and cozy guest lodge from the outside, but the fact remained it was a treatment facility and she did not feel comfortable leaving the children in a place where women didn't have complete control of their emotions. "I have guardianship and that's not going to happen unless I say so."

Millie's brows arched as she lowered Audra's car seat next to her sisters. "It's part of her treatment plan. Don't you want your sister to improve?"

"I find that question rather insulting." Jade folded her arms across her chest, annoyed she was put on the defensive so soon after arriving. "Of course I want my sister to get better, but unless I'm a hundred percent comfortable with the girls' safety here, they will not stay overnight. Honestly, I find this conversation premature. I haven't even spoken with my sister or her physician yet. I didn't even know where she was until this morning."

Millie calmly clasped her hands in front of her. "I apologize. I was not aware of that. Dr. Stewart will be in shortly to speak with you. Until then, do you have any questions?"

Only a million. "How is my sister?"

"Olivia is relaxed and learning new coping skills. Her situation is more unique than most of our patients because her children aren't biologically hers."

"Liv. No one calls her Olivia." Millie's ultracalm demeanor irked her. "Relaxed as in medicated or relaxed as in Zen?"

"Your sister is not medicated. She had the option and she refused, as do many of our patients. Since she is a single parent, it was important to her to not have to rely on medication or worry about its side effects."

A tall middle-aged woman with silvery hair entered the room. "Hello, Jade. I'm Dr. Stewart. It's a pleasure to meet you." She shook her hand before directing her attention to the girls. "And this must be Mackenzie, Hadley and Audra." She crouched in front of them. "I've heard so much about you."

"I wish I knew more about you and this place." Jade swore every emotion known to man coursed through her body. She hadn't even had time to process Wes's goodbye, before having to run out the door with the girls. She'd known he was leaving today, she just hadn't expected it to be so early or so abrupt. Her phone rang in her bag, wrenching her away from this morning's heartbreak. "I'm sorry. I forgot to mute the ringer on the way in."

"That's fine, just understand this is a phone-free zone," Dr. Stewart warned.

"Of course." Jade silenced her phone, but not before seeing Tomás's name on the screen. He'd have to wait.

After a detailed explanation of the treatment center's protocols and a tour of the ten-acre campus and private grounds, Jade felt more confident her sister had chosen the right place. It

was well secured and they even had small cottages with nurseries for the women. By the time they made it back to the visitation room, Jade bore a tinge of remorse for jumping all over
Millie earlier.

"Keep in mind, all visits are monitored. We don't want you
to hold back your feelings, but we do need you to listen to Liv's
feelings. PPD patients have difficulty expressing their emotions, especially when they are overwhelmed. Some exhibit
anger while others retreat into themselves. If at any time we
believe Liv is struggling, we will step in and guide you both
through the process."

"Um, there are a few things I need to tell Liv about the father of her children." Jade had debated having this conversation
today during the entire ride there. She relented, rationalizing
the more they knew up front, the better they could help her sister. "The thing is, I accidently discovered who the father is and,
when Liv had disappeared without a trace, I contacted him in
hopes he might know where she went."

Dr. Stewart's eyes widened. "I was under the impression
she used an anonymous donor. How did you know where to
reach this man?"

"I thought she used an anonymous donor too. When I found
out who it was, I was shocked because not only did I go to
school with him, his siblings live in town and they have children the girls' age. As they get older, they'll have daily contact
with their cousins and not realize it."

Dr. Stewart rubbed the back of her neck and stared at the
floor in silence while Millie sat perched on the edge of her
chair gaping at her.

Okay. Now what?

"And m-maybe I should also tell you that Wes—that's his
name—and his family have been helping me with the girls."

"Helping you?" Dr. Stewart cleared her throat. "So they're
aware of their relation to the children."

"Only Wes is. But he left to go home to Texas today. He

moved there in January." Jade took a deep breath and recounted the past two weeks in detail to Dr. Stewart and Millie. "We had agreed to tell Liv everything, but I didn't think doing it today was a good idea."

"I can't force you to tell her today, but in my opinion, it's better for her to hear everything now so she can process her feelings. I'd rather have her upset here, early on in her treatment, instead of down the road where she might suffer a setback, accuse you of keeping things from her, or both."

"I wasn't prepared for this today." Jade wrung her hands.

"Like we say here, you can't prepare for everything." Dr. Stewart placed a hand over hers to settle them. "Just be open and honest. State the reasons why you contacted Wes, but don't blame her for the reason. Do you understand what I'm saying?"

"But she is to blame," Jade replied sharply. "I'm not talking about her PPD. I'm talking about the way she went about this before she had the embryos implanted. There was a string of bad decisions and it set off a chain reaction. Choosing Wes for starters. What if her kids got sexually involved with one of their cousins years from now? She lied to both Wes and me and said she used anonymous donors. And then the strain of three children at once. She said that was the doctor's idea...now I seriously wonder. I realize there are other mitigating factors, but I truly believe all of this contributed to her PPD."

"And it probably did."

"Thank you." Jade huffed. "I'll be honest...as much as I love my sister, I'm a little angry. My business in Los Angeles is suffering because I'm not there. If she had come to me, I could have moved her out there temporarily and gotten her the help she needed. I think my sister has been a little selfish."

"Millie," Dr. Stewart said. "Set up a few counseling sessions between Liv and Jade. Let's say three for now, the first one today."

"Do you want it before or after she sees the children?"

"Ah." Dr. Stewart pursed her lips and tilted her head from

side to side. "After. I want her to be distraction free when she's with her daughters." Dr. Stewart returned her attention to Jade. "We're going to ask Liv to come in, you two can catch up a little, then we'll ask you to leave for an hour or two. We have a Families Dealing with PPD seminar at eleven o'clock if you're interested. I think you'll find it very informative. Families eat together on Sunday, then we'll regroup in the afternoon and you and Liv will have a session together."

"Okay." Jade mentally ran through her list of things to do. She'd left in the middle of Delta and Garrett's wedding. She still needed to do teardown, on top of readying the linens and other rented items so they could be returned to their vendors. Never mind all she had to do for her own business.

Dr. Stewart nodded to Millie. "We're ready for Liv."

Jade ran her hands over her jeans, not knowing what to expect from her sister. Liv appeared in the doorway, dressed casually in a pair of khaki shorts, a white cotton T-shirt and tennis shoes. Her eyes darted from Jade to the girls and back again. While she looked healthy, her cheeks appeared hollower than they had been when Jade had last seen her. The high ponytail only accentuated her weight loss. She didn't look like someone who'd carried triplets two months ago.

"It's good to see you." Jade rose from the couch and crossed the room to her. "I've missed you. And I love you."

"I love you more." The corners of Liv's mouth lifted slightly at their familiar words. "You must think I'm a terrible person."

"Absolutely not." Jade held her sister's hands between her own, uncertain if a hug would be too much, too soon. "I think triplets are a bit overwhelming for a single, first-time mom. It's impossible to do it all alone."

"How are you managing?" Liv asked, careful to avoid looking in the girls' direction.

"I have a small team helping me."

"A team?"

Jade sucked in her breath. She'd said too much. "Maddie at

night and a couple of sitters during the day. Like you had talked about hiring a nanny once you returned from maternity leave. That's what I've done. I need to work, so I have someone there with me almost all the time to help. I can't do it alone."

"I guess that makes me feel a little better." Liv's face began to brighten. "Who did you get? I had a tough time finding a qualified nanny to take on triplets."

"They're babysitters. Not nannies. There's two of them."

"Who are they?" Liv's eyes narrowed slightly. "What aren't you telling me?"

Why weren't Dr. Stewart or Millie intervening? "They're two local teens. Emma Slade uses them and sings their praises." Jade didn't see the need to add that Wes had referred them to her.

"Slade?" Liv dropped her hands and took a step backward. "What did you do?"

"I uncovered the girls' paternity while I was trying to figure out where you ran off to." There, Band-Aid off. It's out in the open.

"Oh no." Liv covered her mouth with her hands. "Do they know?"

Jade shook her head. "Only Wes does. And he knows I'm their biological mother." She looked at Dr. Stewart. "Is this okay?"

The woman nodded. "It's not how I would have preferred, but it's okay as long as you both continue to communicate effectively."

"Do you have feelings for Wes?" Jade asked.

"No, of course not." Liv's face twisted. "We were just friends."

"According to him, you were good friends. How would that have worked if he had stayed in town?"

"He wasn't staying in town. He talked about leaving constantly. I knew he was leaving before he did. It just would have been nice if he had said goodbye before taking off. That hurt."

"Help me understand something." Jade mentally rehearsed

her words before speaking, not wanting to offend Liv. "Why did you choose a man who comes from Saddle Ridge's largest family to father your children? His brothers have kids close in age. They'd be sitting with, playing with, and possibly even attracted to a relative and they wouldn't know it. I'm having a difficult time understanding your rationale."

"I planned on using a donor. Even after I asked Wes, I still leaned toward one."

"Why did you change your mind?"

"You and I kept having those conversations about medical history and what if something happened to the girls and they needed a donor for whatever reason. You just said it... Wes has a huge family of possible matches. I wouldn't have that with an anonymous donor. I took the risk of losing a great friend in exchange for my children's future health. Especially after watching one of my best friends battle cancer this year. I figured no one would know there was a family connection unless there was a medical crisis. And I would have dealt with it then. It wasn't until after the babies were born and Belle had Travis that I realized one of the girls might want to date him. Garrett moved to town with his children after I was already pregnant. The idea that of one of the girls might want to date his son one day terrified me. It was too late at that point. I just wanted my children to have options. I don't regret that part. When Wes and I first discussed this, there weren't any Slade children in town with the exception of Ivy, and she was seven at the time. The chance of them interacting was slim. Regardless, I regret not being more prepared for the what-ifs."

"Liv, you couldn't have been more prepared. You knew everything there was to know about having children except the emotional aspect of it and I don't think anyone can ever prepare for that. What about Kevin? Did you think he'd come back once you had the children?"

"Kevin." Liv sighed. "He was my one true love. A part of me will always love him, but I knew he wasn't coming back.

Even if he wanted to, I doubt I could ever trust him not to walk out on me again. Besides, he's engaged to be married soon."

"I heard all about it. You're okay with that?" Jade didn't want to bring up the fact she knew Kevin was marrying a woman with children. She assumed her sister already knew.

"It doesn't involve me." Liv's lips thinned and Jade sensed a renewed tension in her words.

"If you weren't in love with Wes, why did you follow him all over the place?"

"Oh, for heaven sake, I wasn't following him." Liv threw her head back and laughed. "Have you seen some of those rodeo cowboys? Those men are hot. I wasn't interested in anyone around town, so I met up with Wes when it was convenient. I enjoyed the atmosphere. I enjoyed getting out of town for a day or two. And I certainly enjoyed the eye candy. So let me reiterate one more time, I'm not in love or attracted to Wes. Are you asking about Wes because you're interested in him?"

Jade opened her mouth and quickly shut it. She didn't want to lie to her sister. She didn't want to hurt her, either.

"Oh wow." Liv paled. "You and Wes. I never saw that coming."

"There is no me and Wes. He's gone and he doesn't plan on returning."

"Ever?"

"That was the original plan, wasn't it?" Jade's defenses began to rise. "You knew he was leaving town, that's why you used him as a donor. How could he possibly come back? It was extremely difficult for him to see the girls." Liv had been in the room with the girls for ten minutes and she still hadn't touched, hugged or even looked their way for longer than a second.

"It sounds like he spent a lot of time with them." Liv's voice remained even and Jade couldn't get a read on her emotion.

"He was a great help to me."

"Liv," Dr. Stewart said. "How do you feel about Wes spending time with your daughters?"

"I don't like it." Liv held Jade's gaze. "She can have any man in the world, just not the father of my children."

Jade inhaled deeply, trying to collect her thoughts. "You should have told me you weren't using a donor. Wes and I have a history."

"You what?"

"We dated in high school. It was brief, but it didn't end well. You would have known that if you had told me you were fertilizing my eggs...with someone from town. Especially someone my age. Didn't you think the likelihood we went to school together was pretty high?"

"All the times I talked about you, Wes never once mentioned knowing you." Liv's voice broke as her hurt turned to anger.

"Because he hated me. We did some terrible things to each other back then. But that doesn't matter now. I had a right to know. You violated our agreement and you violated my trust."

"Okay." Dr. Stewart crossed the room to stand between them. "Jade, you're blaming Liz."

"I don't know how to do this and not blame her." She glared at her sister. "This part happened before her postpartum depression. Honestly, Liv, your actions have terrified me. I'm still trying to figure out why you packed away all the girls' things in the downstairs closet?"

"I needed normalcy. I felt myself spinning out of control and I thought I could regain it if I confined everything baby to the two nurseries." Liv's face reddened in anger. "Clearly it didn't work. And despite whatever you feel you're entitled to, I was under no obligation to tell you who I chose to father my children."

"Our legal agreement says you were going to fertilize my eggs with an anonymous donor. Are you really going to split hairs and say it was anonymous to me and not to you? I think any court would frown on that."

"Oh, so now you want to take me to court?"

"I'm not saying that at all." Jade forced herself to stay calm despite her flaring temper beneath the surface. "Wes and I are the same age and we grew up in the same town. The chances were pretty high we knew each other. The point I'm trying to make is, I may have given you my eggs, but I still had certain rights. You should've told me what you were doing."

"You're right. I had blinders on all through this. I was so excited about finally having a family of my own, I didn't take anyone else's feelings into consideration."

"There is something else I need to tell you."

Liv's body went rigid, bracing herself for another onslaught. "I'm listening."

"I've been living at Silver Bells with the girls in one of the larger family guest cabins."

"You took my children out of their home? Why?"

"Because Maddie and I couldn't do it alone. I am so grateful she offered to stay with me but she has a job and a life of her own. I think you may have forgotten I have a business to run, and it's been difficult to do long-distance. The two girls that babysit for me live on the ranch. It's very convenient for me to stay there."

"I bet," Liv said sarcastically. "Don't you find it a bit hypocritical? You just finished preaching to me about the girls growing up in the same town with their cousins and all these what-if scenarios...yet you have them all living on the same ranch."

"They're infants. They don't know what a cousin or even a relative is. I think there's a difference. If it makes you uncomfortable, I will move back to your house. I only went to the ranch because I needed all the help I could get. I didn't do it to hurt you. I did it for their safety and well-being. If there was a fire, I wouldn't even be able to get the three of them out of the house at the same time. This way there is usually two people watching the girls."

"I'm not asking you to leave. I gave you temporary guardianship because I trust you. So I have to trust you're making the right decisions." Liv crossed the room to her daughters. "With so many people around, they probably don't even miss me."

"They have definitely missed you."

"How do you know?" Liv said in a broken whisper.

"Because they're never settled. Not completely. They always seem to be looking for someone."

"Really?" Liv glanced back at Jade. "You're not just saying that?"

"No, I mean it. You're their mom and they love you."

"But I left."

"You left to get help." Jade wondered if the guilt Molly had told her about was what Liv was experiencing now. "They don't feel the same way toward you that we felt toward Mom. It's different, Liv."

"Thank you. I needed to hear that."

"It's the truth." Jade moved to stand beside her. "I have something funny to tell you." She nudged Liv's arm. "When I first got to your house, I was so afraid I'd mix them up, I wrote their first initials on the bottom of their feet."

Liv tried to suppress a laugh. "You did what? They're not identical."

"All babies look alike to me." Jade shrugged. "I used permanent marker so it wouldn't wash off when I gave them a bath."

"No, you didn't!" Liv said, half laughing, half crying. "Do their little feet still have writing on them?"

"No. It eventually wore off." Jade smiled, relieved to see her sister in good humor. "See, they're very intrigued by you. And I think Audra has your eyes."

"I can't believe how much they've grown in such a short time." Hadley brought her tiny hand to her mouth and smiled up at her mother. "Oh my God, they're smiling now."

"I'm still trying to figure out if it's a genuine smile or gas. They've been a little stinky. They have their two-month checkup on Tuesday so I'll ask the pediatrician about it."

"It's probably the formula again." Liv's shoulders slumped.

"I thought the last one was the right one. It would have been so much easier if I had been able to breast-feed them."

"Liv," Dr. Stewart interrupted. "Remember what we talked about. Your inability to breast-feed was not your fault."

Liv nodded and knelt on the floor in front of them. Jade was glad to see her sister interact with the girls, but it also meant her time with them would soon end. That's what she wanted, wasn't it? Then why did it hurt?

"I'm going to head out for a little while and give you some time with them."

Liv smiled at her over her shoulder. "Thank you for coming today."

"Anything for you."

By the time Jade locked the car seats into their bases in the back of the SUV, she felt physically and emotionally drained. She slid behind the wheel, turned the key in the ignition and switched on the AC to cool the vehicle down since it had been parked in the sun all day long. The clock on the dashboard glowed quarter to four. No wonder she was tired. She'd been going since two in the morning.

"Oh shoot!" Jade dug through her bag for her phone. "I forgot Tomás."

She flicked off the side mute button and tapped at the screen. Thirty-two missed calls, nine of which were from Tomás, twenty-seven text messages and over a hundred emails.

Nothing from Wes.

It wasn't like she had expected him to call. She said she'd call him later and she would once she got home. She glanced at the clock again. He was probably midflight, and if she called him now, she could get away with leaving a voice mail. It would be easier on them both after this morning's emotional goodbye.

She pulled up his contact and pressed Call. Straight to voice mail as she figured.

"Hi, Wes, it's Jade. It's almost four and I'm just leaving the

PPD center. Liv saw the girls, but it was extremely slow going. After about half an hour, she got very overwhelmed. The doctor feels she'll probably need to be there for longer than thirty days. I told her that I knew about you and that you had spent time with the girls. I also let her know we were living on the ranch. She was upset at first, but she understood. Okay, um, well, I just wanted you to know, so I'll talk to you when I talk to you, I guess. I—I miss you, Wes. I'm sorry it had to be this way."

Jade disconnected the call. Maybe she shouldn't have told him the last part. Maybe she should have said more. No. It was better this way. She shifted the SUV into drive when her phone rang. Tomás.

She answered the call. "Hey, I'm sorry. I'm just getting ready to head home from the postpartum depression center, can I call you back when I get there?"

"I hope that means you're sitting down, because we have a problem."

Jade shifted back into Park. "Tell me."

"We lost the Wittingfords."

Jade gripped the phone tighter. "Lost as in they canceled or lost as in they went with someone else?"

"They went with someone else."

"No, no, no." Jade rested her head on the steering wheel. "What happened?"

"Word has gotten around that you're not in town and our competition is poaching our clients."

"But the Wittingfords have been with us for years. Their parties are the cornerstone of our business. Who did they go with?"

"Margot Schultz."

Oh no, not Margot. She was smart, savvy and had a world-class reputation. She was one of the best, if not the best, in the industry. "If she managed to take them, there's no telling who else she'll get. She has the potential to destroy us."

"When are you coming back? I can do a lot of things, but I'm not you."

"I don't know. Liv's first visit with the girls did not go well. And they're telling me she'll be there past thirty days. Possibly sixty or ninety days."

"Wow, love, I'm so sorry to hear that. I still don't understand why you can't check her into a facility here."

"If I had known about this in advance, I would have. She's comfortable where she is and it seems like a great place. I just have to do the best I can from here." She turned in the seat to make sure the girls weren't too cold. "I know you're trying to find the perfect candidate, but I want you to hire two people by tomorrow afternoon. No exceptions, Tomás. I refuse to lose my business because you're picky. You can train whoever you need to train and mold them into mini yous. If you think you need to hire three people, then do it. But I need you to be me. Your reputation in this town is just as good as mine. There is nothing I can do that you can't."

"I appreciate the confidence you have in me, but—"

"But what? Is it money? Is that what you want? More money? I've already given you a raise, but if that's what it takes—"

"Jade, breathe," Tomás ordered. "I was going to say, it's not the same without you here. I miss you, love."

"I miss you too. And thank you. It's nice feeling wanted."

"Uh-oh, problems with your cowboy?"

"He flew home to Texas today."

"And are you okay with that?" Tomás asked.

"I haven't had time to think about it. Dwelling on what could never be is an exercise in futility. We spent some time together, we shared a few kisses and that was all it could ever be. After the way Liv reacted today when I told her Wes was in the girls' lives, I feel even more guilty."

"Whoa, I'll let you tell me about the kisses later, but you two shared a lot more than that. You have children together. Donor or not, you're always going to be connected. I can only imagine that loss. And we don't have to talk about it. You can choose to ignore it all you want, just know, I'm here for you if you need a shoulder to lean on."

More like cry on. Jade missed Wes. Watching him walk out the door hurt more than losing her biggest client. She hung up and steered the SUV onto the highway. She had Tomás, Maddie, everyone on the ranch and she had the girls, yet she'd never been more alone. She did feel a loss. Whether she wanted to or not, she had fallen hard for the cowboy. Her sister was right. She could have any man in the world...just not Wes.

Chapter 10

The warm Texas sun felt good on his shoulders as Wes strode across the Bridle Dance Ranch's parking lot toward the Ride 'em High! Rodeo School's outdoor arena.

"Oh, I know that look," Shane Langtry said from the top fence rail as a teenage version of him demonstrated technique in the center of the ring. "Either you just got bad news or you just got your heart broken."

"What are you, clairvoyant?" Wes watched Shane's son execute a smooth dismount after a successful eight second ride. Something he may never do again. "Hunter looks good out there."

"Thanks. I have no doubt he'll take the championship one day." Shane swung his legs over the fence and jumped down. "Well, am I right?"

"About Hunter? Most definitely. He's the finest young rider I've ever seen."

"I'm asking if I was right about you."

"Yeah, a little."

"From the expression on your face I'd say whatever's on your mind is more than a little. Did you see Dr. Lindstrom?"

"I'm just returning from there. Thank you for the referral. She's really nice, although I didn't want to hear what she said."

"You know who she's married to, don't you?" Shane pushed his hat back and propped an arm on the fence.

"No, who?"

"Brady Sawyer."

"*The* Brady Sawyer? The Brady Sawyer who works here?" The man had been a legend on the circuit until an accident paralyzed him from the waist down. They never thought he'd walk again, but he not only walked, he went on to compete until he retired. Now he works helping others to recover at Dance of Hope, the nonprofit hippotherapy center Shane's mother owned next door. "I had no idea."

"She was one of his doctors who put him back together. They fell pretty hard for each other while he was recuperating. If she could fix him, she can fix you. What did she say?"

"She confirmed what my first doctor had suspected." Wes watched another teen climb into the chute, remembering back to when he was that age. He thought he was invincible. If he got bucked off he just shook it off and got right back on. "There's no way I can compete again unless I have the surgery. And then I'm looking at six months to a year recovery."

"So it's not a matter of if you're going to have the surgery, it's when you'll have it."

"It's scheduled a week from today. Next Wednesday." Wes hadn't even told his agent yet. As much as he had wanted to wait, the pain had become too intense. If it meant his biggest sponsors not renewing his contracts this year, then so be it. He would just have to work twice as hard next year. He'd been debating his options since his last competition. While the surgery alone terrified him, not doing what he loved most terrified him more. "That will leave me without a job though. I won't be able to teach for a while. I guess I'm giving you notice since I can't expect you to keep my position open for that long. But don't worry, I have enough money to cover my rent here on the ranch."

"You're just Mr. Doom-and-Gloom today, aren't you?" Shane gripped Wes's good shoulder. "You need to relax, man. I can temporarily fill your position until you are able to come back to work, however long that takes."

"Thank you."

Wes had feared his only other option would be to move back home and partner with his brothers at Silver Bells, if they still wanted him. After the other day, he never wanted to step foot in Saddle Ridge again. He couldn't risk running into Jade or the girls. She updated him daily through voice mail and text messages and that was enough for him. But Harlan had asked him to be his best man at his and Belle's renewal ceremony, so he had to go back. Why did they have to get married again, anyway?

"There's something I want to run by you. I've been tossing the idea around for a while, but I haven't found the right person to help me with it. Your extensive recovery time may work to both of our advantages."

"Sounds intriguing. What do you have in mind?"

"Between rodeo clinics and my son's competitions I'm on the road a lot. I really need a rodeo school director and if you're interested, I think we can work something out. It would be full-time, more money and full benefits."

"Seriously?" The deal seemed almost too good to be true. "I've only been here six months. Are you sure you don't want to choose someone else?"

"I think you're the best fit. You've shown an interest in the business side of things and that's what I need. Somebody who can see the business beyond today. Walk with me." Shane motioned for Wes to follow him down the wide path leading toward the Bridle Dance Ranch's stables. The quarter-million-acre estate housed three of Hill Country's most successful businesses, including one of the state's largest paint and cutting horse ranches. "Between running the ranch and the rodeo school with my brothers, I can't do everything I need or even want to do. You'd be helping me immensely. And I don't know how much thought you've given to retirement, but you always need to have something lined up past today in case an injury side-lines you. This will give you that opportunity to compete for another year or two after you've recovered and have something solid to fall back on."

"I'd say that sounds like an offer I can't refuse." Wes held out his hand. "Thank you."

Shane shook on it and laughed. "I'll take this as a tentative yes. I want you to really mull it over and get through your surgery before you give me your final answer. From what I understand those initial few weeks after a rotator cuff repair can be pretty painful. You're privileged to have access to some of the best physical therapists and nursing staff here on the ranch. Don't hesitate to ask for help."

"Thank you. I knew moving here was the best decision I ever made."

"Just do me one favor. Don't accept the job because you're running away from that broken heart you're trying to hide. You asked me earlier if I was clairvoyant so don't try to deny it. I've been there, done that and then some. If you have something unresolved with your woman, you owe it to both of you to see it through."

"There's nothing left to resolve." Wes's mind still burned with the final images of Jade and the girls. Despite the love he had for them, he wouldn't—couldn't—go through that pain again. "It's over."

Jade froze at the sight of Emma and Belle pushing their baby carriages down the road toward the cabin. She had just returned from her second family day at the postpartum depression treatment center and hadn't even had the chance to get the girls inside. She fumbled with the latch release on Mackenzie's car seat, trying desperately to separate it from the base.

"Need some help?" Harlan's wife asked. Without waiting for an answer, she opened the door on the other side of the SUV and released Audra's car seat. "They are so adorable. I never get a chance to see them."

Mackenzie's seat finally popped free. "I know. Between your schedule and my schedule—" *and the fact I'm trying to hide the girls' paternity from your family* "—we keep missing each other. We just came from visiting Liv."

"Here, I'll take her." Emma startled Jade as she reached for the car seat's handle.

Jade snatched it back. "Would you be able to get Hadley instead? This one has a dirty diaper I need to change."

"Sure."

Jade quickly climbed the porch stairs and shoved her key in the lock. She needed to get Mackenzie out of sight as quickly as possible. The whole "hide the baby" routine had worn thin and a part of her wished the truth would come out now. Because regardless of what Wes and Liv wanted, it had to come out eventually. Whether on purpose or by accident it would happen one day and it was better for the girls if it happened before they were old enough to understand what was going on.

Jade sat the car seat next to the changing table and unfastened Mackenzie. How could such a sweet, innocent child have so much drama surrounding her? She eased the infant into her arms, kissing the top of her sleepy head before laying her down. She unsnapped her pink-and-white unicorn pajamas and checked her diaper. Surprisingly, she didn't need a change. Ever since the pediatrician had switched their formula, the girls had been significantly less gassy and odiferous. Liv had been right. They were having a reaction to the formula and Jade had missed it.

"Do you need me to heat their bottles or anything?" Belle asked from the nursery doorway. "I'm exhausted just running around with one baby, never mind three."

"Um, actually, that would be great." Jade choked back the tears threatening to break free.

"Hey, what is it?" Belle wrapped an arm around her. "What happened?"

Jade shook her head, fearing she'd cry if she opened her mouth.

"It's okay." Belle pulled her into a hug. "This has to be so hard on you."

If she only knew all the reasons why.

"I'm sorry." Jade pulled away from her. "I'm just a little overwhelmed today. Of course it's nothing compared to my sister, so I just need to quit my complaining."

"How is Liv doing?"

"Better, but not great. Today was her third session with the girls. We went in the middle of the week for a brief visit, but on Sundays the residents spend the entire day with their children, including feeding and changing them. She's capable of doing that, but she worries she's doing it wrong. If she's with one child and the other starts crying, she feels guilty because she's not there for both of them or not doing something fast enough. She gets very overwhelmed with it and blames herself for everything."

"Wow, I can't imagine. I mean as a new mom I always wonder if I'm doing the right thing. Even with my animal rescue work, I'm constantly questioning myself."

"And that's normal." Jade finished changing Mackenzie's diaper and refastened her pajamas. "A lot of it is a hormonal imbalance and Liv refuses to take any medication. I respect her reasons for not wanting to, but it's delaying her progress."

"And the longer she's there, the more stress on you."

Jade didn't want to think that way. She was the only family her sister had and she needed to be there for her, regardless of the sacrifice. "I can't worry about me. I have to worry about her and the girls."

"You are allowed to worry about you. Let me tell you something. I don't feel the least bit guilty leaving Travis with Harlan so I can go out with my friends. Do I do it every night? Absolutely not. But every couple of weeks, I need a girls' night out. And Harlan and I need our date nights. That's the beauty of having family so close. We all watch each other's kids. In fact, you need to come out with us. Between Harlan, Garrett and Dylan, they are more than capable of watching the kids and you, me, Emma and Delta will go out."

"I wouldn't want to intrude on your family time." Nor did she think the Slade men could handle Audra, Hadley and Mackenzie at the same time.

"Honey, above all else, we're friends and friends support one another. Friends have dinner and drinks together. Besides, I don't think this one will mind you going out for a few hours." Belle smiled down at Mackenzie. "Hmm. I hadn't realized how much she looks like Travis."

"Really?" Jade held her breath. *I'm sorry, Liv.*

"Babies are funny that way." She trailed the back of her finger down Mackenzie's cheek. "I ran into a woman just last week at the pediatrician's office whose daughter looked identical to Holly. You would've sworn they were the same child."

"Wow." Jade tried not to show the relief leaving her body. "That had to have been unnerving."

"It was a little." Belle spun around and headed to the door. "I'll start on their bottles."

"I'm right behind you."

Just as soon as I pick myself up off the floor.

After she'd finally managed to get her pulse under control, Liv joined Emma and Belle in the living room. They already had the girls out of their carriers and on the play mats next to Emma and Travis.

This was why her sister and Wes needed to tell everyone the truth. Not only did Audra, Hadley and Mackenzie deserve to grow up knowing their extended family, Liv needed the companionship of other moms.

"I hear you're going to join us for girls' night this week."

"I'm considering it." Jade lowered Mackenzie to the play mat, burying any fear she had of the women discovering the baby's paternity. If the truth came out, it came out. She would deal with the fallout later. "I'm still trying to juggle everything in Los Angeles, although my assistant managed to bring in one of Hollywood's biggest producers. I'm not going to name names, but let's just say he has billions to spend."

"Oh! I know, I know." Emma raised Holly's little hand in the air. "Do you want to tell us or should we *phone home* for the answer?"

"I can't tell you that." Jade was barely able to keep the laughter from her voice. "At least not yet. Nothing is finalized—but fingers crossed—by tonight it will be."

"What kind of event is it?" Belle lifted Hadley in her arms and held the bottle to her lips.

"An award show after party." Jade grabbed a few towels from the kitchen and joined them on the floor. She placed Mackenzie in one of the chairs Wes gave them, tilted it back slightly so she could prop a towel under the bottle, allowing Mackenzie to drink on her own.

"Okay, now I'm jealous." Emma frowned. "That means you'll get to meet all the stars that night?"

"Would you guys hate me if I told you I've already met a lot of them?"

"No wonder you're anxious to get back to California," Belle said. "That makes what I was going to ask you kind of underwhelming."

Jade cradled Audra and offered her the third bottle. "Don't be silly. Go ahead and ask."

"Harlan and I are planning to renew our vows on August 1. Last year's wedding was a little rushed and unexpected. We didn't even have a chance to invite anyone. People heard about it through word-of-mouth and showed up, but it wasn't exactly our dream wedding. Our anniversary is on a Wednesday so we don't want a full-fledged wedding, but we want to have a really big party here at the ranch."

"Basically the wedding reception you never had."

"Exactly." Belle gently rocked back and forth on her knees as Hadley sucked happily on the bottle. Jade had always sat rigidly still while feeding them. "I was going to ask you for some ideas, because I know you're busy and I'd really like to plan this party with Harlan. We just want to make it special. Our track record with weddings isn't exactly the greatest."

"I'd be happy to help you."

"Really? Thank you. I have some ideas, but I'd like some professional input. And we'll pay you. I don't want you to think we're taking advantage of your knowledge."

"You'll do no such thing. Your family stepped in to help me in place of the family I don't have. I've never experienced that before. All of you have shown me a different side to family life. A happy side I wasn't sure existed."

"Does that mean you're ready to settle down and have children of your own? Because you and Wes would have beautiful kids."

Jade began to cough. "Wes and I—" She cleared her throat. "Wes and I are not a couple."

"You two sure looked like a couple at my wedding. That was some kiss." Emma winked.

"And sometimes a kiss is just a kiss."

"I call baby doody on that one," Belle laughed. "There is definitely something between you two and you'll have another chance to find out when he comes home for our ceremony. Harlan asked him to be his best man."

"Will he be able to fly so soon after surgery?" Emma asked.

"Surgery?" Jade looked from Emma to Belle. "What surgery?"

"I'm sorry, I thought you knew." Belle grimaced. "Wes is having rotator cuff surgery on Wednesday. He'll be out of commission for six months to a year."

"I didn't realize he had made a decision already." Wes's shoulder must've gotten worse for him to abandon his plan to wait until the end of the season. "What is he going to do for work?"

"His boss in Texas offered him a director position," Belle answered. "But he's taking a few weeks to decide."

"I know Dylan wishes he would move home, but he's already offered him a partnership twice and he turned it down. It's a shame you and Wes both don't live here permanently." Emma stretched out on the floor next to her daughter. "Silver Bells and Saddle Ridge could really use an event planner. I don't mean just little small-time weddings like ours. We're surrounded by ski resorts and other large guest ranches that would benefit from your services. Plus, I think Wes would move here if you did."

"Can't you open a second location?" Belle asked. "Saddle Ridge can be your satellite office."

Leave Los Angeles? Even if she wanted to—and a small part of her was excited by the prospect of opening a second office—she couldn't. It would be great for her sister, but horrible for her. Saddle Ridge already held too many memories. And while she had made some sweet ones during this visit, it was just that…a visit. Saddle Ridge would never be home without Wes and there was no way he would ever move back.

Chapter 11

Wes knew it would be difficult seeing Jade after five weeks away, he just hadn't expected her to take his breath away when he did. He'd managed to avoid her during Harlan and Belle's vow renewal, but once the reception was in full swing, he found her repeatedly in his line of vision. And what a vision she was. Her vintage cream-and-pale-pink dress caused his heart to flutter. And nothing on a man should ever flutter.

Despite his family's best attempts to get them together, Wes and Jade had managed to stay on opposite sides of the wood plank dance floor. The sun had just begun to set and he finally understood the meaning of the phrase *golden hour*. It was as if an ethereal light shone upon her, making him long for the kisses they had once shared.

Wes shook his head and reached into the front pocket of his jeans and pulled out his prescription bottle. "What the hell did they put in these things?" Dr. Lindstrom had renewed his painkillers before his flight despite his protests. He was glad she had. The cabin pressure and change in altitude had bothered his shoulder to the point he'd had to take one earlier that day. It should've worn off by now.

"Have you given any more thought to our offer?" Garrett handed him a bottle of Coke. He would've much rather preferred a beer or two, but he didn't want to chance mixing alcohol with his meds. "It's a serious offer, Wes. We don't want you to think it's out of pity."

"I know it's not. And I appreciate it, but I just can't move back here. It's too hard."

"Believe me, I totally understand. I felt the same way before I moved back. I saw Dad on every street corner. Everywhere I turned…he was there. Now that I've been home for a while, other memories, new memories, have taken their place. When I walked past the feed and grain, I don't see Dad with the sack of feed over his shoulder. I see Bryce racing through the door to see the baby chicks they have in the back. Just like when I used to go to the Iron Horse for dinner, I saw Rebecca and me on the dance floor." Garrett swallowed hard at the memory of his deceased wife.

"I know you did." Wes slung an arm around his brother's shoulder feeling the distance close between them for the first time in years.

"The point I'm trying to make is you can create new memories. Now when I walk in there, I still see Rebecca, but I also see my first date with Delta."

Wes wanted desperately to confide in his brother. To tell him exactly why he couldn't move home. He loved his brothers. And as their families grew, he had more people to love. But it wasn't enough to make him stay. The love he desperately wanted would never be his.

"I still want you to consider it. Please give us the same courtesy you're giving your job offer in Texas. Look at all the pros and cons. And talk to us. Every time I see you, you seem more distant. Let me tell you something, life is short. No one knows that better than me. You remember that. We are your family and we love you." Garrett took a step to the side. "I believe this lovely woman is waiting to speak with you."

Wes turned around to see Jade standing there. It reminded him of the first time he saw her when she came back to town. Only a month and a half had passed since then, but it seemed like a lifetime ago. He wanted to ask his brother to stay and tell Jade he had nothing more to say, but he needed something from her and it couldn't wait.

"Hi," Jade said.

"Hi," Wes replied.

"Oh, come on. Please tell me you two have progressed further than this over the past couple months." Garrett placed a hand on both their shoulders. "I have an idea...try to com-mun-i-cate with one another. Take it from an old pro like me. It'll get you places." He winked and walked away.

"How have you been?" Jade absentmindedly twisted the ring on her middle finger. "Emma and Belle told me about your surgery. I tried to call you, but I always get your voice mail."

"I got your messages and thank you." Wes had wanted to return her calls, but self-preservation had come first.

"Why didn't you call me back?"

"Because talking to you...texting you...looking at you now just reminds me of what I'll never have. I didn't want a family or to settle down, yet that's all I can think about. You complicated my life."

Jade's eyes blazed. "I complicated your life? Oh no, no. You did that on your own when you went along with my sister's plan."

"Your sister's plan didn't involve me falling in love with you."

Dammit. He hadn't meant to say the words. He tried not to even think them. But they were there, every day at the forefront of his mind.

"Wes, I—"

"I need to see Liv." Wes purposely cut her off not wanting to hear that she didn't love him in return. "I tried calling the treatment center, at least the one that I think she's at, but she's never called me back."

"They're not allowed to talk on the phone. They have computer and email privileges along with old-fashioned snail mail, but most of their communication takes place in person and is supervised."

"Sounds more like prison."

"I wasn't a fan of it myself at first, but I've gotten used to it over the past five weeks."

"I take it things are improving." Wes kept hoping Liv would see that moving to California was best for all of them and leave Saddle Ridge for good. No Jade, no triplets, no heartbreak.

"Definitely. She'd even had a few overnight visits with them and while they were difficult, they went well. She'll be ready to come home soon, and then I'll head back to California. Out of all the crap I've been through in my life, that will be the hardest. I never wanted children and now that I've been caring for them, I don't want to give them up." Jade held up her hands. "I know, I know. I'm perfectly aware that they're not mine to keep, even though they are mine."

"They're ours." Wes wanted to hold her, to console her, but any touch would be too much to bear. "I want to talk to Liv. I need answers."

"I can tell you exactly what she said." Jade's tone flattened.

Wes sensed an argument about to erupt if he wasn't careful. "I need to hear them from her. We were each other's confidants. She was my best friend and there were a lot of times I was closer to her than to them. We owe it to each other."

"I will call the center in the morning and see if I can get it approved. If they say yes, you can come with us on Friday."

"'Us' as in you and the girls?" How could she still not get it?

"Yes."

"No. I can't see them again." His heart squeezed at the thought alone. "Please respect that. I appreciate you keeping me updated, I hope you never stop doing that, but I can't continue to talk to you."

"So that's how it's going to be? You tell me you love me and then nothing. What is there, then?"

"Nothing. There's nothing. There can never be anything more than that unless…" Wes couldn't say the words out loud. He couldn't risk his heart turning to dust in case Liv refused to allow him to be a part of the girls' lives. The chance was small, but he had to try. "I fly home on Saturday. Please let me know when I can see her."

"Fine." Jade stiffened her spine, her face a bright shade of pink. "I'll text you. Don't worry, I don't expect a reply."

She spun away from him and stormed across the dance floor, almost taking out a couple in the process. He'd rather she be mad at him than hurt. He'd take anger over heartbreak any day.

Wes hadn't expected Liv to meet with him so soon, if at all. After meeting with her counselor and physician, a woman named Millie escorted him to a sitting area that reminded him of his old living room at Silver Bells.

When she walked in, he was surprised by how great she looked. He hadn't known what to expect, but based on what Jade had told him, he assumed she'd either be in a hospital gown or some sort of a uniform.

"You look fantastic." Wes took a step closer to give her a hug, then froze when she crossed her arms. "No? Okay. I gotcha." He cleared his throat. "So, um how does this work?"

"You talk to me like I'm a human being."

Liv's words smacked him like a hot tuna on a grill. "Haven't I always?"

"I thought you moved to Texas. What are you doing here and what happened to your arm?"

"Harlan and Belle renewed their wedding vows so I'm here for that and I had to have rotator cuff surgery."

Concern flashed in her eyes. "What does that mean for your career? When will you be able to compete again?"

"Hopefully by next season. I'm being cautiously optimistic and realistic at the same time. I may be forced to retire early."

"What are you going to do?" Liv sank onto the couch across from him.

"I have a few options." Wes sat in the chair in front of her. "The rodeo school I work at in Texas offered me a director position that would still give me the time to compete if I'm able to."

Liv's shoulders dropped slightly. "That sounds like a nice opportunity."

"It's not the only offer on the table. My brothers asked me to partner with them again." Wes watched Liv's left eye twitch ever so slightly as she white-knuckle-gripped her thighs. Now it made sense. She wasn't concerned about his well-being. She wanted to make sure he wasn't moving home.

"So you haven't decided yet?"

"I'm leaning in one direction, but I promised my brothers and my job in Texas that I would take the next couple of weeks to think it over. It's a big decision." Wes inhaled deeply. "I didn't come here to talk about that. I came here because when I agreed to father your children, you told me you were using an anonymous egg donor. I would like to know why you didn't tell me the truth."

"I told Jade all of this."

"I haven't spoken to Jade other than asking to meet with you. You and I were best friends. I think I'm owed some sort of an explanation."

"And I was owed a goodbye."

Hurt registered in her eyes. He had known their friendship would end, but he never meant to hurt her in the process.

"I couldn't say goodbye to you, Liv. If I saw you…pregnant with my children, I was afraid I'd want to be a part of their lives. It was better for both of us if I just left and told you afterward."

"Now that you've seen them, you do want to be in their lives?"

"Most definitely."

Liv inhaled sharply at his admission.

"But I know I can't be, despite my love for them. Unless for some reason you've changed your mind." He had hoped to ask her more delicately, but no matter how he chose to do it, he feared she'd see him as a threat.

"Why, because you're dating my sister? That was inappropriate. You knew she was the biological mother and you put the moves on her."

"For starters, I did not put the moves on Jade. Second, your sister and I are not dating, and third, my attraction to her grew out of the bond we have over those children and the concern for your well-being."

"You're telling me the kids and I are the reason you're attracted to my sister." Liv rolled her eyes, her voice heavy with sarcasm.

"I'm telling you it was an impossible situation. I'm not blaming you. I just want to know why you didn't tell me the truth."

"Because I was afraid you'd say no. I had an anonymous donor picked out. He was perfect on paper. Except he was as cut and dry as Jade and I are, meaning there was no family to fall back on in case my children got sick one day."

"I don't understand, you mean if something happened to you and Jade?"

"No, like if they needed a kidney or bone marrow transplant. I know it sounds illogical, but I've read so many things about donors being hard to find and children who die because they were on a waiting list for years. I wanted to make sure my daughters were covered for everything so they can have the best possible life. And if that time ever came, God forbid, I would have told the girls and your family the truth."

Wes leaned forward. "I just wish you had been open and honest with me. I wasn't just an anonymous donor from the fertility clinic. I was your friend and I had a right to know who I was creating a child with, even though I signed my other rights away, I did still have that right."

"It wasn't the perfect plan I thought it was. It's taken me a while to realize how selfish my actions were." Liv pushed her shoulders back and stared directly at him. "I realize I was wrong. I apologize, and I hope one day you can forgive me."

"Apology accepted. That doesn't change how I feel about Audra, Hadley and Mackenzie."

"They're my children and I decide who is and isn't in their lives. You were so determined to move away from Saddle Ridge, I knew you were leaving when I chose you. I always knew Jade would be a part of their lives. She's their aunt. But I can't have both of you involved or involved with each other."

"Why not?"

Liv ignored his question. "I thought you were dead set against having children."

"I've changed my mind." Wes stumbled for a way to explain it to her. "It's like the couple who has the wild hookup and the woman gets pregnant. Just because the guy never planned on having kids doesn't mean now that he has one on the way that he doesn't love his child."

"You're conveniently leaving a few factors out. You knew what you were doing at the time, so the fact that I was carrying your children wasn't a surprise. And then there's Jade. What do you think it does to me knowing the biological mother and the biological father of my children…the children I carried and gave birth to, are in love with each other?"

"Who said anything about love?" Wes couldn't believe for one second that Jade had emailed her sister and told her what he said last night.

"Sometimes you really are clueless. My sister's in love with you. I can see it in her eyes. I can see it every time she mentions your name, which thankfully isn't all that often. Your involvement with my sister makes me feel like an outsider with my own children. I can't have that. I've worked hard to recover from my postpartum depression. I haven't told my sister this yet, but they're releasing me tomorrow. I'm going to go home to my children and resume my life at my house. Not Silver Bells. I'm sorry, Wes, but I need you to honor our agreement. I don't want you in my daughters' lives."

Chapter 12

Sunny Southern California had never seemed so gloomy. Jade had been home for a month and despite trying her hardest, she still couldn't shake her Montana routine. She constantly checked her watch to see if it was time for the girls' feedings. She carefully listened to every sound in the middle of the night thinking one of them had woken up. And she hugged her pillow tight as she lay alone in her bed, wishing Wes was by her side.

She wanted to fly to Texas and tell him how much she loved him. She should have said it the night he told her, but she had been so scared. She'd never said the words to anyone except her sister. Loving Wes meant hurting Liv. And her sister had been hurt enough.

The day Liv came home had been one of her proudest moments. Saying goodbye to Wes and leaving the ranch had been one of Jade's saddest. After two weeks with her sister and the girls, Liv sent her packing…in the nicest way possible. She had hired a full-time nanny and was receiving outpatient therapy. Jade had no doubt her sister would be a wonderful mother to the girls. It didn't make missing them any easier.

The doorbell rang and Jade forced a smile on her face as she crossed the cold marble foyer of her Hollywood Hills home. She had everything she'd ever wanted. Turned out it wasn't what she wanted, after all.

"Hello, love," Tomás said as she answered the door. "You look simply smashing tonight."

The epitome of tall, dark and handsome, her new business partner kissed both her cheeks and offered her his arm. "Shall we? I still can't believe Margot Schultz invited us to one of her parties."

"I still say she's up to something."

Jade had promoted her longtime assistant to partner when he began snagging Hollywood's wealthiest clientele. Despite losing some clients in the beginning, in the two months she had been gone, he took her business to immeasurable heights. Nobody deserved a promotion more than him. With the addition of their three new employees, Jade had a chance to step back and breathe a little.

"I think tonight's the night we'll find you Mr. Right," Tomás giggled as they slid into the limousine waiting at the curb. "Listen to me. I'm a poet."

"There is no such thing as Mr. Right." The only man who came close was gone forever. Jade's clutch vibrated in her lap. She pulled out her phone and tapped at the screen. "Liv sent me a text message."

"I hope it's another picture of those adorable girls." Tomás leaned closer as she opened the message.

Need you here...please come now.

"Oh my God." Jade covered her mouth and quickly dialed her sister.

"Driver," Tomás called up front as he typed wildly on his phone. "Turn the car around."

Please answer the phone, Liv. Please answer the phone. Voice mail. "She's not picking up."

"I'm booking you on the next flight out of here." Tomás gave her hand a quick squeeze before returning to his phone.

Jade frantically dialed Maddie. Again, voice mail. "What the hell is going on?"

"Driver...take us to LAX. It looks like there is only one flight and it's leaving in an hour. You're going to be on it."

Jade looked down at her black evening gown. "I'm not exactly dressed for the occasion." There was nothing like trying to get through airport security with strappy four-inch Christian Louboutin stilettos.

"At least they won't accuse you of concealing any weapons in that dress."

"Give me your jacket," Jade said as she tried her sister again. "Where can she be? She just sent me a text message."

She called Delta next. No answer. By the time she got on the plane and had to turn off her phone, she'd exhausted her Saddle Ridge contacts. "Something's not right."

Eight hours later, she swiped her credit card on the cab's handheld reader in front of her sister's house. "Thank you for getting me here so fast." She palmed him a fifty-dollar bill. It was the only cash she had left in her small clutch.

Gathering the hem of her dress in her hand, she climbed the porch stairs, careful not to break her neck. Just as she reached for the doorknob, Liv swung the door wide.

"It's about time you got here." Liv's eyes widened. "Wow! Where were you coming from in that dress?"

Jade pushed past her and down the hall to the first-floor nursery. "Where are the girls?"

"They're upstairs sleeping." Liv sucked in her lips. "Um... I need you to come into the living room."

"No." Jade stomped past her. "I need to see them." As she flew past the living room archway, a familiar cowboy hat caught her eye. She spun on her heels, twisting her ankle in the process. Before she had a chance to hit the hardwood floor, Wes wrapped his arm around her and pulled her hard to him. "Wh-what are you doing here?"

Wes stared down at her, his mouth inches above hers. "That's what I'd like to know."

"The girls..." Jade whispered, her mind reeling from the man holding her upright and the pain in her ankle.

"I've already checked on them. They're sleeping peacefully."

"You saw them? You physically saw that they're okay?"

"Yes."

Jade turned her head to demand answers from Liv, only her sister was gone. "What is going on?"

"I don't know." Wes helped Jade into the living room and eased her onto the couch. "I got a text message last night telling me to come right away," he said as he unlaced her shoes. He held her calf as his eyes trailed up her thigh, exposed by the high slit in her gown. "That's some dress." He stopped just shy of her cleavage, closing his eyes and cursing under his breath. "I tried calling Liv and then Maddie, but no one answered."

"I even tried calling your sisters-in-law, but there was no answer there, either. I was about to call Harlan when I had to board the plane."

"I'm glad you didn't call the police," Liv said from the doorway, holding an ice pack and a towel. "That would have been awkward to explain, even though your family is well aware of why you're here."

"They're what?" Wes sat back on his haunches as Liv handed him the ice pack.

"Sorry about your ankle." Liv wrinkled her nose. "That wasn't part of the plan."

"What plan?" Jade and Wes said in unison.

"After you both left and I started getting out more with the girls, a lot of people came up to me and told me how you two made a lovely couple. Maddie had already been singing both of your praises, but she filled me in on all Wes had done for the girls. And then Delta came over, and Emma called." She nervously laughed. "And then it hit me...the family that I wanted was much bigger than me and the girls. It was you." She pointed at Jade. "And all of the Slades, including you, Wes."

The sun had just begun to rise and filter into the room as Liv rose from her chair and looked out the window. Was her sister having a relapse? Was that possible with PPD?

"Liv, sit next to me." Jade patted the couch. "Oh, that's cold." She jumped when Wes rested the ice pack against her ankle.

"It's already starting to swell." Wes held her foot firmly. "Liv, I can't tell if you're trying or not trying to tell us something, but my patience is wearing a little thin. When we last spoke, you told me you didn't want me in your daughters' lives. Now you're saying their family is my family. You didn't tell them, did you?"

"Well..." Liv gnawed her bottom lip. "Yes, I did. I felt I owed them the truth. My actions not only threw your lives into total chaos, it had the potential of hurting the girls and Wes's family in the future. I hadn't thought about the school issue, or that the girls and their cousins would be friends. I was laser focused on having a baby. In hindsight, that destroyed my marriage more than our inability to have children."

Jade felt Wes's grip tighten slightly on her foot. "Liv, I love that you did the right thing, but that was Wes's place to tell his family. Not yours."

Wes exhaled slowly and stood. "I'm not concerned that you told them. I'm more concerned with what comes next."

The front door opened, and Harlan poked his head in. "Is it okay for us to come in now?"

"What's going on?" Jade tugged on Wes's arm. "Help me up. What are they doing here?"

"I called them."

Wes slid his good arm under her and lifted Jade beside him. "I'm almost afraid to believe what this might mean," Wes whispered.

One by one, the entire Slade family filed into Liv's small living room.

"Thank you for coming. And, Jade and Wes, please forgive my little trickery. I didn't think you would come otherwise. Especially Wes." Liv walked over to him and held his face in her hands. "Dear Wes. I am so sorry for the way I treated you. You gave me the greatest gift in the world, and I was so cruel. You asked to be a part of their lives. And today I'm giving that to you." Liv cupped her sister under the chin. "To both of you."

"Liv," Jade sobbed. "What are you saying?" She knew her sister would never relinquish her rights to the girls. If that's what she was doing, then there was something seriously wrong. "Liv, please."

"I've already contacted my attorney and he will meet with us later today to explain in further detail, but…"

"Liv, no." Jade pulled her sister into her arms. "You can't. I won't let you. You love those girls." She didn't care what she had to give up in California, she'd stay by her sister's side every day and make sure she was okay.

"Jade, sweetheart." Liv soothed her hair. "Because I love them, I'm asking you to become de facto parents."

"De what?" Jade released her sister. "I don't understand."

"De facto parents. In Montana, a child or children can have more than two parents. You and Wes would assume day-to-day parental roles with me."

"This isn't a sister-wife thing, is it?" Wes asked.

"I think I might be able to explain this." Harlan stepped forward. "If you two choose to reside here in Montana, and like Liv said, assume the day-to-day parenting of the girls alongside her, her attorney can petition the court to have you named de facto parents. Because you're their biological parents, you have an excellent chance a judge will sign off on it."

"And considering my father is the judge—" Belle winked "—your odds are pretty good. We took Liv to meet with him and he detailed everything that needed to happen in order for the court to grant the arrangement."

"You both have to live in Montana though," Dylan said. "That partnership is still open if you want it."

"And I still say Saddle Ridge needs an event planner," Emma added.

Jade blindly reached behind her for Wes's hand. She needed to feel his touch, to know she wasn't dreaming.

"And you need a place to all live that's not too sister-wifey." Garrett laughed. "We talked it over with Liv, and we have two side-by-side guest cottages on Silver Bells that we'd like to offer you. They need to be renovated, but—"

"But the sale of this place will more than pay for them," Liv said. "You two would have your space, and I would have mine. The girls would have both houses to call home."

Jade's heart hammered in her chest. "Liv, are you sure about this? You love this place."

"I love you more." Liv clasped her hands over theirs. "Do you two love each other?"

"Yes," Wes said as he wiped away a tear. "I love those girls more than life itself." He started to laugh. "And I really wish I had use of both arms right now."

"Oh, Wes." Jade wrapped both of her arms around his waist and looked up at him "I've got you. And I love you."

"I love you too, with all that I am." He looked across the room to his family. "I love all of you. And, Liv, thank you. This means everything to me, but there's just one problem." He sighed heavily.

"What?" Jade pulled away from him. They were so close. How could he possibly back out now?

Wes lowered himself on one knee and took her hand in his. "I don't have a ring or some grand speech prepared, but I have a lifetime that I'd like to share with you and our crazy, unconventional family. That is if you'll marry me."

A wave of euphoria bubbled inside her. "Yes! Yes, I'll marry you!"

The shadows in her heart had finally disappeared and she was happy. Blissfully happy with the father of her children and a family to call her own.

* * * * *

Keep reading for an excerpt of
A Wife At Kimbara
by Margaret Way.
Find it in the
Legends Of The Outback anthology,
out now!

CHAPTER ONE

BROD STRODE FROM the blinding light of the compound into the welcoming gloom of the old homestead's hallway. His whole body was sheened with sweat and his denim shirt covered in dust and grass stains. He and his men had been up since dawn driving a herd of uncooperative cattle from drying Egret Creek to Three Moons, a chain of billabongs some miles off.

It had been a long hot slog filled with plenty of curses and frustration as several beasts in turn tried to break away from the herd. Dumber than dumb in some situations cattle had a decided ability to hold their own in the bush.

He could do with a good scrub but there was scant time for that. His schedule was as hectic as ever. He'd almost forgotten, the station vet was flying in this afternoon to give another section of the herd a general check over. That was about three o'clock. He had time to grab a sandwich and a cup of tea and return to the holding yard they'd set up under the gum trees.

Now he focused on the stack of mail neatly piled on top of the rough pine bench that served as a console. No Kimbara this he thought with bleak humour. Definitely not the splendid historic homestead of his birth.

His father resided on Kimbara. Stewart Kinross. Lord of the Desert. Leaving his only son to slave his guts out running the cattle chain while he claimed all the glory. Not that there weren't quite a few people in the know. Not that it bothered him all that much he thought swivelling to throw his black Akubra onto a peg on the wall. It landed unerringly on the target as it always did but he paid no attention. His day would come. He and Ally together had quite a stake in the diverse Kinross enterprises with ancestral Kimbara, the flagship of the Kinross cattle empire the jewel in the crown.

Grandad Kinross, legendary hero, had seen to that, never blind to his son Stewart's true nature. Andrew Kinross was long gone while his grandson lived a near outcast on Marlu for the past five years. In fact it had been since Alison, hiding her heartache over the breakup of her passionate romance with Rafe Cameron, left home for the Big Smoke, the name the Outback bestowed on big bustling cosmopolitan Sydney.

Alison said then she wanted to try her hand at acting like their celebrated Aunt Fee who had taken off at eighteen full of wild dreams of making a brilliant career for herself on the London stage. And wonder of wonders Fee had actually succeeded despite a well publicised out of control love life. Now she was back on Kimbara writing her sensational memoirs.

Fee was quite a character, too famous to qualify for black sheep of the family but with two big-time broken marriages behind her and the legacy of an exquisite English rose of a daughter. Lady Francesca de Lyle, no less. His and Ally's cousin and from what they'd seen of her as good as she was beautiful. Couldn't have been easy with the arty oversexed Fee for a mother.

Now Fee was telling all, convinced her biography would be a huge success in the hands of one Rebecca Hunt, an award-winning young journalist from Sydney with another well received biography of a retired Australian diva under her belt.

Just to think of Rebecca Hunt lit a dangerous flame somewhere inside him. Such was the power of a woman's beauty he thought disgustedly when he distrusted her like hell. He had no difficulty summoning up her image. Satiny black hair framing a lily cool face, but with one hell of a seductive mouth. The mouth was a dead give-away. Yet she was so utterly immaculate and self-possessed she was darn near mysterious. He could never imagine someone like him for instance mussing that sleek hair or laying a finger on her magnolia flesh. She was way too perfect for him. Brod gave an involuntary laugh the fall of light in the hall giving his lean handsome features a brooding hawk-like quality. In reality the patrician Miss Hunt was just another mightily ambitious woman.

It wasn't his father that had her in thrall. No way would he accept that. Not that his father wasn't a big handsome guy, assured, cultivated, filthy rich, fifty-five and looking a good ten years younger. Forget the meanness there. No it was the wild splendour of Kimbara that interested Miss Hunt, of the large ravishing grey eyes. Eyes like the still crystal waters of a hidden rock pool, yet he had divined instantly Miss Hunt would discard her promising little career any day to become mistress of Kimbara. From a fledgling career to riches beyond her imaginings. Only one catch: She could only have it all while his father lived. After that it was his turn.

The Kinross tradition had never been broken. Kimbara, the Kinross's ancestral home was passed directly from father to firstborn son. No one had ever abdicated in favour of a brother though Andrew Kinross had been a second son, surviving the Second World War when his elder brother James hadn't. James had died in his brother's arms in a far distant desert, very different from their own. One of the countless terrible tragedies of war.

Shaking his head sadly, Brod moved to pick up the mail riffling through it. It had been flown in that day while he was far out on the run. Wally his loyal, part aboriginal ex-stockman had brought it up. Since he had badly smashed his leg in a fall from his horse, Wally's duties revolved around the small homestead and the homestead's vegetable garden, which was currently thriving. Wally wasn't turning into a bad cook, either. At any rate better than him.

Only one piece of correspondence really caught his eye and somehow he had been expecting it. He ripped it open smiling grimly at the contents. Why would the old man contact him directly when he was so good at letters? He took a harsh breath. No "Dear Brod." Nothing like that. No enquires as to his health. It appeared his father had arranged a gala event to impress and entertain Miss Hunt. A polo weekend at the end of the month. In other words ten days' time. Matches starting Saturday morning with the main event 3:00 p.m. Usual gala ball in the Great Hall Saturday night.

His father would naturally captain the main team, read, hand-pick the best players. His son Brod would be allowed to captain the other. His father hated like hell that his son was so damned good if a bit on the wild side. God pity him, his father seemed to hate everything he did even as the chain thrived. If the truth be known his father didn't look on him as a son at all. Since he had grown to manhood his father had treated him more like a rival. An enemy at the gate. It was all so bloody bizarre. Small wonder he and Ally were emotionally scarred, but both of them had confronted it.

Their mother had run off when he was only nine and Ally a vulnerable little four-year-old. How could she have done it? Not that he and Ally didn't come to understand it in time. Getting to know their father so well, his black moods, the colossal arrogance, the coldness and the biting tongue they reckoned their mother had been driven to it. Maybe she would have fought for their custody as she swore she would but then she had gotten herself killed in a car smash less than a year later. He vividly remembered the day his father had called him into his study to tell him about the accident.

"No one gets away from me," Stewart Kinross had said with a chilling smile on his face.

That was Brod's father.

He shook his head in despair. At least he and Ally, the closest of siblings, had had Grandfather Kinross to turn to. For a while. A finer man had never been born. The best thing that had ever been said to him had come from one of his grandfather's closest friends, Sir Jock McTavish.

"You have all your Granddaddy's great fighting heart and spirit, Broderick. I know you're going to live up to the legend!"

Jock McTavish knew how to size a man up. In the many shattering confrontations Brod had had with his father over the years he tried to hold fast to Sir Jock's words. It hadn't been easy when his father had never ceased trying to grind him down.

Brod sighed and thrust his father's letter into the pocket of his jeans. He had no desire to travel so far, he told himself. It was one hell of an overland trek from Marlu to the Kinross stronghold in the Channel Country in the far south west of the giant state of Queensland. Plus he was too damned busy. If he went at all he would have to fly. His father sure hadn't offered to pick him up in the Beech Baron. He'd have to call up the Camerons as he did frequently even after Ally's breakup with Rafe.

He'd grown up with the Cameron brothers, Rafe and Grant. The history of the Kinross and Cameron families was the history of the Outback. It was their Scottish ancestors themselves, close friends from childhood who had pioneered the fabled region in the process turning themselves into cattle barons. Both dynasties had survived. Not only survived, flourished.

Sudden frustration seized him. He remembered as vividly as yesterday the time Ally had come to tell him she couldn't marry Rafe. She was going away. A journey of self-discovery she called it. Her romance with Rafe was simply too overwhelming for comfort.

"But hell, Ally, you love him!" He could hear his own disbelieving voice. "And he sure as hell is crazy about you."

"I love him with every breath that's in me," Ally had responded passionately, fiercely wiping tears from her face. "But you don't know what it's like, Brod. All the girls fall for you, but not a one of them has touched your heart. Rafe squeezes the heart out of me, do you see? I'm sick of him and sick with him. He's more than I can take on."

Bewildered he had ploughed on. "So he's forceful? A man's man. He's not in the least like our father. There's nothing dark and frightening about Rafe, if that's what you're worried about. He's one hell of a guy. What's got into you, Ally? Rafe is my best friend. The Kinross'es and the Camerons are damned near related. We all thought your marriage to Rafe would finally unite our two families. Even the old man is all for it going ahead. Marvellous choice and all that. Couldn't be more suitable." He aped his father's deep, polished tones.

"I can't do it, Brod," Ally had insisted. "Not yet. I have to learn a lot more about myself before I take on Rafe. I'm terribly sorry to disappoint you. Father will be furious." Her beautiful clear green eyes darkened at the prospect.

He had taken her in his arms then, hugging her to him. "You could never disappoint me, Ally," he told her. "My love for you is too great. My respect for your wisdom and spirit. Maybe its because you're so young. Barely twenty. You have your whole life in front of you. Go with my blessing but for God's sake come back to Rafe."

"If he'll have me." Ally had tried to smile through her tears.

It hadn't happened. Rafe had never seriously been drawn to another woman but the one person they never talked about was Alison. That subject was taboo. Tough, self-sufficient as he was giving no sign of hurting, Brod knew. Ally had dealt his friend a near mortal blow.

Momentarily disconsolate he stared sightless through the open doorway. Five years later and Ally still hadn't returned home. Ally like Fee had developed quite a talent for acting. Something in the genes. Ally had just won a Logie for best actress in a TV series drama playing a young doctor in a country town. She was enormously popular for her beauty and charm, the way she gave such life and conviction to her frequently affecting role. He was full of admiration for her but he really missed her; the comfort and humour of her company. God knows how Rafe, being Rafe, coped with the bitterness of rejection that must have accumulated in his heart? He didn't take it out on him though Grant, the younger brother had been known to fire off a few salvos. Rafe and Grant were as close as he and Ally. To hurt one was to hurt the other. Both brothers would be certain starters in the main polo match the coming Saturday afternoon. Both excellent players though Rafe had the edge. But neither was going to faze him.

He liked the going tough and dangerous and he didn't think he'd have too much trouble persuading one or both to join his team despite his father and he'd need their help getting to Kimbara.

The Cameron's historic station Opal Plains bordered Kimbara on its north-northeast border. Grant ran a helicopter service from Opal that covered their part of Outback while Rafe was master of the vast station. Aristocrats of the Outback, the press called all three of them. They presented a polished front to the world, but there had been plenty of sadness and tragedy in their lives.

No, even if he could cadge a ride with Rafe and Grant he had no desire to confront either his father or the magnolia skinned Rebecca. If the truth be told he couldn't bear to see them together. His father showing that seemingly flawless young woman all the exquisite care and consideration he had never accorded his daughter, let alone his wife.

Often to amuse as much as torment himself he conjured up the ridiculous picture of Stewart Kinross down on his knees before the luminous eyed Miss Hunt begging for her hand in marriage. His father so rich and powerful he thought he was invincible. So sure of his virility, he thought he possessed such sexual magnetism he could easily attract a woman half his age. If it weren't so damned likely it would be funny. Women couldn't resist power and money. Especially not adventuresses.

He'd have to find out a little bit more about Miss Rebecca Hunt, he decided. She was remarkably close lipped about her past though he knew from the blurb on the back of the recent biography she'd been born in Sydney in 1973. That made her twenty-seven. Three years younger than he. The rest went on to list the not inconsiderable achievements of her short career.

She had been named Young Journalist of the year at the age of twenty-four. She'd worked with the Australian Broadcasting Commission, SBS and Channel 9. Two years with the British Press. A book of interviews with the rich and famous. The diva's biography. Now Aunt Fee.

Next to nothing about her private life, though. It might have been as blank as a nun's only Miss Rebecca Hunt behind the cool facade was so absolutely fascinating she couldn't have escaped at least a few sexual encounters. If she was footloose it had to be by choice. Was she waiting for the right man? Charming, clever, rich and powerful.

Most people thought Stewart Kinross was just that, until little bits of him occasionally seeped out. The ego, the self-centeredness, the caustic tongue. But when he set out to, Brod had to admit, his father could be dazzling. A young woman like Miss Rebecca Hunt was bound to be socially ambitious. If she took on his father she would get more than she bargained for, the conniving little witch. He almost felt a stab of pity.

No, he didn't want to go, he told himself, suddenly realising he wanted to go very much.

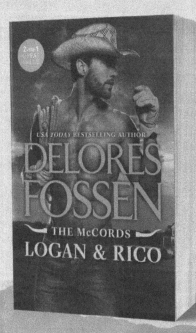

Subscribe and fall in love with a Mills & Boon series today!

You'll be among the first to read stories delivered to your door monthly and enjoy great savings.

WE
SIMPLY
LOVE
ROMANCE